THE REVIEWERS RAVE OVER KAT MARTIN

"Kat Martin is pure entertainment from Page One!"
—Jill Marie Landis

"Kat Martin shimmers like a bright diamond in the genre."
—*Romantic Times*

DANGEROUS PASSIONS

"*Dangerous Passions* is a brilliantly written historical romance fans will relish . . . a tremendous reading experience that will captivate its readers." —*Affaire de Coeur*

NOTHING BUT VELVET

"*Nothing But Velvet* is nothing but brilliant. The lead characters are super, and the villain as vile as they come. The story line is fast-paced and extremely interesting."
—*Affaire de Coeur*

"What more could a romance reader want? . . . [*Nothing But Velvet*] is a boisterous carriage ride in which Martin shows herself to have a firm grasp on the reins."
—*Publishers Weekly*

MIDNIGHT RIDER

"Kat Martin weaves a marvelous western romance that sizzles with unbridled passion and a heated battle of wills. Readers will be enraptured by the heart-pounding adventure

More . . .

and warmed to their toes by the sensuality of *Midnight Rider*." —*Romantic Times*

"Another winner . . . Kat Martin keeps on getting better and better." —*Affaire de Coeur*

"What an outlaw! Dark, daring, dangerous, and delicious! *Midnight Rider* is a rich panorama of old California. I couldn't put it down!" —Georgina Gentry

DEVIL'S PRIZE

"Tempting, alluring, sensual, and irresistible—destined to be a soaring success." —*Romantic Times*

"Kat Martin is a premier historical romance author . . . and *Devil's Prize* enhances her first-class reputation." —*Affaire de Coeur*

BOLD ANGEL

"This medieval romance is a real pleasure . . . the romance is paramount." —*Publishers Weekly*

"*Bold Angel* moves quickly through a bold and exciting period of history. As usual, Kat has written an excellent and entertaining novel of days gone by." —Heather Graham

"An excellent medieval romance . . . Readers will not only love this novel but clamor for a sequel." —*Affaire de Coeur*

WICKED PROMISE

KAT MARTIN

St. Martin's Paperbacks

This is a work of fiction. All of the characters, organizations, and events portrayed in this novel are either products of the author's imagination or are used fictitiously.

WICKED PROMISE

Copyright © 1998 by Kat Martin.

All rights reserved.

For information address St. Martin's Press, 175 Fifth Avenue, New York, NY 10010.

ISBN: 978-1-250-05506-4

Printed in the United States of America

St. Martin's Paperbacks edition / October 1998

St. Martin's Paperbacks are published by St. Martin's Press, 175 Fifth Avenue, New York, NY 10010.

10 9 8 7 6

To my editor, Jennifer Weis, for her help on this and others of my books. May the Force be with us!

ONE

*N*icholas trailed a long dark finger down the small indentations that marked the viscountess's spine. Absently he fondled her bottom, admiring the luscious curves, the way her glossy black hair fanned out across his pillow. Perhaps he should take her again, he thought as his body began to harden and press against the sheets.

A glance at the ormolu clock on the marble mantel and reluctantly the notion slid away.

His solicitor was due within the hour, and though Nick rarely gave a damn what other people thought, he respected Sydney Birdsall and considered him a friend. He didn't want to add to the man's already dubious opinion of him.

Leaning over the woman curled contentedly in his bed, Nicholas Warring, fourth Earl of Ravenworth, pressed a kiss against the nape of her neck. "Time to go, sweeting."

She stirred and her head came up from the pillow. Inkblack hair trailed seductively over a rose-tipped breast. "Please, Nicky, not yet. It's still early. I thought we'd have the rest of the afternoon."

He only shook his head. "Sorry, not this time." He toyed

with a lock of her thick black hair, watched it trail over his hand. "My solicitor is on his way from London. He's due within the hour."

She languidly turned over, her breasts heavy and inviting, yet already his attention had begun to slip away. She ran her fingers through the curly black hair on his chest, circled a flat copper nipple.

"Tell him you're busy. Tell him he'll have to come back later in the evening."

Nick caught her hand, irritation threading through him, impatience rising with it, replacing the last vestige of his desire. Now that it was time for her to go, he simply wanted her on her way.

"Sidney doesn't come often. Apparently this is important." He rolled her over, slapped her gently on the bottom. "Be a good girl, Miriam. Get dressed and go on home."

Her eyes turned a faint shade darker. She made a huffy little sound in her throat. Displeasure hardened the look she cast his way as she reached for her clothes. She dressed with jerky little motions and took her good sweet time about it. At five and twenty, Miriam Beechcroft, Lady Dandridge, was spoiled and selfish. Most of the time, Nick ignored her outbursts of temper and childish manners, but at times like these, he wondered how much longer he'd be able to put up with them.

"I shan't be back for a while," Miriam called over her shoulder as Nick did up the buttons at the back of her plum silk gown. "Max will be arriving on the morrow. He'll be staying at Westover until the end of next week." Maxwell, Viscount Dandridge, was Miriam's aging husband. Much of the year they resided at Westover, the viscount's country estate just a short ride north of Ravenworth Hall. Convenient. For them both. Since Max was often away.

Nick gave her a mocking half-smile. "I'm sure he'll be eager to see you. Be sure to give him my best."

Her pretty lips thinned but Nick didn't care. Aside from

her beauty and skillfulness in bed, Miriam had little to recommend her. Of course Nick didn't say that. Thin as it was, the veneer of a gentleman remained in place, even after the last nine years.

"You're going to miss me," she pouted, turning her face up to his for a kiss, her long black hair coiled once more into a knot at the nape of her neck. "You'll be sorry you sent me away."

A corner of his mouth edged up. "Perhaps I will. I suppose I shall have to console myself with gaming and drink until your return."

She smiled at that, certain that the promise of her charms would be enough to keep him out of another woman's bed. In truth, he would do as he damned well pleased. Just as Miriam did.

They left his bedchamber by the back stairs as they always did, appearing in the downstairs hallway as if they had just left one of the drawing rooms. It was a useless ruse that fooled no one and wasn't necessary among his trusted servants, but if it satisfied Miriam's somewhat tarnished sense of propriety, it was a small concession to make.

When they reached the entry, she turned to face him. "Well, then, I shall see you in a fortnight." She smiled up at him, her lips still slightly bruised from his kisses, her cheeks prettily flushed against the creamy hue of her skin. "Adieu until then, Nicky, my love."

As beautiful as she was, Nick watched her disappear into her carriage with an odd sense of relief. As much as he enjoyed her in bed, Miriam could be tedious at times. Perhaps her absence of the next two weeks would help rekindle the passion for her that seemed to be slipping away.

He turned to the tall, nearly bald butler who stood stiffly in the entry, Edward Pendergass, a longtime. Warring retainer, one of the few who had not defected over the last nine years. "I'm expecting a visit from Sydney Birdsall. When he gets here, I'll be in my study."

"As you wish, my lord." He made a slight inclination of his liver-spotted head, his posture as perfectly correct as it had been in the days *before,* when he had worked for Nick's father, the third Earl of Ravenworth. It was a far different household then, Nick thought, with the earl and his mother still living, doting on him and his younger sister, Maggie.

It was a painful memory Nick let slide away, replaced with thoughts of the upcoming meeting with his solicitor. He wondered what in blazes was important enough to compel Sydney Birdsall to travel from London to Ravenworth, a place his friend referred to as "a fresh-air den of iniquity."

Whatever it was, Nick wouldn't have long to wait before he found out.

Dressed in a gray kerseymere traveling dress cut in the military style, piped in black with matching brandenburgs across the bodice, Elizabeth Abigail Woolcot perched nervously on a sofa in the Gold Drawing Room at Ravenworth Hall.

Her stomach swirled with nerves and her palms felt damp. She straightened her narrow-brimmed gray bonnet, tucking a strand of dark auburn hair up underneath, and shifted on the gold brocade sofa. Determined to keep her mind off what was happening down the hall, she nervously surveyed her surroundings.

Ravenworth Hall was immense and impressive, the salon where she waited richly decorated with ebony gilt furniture and high carved painted ceilings. Heavy Aubusson carpets covered the black marble floors and the walls were hung with gold flocked paper. Gold damask curtains hung at the windows yet somehow managed not to block out the sun.

In fact, the Gold Room glittered against the light that streamed in, touching on the gilded mirrors, forming rainbows of color in the cut-crystal sconces that lined the walls. It was beautiful beyond belief, but in truth, she didn't want to be there. Didn't want to be in the house at all.

Elizabeth sighed, reached down and smoothed a nonexistent wrinkle from the folds of her traveling gown. She knew more than enough about this place she had come to and the man who lived here—the Wicked Earl, they called him, the villainous Earl of Ravenworth—and spending time in his house—in his company—was the last thing she wanted to do. Unfortunately, it appeared she had no other choice.

Elizabeth flicked a glance toward the doorway she had come in through, remembering the earl as she had first seen him, tall and dark and nothing at all like the man she had imagined.

Not that he wasn't just as daunting. If anything, with his slightly overlong wavy black hair, high carved cheekbones, and silvery blue-gray eyes, he looked even more formidable than she had imagined. He was also younger, perhaps not yet thirty, and he was far more attractive. In truth, the Earl of Ravenworth was possibly the handsomest man Elizabeth had ever seen.

Which made him no less a villain, she reminded herself. Nicholas Warring was a murderer—convicted and imprisoned—a man who had served seven years' indenture in Jamaica. Only his powerful father's intervention and what Mr. Birdsall referred to as "mitigating circumstances" had saved the man from hanging.

She thought of him now, tall and lean, yet his shoulders were broad, and his breeches hugged powerful thighs corded with long, sinewy muscle. Though the earl had been back in England for less than two years, he was a notorious rake with a despicable reputation.

Now that his father had passed away, he was also the fourth Earl of Ravenworth.

Which meant he was her guardian.

Elizabeth shuddered to think of it and her eyes slid away from the open doorway. Even seated as she was in the drawing room, she could hear the sound of men's voices drifting in from the study, and a tight knot formed in her stomach. What were they saying? Sydney had assured her the earl would help her, but the look on his face said he wasn't really that sure. The voices rose and fell. Her heart picked up its tempo. What in heaven's name was going on in there?

Knowing she shouldn't, unable to stand the suspense a moment more, Elizabeth rose from the sofa and crossed to the open door. None of the servants were about. With a quick breath for courage, she crept down the hall, paused in front of the study door, and pressed an ear to the ornately carved surface.

"Surely you are jesting," Nick said, rising from behind his desk to pace in front of the marble-manteled hearth. "You cannot possibly mean for me to keep the girl here at Ravenworth."

Sydney Birdsall, a slender, white-haired man once Nick's father's best friend, shifted uncomfortably but didn't look away. "No one knows better than I your sordid reputation, Nicholas. Since your return from the Indies, you have made a point of singularly destroying what little good name you had left."

Nick eyed him coldly. "Then how can you possibly suggest a young girl like Elizabeth Woolcot live under my roof?"

Sydney sighed. "If there were any other way, you may be certain I wouldn't be here. The fact is, the girl is your ward and she is in danger."

"The girl was my father's ward. Until she walked into the house, I had never laid eyes on her."

"No, but you've been sending money for her expenses. You've seen to her education and made certain that she and her aunt are well cared for."

"All of that was done through you."

"Nevertheless, you've stood by your obligations thus far and I am asking you to continue in that vein."

Nick gave up a sigh of frustration. "You know what goes on in this house, Sydney—the sort of life I lead. What you're asking is impossible."

"Elizabeth has no one else to turn to. You know Oliver

Hampton. The man is ruthless in the extreme. For whatever reason—her beauty perhaps, or simply because she has refused his suit—Lord Bascomb wants her and he'll go to any lengths, do anything in his power, to have her."

Nick turned away from the slender little man with the intelligent, perceptive eyes. Returning to his rosewood desk, he sat down wearily and leaned back in his chair. He knew Bascomb, all right. The earl was the wealthy owner of Hampton Shipping, a conscienceless bastard who took what he wanted regardless of the consequences. He used people to further his own ends, then ground them up like so much fodder under the heel of his boot.

He was also the lying whoreson who had helped send him to prison. The thought of the Earl of Bascomb with an innocent young girl like Elizabeth Woolcot made the blood turn to ice in his veins.

He fixed his gaze on the man seated across from him. "The girl is obviously in a bad situation," he said. "I presume you have been to the authorities. What does the local justice have to say?"

Sydney made a tight sound in his throat. "The justice is in Bascomb's coat pocket. The earl is the richest man in Surrey—one of the richest in England—and technically he has done nothing wrong. Aside from that, you know as well as I do, even should Bascomb abscond with the girl, his intention is marriage. Considering Elizabeth's circumstances, every magistrate in the country will view her becoming the Countess of Bascomb as the answer to a prayer."

Nick sighed, feeling defeat creeping into his shoulders. "All right, Sydney. The case you've made is a strong one. I'll do whatever I can to help her, but she simply can't stay here."

Sydney leaned forward, his hands nervously fisted on his thighs. "You met her for only a moment. Let me bring her in so that you might talk to her yourself. Surely that isn't too much to ask."

Nick glanced away, uncomfortable with the beseeching

look on Sydney's face. Reluctantly he nodded. His friend had come a good long ways. Talking to the girl was the least he could do.

The smaller man hurried to the door and jerked it open. To Nick's amazement, Elizabeth Woolcot, caught off balance, tilted precariously forward then stumbled into the room. Only Sydney's quick reactions kept her from landing in a heap on the inlaid parquet floor. As it was, the ribbon on her hat came loose and her bonnet went sailing into a corner, leaving her head bare, strands of glossy auburn hair floating loose around her cheeks.

For the first time Nick realized why it was Oliver Hampton was so determined to have her.

"I—I'm sorry," she stammered. "I was just . . . I was just . . ."

Nick came out of his chair. "You were just what, Miss Woolcot? Eavesdropping, I believe it is called. Isn't that the term?"

Soft color rose into her cheeks. They were high and finely carved. "No, not . . . not exactly. I was . . . I was merely waiting outside in case you wished to see me."

Amusement curved his lips. She was lovely in the extreme, with big green eyes and hair the color of a dark winter fire. It was pulled back in a coil at the nape of her neck, but every time she moved, sparks of copper flashed in the lamplight. Her lashes were thick and dark, her skin as pale as fresh cream. She was slightly taller than average, with an elegant figure, ripe yet not overblown, alluring yet refined, and infinitely tempting.

Sydney Birdsall was frowning, struggling to defend the girl's unorthodox behavior. "Elizabeth is young and at times can be impetuous. She might be a little stubborn and perhaps a bit willful, but she is also keenly intelligent, loyal and caring, and generous to a fault."

Nick's eyes remained fixed on the girl. "I'm certain she is, but as I said, she can't possibly stay here."

"It wouldn't be for long," Sydney pleaded. "Your father made provisions for a sizable dowry. The Season will be starting in a couple of months. Once we find her a suitable husband and she is married, she'll be safe from Oliver Hampton and whatever dubious fate he might have in mind for her."

Nick shook his head. "It wouldn't work. Her reputation would be so blackened living under my roof she would never find a husband."

"She wouldn't come unchaperoned. Her aunt would accompany her. And for all your sins, you're still an earl and one of the wealthiest men in England. With careful planning, a proper match could be made."

"I'm sorry, Sydney. If you were asking anything else—"

A slender foot stomped down. "I wish you would both stop talking about me as if I weren't in the room. It is highly rude and no little discomfiting." Big green eyes locked with his and didn't look away. There was fire in those eyes, Nick saw, and perhaps a hint of desperation.

"At last she speaks." But she said nothing else, just stared straight ahead, her eyes fixed on the wall. Nick approached her, sizing her up from head to foot, admiring the lovely picture she made. He stopped directly in front of her, forcing her to tilt her head to look at him.

"Sydney tells me you are stubborn. That at times you can be willful. What do you say, Miss Woolcot?"

Her chin angled up. There was a tiny cleft at the bottom, he noticed, shadowed by the fullness of her wide bottom lip.

"If stubborn means I refuse to marry a filthy piece of trash like Oliver Hampton, then I must be stubborn. If willful means I have a will of my own, then I am that as well."

Amusement lifted the corner of his mouth. His gaze roamed over her. He didn't miss the tiny tremor that shook her hands. "I presume Sydney has told you about me."

"I am not ignorant of whom you are, if that is what you are asking. I am aware you were convicted of Stephen Hampton's murder nine years ago. I know you were transported for the crime and that you've been returned to England less than two years."

"And you still wish to stay beneath my roof? Surely you are afraid. Surely you would worry your life might be in danger."

Her shoulders subtly squared. "I am in danger from Bascomb. I believe he will force himself on me at the earliest opportunity in order to press me into marriage. I cannot fathom his reasons, since I make no secret of my disgust of him. But I will do anything to keep that from happening. Aside from that, Mr. Birdsall assures me I have nothing to fear from you."

Sydney's voice rose from a few feet away. "As I said, Nicholas, I know your wicked reputation. I also know that behind that rakehell façade is a man of courage and honor, and that if you were to take this young woman into your care you would protect her with your very life."

Nick said nothing. What Sydney said was true—if he took the girl in, there was no way in hell he would let her fall prey to an animal like Bascomb.

He returned his gaze to Elizabeth Woolcot. "Your home in Surrey is next to the earl's. Is that not correct?"

"Yes. That is why I know the sort of man he is. Lord Bascomb is a cheat and a liar. He takes what he wants without the slightest qualm. Even now our upstairs maid, Priscilla Tweed, is heavy with his child. The poor girl was a servant in his household. Bascomb forced himself on her then cast her out when he discovered she was increasing."

Nick's jaw clamped shut. The story sounded all too familiar. But then Oliver and Stephen had both been cut from the same rotten cloth.

He took another long look at the girl, caught the faintest trembling of her full bottom lip. His attention turned to his solicitor. "All right, Sydney, you win. For reasons even I am loath to explain, I will let the girl stay and see that she is kept safe—on one condition."

"Which is?" Sydney asked with a hopeful glance at the girl.

"She and her aunt will occupy the far west wing, and except for meals when guests are not present, or unless they are invited, they will remain there. I refuse to change the way I live for Miss Woolcot or anyone else. If she can live with those arrangements—"

"I can," she broke in, her eyes suddenly bright with relief. "I mean . . . thank you, my lord, those conditions would be quite agreeable to my aunt and to me."

He almost smiled. "Good. Then perhaps this will all work out."

"Yes," Sydney said, smiling for the first time since his arrival. "We shall make certain it does." He clapped Nick on the shoulder. "I knew I could count on you, my boy. Thank you, Nicholas. I can rest easy now, knowing dear Elizabeth is safe in your care."

Nick made no comment. The girl was his ward and she would be safe at Ravenworth. He had given his word and he meant to keep it.

Turning, he walked away, determined to forget those big leaf-green eyes and the dark burnished sheen of Elizabeth Woolcot's hair.

Aunt Sophie arrived at Ravenworth Hall three days later. The earl had sent his plush traveling carriage to Elizabeth's home, and her plump, gray-haired aunt, Mrs. Sophia Crabbe, appeared on the front porch steps of the hall looking none the worse for the two-day journey from West Clandon, a small village three miles east of Guildford.

Hurrying in her direction, Elizabeth hugged the little woman just entering her sixty-fifth year, her mother's older sister, Elizabeth's closest living relative.

Aunt Sophie appraised her from top to bottom, then nodded, apparently satisfied with whatever it was she saw. "Well, child, apparently you've survived your first few days without a mishap." The butler accepted Aunt Sophie's woolen cloak while the heavyset woman turned to survey the entry. "All right, where is he? I should like to meet this ogre who has instead turned out to be our savior."

Elizabeth flushed as Nicholas Warring materialized like a ghost out of the shadows. It was the first time she had seen him since the day they had spoken in his study.

He smiled, though rather thinly, apparently nonplussed by Aunt Sophie's words. "Nicholas Warring," he said with a slight bow of his head. "A pleasure, Mrs. Crabbe."

He sounded as if he meant it, which she knew he did not. He wasn't the least bit happy about either of his most recent guests, but at least he was gentleman enough not to show it.

Aunt Sophie beamed, spots of red appearing in her apple-round cheeks. "Well, aren't you just the image of your father, and every bit as handsome, too."

A slashing black brow arched up. "I had forgotten that you knew my father."

"And your lovely mother, Constance, as well, God rest their poor, dear, departed souls. Good people—the salt of the earth—were your mother and father. I imagine you must miss them very much."

Something flickered in the earl's silver-blue eyes. His posture grew a little more erect. "Yes. I am sorry I wasn't here when they died."

"Yes, yes, terrible thing your being sent away like that, and all for killing that awful Hampton boy. No doubt he deserved it. No doubt at all."

"Aunt Sophie—" Elizabeth gently gripped her aunt's plump arm, hoping to steer her away from an unpleasant subject, but the older woman kept on talking.

"And what of your lovely sister?" she asked. "Does Lady Margaret fare well?"

Any pretense of a smile slid from his lips. "My sister has chosen a life in the Sacred Heart Convent. Though I haven't seen her in quite some time, from the letters I receive, I presume she is faring quite well."

But for whatever reason, Nicholas Warring didn't seem

happy she was there. Aunt Sophie opened her mouth to say something else, but Elizabeth cut her off before she could speak.

"I'm certain my aunt is tired after such a long journey. If you don't mind, my lord, I would show her upstairs and help her get settled in her rooms." It was obvious the subject of his sister wasn't a pleasant one. Elizabeth couldn't help wondering why.

Ravenworth nodded stiffly and bent to take the old woman's white-gloved hand. He frowned slightly when he noticed the dirty ball of string she clutched like gold against her bosom.

Elizabeth forced herself to smile. "My aunt . . . ah, likes to collect things." She grimaced to think of the filthy bits of string, wrinkled scraps of paper, shells and odd-colored stones that would, if left unattended, soon fill every corner of Aunt Sophie's room.

The earl stared down at the string. "So I see," he said dryly. He flashed her a pointed glare. "I'm expecting some friends from London this evening. Since I'm sure you and your aunt would prefer your privacy, I'll have supper sent up to your sitting room."

Elizabeth smiled thinly. "How thoughtful." He didn't miss the sarcasm and she didn't miss the warning in his eyes. *You know the rules,* that dark look said. *I'll expect you to obey them.* She nudged her aunt toward the stairs. "Have a good evening, my lord."

Two

$\mathcal{N}$ick stood at the window of his study. A watery late February sun shone down between the branches of the trees, casting fingerlike shadows over the stark winter landscape. Strolling the gravel paths between the hedgerows, Elizabeth Woolcot's cloaked figure paused to study the hollyhocks and ivy beds, the skimmia and carpets of heath that made up the winter garden.

She wandered a little farther, toward a small meandering stream that tumbled over rocks, formed a pool, then disappeared into the rolling grassy fields beyond. Nick had seen her there before, heedless of the chill in the air, the blustery breeze, or even an occasional light fall of rain. It was obvious she liked the out-of-doors, and equally clear from the bloom in her cheeks that the fresh air agreed with her.

He couldn't help comparing her to his latest mistress, the self-centered Lady Dandridge, a woman who hardly set foot out of doors for fear of dampening her perfectly coiffed hair or freckling her flawlessly white, unblemished skin. He wondered what Elizabeth Woolcot would think of Miriam but he was fairly sure he knew the answer.

Footsteps sounded. Nick's gaze slid past the heavy walnut paneling, the rows of gold-lettered, leather-bound books, to the place where Nigel Wicker, Baron St. George, had just walked in through the open study door.

"Ah . . . so there you are, old boy. We were wondering where you'd got off to." He was a florid, overweight man in his early forties, prone to gout and somewhat foulmouthed. But he liked to gamble and he liked to whore. He was a friend of Lord Percy's, who was a friend of Lord Tidwicke's, and somewhere along the way they had all become friends of Nick's.

"Percy is looking for you," the baron went on. "Got a game of whist going in the Oak Room and they want you to join the play."

"It's early yet. I was just finishing up in here." Going over the ledgers, checking on his tenants, getting ready for the spring barley sowing, for planting vegetables, peas, and beans. But he didn't say that. It was no one else's business and it hardly fit his image.

"Richard's winning," the baron said, "feeling quite the thing. He says his luck is running. Tidwicke and I have a bet. I say you'll have Richard's winnings cleaned out and a marker to boot before it's time for supper."

His mouth curved at that. He could beat Richard Turner-Wilcox six ways to dawn if he put his mind to it and stayed off the drink. Then again, where was the fun in that?

"All right, I'll be there in a minute. Ask one of the servants to bring me some gin, would you?" He grinned. "Suddenly I'm feeling very thirsty."

"Gin." St. George grimaced. "Most uncivilized." He went out muttering something about the evils of blue ruin, the cheap liquor Nick had developed a taste for during his years of indenture.

Nick didn't care. He'd given up worrying about what other people thought of him years ago.

A few minutes passed and a light knock sounded. Theophilus Swann, his number-one footman, appeared at the door.

"Yer gin, milord." Dressed in Ravenworth black and scarlet livery, blond and fair-skinned with a receding hairline, Theo lifted a crystal decanter and a thick-bottomed glass off a silver salver and set it on the desk. "Will there be anythin' else, milord?"

"Nothing at present. Thank you, Theo." The footman backed away and Nick took a long sip of the cool, clear liquid, enjoying the burn as it began to warm his stomach. He gazed back out the window, easily finding the slender figure now perched on a wrought-iron bench beneath a willow tree at the far end of the garden.

Undoubtedly Elizabeth Woolcot would frown on his drinking. She didn't approve of him, he knew. He had seen it in her eyes at their first meeting and several times since. His mouth thinned. He downed the liquor in a single swallow, lifted the lid off the decanter, and refilled his glass to the brim.

From her place in the garden, Elizabeth studied the spires and towers, the pediments and gables, of Ravenworth Hall. It was fashioned of smooth gray stone with tall mullioned windows and ornately carved doors. It was completed in the sixteenth century, according to the butler, and owned by the Warring family ever since. It was a huge house, with a hundred and forty lavishly furnished rooms, sixty of which were bedchambers.

Currently much of the hall was not in use, but all of it was surprisingly well maintained, and the grounds, an almost park-like setting, were as beautiful as any Elizabeth had ever seen.

She trailed a finger over the scrollwork on the wrought-iron bench where she sat and tried not glance up at the second floor, at the window that was the Earl of Ravenworth's private study. She knew he was watching. She had seen him there at the window nearly every day since her arrival.

She wondered what he did in the room during the hours he was there—certainly not the same sorts of things he did later on in the evening. Elizabeth knew what went on in the house after dark, even though she was supposed to be banished to her suite. On more than one occasion, she had crept down the servants' stairs and watched the earl and his drunken friends playing cards, had listened to them tell their bawdy jokes, seen them gaming away an indecent amount of money.

The earl would join in their drunken laughter, but there was something in his eyes that made her wonder if he were truly enjoying himself. She wondered as well at the earl's choice of friends. Elizabeth didn't like a single one of them. They were nothing but a bunch of preening peacocks and worthless hangers-on, sponging off Ravenworth's generosity.

Then again, who was she to criticize? Wasn't she doing the very same thing?

Elizabeth glanced up at the window, but the shadowy figure of the dark earl was gone. Without him there, the garden seemed somehow less intriguing and she wandered back up to her room.

Mercy Brown was waiting, the lady's maid Ravenworth had assigned her. "Look at ye—Lord luv ye. Yer chilled to the bone." With a ripe, full figure that Mercy did everything in her power to display, a thick Cockney accent, and almost nonexistent knowledge of feminine etiquette, Mercy Brown was the furthest thing from a lady's maid Elizabeth could imagine.

"To tell you the truth, I rarely notice the cold. The day was sunny and the sky full of fluffy white clouds. It was simply too nice to stay indoors."

Mercy clucked and coddled her like a mother hen, though she was only four or five years older than Elizabeth. "You'll catch yer death, ye will. 'Is lordship would 'ardly be pleased."

Elizabeth draped her cloak over the foot of the big four-poster bed and Mercy began helping her out of her clothes. "I'm sure his lordship couldn't care less whether or not I caught a chill."

"'E cares, all right. 'E don't show 'is feelin's much, but 'e cares about people, and 'e 'elps 'em whenever 'e can."

"I'd say he spends most of his time helping himself to another glass of gin and gaming away his coin." Elizabeth knew that by now the earl would be readying himself for his evening of drinking and cards. He'd be drunk by midnight and losing endless sums of money.

Mercy Brown gave up a sigh. "'E lets 'em take advantage, Lord luv 'im. 'E's as good a man as ever come down the pike—not a whit like them others. I don't know why 'e puts up with 'em. Sometimes I just don't think 'e cares."

It was an interesting observation. Elizabeth wondered as well. "Perhaps he is lonely. The earl is an outcast from polite society. Perhaps the company of these men is better than having no friends at all."

The buxom little maid merely scoffed. "'Is Lordship 'as a number of friends. Not such 'igh-and-mighty nobs as them 'e drinks with downstairs, but fine men all the same."

Elizabeth started to ask which men it was Mercy spoke of, but the girl was already off to her chores, bustling busily around the room, trying to assemble a change of clothing for supper. Whatever men they were, surely they were better than the dandies, coxcombs, and sycophants downstairs, insects out of the woodwork, a blight on Ravenworth Hall.

Mercy's voice drew Elizabeth's attention. "'Ow bout this one?" She held up a beaded gold satin gown more suited to a ball than a quiet evening supping with her aunt in their private sitting room. "Lord, is it perty."

"Too pretty for an evening in my suite, I'm afraid." She pointed to the gown beside it. "The apricot muslin should do nicely."

Mercy still held the gown. "Ye ain't takin' supper with 'is lordship? I though mayhap tonight—"

"I'm not invited, which, considering the caliber of his lordship's guests, I am not at all unhappy about. I assure you Aunt Sophie will be far better company."

Mercy grumbled something she couldn't hear and marched toward the rosewood armoire, her hips swaying with every step. Elizabeth watched her begin to lay out a fresh chemise and her mind turned to Nicholas Warring. She couldn't help wondering why a man as handsome and intelligent as the Earl of Ravenworth would choose to throw his life away.

The earl was still on her mind when she saw him the following morning. Having always been an early riser and certain that none of the dissipates who had gamed in the hall the night before would be up before noon, Elizabeth had begun taking her morning meals in the sunny little breakfast room at the rear of the house. It was a quiet, pleasant place, done in saffron and olive green, with windows that overlooked the garden.

This morning, however, as she seated herself on a yellow-striped chair in front of the oak table, the door swung open and in walked the earl. Surprise arched his sleek black brows while Elizabeth's own eyes widened.

"My lord, I . . . I didn't think you'd be up quite so early." A thin smile lifted a corner of his mouth. He closed the door and strode toward the place where she sat suddenly fidgeting with nerves. "And I thought we had an agreement. You were to take your meals in your suite while I had guests."

Her chin inched up. "Your *guests* are hardly likely to be downstairs at this hour, considering the drunken state they were in last night. And even if they were, by some miracle, to appear, I doubt my presence would offend their delicate sensibilities."

"I am not concerned with *their* sensibilities, Miss Woolcot. I am concerned with *yours*. Though some of them may be peers, they are definitely not of the first stare, hardly the sort of acquaintance for an innocent young girl." He braced his hands on the opposite side of the table and leaned forward. "And how is it you know *what* state my guests were in last night?"

She flushed a bit and unconsciously smoothed a wrinkle

from the skirt of the same apricot muslin gown she had worn the night before. "I am not a fool, my lord." She met his unrelenting gaze. "Your friends drink all day and well into the evening. They stagger through the halls as if Ravenworth Hall were their own private alehouse, and you expect me not to notice? It is a miracle our paths have not already chanced to meet."

Ravenworth leaned farther across the table, his blue-gray eyes skewering her to the seat. "Do not make me regret my decision to let you stay, Miss Woolcot. There are a hundred and forty rooms in this house. Should you choose to, you could disappear for days. From now until my guests return to London, I'd advise you to stay out of their way."

She shoved back her chair and stood up. "I shall do so, my lord. And out of your way, as well." She brushed past him and started for the door, but the earl caught her wrist before she could escape.

The eyes on her face were gentler, more a soft blue-gray. "You have come for breakfast. There is no need for you to leave before you have had the chance to eat." He turned to a servant who stood near the door to the kitchen. "Miss Woolcot and I will be breaking our fast together this morning. Have Cook send a pot of chocolate and some cakes." He glanced in her direction, his gaze even lighter, skimming over her face. Elizabeth could feel it almost as if he touched her.

"Would you care for some eggs, Miss Woolcot, or perhaps a slice of meat? 'Tis a habit I acquired since my return from the West Indies." He smiled, a flash of white in a dark, compelling face. "There are times even now, I wonder if I shall ever get enough to eat."

Something pulled in Elizabeth's chest. For the first time it occurred to her how much he must have suffered during the years of his indenture. It surprised her he could speak of it with such ease, that the smile he wore seemed so unexpectedly genuine. She could hardly believe the transformation. If he was handsome before, when he smiled that way, he was devastating. Absently, she rubbed her wrist, which still tingled where his fingers had wrapped around it.

"Miss Woolcot?"

She dragged her gaze from his face. "No . . . no, I prefer to eat light until later in the day. Chocolate and cakes will be fine."

He nodded and turned to the servant, who bowed and hurried away. Elizabeth returned to her chair and the food arrived a few moments later. It occurred to her this was the most time she had ever spent in his company. Feeling the odd thud of her heart, the dryness in her mouth as she looked at his darkly handsome features, she vowed she would not do so again.

Nick studied Elizabeth Woolcot over the porcelain rim of his coffee cup. "How old are you, Miss Woolcot?"

Her head snapped up. She looked him in the face. "I turn twenty the end of next month."

Twenty. Older than he had thought. Nine years his junior but certainly not the child he kept trying to convince himself she was. "So why is it you have not married before this? Surely you have had plenty of suitors." No doubt of that, not with the face of a fiery-haired angel and the spark of the devil in those pretty green eyes.

She took a sip of her chocolate. "To tell you the truth, marriage never really occurred to me. When my father died three years ago, I was devastated. I spent the first year deeply in mourning, and the year after that, trying to sort out my situation. Six months ago, Aunt Sophie came to live with me and my life took another, different turn. That is about the same time Oliver Hampton began his efforts to court me."

He wiped his mouth with a white linen napkin and leaned back in his chair. "Tell me about it."

She sat up a little straighter, carefully set her cup back down in its saucer. "As you mentioned before, Lord Bascomb lives in Surrey, just as I do. His property borders the small estate my father owned, which now belongs to me. Perhaps owning the adjacent property was part of his motivation."

Perhaps, Nick thought. Or perhaps he was simply entranced by Elizabeth Woolcot's beauty and fierce determination.

"My father never liked him," she went on. "He caught Lord Bascomb cheating at cards. Papa said a man like that hadn't the least amount of honor."

"Your father was a remarkable man. My father had a great amount of respect for Sir Henry."

Sadness flickered for an instant in her eyes, then it was gone. "I am grateful for the help your father gave me through the years . . . and of course for your help as well."

"Of course," he said dryly.

She flushed a little, glanced toward the window then back again. "At any rate, my father would never have approved a marriage between Lord Bascomb and me. But after Papa was gone and the period of mourning had ended, there was nothing to stop him from making advances. He appeared at my door on any number of ridiculous pretenses, and at first I was cordial to him. As soon as I realized his intention, I started refusing his calls, but by then it was too late. Lord Bascomb had decided he wanted me for his wife and he was determined to have me."

"Sydney said there was an incident . . ."

Twin spots of color settled high into her cheeks. He noticed they were the same rose shade as her lips. "There were several unpleasant incidents with his lordship, but the one Mr. Birdsall is referring to is the time Lord Bascomb managed to elude the servants and discover me alone in the study. He was attempting to . . . to compromise my person when my aunt walked in." She shook her head at the unpleasant memory.

She smiled but it looked a little tight. "Aunt Sophie may be somewhat eccentric, but she is quite clever. When Bascomb began to apologize for his behavior and speak of marriage to set the matter aright, my aunt simply acted as though she had witnessed nothing untoward happening between us. I did the same, smiling all the while, and Bascomb had no choice but to leave. He stormed out of the house—brideless again, I am happy to say—and I went to see Mr. Birdsall shortly thereafter. Sydney agreed to intercede with you."

He pondered that. She made it sound quite painless, simply an "unpleasant" encounter with Bascomb. Nick had a feeling it was far worse than that. "There is little Oliver Hampton holds sacred, Miss Woolcot. You are fortunate to have escaped him as you did."

"As I said, my lord, I am grateful for your help. I realize I am a burden, but—"

"Hardly that. A bit of an inconvenience at times, perhaps, considering the life I am used to, but I imagine we will all survive." He shoved back his chair and stood up. He was beginning to feel an unwelcome desire to linger in her company and that was the last thing he wanted. "Thank you for being so forthright. It is a rare quality in a woman. Now, if you will excuse me, there are matters I must attend. Have a pleasant day, Miss Woolcot."

She bowed her head slightly as he departed. "And you, my lord."

Two days passed. More guests arrived, two gentlemen and their ladies who had been taking the waters at not-too-distant Tunbridge Wells. Elizabeth knew who they were. Mercy Brown turned out to be a wellspring of information. For a simple vow of silence, Elizabeth had access to every bit of gossip in the house.

It was late in the morning when the carriage arrived. The jangle of harness alerted them, and Elizabeth and Mercy went over to look out the window.

"Lud, the nerve o' them hussies." Mercy shook her head, tilting the mobcap she wore over her dark hair at a precarious angle. "Comin' 'ere like they was royalty instead of some expensive London light-skirts no better than the poor gels who works the streets."

Elizabeth felt the color rise into her cheeks. "You . . . you are saying those women are . . . are . . ."

"High-priced wagtails, to be sure. Old Lord 'Arry's mistress, Emma Cox, and the viscount's woman, an actress named Jilly Payne."

"How . . . how do you know?"

Mercy waved her hands as if it were a stupid question. "They been 'ere a'fore. Lots of folks goes to Tunbridge Wells. They stop to see the earl 'cause they know 'e don't care who it is they bring with 'em."

Elizabeth watched them through the panes of the mullioned window, the women stepping down from the carriage in gowns of lace and silk, careful to keep their skirts up off the muddy ground. "They're very pretty," she said.

Mercy made a throaty, harrumphing sound and turned away from the window.

Elizabeth still stared at the women, who were being led inside by a tall blond man in his early thirties and an older, dandified man wearing an old-fashioned silver wig. The woman beside him, blond and fair but sporting a bit too much lip rouge, bent and whispered something in his ear and he gave up a husky laugh that faded as the front door closed behind them.

"Does . . . does Lord Ravenworth also have a mistress?" Elizabeth inwardly cringed to think she had come right out and asked.

Mercy's dark eyes rolled skyward. "'Andsome man like 'is lordship, 'e's got 'imself plenty of women. That prissy little piece from Westover—she's 'is latest bit of fluff. That 'igh and mighty, Lady Dandridge. But she won't last long. None of 'em do."

Elizabeth said nothing more. For some inexplicable reason it bothered her to think of Nicholas Warring with a woman like the two who had just gone into the house. With any woman for that matter.

Even his wife.

* * *

"Hurry up, Aunt Sophie—the race will be starting and we're going to miss it."

Aunt Sophie waddled forward down the hall. "Coming, my dear. I'm hurrying as fast as I can."

Elizabeth hurried, too, tying the strings of her bonnet beneath her chin, then swirling her cloak around her shoulders. Holding open the door at the side of the house, she helped her plump aunt down the steps to the gray stone walk, then led her off toward the stables at the rear.

The day had turned blustery, but it wasn't really cold. A few scattered clouds drifted across the sun, but the fields were dry, and the green of spring was beginning to poke through the rich Kentish soil.

"I hope you know what you're doing," Aunt Sophie said. "His lordship doesn't like us to mingle with his guests."

"We aren't going to mingle. We are simply going to watch." And what a sight it would be! The earl and the newly arrived Viscount Harding were staging a carriage race. Mercy Brown had told her about it—all of the servants would be watching—and Elizabeth determined so would she.

With that goal in mind, she made her way to the south wall of the barn and pressed herself against it. The stones felt cold and rough behind her back, and the earth smelled damp and musty at her feet. Peering around the corner, she checked to be certain no one was near and was relieved to see the space was empty.

A number of servants stood across from the starting line, where two smart black phaetons, one a sporty, high-perch model drawn by a pair of matched blacks, the other a lighter, drop-front phaeton pulled by a pair of glossy bays, were lined up side by side on a makeshift track. The guests formed a cluster around them, all of them, she noticed—even the women— well into their cups. Ravenworth was nowhere to be seen, off somewhere apparently making ready.

She motioned around the corner for Aunt Sophie to join her, but the old woman didn't appear. Backtracking to the side of the barn, Elizabeth found her aunt bent over, plucking bits of shiny red glass up off the ground.

"Isn't it pretty?" Aunt Sophie held a pudgy hand up to the light so the broken glass sparkled in the sun.

Elizabeth sighed. "Very pretty, Aunt Sophie, but we're going to miss the race if you don't hurry up."

"I know, I know." But she carefully filled the pocket of her cloak with the broken bits of glass before she lumbered forward. Elizabeth gripped her hand and tugged her along in her wake, rounding the corner full tilt and slamming headlong into the tall man walking the opposite way.

He caught her easily, steadying her against him to keep her from falling. "Well—look who we have here. Miss Woolcot. Why am I not surprised?" The Earl of Ravenworth stared down at her from his considerable height. Elizabeth's palms still rested on his chest while his long dark fingers encircled her waist. They felt warm and strong and for a moment she found it hard to breathe.

"I—I . . . we heard about the race. We wanted to watch." She lifted her chin. "Surely there is nothing wrong with that."

He let go of her and she took a step back, trying not to think how solid his chest had felt, how the muscles had flexed when he moved. Her glance strayed down from his full-sleeved white lawn shirt to the tight buckskin riding breeches that molded the lines of his body. She noticed the way they gloved the heavy bulge of his sex, and heat raced up her neck and into her cheeks.

Something glinted in his eyes, as if he knew where she had been looking, then it was gone. "You may watch—as long as you content yourselves with staying over here out of the way." She could smell a hint of the gin he had been drinking and beneath his dark skin his cheeks looked a little bit flushed. She didn't know if it was excitement or the spirituous liquor he had consumed.

She turned toward a small wooden shed near the racecourse. "If it's all right with you, we will watch from just over there." She pointed toward the shed, and Ravenworth nodded.

He turned his formidable gaze on her aunt. "I leave it to you, Mrs. Crabbe, to see your niece stays out of harm's way."

"Of course, my lord. You know you can always count on me."

Ravenworth's mouth curved faintly. He made a curt bow of his head, flashed a last warning glance at Elizabeth, and turned to leave. She watched him walk away, his long strides eating up the distance toward where the carriages sat, and her mouth opened up of its own accord.

"Good luck, my lord!" she called after him.

The earl stopped and turned, smiled that devastating smile she had rarely seen. "Thank you, Miss Woolcot. Since you are watching, I shall make it a point to win."

She returned the smile in spite of herself. In spite of the fact she didn't approve of gambling, even in sports, and she certainly didn't approve of a man who was half-foxed in the middle of the day.

And yet as she watched him pause in front of his carriage and speak softly to his magnificent black horses, a little thrill shot through her. With his wavy jet-black hair and silvery blue-gray eyes, his dark olive skin and flashing white teeth, he was a sight even more stirring than his magnificent horses.

"I wish we could wager," her aunt said. "I would stake my last shilling his lordship will win."

"Then 'tis probably a good thing there is no one here with whom you might bet."

"Except for you," Aunt Sophie corrected with a rise in her wobbly double chins and an arch of her thin gray brows.

Elizabeth gave up a reluctant smile. "Yes, but I also believe the earl will win, and it would be disloyal to wager against him." She watched him climb into his fancy black phaeton, his breeches tightening over his rounded buttocks. He was broad shouldered and lean hipped, and where he had rolled up the sleeves of his shirt, she could see the long, thick muscles in his forearms.

Leaning back against the seat, he clamped a thin cigar between those straight white teeth, laced the reins between his fingers, and grinned at the man who held a pistol in the air at the starting line.

He made such a rakish picture, Elizabeth found herself staring, unable to look away. The starting weapon sounded with a loud report and her heart leapt inside her. The carriages lurched off the mark, their wheels spinning, Ravenworth leaning forward, his legs braced apart on the footrest. Harding matched his aggressive drive off the mark, cracking his whip over the heads of the bays, urging them into a flat-out run. He was a big man, tall and lithe, with sandy-brown hair and hazel eyes. He was perhaps two and thirty, and according to Mercy Brown had a wicked reputation with the ladies.

He was not unpleasant to look at, Elizabeth admitted, her excitement mounting as she watched the phaetons streak down the track, but he didn't have the dark, hard-edged, masculine beauty of Nicholas Warring.

"Lord Harding just might win," Aunt Sophie pointed out. "Perhaps you should have wagered after all."

Elizabeth said nothing. Her palms were damp and she nervously chewed on a finger of her white cotton glove. The first turn loomed ahead. The horses rounded the mark, straining forward, almost neck and neck. Harding on the inside drew ahead, but Ravenworth's team caught up with him on the straightaway and pulled into the lead. The second turn put Harding back out front and Elizabeth bit down on her bottom lip. He stayed there through the straightaway but his horses were beginning to tire, sweat and lather erupting on their neck and withers.

By the time they approached the third turn, slinging mud and dirt up beneath their wheels, Elizabeth's heart was roaring in her ears. Harding was still out in front, but the earl was closing fast and it looked like the viscount's bays were slowing.

"Come on," she whispered beneath her breath. "You can do it."

They passed the fourth turn, Harding ahead again. The earl was half standing, his cigar long gone, his fingers handling the reins with a skill she hadn't expected. For an instant he turned in her direction and their eyes met across the distance. She wondered what he had seen in hers for he slapped the reins down sharply on the horses' rumps, shouted something she couldn't hear, and just as the animals reached the finish, Ravenworth's blacks surged across in the lead.

Shouts went up all round. Elizabeth was grinning, laughing out loud.

Aunt Sophie clapped her hands. "I told you he would win."

She started to wave, but her smile slipped a little and her hand stilled midway there as she watched the dark-haired earl being engulfed by his cloying group of admirers.

"Yes . . ." she said, "so you did." For a moment, she wished she could join them, wish him congratulations and share in his moment of triumph. She couldn't, of course, and the knowledge somehow made the joy she had felt only moments before begin to fade.

"We had better go back in," she told her aunt, but couldn't resist a last glance over her shoulder to where the earl held court. To her surprise, she found him watching, his gaze fixed on hers as if he sent her a silent message: *I won this race for you,* it said. Silly, she knew, yet she couldn't shake the notion. She glanced away and when she looked back, he was grinning at the woman in ice-blue silk, the actress Jilly Payne. Someone handed him another thin cigar and he bent his head while a servant struck flint to tinder.

The viscount pressed a glass of liquor into his hands and slapped him on the back in congratulations, though she wondered at the man's sincerity. It was obvious Lord Harding had expected to win and the tightness around his mouth said his loss to the earl didn't sit well.

Ravenworth lifted the glass and quickly drained the contents, and Elizabeth turned away, her mood growing darker still.

A sigh escaped her. The Earl of Ravenworth was a rogue of the very worst sort, yet there was something about him. If her father had imagined for an instant his daughter's fate would rest in the hands of a wicked, undisciplined man like the earl, he never would have given her into his good friend, the third earl's, care.

As it was, oddly enough, the days since her arrival at Ravenworth Hall, under Nicholas Warring's protection, were the first she had felt truly safe since Oliver Hampton had begun his relentless pursuit.

Her aunt chuckled softly. "Lord Ravenworth . . . he is really quite something."

Elizabeth gazed at him one last time, saw him receive a victory kiss from the lovely Jilly Payne. "He is definitely that," she agreed, ignoring the odd, unwelcome tightness that rose in her chest as they started back to the house.

THREE

$\mathcal{N}$ick's guests were still abed. They rarely arose before noon, and with the excitement of the carriage race, last night had been a particularly rousing evening.

Nick never slept in. His mental clock wouldn't allow it. Too many years of being roused before dawn to face another day of backbreaking labor. At the first whisper of sunlight, his eyes popped open and he could no longer sleep.

This morning, although a thick mist had settled over the rolling hills and his head pounded mercilessly from the gin he had consumed, he had already breakfasted and ridden out to check on one of his tenants, a man named Colin Reese whose wife was with child and due to deliver any day.

He was just now returning, walking out of the shadows of the barn into the sun beginning to break through the mist when he spotted Elizabeth Woolcot standing in the doorway of the blacksmith's shop in the low stone building across the way. Curiosity pulled him in that direction. He could see Silas McCann, the blacksmith, nodding his big shaggy head at whatever she was saying.

Nick strode up then paused beside the heavy oaken door. As yet they hadn't seen him.

"Thank you ever so much, Mr. McCann. Yesterday I spotted the perkiest little whitethroat perched on the garden wall. Perhaps with your help, we shall entice him to return."

A slight flush rose in the huge Irishman's ruddy cheeks. "A whitethroat, is it now?" He grinned. "And a lass like you knowin' which bird is which. 'Twill be my pleasure to build ye a feeder, Miss Woolcot."

She turned just then, spotted Nick lounging nonchalantly against the wall. Soft color rose in her cheeks. "I hope you don't mind, my lord. I asked Mr. McCann if he might have time to build me a bird feeder to hang outside my bedchamber window. I shall have to figure a way, of course, but I do so enjoy to watch them."

He shoved away from the wall. "And I take it you know their names."

"Quite a number of them, yes. I have always been partial to birds."

He smiled at her, thinking that she had surprised him again. He liked that about her, that he hadn't quite figured her out. He wondered how long it would take him.

He turned to Silas McCann, the big beefy Irishman he had known in Jamaica, once a convicted man like Theophilus Swann and several others in his employ. "You might as well build three or four. She can hang them in the garden."

She smiled with such pleasure a dimple appeared in her left cheek. "Thank you, my lord."

"I was just going in," he found himself saying. "But I believe I might enjoy a lesson on birds, if you would care for a walk in the garden."

For an instant he thought she might refuse, almost hoped she would, but instead, she simply smiled and accepted the arm he offered. Several species flittered past as they strolled the gravel paths and she amazed him by knowing the names of each one.

"See that speckled brown bird over there?" She pointed toward a small bird perched on the branch of a beech tree.

He smiled. "Even I know that one, Miss Woolcot. That is a common wren."

Elizabeth laughed and shook her head. "That, my lord, is a spotted flycatcher. He merely looks like a wren. One mustn't be too hasty when it comes to identifying birds."

His gaze ran over her incredible burnished dark hair, fine-boned face, and elegant, womanly figure, and he thought of the first time he had seen her, hardly noticing she was there. "As I have learned on several occasions, first impressions can often be deceiving."

"My, yes," she continued brightly, "especially with birds. Take that little blackcap over there. Most people mistake him for a blackbird."

"But not you, Miss Woolcot."

She smiled, a warm, sweet, youthful smile, yet there was an underlying strength in Elizabeth Woolcot that always seemed to shine through. "My father loved birds. He taught me to love them as well. After he died, I spent a great deal of time in the garden and they never failed to lift my spirits."

Nick smiled. "I'll remember that, should my spirits ever need lifting."

She started to speak, paused to peer around his shoulder, and he realized they were no longer alone. Roger Fenton, Viscount Harding, approached, his eyes fixed on Elizabeth and shining with an unholy gleam. Nick cursed beneath his breath. Instead of encouraging his ward to walk with him, he should have insisted Elizabeth go in.

Harding appraised her from head to foot. It was obvious he approved. "So this is the lady you've been hiding away."

Unconsciously, Nick stepped a little in front of her. "Miss Woolcot was just going in." He flashed a look of warning she could not pretend to miss. "Isn't that right, Miss Woolcot?"

"Well, yes . . . I suppose . . ."

"Viscount Harding at your service, Miss Woolcot." He

made an extravagant bow. "Nicholas mentioned his ward was in residence here at Ravenworth. Now I realize why he has been secreting you away."

"I was attempting to protect the lady's reputation—which is already tilted precariously simply by being my ward."

Elizabeth extended a white-gloved hand. "I watched you race. You were very good. You nearly beat his lordship."

Roger smiled. "Actually I usually do. Nick rarely puts his heart into the contest as he did the other day."

"Elizabeth," Nick said with warning. "I believe it is past time for you to go in." She looked up at him and a dark brow arched in surprise. He realized it was the first time he had ever used her Christian name.

"As you wish, my lord." She flashed Roger Fenton a remote, well-bred smile. "Good day, Lord Harding."

"A pleasure, Miss Woolcot." Harding watched her all the way back to the house, and with every second that passed, Nick's temper heightened.

"Whatever it is you are thinking, the girl is off limits. She is young and naïve, and while she is here, she is under my protection."

The edge of a smile tilted the viscount's lips. "She is remarkably lovely. Perhaps you have an interest in her yourself."

A jolt of heat rose at the back of Nick's neck. "The girl is my ward. Her father entrusted her into my father's care. Whether I like it or not, that means she is now under my care. That is the only interest I have in Elizabeth Woolcot."

Harding said nothing more and neither did he. But he didn't like the glint in the viscount's eyes as they followed Elizabeth's retreating figure back inside the house. Harding was handsome and eligible, but he was also an obsessive gambler with a penchant for losing. He had lost his family fortune, driven his first wife to an early grave, and was still unable to stay away from the tables. He drank overmuch and felt no qualms in seducing the naïvest young virgin.

God's blood, men like Harding were the reason he had

warned Sydney Birdsall against bringing Elizabeth Woolcot to Ravenworth in the first place. Thank God Harding and several of the others would be leaving on the morrow. Suddenly, he found himself wishing the rest of his guests were departing as well.

Dressed in a simple navy blue day dress, Elizabeth descended the sweeping marble staircase and headed down the hall toward the door at the rear of the house. She was on her way to the stables in search of the earl, familiar now with his habit of rising early just as she did. She had seen him ride out on several occasions and, this morning, spotted him through her bedchamber window dressed in his riding clothes and heading off toward the barn.

She found him there, working next to his groom, Freddy Higgins, both of them bent over, examining the hoof of one of his brood mares. Elizabeth watched them from the shadows, the barn smelling of hay and horses, of well-oiled harness, and the liniment they were using on the horse's leg. She studied them in silence for a while, surprised by the concern in Nicholas Warring's voice, drawn to its smooth, deep cadence as he carefully delivered his instructions.

"I'll take care o' it meself," Higgins said. "She's a strong'un. She'll be right as rain in a fortnight."

"Thank you, Freddy." Ravenworth turned to leave then stopped when she stepped out of the shadows. "Miss Woolcot. Up early as usual, I see."

"As are you, my lord."

"I was worried about the mare. She's been sickly of late and with the foal coming soon I wanted to be sure she was on the mend." Dressed in tight black riding breeches and a full-sleeved white lawn shirt, he assessed her with those cool, silvery eyes. "Was there something you wanted?"

Her gaze fixed on the length of rope coiled in his long dark hands and she realized how close he stood. Her heart picked up its tempo, began an uncomfortable rhythm, and her mouth felt suddenly dry. Turning away, she walked over to look at the mare.

"You have some very fine horses, my lord."

Ravenworth joined her, propping a boot on the bottom slat of the stall. "You like horses, Miss Woolcot?"

"Oh, yes, I like them very much. Actually, that is the reason I came out here this morning. I was hoping you would allow me to ride."

Amusement lifted a corner of his mouth. "Horses as well as birds, Miss Woolcot?"

"I love to ride, my lord. There is nothing more enjoyable than an early spring morning with the sun beating down and the wind in your face."

He pondered that, seemed to agree. "Do you ride well, then?"

She shrugged her shoulders. "Better than average, I suspect. I have ridden for a number of years."

"I suspect you are better than average at a lot of things. As to the riding, I see no reason why not. One of the grooms can accompany you, show you around the estate. There is a pretty little dappled gray mare, an Arabian named Sasha, who ought to suit. Just let Mr. Higgins know when you are ready."

He was standing so close she could feel the heat of his hard, long-limbed body, and the beating of her heart increased. "Thank you, my lord." He nodded and she watched him walk away. His shoulders were so wide they nearly filled the door frame, and muscles flexed in his legs with each of his long, graceful strides.

He was so very handsome. Mr. Birdsall had told her that his wife had abandoned him nine years ago when he had been convicted of Stephen Hampton's murder, yet Elizabeth couldn't help thinking that perhaps if Lady Ravenworth had stayed by her husband's side, if she had been awaiting his return from prison, his life might have turned out far differently.

She sighed to think of it. The Earl of Ravenworth and his decadent life were hardly her concern. Besides, he wasn't as bad as she had first imagined. He was kind to his servants and conscientious about his duties as earl. Perhaps there was hope for him yet.

At least she thought so until Lady Dandridge arrived.

Elizabeth stood at her bedchamber window that chilly, wind-blown afternoon, watching as the viscountess stepped down from her stylish black calèche. Lady Dandridge was dressed modishly in a high-waisted ice-blue silk gown trimmed in small embroidered roses. Beneath the brim of her hat, her hair was as glossy and dark as Ravenworth's, though her skin was pale instead of dark, and her mouth was full and the same rosy hue as the flowers in her dress.

The earl took her hands and bent to kiss her cheek. Lady Dandridge cupped his face between her palms, and her dark, sensuous gaze said exactly what she had in mind for the balance of the afternoon.

Watching them, Elizabeth felt her stomach suddenly tighten. Her chest felt heavy and she had to look away.

"I tell ye, she's worse than the rest." Standing at the opposite side of the window, Mercy Brown clucked her disapproval. "Always comin' round, chasin' after the earl, hoistin' 'er skirts like a trollop. And that poor ol' Lord Dandridge believin' she be the saint of motherhood."

Elizabeth's head snapped up. "Lady Dandridge has children?"

"What ye think? It's the way of them rich nabobs. She's done give 'er 'usband a bloody 'eir, now she can do what she pleases. It were 'er, not 'is lordship what started all this. She come round till 'e finally give in."

Elizabeth thought of the pair downstairs—or were they upstairs by now, ensconced in Ravenworth's suite of rooms, perhaps already naked in his big four-poster bed?

The thought made her overly warm, her skin tight and tingly. "Whatever sort she is, his lordship certainly doesn't seem to mind."

Mercy grunted. "No doubt of that," she agreed, and with the words Elizabeth felt a jolt of something that seemed very close to jealousy. She prayed that it was not.

"You goin' out?" Mercy asked. "'Bout time you usually do."

Elizabeth absently shook her head. "Not today. I don't . . . I don't feel much like going out."

Mercy said nothing, but those keen black eyes stayed a little too long on her face. "If there's anythin' else ye need, just give a ring downstairs."

"Thank you, Mercy."

Elizabeth read for the balance of the afternoon, snuggled into a chair in the corner of her sitting room in front of a cozy fire. But it was hard to concentrate on the words. Her mind kept shifting, imagining Nicholas Warring, his long lean body lying naked beside that of Lady Dandridge. It made her cheeks go warm to think of it, yet she couldn't seem to stop.

Anger filtered in behind the image. It was in the very worst taste for a man to bring his mistress into the house. On the other hand, the viscountess was a married woman and a peer, the ruse of a neighborly visit perfectly acceptable.

And in truth, the earl had warned her. Ward or no ward, he didn't intend to change his sordid way of life one little bit.

The knowledge put a blight on an already dreary afternoon.

Ravenworth's guests came and went, though it seemed as though there was always someone in the house. On several occasions, Elizabeth had chanced upon the earl in the breakfast room, and though he rarely spoke of his friends and never of Lady Dandridge, she found herself more and more intrigued by him. She couldn't quite say what it was, yet she sensed there was a great deal more to Nicholas Warring than the image of decadence he wore like a bright purple cloak.

A good deal more, she continued to discover, as she had the night she had come upon him in the library. It was well past midnight, the house, for once, dark and silent, but Elizabeth still couldn't sleep. It was raining hard, a gale wind blowing in from the cold North Sea, lightning flashing its ragged tentacles just outside the window.

Dressed in a heavy quilted wrapper that covered her from neck to toes, Elizabeth lifted a branch of candles off the ornate rosewood dresser and quietly made her way downstairs. Thunder clapped, echoing eerily through the house, and a slight shiver ran through her.

Standing at the door to the library, she reached for the silver doorknob, intent on finding something new to read. The knob turned, the heavy door swung wide, and for a moment, she stood frozen in the opening. A lamp was lit and the room was far from empty.

"Good evening, Miss Woolcot." Nicholas Warring leaned back in a black leather chair, a glass of gin in one hand, a thin cigar in the other. The florid, foulmouthed Nigel Wicker, Baron St. George, sat like a puffed-up toad in the seat across from him.

"Good evening, my lord. I didn't mean to intrude. I didn't realize you were in here."

They appeared to be playing cards. Stacks of money rested in haphazard piles on the polished mahogany table, and a fresh hand had been dealt facedown in front of each of the men.

Elizabeth hesitated only a moment, then walked farther into the room, determined not to be intimidated this time. Whether his lordship approved or not, she had come for a book and she didn't intend to leave without one.

She set the branch of candles on the table next to a row of leather-bound volumes behind the two men. "Gambling again, I see," she couldn't resist saying to the earl. "I don't suppose this time you are winning."

He grinned at that. "Not so you'd notice."

"Nick's a demmed fine player," St. George slurred, "when he puts his mind to it." The baron's thick lips curled up in the semblance of a smile. "Fortunately, that doesn't happen all that often."

Ravenworth took a draw on his cigar, blew several floating

gray rings, and watched them linger in the air. "Miss Woolcot doesn't approve of my gaming, do you, sweeting?"

The unexpected endearment rolled through her, curled warmly in her stomach. Elizabeth resented the intrusion, the ease with which he could affect her. "You know I do not."

St. George took a gulp of his drink, sat back, and belched loudly.

Ravenworth arched a sleek black brow in the man's direction. "I believe you met the baron a couple of days ago." He took a sip of his drink. His hair was mussed, his cravat missing, his frilled shirt undone several buttons down. Smooth dark skin covered with curly black chest hair appeared through the opening. He looked roguish and handsome and he was obviously foxed, though St. George was even more in his cups than the earl.

Elizabeth straightened her spine. "Yes, I believe we met just yesterday afternoon." She had encountered Nigel Wicker walking with Ravenworth in the maze of hallways running through the house, and the earl had been forced to introduce them.

She pasted on a smile for the overweight baron. "Good evening, my lord." But her gaze remained fixed on the earl and she thought what a waste it was for a man like him to fall into such ruin. "As I said, I'm sorry if I'm interrupting. I finished the book I was reading, but still couldn't seem to fall asleep. I promise I shan't be long."

"Take as long as you like, my dear," slurred the baron, leaning precariously toward her. "Pretty little thing like you can disturb me anytime she likes." Until his arm snaked out toward her waist, she hadn't realized how near to him she was standing. "By jove, Nicky, old boy, she's a comely bit of bag—"

In an instant, Ravenworth was out of his chair, the cigar dropped onto the floor, his drink spilled onto the table. St. George's blunt hand never reached her. Instead the dark, long-boned fingers of the earl curved painfully around the man's thick wrist.

"I told you before, the girl is out of bounds to you and anyone else who comes here. I thought I made myself clear."

The baron's fleshy lips curled in a grimace of pain and Nick released his hold. Elizabeth backed away, pressing herself against a row of books. Watching her, the baron gave up a slow, lecherous smile. "Very clear, my friend. I didn't realize you had a claim on the lady yourself."

Ravenworth's mouth thinned into a tight warning line. "The girl is my ward, nothing more. Remember that, St. George, and we won't have a problem."

Elizabeth just stared. Her mind kept replaying a picture of the earl rising out of his chair with the swift grace of a panther—and not a single trace of the drunken man he had appeared.

"Elizabeth?" he said softly. "Are you all right?"

She blinked several times, dragged in a soft breath of air. "Yes . . . yes, quite all right. I shall simply get my book and return upstairs."

"Fine, but do it quickly."

She didn't dawdle, just picked up one of Mrs. Radcliffe's Medieval novels she had spotted on the shelf two days ago, turned and hurried out of the room.

The sound of men's voices followed. She wondered what they were saying, but mostly she thought about Ravenworth. He hadn't been drunk—not really. Her suspicions grew more pronounced that the earl was a far different man than he appeared. He intrigued her, more than any man she had ever met.

Interest quickened her pulse as she decided, one way or the other, she would discover the truth about the Wicked Earl.

Clouds drifted by overhead, throwing the distant fields into momentary shadow. Then the sun slipped out once more and Nick felt the warmth on his face through the glass of his second-floor bedchamber window. Standing next to the dark blue velvet curtains, he looked down at the garden, watching Elizabeth Woolcot as she made her way along the gravel paths.

Today she wasn't alone. Two of the servants' children, Silas McCann's son, Petey, and Theo's little girl, Tildy, were holding on to her hands. She was telling them about the birds, he imagined, and the notion made him smile.

She's good with children, he thought, seeing her bright indulgent smile, hearing the faint sound of her laughter as little Tildy stooped to pick up a snail then hold it aloft as if she had discovered some grand prize. Someday she would make a good mother.

The notion slipped through him, tugging at his insides. Not like Rachael. Not like Miriam Beechcroft or so many of the other women he knew. More like his mother or perhaps his sister, Maggie.

Nick had always liked children. To him they were the essence of life, the true joy of living. Without them, the world was a duller, less sparkling place. He watched the children below, darting between the immaculately tended hedgerows where the gardener usually forbade them to play, and thought of the days when he had imagined his own brood playing tag among the Ravenworth shrubs and flowers, laughing and getting into mischief as he and his sister once had done.

In the months after his marriage, Rachael had been willing to do her duty, though he'd discovered that she, like Miriam, was far from the motherly type. Fate had intervened and spared her the task. A husband convicted of murder. Seven years' indenture. Rachael had moved into Castle Colomb, his estate north of London, and was living life on her own by the time he came back.

There would be no children for him, he knew, no heir to carry on the family name. For the most part, he was resigned to the fact, but it bothered him at times like these, times he watched little Petey and Tildy play and imagined what his life might have been if he hadn't killed Stephen Hampton.

A muscle flexed in his jaw. He didn't like to dwell on the subject. The past was over and done, and there was nothing he could do to change it. In truth, there had never been any choice for him, and even if there had been, he would have done the same thing.

He stared down at Elizabeth Woolcot, laughing with Tildy, her bonnet long gone, a single long dark auburn braid teasing an impossibly narrow waist, her face turned up to the afternoon sun. He frowned to recall the anger he had felt last night when St. George had tried to touch her. He'd reacted out of instinct, he told himself. She was his ward, his responsibility. It was only natural he felt protective of her.

In truth it was far more than that. Elizabeth Woolcot was the only good and decent thing he had allowed into his life in years. She deserved better than the pawing hands of a lecher like the baron, or a rake like Viscount Harding.

He would send her away if he could, if he trusted that Hampton had ended his pursuit, but Nick couldn't convince himself to believe it. He knew Bascomb's obsessive nature far too well to think he would quit when there was something he wanted so badly. Nick wasn't about to let the whoreson have her, nor any of his other sordid friends.

Not that he intended to change his way of life. He wasn't about to do that for Elizabeth Woolcot or anyone else. Why should he? He was an outcast, unworthy in the eyes of his peers no matter what he did. He had lost seven years of his life and he intended to make up for them, to indulge himself in any way he wanted.

In a few months' time, Elizabeth Woolcot would be gone, married to whatever man he and Sydney Birdsall chose for her. In the meantime, he intended to live as he had since his return to England. He had warned her of that before she had decided to stay.

Nick turned away from the window, determined to put Elizabeth Woolcot out of his mind, at least for the balance of the afternoon.

"Elias!" he called to his valet, whose long, solid frame

sauntered lazily into the bedchamber. Elias Moody had been his friend through the last four years of his indenture. The kind of friend a man could count on with his life.

"Yeah, Nick?" He was taller than Nick, a big, beefy man, muscled in the chest and shoulders. He had killed a man in a brawl over a woman, but he'd served time instead for stealing the dead man's watch.

"I need a drink," Nick said. "Have Theo bring me up some gin."

"Not a problem," Elias agreed. "Me work's all done. Mind if I join ye?"

Nick grinned. "Good idea." It occurred to him he had to be the only man in England who preferred the company of his servants to most of the guests who came to his house.

FOUR

        Elizabeth stroked the smooth, velvety muzzle of the little Arabian mare the earl had said she could ride. She was a beautiful horse, her coat a sleek dappled gray, darker around the eyes and feet, her head small and perfectly formed, her ears perked forward at attention.

Elizabeth loved her on sight and today she meant to ride her. Dressed in a plum velvet habit with a jaunty narrow-brimmed hat, she walked beside the groom, Freddy Higgins, who led the mare to a mounting block and helped her into the sidesaddle.

"Are ye sure ye don't want me to come with ye?" Freddy asked. He was a short man, small and wiry. In his youth he had jockeyed at Epsom Downs. His small frame was slightly stooped now, but he still knew more about horses than any man Elizabeth had ever met.

"I'll be fine, Freddy."

"'Is lordship might not like ye goin' off by ye'self."

She leaned down to pat the mare, whose pretty little head came up. "I won't go far, just to the edge of the forest and back." Sasha blew and pawed the ground, as ready as she to be off. "I've been cooped up for so long. I'd really like a little time on my own."

Freddy smiled as if he understood. "Whatever ye say, miss."

She reined the mare away, eager to be off. It was the first time she had ridden in a while, and it took a few minutes for her legs to conform to the saddle, to find the horse's stride and tune in to its rhythm.

As she galloped along, Elizabeth smiled and tipped her head back, enjoying the feel of the sun on her face and the wind against her cheeks. She rode away from the house across the rolling fields, pausing now and then just to look over the fertile landscape. Too soon she reached the edge of the forest. She surveyed the dense copse of trees then glanced back in the direction she had come.

She had promised not to go far, but the day was so lovely she just wasn't ready to go in. Deciding to continue a little bit longer, she had just topped a knoll when a flash of something glinted in the sun and Elizabeth shaded her eyes to see. Emerging from the trees at the edge of the forest, two riders galloped down the hill in her direction.

She wondered who they were and why they were riding so fast. Surely they were tenants, or perhaps friends of the earl's, but as they drew nearer, she could make out their unkempt beards and the muddy, ragtag appearance of their clothes, and a trickle of unease filtered through her.

For the first time, it occurred to her just how far she had ridden from the house. She stared at the two approaching men and her unease turned to fear. Dear God, what if they meant to harm her? What if they were highwaymen or footpads and she was out here all alone?

They were bearing down on her now, riding full tilt, and her growing fear jolted Elizabeth into action. Whirling the mare, she leaned over the animal's neck, and the horse leapt forward, breaking into a fast-paced gallop. Now that she was riding away, she told herself, surely the men wouldn't follow.

But when she looked over her shoulder, she heard one of them curse while the other brought his riding crop down with a vicious wallop. The thunder of hoofbeats increased as their horses broke into a flat-out run.

Her heart slammed hard. Dear, sweet God! There was no mistaking the men's intent—they were trying to catch her and God only knew what they would do once they did. Elizabeth leaned farther over the mare, whispering words of encouragement, urging the little horse faster. Dear Lord, what could they possibly want with her?

With a sudden flash of clarity, she knew what she should have guessed from the start. God's breath, it was Bascomb! Or more accurately, Bascomb's men, and they were trying to abduct her! Elizabeth's stomach knotted. She had convinced herself she was safe at Ravenworth Hall, but deep down she'd been afraid the earl might try something like this.

Her hands were damp inside her kid gloves, while her mouth felt as dry as parchment. Elizabeth glanced over her shoulder. Sweet Jesu, they were gaining on her!

"Pull up!" one of the two men shouted. "Dammit, do what we tell you before you get hurt!"

Pull up? Elizabeth thought, her breath coming hard, her heartbeat thundering as loud as the horses' hooves. Not on your life! She caught a quick glance of the men, who were beginning to hem her in, shortening the distance between them. Then, on the rise up ahead, she spotted the tall spires and big stone towers of Ravenworth Hall and her hammering heart leapt with hope.

She pressed the mare. The thought of her fate at the hands of Oliver Hampton made the bile rise up in her throat. She fixed her gaze ahead, silently praying, her breathing as ragged as the mare's. A stone wall lay between her and the house, a tricky jump, since a high box hedge rested in the path just before it. Still, if she could clear the hedge, she just might make it.

Elizabeth gathered the reins, her gloves damp and sticking

to her hands, her hat long gone, the braid she had coiled at the nape of her neck flying free down her back in the wind. The little mare was lathered, but she was strong and stout of heart. The hedge loomed ahead. Elizabeth pulled the riding crop she rarely used from its place beside the saddle and brought it down firmly on the animal's rump. The little mare leapt forward, took several well-placed strides, and soared over the hedge.

Sasha landed hard but stayed on her feet, and Elizabeth managed to stay aboard her. They cleared the stone wall without effort and stormed through the gate leading into the stables. Sliding the mare to a halt at the side of the barn, Elizabeth swiveled her head to look back over her shoulder. Praise God, the men had turned off to the side and were riding like fury the opposite way, into a copse of trees.

A long shaky breath whispered out and her eyes closed in relief. When she opened them again, she blinked at the sight of Nicholas Warring's tall frame standing at the horse's withers, his face a dark mask of rage.

He gripped her waist and hauled her down from the mare, his silver gaze glinting as it traveled over the animal's sweaty coat and he took in its labored breathing. Jerking the riding crop out of Elizabeth's hand, he slashed it down against his high black boot.

"What in God's name did you think you were doing? We don't treat our animals that way at Ravenworth. If I ever find out you've mistreated a horse that way again, I promise I will take this riding crop to your backside and enjoy every minute I am doing it."

She blinked several times, swayed a little on her feet. "I'm sorry. I didn't . . . I didn't mean to hurt her. I would never do that, I just—" She swayed again and Ravenworth caught her arm.

His expression changed, the anger instantly gone. "What is it? What's wrong?"

Elizabeth wet her dry lips. Beneath the skirt of her habit,

her legs were shaking so hard she was afraid they wouldn't hold her up. "It . . . it was Bascomb."

"Bascomb!"

"His men were waiting. If it hadn't been for Sasha—" She shook her head, stroked the nose of the brave little mare. Something burned behind her eyes and before she knew it, tears were sliding down her cheeks. "I had to get away. There was nothing else I could do. I was so terribly frightened."

The earl swore an oath, then she felt his arms around her, gathering her protectively against him. "It's all right, love, you're safe now. I won't let anyone hurt you."

She didn't mean to cry, but somehow, there in his arms, held tightly against his chest, the tears just spilled out. She felt his hand stroking gently over her hair, heard him whispering soft words of comfort. She knew she should pull away, but in that moment she didn't want to be anywhere but exactly where she was.

She sniffed several times and her tears finally abated. "I'm sorry." She hiccuped softly, beginning to pull away. "I don't usually cry."

"It's all right. I don't usually behave like such a bloody fool." The earl reached into his pocket and handed her a handkerchief, and she dabbed it against her eyes. "I apologize for misjudging you. I shouldn't have jumped to conclusions."

"It wasn't your fault." A shudder passed through her. "It's just that when I think of what those men meant to do . . ."

Ravenworth gently lifted her chin. "I want you to tell me exactly how all of this happened."

Elizabeth closed her eyes, picturing once more the men riding toward her. She dragged in a slow breath of air and nodded, began to relate the morning's events. She told him about the flash of light that had glinted in the sun and how, a few minutes later, the pair had started riding out of the forest.

"They must have been using a spyglass," Ravenworth said. "That is probably the reflection you saw. That was how they knew it was you."

"I wonder how long they had been waiting."

He stiffened then, his jaw going tight, and she realized he was angry all over again. "Probably for quite some time." He swore softly. "I should have known something like this would happen. I convinced myself Bascomb would leave you alone as long as you were here, but I should have known better." He turned a hard look in her direction. "And you should have known better than to ride off on your own. I specifically told you to ride with a groom."

True, but she hadn't realized why. She hiked up her chin. "I needed some time on my own. Next time, I shall take Freddy and—"

"There isn't going to be a next time. Obviously it's too dangerous. From now on you will stay near the house."

"But surely if Freddy goes with me—"

His fingers bit into her shoulders. "You saw what happened today. You've had a taste of Bascomb, more, I think, than what you've let on. The man is cruel and ruthless. If he gets his hands on you, he'll take what he wants—make no mistake about it. And I don't believe you will enjoy it."

Elizabeth's cheeks went hot and then cold. She trembled at the memory of Oliver Hampton pressing her down on the sofa in the study, his hot, damp hands feverishly shoving up her skirts.

Her eyes slid closed and slowly she nodded. "I'll stay close to the house," she said softly. "I won't go riding again."

She thought she saw a softening in the hard planes of his face, just before she turned and started walking back to the house.

Nick watched her leave, anger still pumping through him. Fury at the men who had ridden onto his land and tried to accost her. Rage that Bascomb would go so far.

Anger mostly at himself for failing to protect her.

He had given her his word that he would keep her safe, yet she hadn't been safe, and in truth it was entirely his fault.

Watching Freddy Higgins lead the tired little mare into the barn, Nick swore a long, fluid oath. He had underestimated Bascomb just as he had so many years ago. It had been a costly mistake—one he vowed not to make again. He watched Elizabeth Woolcot climb the steps to the house, her shoulders not nearly so straight as they usually were, her head drooping forward like a wilted rose. She was worried and he didn't blame her.

Thank God she'd been the capable rider he had suspected. His stomach tightened to think what would have happened if the men had succeeded in their scheme to abduct her. Thinking of Elizabeth with Oliver Hampton, of his big hands on her body, of him thrusting himself inside her, made him want to squeeze a hand around the bastard's throat.

A memory of Elizabeth appeared and he couldn't help remembering how soft and feminine she'd felt when he had held her, how her high, full breasts had pillowed against his chest as she had clung to him and sobbed out her fear. Too easily he recalled the silk of her auburn hair beneath his hand, the deep green of her eyes, round and luminous with her tears.

There was something about her, something strong yet vulnerable that touched him in some strange way. He felt protective of her as he never had of another woman. Why she affected him so, he could not say, only that for some odd reason he was beginning to care about Elizabeth Woolcot.

It was dangerous, he knew.

Dangerous for both of them.

Elizabeth returned to the stable the following day, worried that her madcap ride might have injured the little gray mare in some way.

"Sasha is fine," Freddy assured her. "A little run is good for her once in a while." He led her toward the animal's stall and the saucy little Arabian nickered a greeting and ambled over. "See, she's fit as a fiddle."

Elizabeth extended her hand, holding out a chunk of sugar.

Sasha lipped it off her palm and her perky little ears went up. "Such a good girl," Elizabeth crooned, hating the fact she had ridden the horse so hard. "So brave and strong."

She turned away with some reluctance, the animal's presence reminding her of the earl's forbidding words. "I guess I won't be riding her anymore."

"Don't ye be thinkin' that way. 'Is lordship, 'e'll have them blighters on the run in no time. 'E won't let nothing like that happen to ye again."

"Bascomb won't give up."

Freddy grinned. "Neither will our Nick."

Our Nick. It was an odd way to refer to an earl, yet she had heard others in his employ speak of him with the same strange note of familiarity. "You think a lot of him, don't you?"

"'Is lordship—'e helped me. Hired me when nobody else would. Me and a lot of the others, Theo and Elias, Silas, and Jackson, 'e's the coachy. Maybe 'alf a dozen more. And o' course there's Mercy Brown."

Elizabeth frowned. "Mercy? Why wouldn't anyone hire Mercy? She certainly seems capable enough."

Freddy's mouth flattened out and his short frame went stiff, his fingers tightening around the just-oiled headstall he held in one hand. "I thought ye knew or I wouldna' said. Me and them others . . . we're all of us ex-convicts. Some of us was indentured with Nick in Jamaica. If that bothers ye, ye don't have to talk to me no more." He watched her, his eyes fierce as he waited for her reaction. There was something in his wrinkled, weathered face that told her how important this was, how much he hoped she could see him for the man he was now, not the man he had been.

Elizabeth met his gaze squarely. "I'm a little surprised, I have to admit. But you've always been kind to me, Freddy. `Judge not that ye not be judged'—that's what it says in the Bible. That is good advice, I think." Besides, it was obvious the men who worked at Ravenworth Hall had reformed. Most likely far more than the earl himself.

Freddy seemed to relax, so Elizabeth pressed on, more curious than ever about Nicholas Warring and the people who worked for him. "Earlier you mentioned Mercy Brown. Surely Mercy wasn't in prison."

"Aye, that she was. She were arrested for stealing her employer's fancy jeweled brooch. Mercy claims she didn't do it. Swears she were wronged."

Elizabeth thought of the robust young woman upstairs. She was so forthright it was hard to believe she could possibly be a thief. "I take it you believe her, and obviously the earl did, too."

Freddy nodded. "'E knows what it's like out there, how 'ard it is to start over. Even for him, it weren't easy."

For the first time Elizabeth thought of Nicholas Warring and the life he must have led. Of the wife who had abandoned him, of the seven years he had spent at hard labor and how it must have felt to come home to a world that shunned him. A memory arose of his arms around her, gently stroking her hair. She could still recall the smell of him, of tobacco, horses, and leather. The tips of her fingers still tingled with the memory of his hard-muscled chest beneath her hands.

More and more she was beginning to believe she had misjudged him. If she had, heaven help her. She would be even more drawn to him than she was already.

"Thank you for telling me, Freddy. I think perhaps I understand his lordship a little better now." She smiled. "And I believe you should all be proud of yourselves for accomplishing what you have and turning your lives around."

Freddy grinned and a great dark hole appeared between his two front teeth. "Ye come out to the barn anytime, Miss Woolcot. Any time at all. Me and the little gray mare, we'll both of us be glad to see ye."

Elizabeth smiled even wider, feeling as if she had just made a friend. She said nothing more as she turned to walk away but she was suddenly glad that Nicholas Warring had given a man like Freddy Higgins a second chance.

Oliver Hampton, Lord Bascomb, slammed a meaty fist down on the walnut desk in his study. The motion scattered a stack of papers sitting on the corner and they floated to the polished oak floor.

"I'm tired of your whining and I'm sick of your lame excuses. It doesn't matter a whit that the girl was a more capable rider than you had guessed or that her horse had too big a lead. The fact is, the two of you have been waiting for weeks for a chance at the girl and when you finally got it, you muddled the whole affair."

Both Charlie Barker and Nathan Peel, the two ruffians he had hired to return Elizabeth Woolcot to Parkland, his estate in Surrey, had the good grace to look embarrassed.

"But we was only—"

"I've heard what you have to say. Now you will listen to me and you had better listen well. I want that girl. I don't want excuses; I don't want to wait another six weeks. I want Elizabeth Woolcot and I want her now. If that means going onto Ravenworth property—if it means going onto the grounds of the hall itself—then that's what you will do."

"But you told us not to get too close," Charlie argued, scratching his burly red beard. "You said for us to wait for the girl, catch her on the way to town or when she's out ridin'."

"Well, obviously I've changed my mind." Oliver was a big man, tall and imposing. He was used to giving orders and expecting people to follow them without question. These two were no different.

"We'll have to be careful," Nathan put in, "watch her a while and get to know her habits better. It might take a couple more weeks."

"That's right," said Charlie. "Got to do this right. Ain't no amount of coin worth facing the three-legged mare."

Reluctantly, Oliver nodded. He had waited for years. A

couple of weeks, more or less, would hardly make a difference. "Just don't take too much time. The London Season will be starting, and I want her married and settled in my bed long before that happens."

Charlie nodded and Nathan seemed to agree. "We'll get it done, milord. You can count on Nathan and me."

Perhaps he could—for enough coin to keep them in trollops and gin, they were willing to do about anything. "That'll be all, then. Bring me the girl in the next two weeks and there'll be an extra measure of guineas for both of you."

Charlie gave up a yellow-toothed grin and Nathan's thin face split with a smile of anticipation. They left through the servants' entrance at the rear of the house and Oliver went back to work, rounding his desk to pick up the papers that had sifted onto the floor.

For the next two hours, he worked over his shipping ledgers, checking bills of lading, sailing manifests, and shipping invoices. He was more than halfway through the stack when his mind began to wander, turning to thoughts of Elizabeth Woolcot, straying back to the day she had arrived home from Mrs. Brewster's very fashionable finishing school.

He had been visiting Sir Henry that day, trying to settle a boundary dispute, but he could still remember the moment she had walked through the door. His breath had caught at the sight of her. No longer the saucy little girl who had gone away, this Elizabeth was a woman, a delicious blend, he came to discover, of sensuous femininity and cleverness, of naïveté and determination.

He had decided to have her almost from that very moment, the notion more pronounced as the years went by and the proximity of their estates put them in such close contact. From the start, he had known her father would not approve, but the fact had never deterred him. He had devised at least a dozen methods to force Sir Henry to accept the marriage, each of them requiring Elizabeth to be compromised in some fashion, and the need for that had not changed.

Even with Sir Henry gone, Elizabeth had not been able to see the rightness of a union between them. In time she would, he was sure. Once they were married and Elizabeth firmly resigned to a future as the Countess of Bascomb, the trouble he had gone to would all be worthwhile. His wife might require a bit of discipline on occasion, being as strong-minded and willful as she was, but Oliver looked forward to the challenge.

A memory surfaced of Elizabeth's fine young body struggling beneath him on the sofa and his body began to grow hard. He imagined what it might have been like to fondle her lovely white breasts and take them into his mouth, to spread her shapely legs and thrust himself inside her.

Oliver groaned, his hands shaking and his body hard. He had wanted Elizabeth Woolcot for as long as he could remember. As the time drew near for him to have her, his need for her seemed to expand until it was all he could think of. He ground his teeth together until a muscle ached in his jaw.

God help his men if they failed him again.

Elizabeth thought the earl must surely have taken pity on her, must have realized how trapped she felt, even in the seemingly endless, sprawling chambers of Ravenworth Hall.

Perhaps he remembered what it felt like to be a prisoner, no matter that Elizabeth's prison was hung with satin draperies and furnished with deep feather beds. Whatever his motivation, it was early the following morning that he suggested an outing, a trip into the village for her and Aunt Sophie.

"Surely there are things you need," he said from his seat across from her in the breakfast room, "sewing supplies, ribbons—whatever it is that women buy when they spend half the day out shopping."

Elizabeth laughed. "To tell you the truth, there is nothing I need, but I shall be happy to pretend there is if it will provide an excuse for a trip into the village."

His mouth curved up. A silvery glint appeared in the pale

blue of his eyes. "You will have to stay close to me, I'm afraid. Bascomb's men may still be about and I don't want to take any chances."

Her stomach did a funny little twist. Spending time in the handsome earl's company was hardly a burden. In truth, the notion was all too appealing. It worried her, this growing attraction, but not enough to deter her from a day out of the house. She smiled. "I suppose I shall simply have to endure."

Ravenworth flashed one of his charming smiles. "An hour, then, shall we say? I'll have the carriage brought round and await you and your aunt in the Red Drawing Room."

Elizabeth nodded, feeling a surge of pleasure, and two hours later their small entourage was making its way from one shop to another along the busy street. It was market day in Sevenoaks; an area in the middle of the main street of town was filled to overflowing with colorful stalls. Vendors hawked their wares: fruit sellers, knife grinders, coal merchants, rag pickers; there were butcher stalls, cheese stalls, cloth stalls, gingerbread men, oystermongers, and a variety of arts and crafts.

As Elizabeth had told the earl, there was little she needed, but that didn't lessen the joy of being out among people again, or if she were honest, the pleasure of having Nicholas Warring all to herself.

Not that they were actually alone. The footman, Theophilus Swann, had come with them, as well as Ravenworth's valet, Elias Moody. Both of them, she recalled, were acquaintances of his from the days of his indenture, capable, hard-edged men who were obviously there for protection.

She glanced at the earl, who was dressed in a dark plum tailcoat and tight black breeches. A lacy white cravat nudged the dark skin at his throat and she found herself staring at the long lean muscles that moved whenever he spoke.

"I am so enjoying myself," Aunt Sophie said, blessedly interrupting the train of her thoughts. "And such a marvelous day it is." She wandered into a corner of the cloth merchant's stall to examine a length of scarlet ribbon, and the earl led Elizabeth away to look at a painted fan in the stall next door.

"Do you like it?" he asked, his eyes on hers instead of the fan.

Elizabeth had to force herself to look down at the object in her hand. "It's magnificent." She turned the fan over, lightly touched the tiny seed pearls that were sewn into the silk. The artist had incorporated them into the scene he had painted, a shimmering accent to the moonlit landscape on the fan. "I've never seen anything quite like it."

Ravenworth smiled. "Then it's yours."

"Oh, no, I couldn't possibly—"

"You're my ward, Elizabeth. I have every right to buy you whatever I wish, and I wish for you to have it."

A rush of pleasure spilled through her, curling warmly in her stomach. "Thank you, my lord."

Nicholas Warring smiled again, and her eyes fixed on his mouth. It was finely carved, yet she thought that his lips might be softer than they appeared. The thought made her stomach flutter in an odd, unexpected manner and her mouth felt suddenly dry. She dragged her gaze away and studied her surroundings.

"I wonder where Aunt Sophie has got off to?" She surveyed the overflowing stalls and the milling crowd but didn't see her. Aunt Sophie was in no danger and she often wandered about, yet a thread of worry began to niggle at her insides.

Ravenworth also scanned the crowd. "She has probably just wandered away, but perhaps we had better go and find her." He turned to the men he'd brought with him. "Elias, you and Theo split up. See if you can find Mrs. Crabbe. We'll meet back here in half an hour. And remember to stay alert, keep an eye peeled for anyone who might look suspicious. There is every chance Bascomb's men have been watching the house. If they have, undoubtedly they followed us here."

"We'll keep a sharp watch, milord." The fair-haired Theo grinned. "Won't we, Mr. Moody?"

"Right ye are, old son." His eyes swung to the earl's. "With any luck, one of us will 'ave your missin' lady in tow by the time we meet again."

Nicholas nodded and took hold of Elizabeth's arm. "You come with me and remember to stay close. I don't want to lose you, too." They started through the streets, both of them quietly searching.

"Perhaps she got hungry," Ravenworth said. "I smell something roasting. We'll follow the scent and see if she is anywhere near." Resting a hand at Elizabeth's waist, he urged her off toward the aroma of roasting meat. Outside the Fat Ox Inn, a big boar turned over the hot coals of a fire pit. For a few shillings, a portion of meat was carved off and served with a chunk of coarse brown bread.

Elizabeth's stomach growled but worry overrode her rising appetite. Aunt Sophie wasn't among the people standing in line for food and she wasn't at any of the tables inside the inn. It wasn't until they stepped into the alley at the side of the building that Elizabeth spotted her aunt's bulky figure bent over a heap of garbage, busily retrieving parts of a rusted hinge.

Ravenworth stopped dead in his tracks. "Good God, what on earth is she doing?"

Elizabeth's face went warm and her heart went out to her aging aunt. "Something in the trash has caught her eye. Please don't be angry. Aunt Sophie can't seem to help herself. It is some sort of odd compulsion."

Ravenworth snorted. "That is ridiculous. Your aunt feels compelled to pick through other people's trash?" But he didn't move from his place in the shadows, and as he stood watching the woman gowned in pink silk who rummaged in the alley, a look of pity shifted across his features.

He had taken a single step forward when a group of children

appeared a few feet away. Apparently they also had been watching.

"Crazy old woman," one of them shouted. "Are ye daft? Whot's a lady like you want with pieces of a rusty old hinge?"

Aunt Sophie looked offended. "Well, I . . . with a little effort it can be mended. It can be fixed good as new."

"Crazy old woman," a skinny blond boy sneered. "Notty in the noodle, ye are." They started a singsong chant, calling her names, picking up small stones and twigs and tossing them in her aunt's direction.

Ravenworth's face went hard, his bold black brows drawing together over eyes that had suddenly gone cold. He stepped out of the shadows and strode toward the children, his tall frame rigid. He opened his mouth to unleash an angry tirade, then paused.

Watching him, the children stood frozen, as caught in the unfolding drama as Elizabeth was. Suddenly Ravenworth smiled. Turning away from the children, he made a slight bow to Aunt Sophie.

"Good afternoon, madam. Would you mind very much if I examined that hinge?"

"Wh-why, no," Aunt Sophie sputtered, "of course not, my lord." Carefully, one by one, she rested the broken pieces in his palm.

"This is an extremely excellent hinge, madam. Yes . . . a very nice hinge, indeed. I should be happy to offer you a shilling apiece for each of the parts."

"A shilling apiece? But surely—"

"Two, then. You drive a hard bargain, madam."

"You are offering me two shillings? But surely they are not—"

"All right, three shillings for each, but not a penny more."

For a moment Aunt Sophie looked dumbfounded, but whatever her problems, she was not dumb. It took only a glance at the children, whose mouths were gaping open, to catch on to the ruse.

Grinning at the earl, she nodded. "All right, milord, three shillings it is."

Elizabeth's chest hurt with the effort to stifle her laughter. She hid it behind her hand.

"If you wouldn't mind," said the earl to her aunt, "perhaps we might conclude our business in the tavern. I find that I am quite hungry. Perhaps you would care to join my companion and me?"

"Yes," Aunt Sophie said, "as a matter of fact I would." The children continued to stare at the woman in pink. Aunt Sophie accepted his arm, Elizabeth took the other, and he ushered them into the inn.

It was in that moment, with her aunt smiling up at him with obvious adulation, that Elizabeth realized the true peril she had stumbled into in coming to Ravenworth Hall.

In truth, it wasn't Lord Bascomb she needed to fear but the Earl of Ravenworth, who, with only the slightest effort, had just managed to capture another small piece of her heart.

FIVE

*N*icholas looked down at the naked woman beneath him in his big four-poster bed. Long black hair streamed like silk across her shoulders. Her face was flushed and her eyes were closed, the lids fringed with thick black lashes. Small white teeth bit into her lush bottom lip.

Braced on his elbows, he surged into her again and heard her moan. He felt her body tighten around him, felt the tiny ripples of her climax. His own body tightened, straining toward release, yet his mind remained oddly numb.

He closed his eyes and for a moment it wasn't Miriam he saw but another. A woman with fiery dark auburn hair and eyes that sparkled with a touch of the devil. Her legs were longer, her body more graceful than the one beneath him, yet her breasts were full and firm. He wondered if her nipples were small and tight, or large and dusky like Miriam's. He wondered how her skin would taste, wondered if the warmth of the sunlight she loved had seeped into her pores, if the freckles scattered across her cheeks would be slightly rough against his tongue.

He wondered how it would feel to be inside her, to touch the innocence of her, the joy of living that surrounded her like sweet perfume, a joy he had lost long ago. He wondered, and as he did, his body spasmed. Release hit him hard, washing over him like a wave. He thrust deeply two more times, taking what he once thought he wanted, wasting his seed inside a woman he cared nothing about.

He lay there in silence as she climbed from the bed, taking care of her needs, wiping away the evidence of a passion that had left him feeling cold. He watched her dress, watched her leave.

But this time he did not follow.

Elizabeth sat on a wrought-iron bench along a high stone wall of the garden. The budding leaves of a plane tree cast fingers of shade over her head. A small wooden bird feeder built in the shape of a castle hung from one of the branches. A little garden warbler, a plump brown bird with pale underparts and a stubby tail, sat on the miniature drawbridge plucking up seeds.

Elizabeth smiled to watch him, enjoying the slight, jerky movements of the small bird's head as it studied her in return.

Light footfalls sounded along the path and, like the warbler, she hastily turned her head.

"I'm sorry. I didn't mean to disturb you." The woman smiled, but it held no warmth. "You must be Miss Woolcot."

Elizabeth came to her feet. "I'm Elizabeth Woolcot." Her stomach suddenly tightened, knowing only too well that the beautiful silk-gowned, black-haired woman was Miriam Beechcroft, Lady Dandridge—Nicholas Warring's mistress.

"I've been hoping to meet you," the viscountess said with another of her slightly brittle smiles. "I'm Lady Dandridge, a close friend of the earl's."

"Lady Dandridge . . . yes, I know who you are. I've seen you here before."

A fine black brow arched up. "Have you, indeed?"

Elizabeth merely smiled. The last thing she wanted was a lengthy conversation with Ravenworth's mistress. "I'm afraid his lordship isn't home at present. I believe he had some business to attend with one of his tenants."

"So I've been told." Lady Dandridge glanced back toward the gray stone house. "The whole place is empty. That isn't like Nicky at all. He usually has any number of people about. Apparently they have all returned to the city."

"I'm sure they'll be back," Elizabeth said with a touch of sarcasm she made no effort to hide. "You know what they say about bad pennies . . ."

Thick black lashes lowered over eyes a perfect sapphire-blue. "I gather you don't approve."

"I'm a guest here. I haven't the right to approve or disapprove of any of his lordship's friends. Besides, I've only met a few of them."

The viscountess waved an immaculate white-gloved hand, and Elizabeth glanced down at her own bare hands, the backs lightly freckled from the hours she spent in the sun.

"I'll grant they are not exactly diamonds of the first water," the woman said. "Why Nicky puts up with them I cannot imagine." She gave Elizabeth a knowing, slightly condescending smile. "Of course, there are any number of people who try to take advantage of a man of Ravenworth's wealth and position."

The needle found its mark and Elizabeth's head went up. "I'm certain there are."

"His wife was that way." The viscountess toyed with the fingers of her glove. "You did know he was married?"

Something sharp stabbed through her. "Of course I did." But she never really thought of him that way and the reminder felt like a barb beneath her skin.

Miriam sighed, plucked up a pale pink blossom that had fallen onto the sleeve of her high-waisted gown. "A number of people don't know. Nick never mentions Rachael and neither does anyone else—not if they wish to remain in his good graces."

"How did his wife take advantage? That is what you were implying."

"Rachael wanted his money. Nick was the Ravenworth heir, after all. That is the reason she married him."

Elizabeth shrugged. "Marriages are often arranged for such reasons. That is simply the nature of things."

"True. I am merely pointing out that there is always a motive for one's behavior. I don't know what you are interested in, but if you think—"

Elizabeth slashed a hand upward through the air, anger making the movement jerky. "I want nothing from Nicholas Warring but his protection. He has been kind enough to grant it. If you are concerned that I shall somehow interfere in your . . . friendship . . . with the earl, you have nothing at all to fear. As I told you, I am in no position to approve or disapprove of the people Lord Ravenworth chooses for friends."

Lady Dandridge seemed to mull that over. "Perhaps I was mistaken." Her gaze traveled over Elizabeth's simple muslin gown, noting the traces of dirt on the hem, the grass stains on the underskirt. "You are quite different than I imagined. Now that we have met, I shall make no more presumptions." Which meant the viscountess had decided Elizabeth posed no threat to a woman of her far greater beauty and sophistication. "I hope you understand I was only concerned for Nicky's welfare."

Lady Dandridge smiled her stilted, self-serving smile. "It might be better, however, if you didn't mention our conversation. We did discuss the earl's wife, after all, and I am certain his lordship wouldn't approve."

"No," Elizabeth agreed, "I'm sure he wouldn't." Neither discussions of his wife nor conversations with his mistress would be something the earl would approve.

"I shall leave you, then. Enjoy your birds, Miss Woolcot. I'm sure Lord Ravenworth will find them a stimulating topic of conversation." She laughed then, a clear, smug, satisfied sound matched by a confident stroll back up the path that left Elizabeth feeling oddly deflated.

It was nonsense, of course. Utterly ridiculous. What did she care if the Earl of Ravenworth had a mistress? What did it matter if he had a dozen?

But Elizabeth did care. And watching the exquisitely lovely Miriam Beechcroft enter the house as if it were her domain made her feel slightly sick to her stomach.

Charlie Barker looked over at Nathan Peel, each of them hidden behind a tall green cypress at the far end of the garden. It was late in the afternoon, blustery but not really cold, the sun streaming down between fat white intermittent clouds.

"Did ya see her? She comes here just this time every afternoon. We could nab her easy enough right here in the garden."

"Too bloody risky," Charlie argued. "His bleedin' lordship's guards might see us."

"They're posted farther out along the forest. He don't think we'd be smart enough to get past 'em."

"He doesn't think we'd be dumb enough to come in this close."

"But we are dumb enough, ain't we?"

Charlie looked at him and his mouth flattened out beneath his thick red beard. "Yeah, only we ain't gonna be stupid enough to get caught. We don't take her in the daytime, we wait until dark. The girl comes out here after supper. We nab her then. Be easier to get away."

"Yeah, but we don't know which night she'll come. We might have everything ready, the horses waitin', and that night she don't show up. Better to do it during the day."

Charlie scratched his beard. "I ain't chancin' it. I say we wait a little longer, watch how things shake out, then grab her out here when its dark."

Nathan started to argue, but Charlie pinned him with a

glare. "You want an earth bath, you idiot? You wanna dance the bloody hangman's jig?"

Nathan's ugly face went pale. "No, a' course not."

"Then dammit, man, use your head. We wait a while, watch a little longer. When the time is right we take her—catch her alone one night out here."

Nathan nodded with surprising vigor, the image of his thin body limp and swinging in a London breeze all too clear. "All right then, we'll wait. But you just remember, even if ol' Jack Ketch don't hang us—we don't get the girl and that cold-hearted sod we work for'll still see we cock up our toes."

Nick found Elizabeth curled in a window seat in the library. He was still wearing his riding boots, which were dusty and scuffed. He'd untied his cravat and slung his jacket over one shoulder. He tossed them across a chair as he strode through the house and opened the library door.

She was reading when he walked in, her hair bound into a thick auburn braid that hung down her back, a few wispy strands hanging loose beside her ears. Her eyes swung to his, and it occurred to him that he had missed her in the days since their journey into the village. The knowledge, and the sudden tightening in his groin at the sight of her, was not a pleasant discovery.

"Reading again, I see. I thought I might find you in here."

She straightened, unfolded her legs and stood up. "You were looking for me, my lord?"

"As a matter of fact, I was. I was told I had a visitor earlier in the afternoon." Elias had told him of Miriam's visit. His staff was loyal to a fault. They kept him well informed of what went on at Ravenworth Hall. "Since you spoke to her in my stead, I was curious what she might have had to say."

Elizabeth's posture grew more erect. Her lips went a little bit thin. "Lady Dandridge appeared in the garden, as apparently you have heard. She was looking for you, of course. We spoke only briefly. I imagine she was hoping for her usual afternoon's diversion."

His mouth curved faintly. "Was she, indeed? And what would you know of such diversions, Miss Woolcot?"

She closed the book but kept a finger between the pages to mark her place. William Blake, he saw, *Songs of Experience,* one of his favorites.

"I am no fool, my lord. I know what goes on between you and the viscountess when she is a visitor here."

His brow arched up. "Do you?" Somehow he didn't think so. She might have a good idea, but he didn't believe she knew for sure, and he didn't imagine she had guessed he would far rather be diverted by her. "I take it you don't approve."

She pulled her long thick braid over one shoulder and casually twisted the end. "As I told Lady Dandridge, it is not my place to approve or disapprove of what you do or with whom you do it."

"But if it *were* your place," he pressed, "you wouldn't approve of Lady Dandridge."

Elizabeth glanced away, her expression suddenly unreadable. "She is beautiful in the extreme."

"True enough." He wandered in her direction, paused beside a small rosewood table a few feet in front of her, toyed with a white beeswax candle in the candlestick on the top. "She is also selfish and spoiled."

Elizabeth didn't argue. Her look said she was surprised he had noticed. "What else did her ladyship have to say?"

Elizabeth twisted her braid. She was dressed in a sprigged green silk gown several shades lighter than her eyes. It made her look young and at the same time womanly and not young at all.

"I believe, upon making my acquaintance, her mind was put at ease. It was obvious to both of us I pose no threat to her position."

Surprise filtered through him. She really didn't know what a man saw when he looked at her? That one glance from those bold green eyes could make the most jaded rake grow hard with desire for her, make him want to know the secrets of her body. Then again, perhaps it was better she didn't suspect.

"Lady Dandridge *has* no position," he said. "As a matter of fact, lately I find I've grown quite bored with her."

He tossed the leather riding gloves he still carried on top of the table. "Odds are, in future, her visits to Ravenworth—if they should occur at all—will be few and far between."

Elizabeth said nothing, just studied him in her usual straightforward manner. "You are angry that she approached me. You're upset because your mistress conversed with your ward. Lady Dandridge said you would be."

"Lady Dandridge's astuteness is amazing. However, that is not the reason I intend to end our relationship."

"If it is because I am in residence—"

"Your presence here has nothing to do with it. I told you I would not alter the way I live."

"Then why—"

"As I said, Miriam Beechcroft is selfish and spoiled. I simply grow weary of her childish behavior."

She cocked her head as if she pondered his words. "I suppose you have someone else in mind, someone who has piqued your interest. A man of your reputation must have any number of women he wishes to seduce."

Bloody hell, she *was* naïve—and thank God for it. If she suspected for a moment the lust he had begun to feel every time he looked at her, fear of Bascomb or not, she would run like a scalded rabbit back to her house in West Clandon. The plain truth was, she needn't worry. His desire for her made not the least bit of difference. He had given his word and he did not mean to break it.

He gave her the answer she expected. "A man has needs, Elizabeth. My wife and I are estranged these past nine years."

"I know about your wife." Something softened in her features. "I am sorry, my lord."

Dammit, he didn't want her pity. Embarrassment made his jaw go hard. "Don't be. My life is my own and for that I am grateful." He turned before she could speak, before she could read the lie in his eyes, the fact that the freedom he had so bitterly paid for only meant he had nothing left to lose.

He started walking. "Enjoy your book, Miss Woolcot." And then he was safely out the door.

Elizabeth sat across from Aunt Sophie in the dining room. A few of his lordship's friends had stopped by but they had all departed, and to her surprise, the earl had invited them both to sup with him tonight.

Seated with the others at one end of the mile-long table, Elizabeth smoothed her napkin over the skirt of her green silk gown and watched the earl in the light of the silver candelabra. He was dressed in a velvet-trimmed dark plum tailcoat over a silver brocade waistcoat, frilled lawn shirt and lacy cravat that looked remarkably white against his dark skin. Tight black breeches disappeared into shiny black shoes.

A footman served him a portion of roasted pheasant. He smiled his approval and Elizabeth found it difficult to look away from his face. Sweet God, surely it was a sin for a man to be so handsome. And yet he was not handsome in the usual sense. There was a harshness to his features, a darkness to his finely carved profile that made him seem unreachable, cold, perhaps even brutal.

She turned her attention to the gold-rimmed plate in front of her, saw the steam rising up and inhaled the mix of delicious aromas. The meal was sumptuous: oyster soup, turbot in lobster sauce, partridge and truffle pie, veal sweetbreads with sweet walnut stuffing, candied carrots, and cabbage drenched in butter. An apple pudding was among the confections promised for dessert.

The earl dug in with great gusto and Aunt Sophie followed suit.

"My goodness," the plump woman said between bites.

"This is utterly delicious. Your cook has outdone herself tonight, my lord."

"Thank you. I shall tell him you said so."

"Him?" Aunt Sophie repeated. "Your cook is a man?"

"Yes."

"Is he also one of those you met while you were indentured?"

Elizabeth nearly choked on the bite of veal she had been eating. "Aunt Sophie, I doubt his lordship enjoys discussing his past. Undoubtedly it is painful for him."

Nicholas wiped his mouth with his napkin, and she found herself staring at his lips. Beautiful lips, she thought, and immediately wished she had been looking somewhere else.

"On the contrary." Ravenworth took a sip of his wine. "I spent seven years of my life in Jamaica. It seems rather ludicrous to pretend they never happened. But as for my chef, no, Valcour was not with me in Jamaica. He was here when my father was still alive. He and Edward Pendergass are among the few who remained with me after I returned from being transported."

Curiosity made her bold, a desire to know more about him. "What was it like, my lord? Was it as terrible as everyone says?"

He leaned back in his chair, stretched those long legs out in front of him. "At first it was. I couldn't believe I was actually there, that I was really a prisoner, at someone else's mercy for the next seven years."

He shook his head. "The transport ship was a nightmare and once we landed on the island it wasn't much better. We were treated like animals, and in truth a number of the men behaved that way. They were murderers and thieves, cutthroats, pickpockets, and sharpers. But a few of them were decent men who had simply made a mistake."

"Like Freddy Higgins," Elizabeth said.

"Like Freddy, and Theo, and Elias. Circumstances forced them down the road they traveled but they were determined the years they spent in servitude wouldn't be wasted. They swore that when they returned to England they would make a better life for themselves than the one they had left behind."

"And you helped them make that happen."

He shrugged his broad shoulders. "I did what I could. In one way or another, each of them has helped me."

"A fine notion, indeed," Aunt Sophie put in, "giving those less fortunate a second chance. Not very fashionable, I vow, but then, you are hardly a member of the fold at any rate."

Elizabeth flushed, but Nicholas merely grinned. "Hardly," he agreed.

"You said at first it was terrible," Elizabeth continued. "Did your situation somehow improve?"

He nodded, took another sip of his wine. As much as he strove for nonchalance, a fine thread of tension had crept into his features, making his face look hard.

"For the first few years I worked in the sugarcane fields. It was backbreaking labor, not to mention the bugs and the heat. Four years into my indenture, the plantation was sold and a new owner took over. His name was Raleigh Tatum. He was honest and hardworking, determined to make his business more profitable. When he learned I could read and write, he took me out of the fields and ordered me to work on his ledgers. In time we became friends of a sort. I helped him manage his business affairs and in return he made my circumstances more comfortable while I served my last few years."

Elizabeth mulled that over. She could only imagine the misery he must have suffered, even though he tried to make light of it. "I should think you would be bitter, but I can see that you are not."

He shrugged again, but the tension remained, a subtle tautness in the muscles across his shoulders. "I knew the consequences of my actions when I went that night to confront Stephen Bascomb. I meant to see him dead—one way or another. In truth, I am lucky I did not hang."

A chill ran through her. *I meant to see him dead.* It should have been shocking to hear him say such a thing, yet knowing him as she had begun to, she wondered what Bascomb had done to deserve the treatment he had received. She wanted to ask, but she was afraid to. The harshness in his features, the stiffness in his bearing, warned her she had pressed him far enough.

"Well, I believe I am ready for dessert," Aunt Sophie said, for once having the good sense to know when it was time for a change of subject. "You promised apple pudding, my lord, and I can almost taste it already."

Ravenworth relaxed, his smile a radiant white against his dark skin. "Then let us see it done, Mrs. Crabbe." He turned to the footman, who nodded, bowed, and backed away, returning a few minutes later with a large silver tray covered with an array of sweets including the promised pudding.

Elizabeth sampled hers while Ravenworth's dark head bent over the plate set in front of him. Little by little she was uncovering pieces of the puzzling Wicked Earl, yet she could not seem to fit them all together. He was a rake and a rogue, a gambler and a womanizer who made no bones about it. Yet there was something in his eyes that said there was another, altogether different man inside.

Perhaps it was simply wishful thinking. Perhaps he was the hopeless rake he usually appeared. Elizabeth was no longer certain—of the earl, or why she so desperately cared.

The evening turned out to be surprising pleasant, at least until the final few moments after Aunt Sophie had retired, leaving her and Ravenworth alone in the drawing room. Their easy conversation turned stilted as the hour wore on, Ravenworth sitting just a few feet away, his eyes turning dark in the lamplight as he watched her.

There was something disturbing in their silvery depths, something that made her breath catch and her heartbeat quicken. She found herself staring at his mouth while his gaze seemed to drift lower, to settle on the curve of her breast. The room felt hot, her skin flushed and damp.

Excusing herself on the pretext she was tired, she retired upstairs to her room, but it was impossible to think of sleep. The solitude of the garden beckoned. Surely, if she were quiet, if she used the back stairs, she could make her way outside and no one would be the wiser.

Pulling a cashmere shawl out of a dresser drawer, Elizabeth slung it around her shoulders and tied it over her breasts. She passed Mercy Brown coming up the stairs, but the girl was used to her occasional nightly treks and merely mumbled a greeting as she passed.

The night was especially dark, the moon a mere crease of light against a backdrop of thick gray clouds. It hadn't begun to rain, but the breeze was heavy with the smell of moist earth, and there was a dampness in the air that wouldn't allow her to stay out long.

Still, she made her way through the winding gravel paths, letting the solitude wash over her, enjoying the crisp night air and the slight evening breeze. An owl hooted softly and she turned to see him streaking above her head, a flash of white against the blackness of the sky, the quiet disturbed by the heavy flap of wings.

Elizabeth smiled. She had always loved owls. They seemed so mysterious. Unfathomable creatures, aloof and independent, governed by no man's law but their own. Rather like the earl, she mused, then smiled to think he would probably not take kindly to being likened to an owl. No, more a falcon, people would say, ruthless and aggressive, a dangerous predator, a creature to be reckoned with. Or the raven of his name, perhaps, sleekly dark and sinister.

Elizabeth thought him more a hawk, dangerous when the need arose, a beautiful, capable bird who hunted only to care for himself and his nestlings. An odd thing to think, she conceded, since the earl unashamedly admitted to willfully murdering a man.

Pulling her shawl a little tighter, Elizabeth continued along the path, pausing here and there to study a newly blossomed flower. A shadow appeared a little to her right, just at the edge of her vision, and Elizabeth started. Surely she had imagined it, yet her heart began to pound, the blood pumping fast through her veins. She listened hard but heard nothing to alarm her. Perhaps it was simply the owl, returning from its foray across the fields.

Certain that must be it yet still a little nervous, she turned and started back up the path toward the house. She'd gone only a few short paces when fabric rustled, footfalls sounded, and a man sprang into the path in front of her.

Elizabeth screamed before he could stop her, turned and started to run, but another man appeared on the path behind her and she collided with his chest. He was a thin man, skin over bones, but he was tall and he was stronger than he appeared. Shoving hard against him, she twisted away from the hand he clamped over her mouth, and screamed again, but it came out muffled and weak.

The first man, larger and rougher than the other, swore an oath and jerked her around. He wrenched an arm up behind her back until pain shot into her body and she thought she might be sick.

"Shut your damned mouth, wench, before I shut it for you." He was a burly man with a thick red beard and it was obvious he meant what he said. "You hear me? From now on you be quiet and do exactly what I say."

She winced at the pain, bit down on her trembling bottom lip and nodded, though as soon as she could muster the courage she intended to scream again.

In the end she didn't have to. A noise sounded in the garden, someone running along the path. A flash of movement, a body hurling through the air, then the skinny man went down as if he'd been hit with a barrel of bricks.

"Nicholas!"

He grabbed the bony man by his shirtfront, lifted him up

and punched him in the jaw so hard his head thumped loudly against the gravel. The burly man gripped her arm and started to drag her away, but Elizabeth dug in her heels and began to fight him. She wasn't going to let him take her to Bascomb, not as long as there was breath left in her body.

Nicholas bolted after them. He gripped the man's shoulder and whirled him around, pried her loose from the bruising fingers and shoved her out of the way, then swung a blow to the stomach that doubled the big man over.

The red-bearded man came up swinging, but so did the earl. Nicholas dodged a heavy blow, then threw a vicious punch to the stomach that had the heavier man doubling over. The earl's knee shot up beneath the man's chin and a loud crunch sounded. He tumbled over backward, landing solidly on his arm, and the crack of bone split the quiet in the garden. A harsh groan was followed by a curse, then the man was on his feet and running, holding his shattered arm, his coattail flapping, his tall, skinny friend pounding along in his wake.

Nicholas didn't follow, just strode to where Elizabeth stood swaying on her feet and gathered her gently into his arms.

His hand stroked over her hair. "Elizabeth, are you all right? They didn't hurt you, did they?" He was breathing hard but so was she. She could feel the last faint hum of energy still running through his body.

"I—I'm fine. Just frightened mostly."

He held her a moment, letting her absorb the heat and comfort of his body. Then he eased himself away. Examining a slight bruise on her cheek, he swore an oath she thankfully didn't catch.

"It's nearly midnight, dammit. What the devil were you doing out here?"

Elizabeth hauled in a steadying breath. "I needed some air. I often come at night to the garden."

"You often—" His jaw clamped down. "Sweet God, woman, have you lost your wits? Those were Bascomb's men.

They must have skirted my guards and found a way onto the grounds of the house. I didn't think the whoreson would be so brazen, but apparently this is another time I've been wrong." Silver-blue eyes bored into her. "And you make it so damnably easy."

Elizabeth swallowed. He was madder than she thought. "I'm sorry. I believed it would be safe."

"Well, obviously it isn't." His fingers dug into her shoulders. A muscle tightened in his cheek. "Bloody hell, Elizabeth, you have to be more careful. Don't you understand—if I hadn't been out on the terrace when you screamed, Bascomb's men might well have carted you away!"

Elizabeth bristled, jerked free of his hold. "I'm sorry this happened, but I can't stay inside all the time. For God's sake, I was only walking in the garden!"

"Yes, dammit—and you were very nearly abducted. From now on you won't go out of the house by yourself. You won't go anywhere unless someone is with you."

Elizabeth's chin shot up. "That is insane. I refuse to live that way. You don't own me, Nicholas Warring. I won't be treated like a prisoner and there is nothing you can do about it."

A dangerous glint appeared in those steel-blue eyes. Bold black brows pulled down, making him look every bit the dangerous man he was. "Isn't there?"

She swallowed hard but didn't look away. "No, there is not. You might scare everyone else, but not me. I'm not the least bit afraid of you."

His expression turned as dark as the thunderclouds overhead. He drew himself up until he seemed to tower above her. "You ought to be afraid of me, Elizabeth." The words whispered out with soft menace. "Perhaps you should fear me even more than you do Lord Bascomb."

For a moment, his gaze held hers and she felt like a bird caught in a net. Then he dragged her hard against him and his mouth crushed down over hers. It was a brutal kiss, punishing in its force. She tried to twist free, but he held her fast, parting her mouth with his tongue. It swept inside boldly, sending little shivers down her spine. Her hands pressed against his chest and she could feel the heat of him, the muscles expanding, the too-rapid beating of his heart.

His knee slipped between her legs, brushing the inside of her thigh, and she told herself to push him away, that what he was doing was wrong, but her hands remained on his chest and the throbbing of her pulse matched the heavy cadence of his.

Something shifted in the air between them. His hard mouth softened, the rough kiss gentled, turned coaxing instead of demanding. His lips were firm yet pliant, giving now instead of taking, as soft as she had imagined, warm and strong, yet somehow oddly tender.

Heat rolled through her, settled low in her belly, spread like warm honey through her limbs. It was a sin, she knew. Nicholas Warring was a married man. He was a rake with a dozen mistresses, a man who took whatever woman he wanted then grew bored and brutally cast them away.

It was wrong, but it didn't feel wrong at all.

Nicholas groaned and pressed her more fully against him, into his heat, the power of his solid frame. She felt the rigid hardness of his desire, but instead of pulling away, her arms slid around his neck and her fingers laced into his wavy black hair.

A small sound came from her throat and Nicholas shuddered. For an instant he deepened the kiss and her whole body burned. Then suddenly he went still. His heart was thundering, his tall lean frame nearly rigid. Clasping her wrists, he carefully freed himself and took a step away. His expression was dark and unreadable, as if the fire she had seen in his eyes had been banked for another day.

"Go back to the house," he said, his voice low and harsh. "Do it now, Elizabeth, and don't come out here alone again."

Elizabeth didn't argue. Her lips still tingled from his kiss; her legs felt wobbly and numb. She managed a faint nod in his direction, turned and raced back toward the house.

This time the fear pumping through her had nothing to do with Bascomb or his men.

Six

ick paced the floor of his bedchamber. For the third time within the hour, he paused beside the window overlooking the garden. On the ground below, anemones, pansies, and tulips had begun to bloom in bright shades of purple, yellow, and pink. Color streamed along every walkway, yet Nick found himself thinking how bleak it all looked without Elizabeth there to enjoy it.

Three days had passed since he had banned her from her favorite place of refuge. It wasn't fair, he knew. It was his fault the men had been able to breach his defenses. He had underestimated his opponent yet again.

Nick looked down from the window. From his vantage point above the garden walls, he could see the men Elias had hired, a veritable army this time, placed at strategic points along the rough gray stone.

Elizabeth would be safe there now. She could pick flowers if she wished or sit and study her birds. She would be safe in the garden. And, he vowed, she would once more be safe from him.

Nick turned away from the window, his strides long and

determined as he crossed the room, turned the silver knob, and pulled open the door.

Elias Moody called out to him from the door of his dressing room. "She's in the conservatory, Nick. I seen her go in there this morning."

His mouth edged up. "How do you do that? How do you always manage to know what I am about?"

Elias gave him a canny smile. "Ain't much of a trick in this case. Miss Mercy seen ye kiss 'er the other night in the garden. Ye been moody and out of sorts ever since. I figured, sooner or later, ye'd be tellin' 'er ye was sorry."

"I am sorry, dammit. I can't believe how badly I lost control."

"You're a man, my friend, nothin' more. She's a pretty little thing and ye've got feelin's for 'er."

"I'm not allowed to have feelings like that. For God's sake, man, I'm her guardian. I'm supposed to be protecting her."

"And so ye did."

"I also scared her half to death. It's a wonder she hasn't packed up and left." He shook his head. "I hope I can convince her it won't happen again."

Elias made a rude sound in his throat. "I hope ye can convince yerself."

Nick gave him a brief sidelong glance, stepped out in the hall, and closed the door behind him. Elias was right. As bad as he felt about taking advantage of Elizabeth the other night, he still wanted her. Now more than ever. Dammit to hell, if only he could send her away, get her out of his life, out of his blood. But he couldn't do that, at least not yet. Thank God the Season was fast approaching. Sydney Birdsall would already be compiling a list of eligible bachelors, suitable choices from which Elizabeth could find a husband.

In the meantime, he would simply stay away from her, do what he had been doing for the past nine years.

Soothe his appetites somewhere else.

The conservatory was humid and warm, a tall glass-enclosed structure sitting off at one end of the house. It wasn't a place he frequented, since he preferred the out-of-doors, but his mother had always enjoyed it. The last time he had been there, it was badly overgrown. He had meant to order the dead foliage stripped away and something green planted in its stead. He had never quite got round to it.

Now, as he pulled open the door, he was surprised to see Barnaby Engles, his chief gardener, furiously pulling weeds, tossing them into a growing pile at his feet. Elizabeth worked a few yards away, carefully scraping the dead leaves from the soil at the base of a row of miniature orange trees.

Nick watched her a moment then made his way in that direction, stopping directly in front of her. When she still didn't see him, he cleared his throat, shifting his weight from one foot to the other, nervous all of a sudden.

"I can see that you are busy. I'm sorry to intrude, but I was hoping I might have a word with you."

She brushed the dirt from the front of her simple blue gown, her face flushed with a hint of embarrassment that he had found her working on her hands and knees. "Of course, my lord."

He waited while she washed in a rusted bucket of water and dried her hands on a scrap of linen, then allowed her to walk in front of him out of the conservatory and back inside the house. He motioned her into a small salon he called the Quiet Room and softly closed the door.

Elizabeth waited for his direction, then took a seat in an overstuffed dark green velvet chair. Nick sat down in a carved wooden chair across from her.

He drew in a steadying breath. "This isn't easy for me, Elizabeth. I'm not a man used to making apologies, but the fact is, as much as I hate to admit it, I owe you one."

Her head came up. Color seeped into her cheeks. "That is the reason you brought me here?"

"Yes. I was out of line the other night. I was completely

in the wrong and I am sorry. My only excuse is the fear I experienced when I saw what those men were trying to do. I was angry at myself for letting it happen and angry at you for putting yourself in danger."

She kept her eyes trained on his face, but her hands were clenched tightly together. "We were both of us upset. I was frightened; you were angry. It was really no one's fault."

Nick shook his head. "I took advantage. What happened between us should never have occurred. I'm your guardian. I am older, and obviously I should be—"

"You are not all that much older, my lord. And if you think I see you as some sort of father figure, you are quite mistaken."

For a long time he said nothing, but he couldn't help wondering just how Elizabeth Woolcot did see him.

"Your rescue was most timely. You were quite brave and I have been meaning to thank you."

"Thank me? Make no mistake, Elizabeth. You owe me no thanks. All I ask is that you forget what happened between us."

She glanced down, studied the smattering of freckles on the backs of her hands. Slender hands, long-fingered and graceful. "No one has ever kissed me that way," she said. "I doubt I shall ever forget it."

Nick felt a surge of heat at the back of his neck. It traveled through his limbs and settled low in his groin. He doubted he would forget it, either. "I've posted guards around the garden. You'll be safe there from now on. You'll be able to enjoy your birds without fear someone may be lurking behind the walls."

She smiled with such pleasure something tightened in his chest. "Thank you, my lord. I admit I have missed it sorely."

Nick simply nodded. "The conservatory was a shambles. I am grateful for your direction in setting it aright. Let me know if there is anything you need." He rose to his feet and she did as well, but she made no move to leave. He left her standing in front of the overstuffed chair, her gown slightly wrinkled, the hem covered with dirt, looking more desirable than any woman he had ever seen.

He headed straight for the decanter of gin in his study. Tomorrow Baron St. George would be returning, along with Lord Percy and Richard Turner-Wilcox. They were bringing something "guaranteed to divert him," their message had said.

He had never been more grateful for such an occasion.

Elizabeth lay awake in her bedchamber, staring at the mauve silk canopy above her head. She was thinking of the earl, remembering his apology that afternoon. It was the last thing that she had expected.

Then again, perhaps it shouldn't have come as such a surprise. The earl took his duties seriously, she had learned, for all his rakish ways and wicked pastimes. Still, it had come as somewhat of a shock. An apology, she had reasoned, would not be forthcoming from a man who took what he wanted from a woman and never looked back.

And in truth, she didn't deserve one. After the first few startling moments, she had enjoyed the kiss. It was every bit as exciting as Nicholas himself, and as much as she knew she should regret it, she did not.

He is married, the voice of her conscience told her.

He is lonely, she argued. *He has been abandoned.* It was silly, she knew. A ridiculous rationale to keep her from feeling guilty, but in truth part of her believed it. Rachael Warring was no wife. The Earl of Ravenworth had no wife, nothing but a name scrolled beside his in the register of some ancient church. In the eyes of God, he was alone.

Elizabeth couldn't stop wondering what he might have been like if he had married a woman who loved him, who had stayed by his side when he needed her.

And she couldn't stop thinking about that kiss.

Elizabeth unbuttoned the top of her nightgown, suddenly overly warm. She could still feel the pressure of his tall, hard body, the movement of the muscles across his chest.

Against the thin cotton fabric, her nipples peaked and her skin grew damp. It was desire, she knew. Desire for Nicholas Warring.

Elizabeth understood little of what happened between a man and a woman, but she knew desire was a part of it. In the hayloft back home in West Clandon, she had seen a couple lying naked, holding each other in a passionate embrace. She had turned away, of course, run like a deer back to the house, but she had never forgotten the rapture on their faces, or the soft sighs of pleasure that seeped from the barn.

She thought of that scene now, but the man she imagined naked wasn't one of her father's grooms. It was tall, dark Nicholas Warring. Brown-skinned and sleekly muscled, a tough man with a hard mouth that softened when he kissed. Sweet God, she wanted him. Wanted him to touch her, to kiss her. To do whatever it was a man did to a woman to make her his.

She was attracted to Nicholas Warring in a way she had never been attracted to a man before. In truth, she was afraid she was falling in love with him.

Sweet God, you must be mad, said the voice. *The earl is the one man you can never have.*

If only she could go home, back to her house in West Clandon. She would be safe from this dangerous attraction she felt for the earl, safe from the riot of feelings he stirred whenever he was near. Elizabeth knew there was no going home. Not yet, not until she was safely married.

Oddly enough, a husband—her salvation from Bascomb, the home and family she had always dreamed of—was the last thing she wanted now.

Oliver Hampton surveyed his beaten and battered men. Nathan Peel had two black eyes and a cut beside his nose. Charlie Barker, with his swollen lip, scabbed-over knuckles, and bruises on his chin, looked as if he had fought in a war, to say nothing of the broken arm in a sling across his chest.

Oliver's lip curled in distaste just to look at them. "You two make me sick. I send you out to do a simple job and twice now you have botched it. I ought to have a go at you myself."

"The man's a bloody maniac, is what he is," Charlie grumbled. "Come at us outta nowhere, fought like some kinda madman."

"Yes, well, the man is a killer. You knew that when you took the job."

"He's got guards all over the place," Nathan said. "Ain't no way we can get to her now."

Oliver came out of his chair, his big hands fisted as he leaned over his desk. "You will *find* a way to get to her—do you hear? I shall hire a couple more men—someone who isn't afraid to use a little force. If you eliminate a few of those guards, you won't have a bit of trouble getting in."

"You ain't askin' us to kill someone?" Barker asked warily.

Oliver ground down on his jaw. "I'm not asking you—I'm telling you. I'm ordering you to get that girl any way you can. If someone gets in your way, you will deal with him."

"We'll have to get in the house," Nathan said. "We can't sit around waitin' for her to come out again."

"All right. We'll need someone to help us from the inside, but I can handle that. With the flotsam in Ravenworth's employ, it shouldn't be all that difficult to find someone with the taste for a bit of gold. It'll take me a little time to get everything lined up. As soon as I do, you'll go after her. I want that girl and I want her soon. And I don't want any more failures."

Charlie looked uneasy, but Nathan simply nodded.

Oliver pinned the bigger man with a glare. "What about you, Barker? Are you in or are you out? The man broke your arm. I would think you'd have a score to settle."

Charlie grunted. "I can still ride a horse and I can shoot. Ravenworth gets in my way, this time he's a dead man."

For the first time Oliver smiled. "That's more like it. You get this done and I'll pay you double what I promised. That'll keep you in women and liquor for a good long time." The words seemed to please them. The two men came to their feet while Oliver sat back down in his chair.

"You get us those men," Barker said, "we'll get you the girl."

"Done." Oliver watched them leave, his thoughts returning to Elizabeth Woolcot. In the eye of his mind, he saw her big green eyes and long dark auburn hair, remembered the feel of her breasts pressing into his chest that day on the sofa, and his body went instantly hard. He would have her. By God, he would have her and soon.

Oliver smiled. Reaching across his desk, he lifted the lid off a cut-crystal humidor sitting near the edge, and pulled out a fat cigar. All the years, all the waiting, would soon be over. Biting off the end, he bent toward the fire and lit the end.

It felt like a moment that needed a little celebration.

"The bloody leeches 'ave arrived." Mercy Brown shook her head, thick dark brown hair spilling over one shoulder. The girl often wore it down, clipped back on the sides, a tantalizing mass of curls that swung seductively against her broad hips as she moved.

"So I gathered," Elizabeth said. "A note came advising us the earl would be receiving guests tonight and that supper for my aunt and myself would be served upstairs in our suite." She plucked a loose thread from the bodice of her blue muslin gown, looked up to where Mercy stood beside the window. "By the way, which leeches are they?"

Mercy made a face, her pretty lips curling in distaste. "That foulmouthed Baron St. George and that no-good Lord Percy. And of course there's that lecher, Richard Turner-Wilcox. 'E's the best of the lot and all 'e thinks of is which of 'is tarts 'e's gonna tup next."

Elizabeth stifled a smile. She was growing used to Mercy's blunt language. In a way it was refreshing. Elizabeth had never known a woman who spoke with such candor. And yet, considering the way she talked and dressed, Mercy was surprisingly prudish. She wanted the men's attention, but she expected them to behave like gentlemen. Elizabeth wondered if perhaps she were angling for a husband.

Several hours passed. A commotion in front of the house announced that a second conveyance had arrived. Elizabeth was standing at the window when Mercy burst into the room, walking with her usual energetic stride toward the place where she stood.

"Turner-Wilcox and 'is bloody tarts—a sodden carriage-load of 'em."

Elizabeth turned back to the scene below, more curious than outraged as Mercy seemed to be. Four silk-gowned women stepped down to the gravel drive, their faces whitened with rice powder, their lips and cheeks reddened with rouge. With their flashy feather bonnets and ruffled silk parasols, they were garishly dressed and overdone, but still, they were pretty, their figures womanly, their breasts high and full, nearly spilling from the tops of their low-cut gowns.

"Wagtails for Turner-Wilcox and 'is no-account friends."

Elizabeth merely shrugged. She was no longer shocked by the earl's unconventional visitors. She didn't particularly like the idea of the house being overrun with ladies of the evening, but the earl was helping her when no one else would, and as she had said, it was not her place to disapprove.

And strangely enough, she wasn't worried about the effect the women might have on the earl. If Miriam Beechcroft was any example, his taste ran to a far more refined, more subtle sort than that.

As handsome as he was, even with—or perhaps because of—his sordid reputation, he was appealing to any number of females. Elizabeth didn't doubt there were a score of beautiful women from whom he could pick and choose.

The thought settled like a weight on her chest.

Moving away from the window, she sat down in a chair in front of the hearth and picked up the book of bird sketches she had discovered in the library. Her aunt would be awakening from her afternoon nap and soon would be joining her. They would take supper together in their suite and retire to bed early.

Elizabeth didn't intend to mention the carriage load of women who had just arrived at Ravenworth Hall.

Joining his friends in the Pink Drawing Room, a large high-ceilinged, ornately gilded salon that he rarely used, Nick took another long drink from the glass of gin he carried. Across the room, Richard Turner-Wilcox sat at a table with Baron St. George, dealing a hand of whist. One of the women, a short, big-breasted blonde, sat on Richard's lap, while another hung around the thick, flabby neck of St. George.

Across the table, Lord Percy sat between the other two women: a tall, blowsy brunette with a set of massive breasts; and a well-built, passably pretty redhead. One of Percy's hands strayed inside the brunette's bodice, stroking over a red-rouged nipple that occasionally peeked from the top.

It was a scene Sydney Birdsall would have expected to find in what he called Nick's "fresh-air den of iniquity." Nick had seen such displays often enough, but he rarely joined in. He preferred his own mistresses to the painted women his friends often brought. Tonight, however, he was already half drunk and badly in need of a woman.

Any woman, he told himself. Even one of Richard Turner-Wilcox's pretty whores.

Baron St. George looked up just then and saw him walk through the door. "Nicky, my boy! We've been waiting for you." St. George waved him over. Nick pasted on a smile and joined the merry little group clustered around the green baize table.

"We've been hoping you would join us," Percy said, a diminutive little man with thinning hair. He was five years older than Nick, looked at least ten, and had an appetite for women that in no way matched his bland demeanor. "Miss Jubil has been wondering where you'd got off to."

The redhead, a woman who called herself Cherry Jubil, rose out of the chair at Percy's side. "Good evening, my lord." She was by far the most attractive, at least to him, with her pale skin and slender figure, her speech more refined than the rest. Perhaps his friends had known she would be.

He took a drink of his gin, felt the welcome burn of it down his throat, and studied the woman, trying not to think how her hair was a little too red, her mouth a little too wide, her eyes dark brown instead of a bright leafy green.

Still, he bowed with great formality over her hand. "I apologize, Miss Jubil, if I have kept you waiting. But I am here now and so are you. I suppose the evening may officially begin."

She laughed as if he had actually said something funny, sidled closer and pressed herself against his long length. She kissed him full on the mouth and he tasted the gin she had also been drinking.

At least they had one thing in common.

A long-nailed hand ran up his thigh and his body began to respond. He would take her and soon. He had made up his mind the moment he had seen the women walk into the house. He would have her this night, cleanse his body of this haunting desire for Elizabeth Woolcot that had been eating away at his sanity.

Once his desire was sated, memories of the kiss they had shared would fade. Things would go back to normal and he could return Elizabeth to her position as his ward and nothing more. He would soothe his desire with the redhead, pound into her until he couldn't remember Elizabeth's name.

Bending his head, he kissed her, wishing her lips were half as sweet as the last pair he had tasted.

Aunt Sophie heaved herself up from the silver brocade sofa in front of the hearth in the well-appointed sitting room of their suite. It was an elegant room, done in dove-gray and blue with silver accents throughout, warmed by a gray marble hearth near the corner.

"Well, dear, I believe I am off to bed. These old bones just aren't as young and spry as they used to be." Aunt Sophie yawned behind a pudgy hand. "Sleep well, my dear, and I shall see you in the morning."

"Good night, Aunt Sophie." The door to the older woman's bedchamber closed, leaving Elizabeth alone. She stared at the fire, watched the low-burning orange and red flames lick over the grate, and wished that she were sleepy. Wished her curiosity hadn't been nagging her all evening, goading her, telling her to creep down the back stairs and see what Ravenworth and his guests were doing.

She shouldn't, she knew. It was hardly appropriate for a well-bred young lady to think of spying on the earl and his odd assortment of friends. But as the next few minutes slipped past, the notion continued to grow, and Elizabeth found herself rising to her feet, crossing the room to the door.

She would simply go down for a glass of milk to help her sleep, making, of course, a quick trip through the halls while she was about it. She would discover where the group was ensconced and take a brief peek inside. She wouldn't stay but a moment—she certainly didn't want to get caught.

What could it possibly hurt?

The question went unanswered as she silently slipped down the back stairs, a trip she had made at least a dozen times. One of the footmen stood at a post near the door leading out to the garden, his head tipping onto his chest, snoring lightly as he dozed against the wall. She tiptoed past and headed down the passage. No one was in the usual array of downstairs drawing rooms. Elizabeth paused and went into the kitchen to fill a crockery mug with milk, then started down a hall leading to another, less-used wing of the house.

Muffled voices carried from the distance, along with the high-pitched squeal of feminine laughter. Elizabeth's breathing quickened and her heart kicked up its tempo. It appeared they were in the Pink Room, a large, ornate, little-used drawing room at the end of a marble-floored portrait gallery. Elizabeth made her way there on silent feet.

She paused outside the tall gilded doors, pressed her ear against the thick slab of wood. Low murmurs interspersed with bouts of silence. She wondered if the earl were inside and battled down the queasy feeling that suddenly rolled in her stomach. Her fingers itched to encircle the big silver doorknob. She reached for it, turned it to the left, heard the soft click of the latch being opened, let the door slide open a crack.

Oh, dear God. Her breath snagged at the sight before her, a sight she was certain never to forget. It was a scene from the pages of Dante's Inferno—painted, half-naked women draped over drunken, half-naked men. Breasts were exposed. Richard Turner-Wilcox groped between one woman's legs. The fat Baron St. George sat with a bare-breasted woman on his lap who was kissing the side of his neck, running her tongue around a puffy, red-veined earlobe.

Elizabeth swallowed hard. Her hands had begun to tremble and drops of milk spilled over the edge of the mug she held, onto the marble floor. She found herself praying, silently beseeching God that she wouldn't find Nicholas in there.

Staring through the crack, repelled yet unable to look away, her eyes searched the room. Her chest squeezed when she saw him, and a raw, burning pain spiraled through her. He was sprawled on a velvet sofa on the far side of the drawing room, pinned beneath the curvaceous body of the slender redhead she had seen getting out of the carriage. The woman lay half on top of him, her gown unfastened, the earl's dark hand massaging one of her breasts. She was kissing him, Elizabeth saw, running her fingers over his bare chest, which was exposed where his white frilled shirt had been unbuttoned and pulled apart.

Elizabeth swayed on her feet, her face going pale, her body suddenly numb. Her fingers fell away from the door and it swung farther open. A soft whimper tore from her throat and the mug of milk slipped from her hand to land with a splintery crash on the floor.

Several heads swung in her direction, but only one pair of eyes remained locked with hers. For a moment Nicholas just stared at her, as if he couldn't believe she was actually there. Tears blurred Elizabeth's vision, but she remained frozen, unable to move, her shocked eyes moving from Nicholas to the redhead. With a savage curse, he came up off the sofa so quickly the woman went sprawling on the floor.

"Bloody hell," the redhead grumbled, but Nicholas ignored her, his long legs striding across the drawing room toward the door.

Elizabeth whirled away from him and started to run, her slippered feet flying along the slick marble floor. She rounded a corner and kept running, turned again and ran some more.

"Elizabeth, wait!" Nicholas's voice echoed down the passageway, his footsteps pounding behind her. From the corner of her eye, she saw him round the corner, his shirt hanging open, his black hair mussed and falling into his eyes. The sight made a hard lump swell in her throat and a shaft of pain slice into her chest.

"Leave me alone!" She turned down the final corridor toward the door leading out to the garden, slammed through it without looking back and kept on running. She didn't stop until she reached a tall, leafy beech tree near the rear wall of the garden and paused to ease the painful stitch in her side. Her face was wet with tears, her chest heaving, her stomach rolling with nausea.

Slumping down on the wrought-iron bench beneath one of Silas McMann's bird feeders, she turned and began to weep against the cold ornate metal.

"Elizabeth?" It was Nicholas Warring. His voice sounded oddly rough. Though she couldn't see him, she knew he stood on the path just a few feet in back of her. She could hear his labored breathing, but she couldn't bear to look at him.

"Go away," she whispered. "Please . . . just go away."

He made no reply but neither did he leave. Long seconds passed. A minute, two, then three. Elizabeth finally turned, saw that he still stood there.

"I'm sorry," he said. "God, I'm so damned sorry."

She simply shook her head, but her heart ached unbearably, felt as if he had crushed it beneath his tall black boots. She didn't want him to know—dear Lord, she couldn't let him guess how badly he had hurt her. Lifting her chin, she forced a hint of steel into her spine.

"You told me to stay in my room. I should . . . should have listened." She dragged in a shaky breath, hoping the darkness would hide the wetness on her cheeks. All the while she was thinking, *How could you do it? How could you kiss me the way you did in the garden then make love to a woman you don't even know?*

Nicholas took a step closer, his hand outstretched as if he might touch her. She recoiled at the movement and the hand fell away.

"Elizabeth, please. I know what you must be thinking and I don't blame you." His voice sounded raw, harsh, as if each spoken word gave him a sharp jab of pain. "Until I saw you standing in that doorway, I never realized the sort of man I had allowed myself to become."

Elizabeth didn't answer. She just wished he would go away. "You warned me," she persisted, hating herself for not listening, for allowing herself to believe he was something that he was not. "The fault is mine." To her horror, her voice broke. "I should not have gone downstairs."

Something flashed in Nicholas's eyes. His hands fisted, though he made no other move. "No, you should not have," he softly agreed. "And I should not have been consorting with whores in the house that was my family's home. I can only tell you they will all of them be gone by first light on the morrow. And I promise you, Elizabeth, nothing like that will ever take place in this house again."

Elizabeth just looked at him, trying not to think of the red-head's hand running over his beautiful chest, of the woman's breasts thrusting up between his fingers.

Nicholas looked away, staring off into the dark night sky, then back into Elizabeth's face. As hard as she tried to hide it, she knew he could see the pain she was feeling. It was etched into her features, a pain she had no right to feel.

"It makes me sick to think what you saw going on in that room." He shook his head, his jaw clamped hard, something very like anguish carved into his face. His next words were so soft she almost didn't hear them. "I didn't even want her."

Elizabeth wiped at the tears on her cheeks. "Then why did you . . . ?"

"I thought it would help me forget." A deep, regret-filled sigh whispered out into the night. "I hoped it would take my mind off the woman I wanted but could not have."

Her heart squeezed. "Lady Dandridge," she said dully.

"No, Elizabeth." His eyes fixed on hers, silvery and intense as she had never seen them. "The woman I wanted was you."

Her heart stopped—she was sure of it. Her breath expanded in her chest until she couldn't draw in a whisper of air. "I'm the one you wanted? Is that the reason you kissed me in the garden?"

"I was angry, but yes . . . in truth that is the reason I kissed you."

Elizabeth glanced away. "It is difficult to believe you were making love to her because you wanted me."

He followed her line of vision, off across the garden to the high stone wall, then returned to settle on her face. "I want you, Elizabeth. I have almost since the first time I saw you. I was making love to her because I was a fool."

Elizabeth said nothing, just stood looking at the tall, dark earl, trying to convince herself what she saw in his face could not possibly be pain.

"I know I have probably frightened you, but you needn't be afraid. I would never take advantage of my position. I don't want to hurt you, Elizabeth. I would do anything to prevent that from happening. Tonight . . . tonight was a terrible mistake."

Still she said nothing.

"I was a fool," he repeated. "I hope that in time you will be able to forgive me." He stood there for several long moments, then he scanned a length of the wall, saw that two of his guards were positioned not far away, turned and started walking back to the house.

Elizabeth watched him go, feeling as if her heart were being squeezed into a painful ball. He wanted her. Just as she had wanted him. But in truth, she now knew, what she felt for him was far more than desire. Like Miriam Beechcroft and a dozen other women, she had fallen beneath the spell of the Wicked Earl.

Elizabeth rose wearily from the bench. She still felt shaky and numb, and images of Nicholas with the redhead burned before her eyes. She had known what he was like and yet she had believed him somehow different.

She was a far bigger fool than Nicholas Warring.

SEVEN

Nick nudged his black Arabian stallion into a gallop, heading home from a day in the fields. It was nearly dark, the moon edging up, yet for him the day wasn't finished. Once he reached the house, there were hours of paperwork he still meant to do.

The horse crested a rise and Nick glanced ahead, saw the lights of the huge stone house like yellow beacons in the distance. He'd been pushing himself all week, working from dawn till dark, till every muscle ached and he felt nearly ready to drop.

It didn't seem to matter. Not even the hours of backbreaking labor could erase the image of Elizabeth's stricken face as she stood at the door of the Pink Room, staring at the debauched spectacle going on inside.

That she had seen him with the whore made him feel like the lowest sort, a man like St. George or Richard Turner-Wilcox. Though his reputation branded him a rogue, Nick had always considered himself above that kind of behavior. It was all right for them, he rationalized, but not for him. In the beginning, when he had first returned to England and discovered

what an outcast he truly was, he had simply taken up the role
they had cast him in, the part of the Wicked Earl. He had
done it to thumb his nose at the society that had so thoroughly
abandoned him.

Since Elizabeth had come—perhaps because she had
come—he'd been determined to continue in that same vein.
But he had never meant for things to go so far.

Her image reappeared as he galloped across the green
rolling hills, her pretty face damp with tears. Two days before, he had been kissing her soft sweet mouth, holding her
slender body against him. His actions with the redhead felt like
a betrayal of the very worst kind and in a way perhaps it was.

Elizabeth was an innocent. He had trod on that innocence
and destroyed her illusions. She saw him now as the kind of
man he had almost become.

Almost, he thought, but not quite.

In that narrow flash of time, that instant when he had seen
her standing there in the doorway, something had snapped
inside him. For months now, he had been restless, bored by
the life he had been leading, finding it more and more dis-
tasteful. He was tired of the role he played, tired of the company he had been keeping. In a single instant, with a shot of
clarity as bright as a shooting star, he had known it was time
for his life to change.

In that vein, he had already taken steps to set things right.
St. George and his entourage had been escorted from the
house and subtly warned not to return. Others of a similar
ilk would receive the same message.

As for Elizabeth, it wasn't right what she had suffered because of him, but perhaps it had happened for the best. Elizabeth knew nothing of the desire that ate into his loins
whenever he looked at her. She didn't understand the lust he
had been trying to hold at bay. She hated him now and she
would stay away from him. What had happened would actually protect her.

The thought settled over him like a shroud, a cloak of bitter loneliness over a long and lonely day.

Elizabeth spent the next few days working in the conservatory. She'd said nothing of the scene in the Pink Drawing Room, nor did she intend to. If her aunt wondered why it was that she had been so quiet, why her appetite had waned to meager portions, the older woman could speculate as she wished. In the meantime, Elizabeth busied herself alongside Barnaby Engles, transplanting anemones, pansies, and tulips from the garden outside simply to give the glass-ceilinged room a little color—and Elizabeth something to do.

In the evenings, she took special care not to go anywhere she might encounter the earl. The thought of seeing him, of hearing his voice, made a painful ache rise in her chest.

As he had promised, his friends had left the house the following day and since then the place had seemed strangely empty. Word had been sent that she and her aunt were free to enjoy the house as they wished, that from now on supper would be served to them in the dining room.

Elizabeth had pled the headache that first night and her aunt had dined downstairs alone, but the earl made no appearance. Apparently he was working late in the fields and had not returned until the household had fallen asleep. The next night was the same. On the third night, stifled by the walls of her room, Elizabeth took courage and headed downstairs. Cook had prepared a delicious meal of succulent roast quail and venison pasties, but again, thankfully, there was no sign of the earl.

Elizabeth began to wonder about him, as she did now, working over a bed of fresh earth, her hands immersed to the wrists in rich black soil. He was avoiding her as she avoided him. That he had a conscience at all seemed a positive sign, and it made Elizabeth question whether the pain she had read on his face that night might actually have been real.

It made her wonder if he might have meant what he had said and was well and truly sorry.

Nicholas sat hunched over his desk, penning a letter to Sydney Birdsall. It was the fourth draft he had written. The other three sheets of foolscap were wadded up and tossed into the waste bin.

> *Dear Sydney,*
>
> *As you and I discussed at our last meeting, the London Season is about to begin. In accordance, it would seem the time is at hand to begin preparations for Elizabeth's introduction into Society and subsequent search for a husband.*
>
> *Having come to know her over the past few weeks, I have discovered that besides being quite lovely, she is a charming, intelligent young woman with a good deal to offer a mate. I believe finding candidates for her hand will not be a difficult task. However, choosing one suitable for a woman such as Elizabeth may be difficult, indeed. I look forward to a report on your progress in this matter, as well as a suggested date for Elizabeth's departure to London.*
>
> *With most sincere regards, your friend,*
> *Nicholas Warring, Earl of Ravenworth*

It would have to do, Nick thought, surveying the letter again, though he still wasn't completely satisfied. He was hoping Sydney would read between the lines and choose very carefully the men he would approach regarding Elizabeth's marriage. It would have to be done. With Bascomb so ferociously determined to have her, there wasn't time to wait for the natural course of events. And Nick wasn't about to leave Elizabeth's happiness in the hands of fate.

He reached for the sand shaker and dusted it over the page, waited for the ink to dry, then folded the letter and sealed it with a drop of wax. He would send it today—the sooner the better. Perhaps once she was gone, he would be able to forget her.

God knew nothing else he had tried had had the least effect.

Elizabeth sat on a polished walnut pew of the small stone chapel at Ravenworth Hall. A glowing stained-glass panel, a scene from the Crucifixion, bathed the chapel in shades of sapphire, rose, and gold. A carved wooden altar covered by a length of embroidered linen stood beneath the window, an aging gold-leafed Bible sitting open on the top.

Elizabeth had been coming to the chapel off and on since her arrival at Ravenworth Hall. At first the place was dusty, the linen cloth yellowed from so little use. Considering the wicked nature of the chapel's owner, Elizabeth had not been surprised. The second week, however, she had found the place clean and polished to a shine, the earl having anticipated her need, since she would not be traveling to the church in Sevenoaks.

The gesture had been mildly surprising, but the real surprise came with the discovery that the chapel was no longer in use because the earl had donated money for the construction of a new church in the village. His servants attended service there as did his tenants and the people in surrounding homes and farms as far away as Tonbridge. It pleased her to think that Nicholas had done such a thing, that the Wicked Earl might yet be redeemed, though she continued to have her doubts.

Elizabeth ran a hand over the empty pew in front of her, enjoying the feel of the polished wood. From the moment she had first walked through the door, she had found the quiet charm of the little chapel comforting. She sat there now, thinking about the earl, missing his dark presence in a way she hadn't expected, a way that made a soft ache throb next to her heart.

She hadn't seen him since the night she had found him with the woman. Since then, he'd been gone from the house every day until late into the evening. Mercy had been clucking worriedly, wringing her hands because the earl was driving himself to exhaustion.

"'E just keeps on workin' night and day. 'E's been actin' strange all week. 'E sent them leeches 'e calls friends a-packin'—and good riddance to the lot of 'em—but now 'e seems bent on workin' 'imself to death."

Elizabeth had felt strangely guilty. She knew he was punishing himself for what had happened. He had sent his so-called friends away. Theo Swann had told her that others of his acquaintance had received the same subtle message. Even Miriam Beechcroft had been barred from the door.

Her guilt slid away on a warm thread of hope. True, Nicholas Warring had hurt her, but he had never meant to, and it seemed he was doing his best to make things right. He had made a mistake, but no one was perfect. And whatever he had done, she couldn't stand to see him suffer. After seven years in prison, he had suffered more than enough.

Clasping her hands, Elizabeth bent her head and whispered a silent prayer for guidance. She cared for Nicholas Warring, no matter what sins he had committed, and for some inexplicable reason, she still had faith in him. She told that to God, and in the soft light of the church the answer to her prayers settled deeply inside her.

Elizabeth smiled for the first time since her fateful journey to the Pink Room and headed back to the house.

It was almost midnight when Elizabeth knocked on the door to Nicholas's study. She found him sitting behind his desk, his dark head bent over a stack of ledgers. He bade her come in, and when he glanced up, Elizabeth was shaken by the lines of fatigue etched into his forehead, the dark purple smudges beneath his silver-blue eyes.

"Elizabeth . . ." His chair scraped against the wooden floor as he came to his feet. "I am surprised to see you. It is late. I thought you would be sleeping."

"I've been waiting for you. I was hoping we might speak."

Tension seemed to ripple through his tall, lean frame. A muscle tightened in his cheek. "Sit down, then," he said formally, retaking his seat. "What is it that you need?"

Elizabeth smoothed the skirt of her mauve silk gown, fighting the sudden swell of nerves in her stomach. "There is nothing I need. That is not the reason I came here. I am worried about you, my lord."

The pen in his hand pressed hard on the page, forming a dark blue stain on the paper. "Worried? Why on earth would you be worried about me?"

"You are working too hard and I am told you are not sleeping. Cook says you are not eating very well. I have come to make certain that from now on you take better care of yourself."

He stuck the pen back in the inkwell, but ignored the wet spot on the page. "Why? Why should you care what I do?"

Elizabeth looked into his eyes and saw what could only be described as despair. It made a painful knot tighten beneath her ribs. "It would seem to me, my lord, that as your ward it should be my duty to look after you, just as you have been looking after me."

The lines around his mouth went thin, making his features seem hard. "I have done a very poor job of it, Elizabeth, as both of us well know."

"You are new to such a position. You are bound to make an occasional mistake."

His troubled eyes searched her face. "It was more than a mistake. My behavior was unforgivable."

Elizabeth smiled. "Nothing is unforgivable, my lord. Not if the person is truly sorry."

Something shifted in his features. His gaze searched her face. "Are you trying to tell me you have decided to accept my apology?"

"Yes, my lord. I believe it was sincere, that it came from the heart."

His expression changed once more, the uncertainty fading, his features lighting with relief. "As indeed it did."

"Then the matter is behind us. I shall return upstairs to my room and trust that you will rest this night. And perhaps, my lord, you will make time for something to eat."

Something warm sparked in his eyes. A faint smile curved his lips. "You called me Nicholas once. I found I rather liked it. Do you think perhaps we might go on in that vein from now on?"

Elizabeth smiled. "Yes, I believe we could. Good night, then . . . Nicholas. Perhaps I will see you at breakfast on the morrow?"

"I shall make a point of it. Good night, Elizabeth. Thank you for coming."

She left him sitting at the desk, but she could feel his eyes on her all the way to the door. They warmed her insides and she believed that she had done the right thing.

Only time would tell, of course.

Elizabeth ignored the voice that warned if she were wrong, she would suffer far worse than she had already.

Nick strode the wide stone path that led from the stable to the garden. Three days had passed since Elizabeth had come to him in his study and, during that time, an easy camaraderie had begun to grow between them. He knew it was dangerous to spend time with her, but he enjoyed her company far more than he had imagined, and he deserved a little happiness, he told himself, just like everyone else.

That he wanted her went without saying. But he wasn't some sort of animal governed by its primitive instincts. He could control himself, keep a leash on his burning desire for her. Besides, he had received a reply to the message he had sent to Sydney Birdsall. In less than two weeks, Elizabeth would be leaving.

He spotted her now in the garden, sitting quietly a few feet away from one of the bird feeders that now hung from the trees along the gravel paths. She was studying an olive-green bird with a yellow-green rump and a yellow tail, listening to its loud, rapid trill.

He stood in the shadows till the bird flew away and Elizabeth rose from her seat, then approached where she stood beside a tall cypress.

Nick smiled, feeling his chest go tight in that odd way it did whenever she looked at him. "All right, don't keep me in suspense—what kind of bird was it?"

She laughed, a sweet, uninhibited sound. "A greenfinch. They're pretty, aren't they?"

"Very pretty." But he was thinking it was she who was pretty, with her fiery dark hair and her pink and white striped gown, the small puffed sleeves making her look so very young.

"You're home from work early today," she said. "You have finished supervising the timber cutting?"

"Actually, I've been here all morning. One of the broodmares foaled last night. I thought you might like to see her new colt."

Elizabeth grinned, her face lighting up. "Truly, I should love to."

He offered his arm and she took it. Together they walked the path leading back to the stable, entering the cool interior, pausing at a stall near the rear.

The mare nickered at their approach, shook her head and tossed her thick black mane. She was a rich blood bay, nearly sixteen hands, bred to his black Arabian stallion, and the colt was as black as its sire.

"Akbar is the father?"

He nodded, resting a boot on the bottom rung of the stall. "I've named him Prince, for his sire is surely a king."

"Prince will surpass even his father, I think." She assessed the blazing white star on the animal's forehead. "Akbar has quite outdone himself with this one."

He smiled, pleased that she saw what he did, that the colt had the makings of a champion. They watched the foal for a while, teetering uncertainly on its new legs, then nuzzling up beneath its mother's belly, searching for something to eat. Then they walked to the little gray Arabian's stall and Nick handed Elizabeth a chunk of sugar to feed her.

Silence fell between them. He was amazed how much he enjoyed even those moments when nothing was said. They walked to another stall and he felt her eyes on him, felt them probing, gently trying to read him.

"There is something I would ask you," she finally said. "If you do not wish to speak of it, I will understand."

"We are friends, Elizabeth. I will tell you whatever it is you wish to know."

"I realize it is not a pleasant topic." She glanced down at the gray stone floor and then back into his face. "I wish to know why it was that you killed Stephen Hampton."

A coil of tension filtered through him, remembered wrongs, regrets about how he had failed his sister. "It's been years since I've spoken of the murder. For my sake, it doesn't matter, but there is Maggie to consider."

"Maggie? Do you mean your sister?"

"Yes. Margaret is the reason I killed Stephen Hampton." His dark gaze drifted away. "Knowing the way he hurt her, I would not hesitate to do it again."

Elizabeth said nothing, but he felt the slight pressure of her hand on his arm.

He took a steadying breath. "She was only sixteen when she met Stephen. I was twenty, supposedly older and wiser." He shook his head. "I should have kept her safe from a man like that, but somehow I failed to see the danger until it was too late."

"Your father was still alive. It was his responsibility more than it was yours. Apparently, he was unsuspecting as well."

Nick sighed wearily. "None of us suspected. Hampton was my age. I was never really close to him, but we were friends after a fashion. Like a fool, I believed it was I he came to visit whenever he came to the house. In truth, it was Maggie who had captured his interest."

He reached down and picked up a stem of straw, smoothed it between his fingers. "She was in love with him—why I couldn't begin to guess. Not that he wasn't handsome—and charming after a fashion. He was also ruthless and self-serving. Stephen was married. He kept a number of mistresses and still wanted Maggie. I don't know what he said, how he managed to seduce her, but he did."

"Your sister was young and impressionable. It could happen to any young girl. That is the reason she went into the convent?"

"Part of it. Mostly it was the scandal. For years I hoped she would leave that place, but I never could make her see. She deserved a different sort of life. God, I wish I could have convinced her."

"Perhaps she is happy. After what happened—"

"That is exactly the point—what happened between her and Hampton never should have occurred." The anger rose up, needling him, prodding him to remember the old hurts, the old pain.

"And that is the reason you killed him?"

Nick jerked hard on the straw, snapping it in two then letting the pieces drift to the ground. "No. I killed him because when she told him she was with child, he beat her so badly she lost the babe. I gave him the same treatment he gave her. In the fighting, Stephen wound up dead."

"You shot him?"

"Yes."

She studied the harshness that had crept into his features and seemed to ponder his words. "There is something you are not saying. What is it?"

She was observant, he had to give her that. Birdsall had said she was intelligent and he was right. "I went there to shoot him, so perhaps it doesn't matter. But the truth is, Stephen pulled a dueling pistol from a pair that was sitting on the mantel. I drew my weapon and shot him in self-defense, but no one believed me—his brother saw to that."

Elizabeth fell silent, absorbing each of his words. "I believe you. And I am glad, my lord, that is the way that it happened."

Nick glanced away. "I would have killed him anyway. It is what I went there to do."

Elizabeth made a negative shake of her head. "I do not think so. I do not think you are the kind of person who could shoot an unarmed man."

The knot of tension began to unravel inside him. Perhaps he wouldn't have. It was a question he had asked himself a thousand times. He would have called him out—there was no question of that. In the end, Stephen Hampton would still be dead.

But perhaps there was a difference, as Elizabeth seemed to believe.

As they walked back to the house, Nick discovered he wanted to believe it, too.

"Come now, dear. What can you be thinking that has got such a serious look on your face?" Sitting across from Elizabeth in the sitting room of their suite, Aunt Sophie pored over a stack of wrinkled foolscap she had carefully set on the table in front of her. She was busy tearing off the written-on portions of the paper and stacking the unused portion in a neat, separate pile, which she obviously intended to keep.

Elizabeth bit back a smile. Her aunt might be eccentric, but she was still one of the warmest, most giving women she had ever known. "I was thinking about Lord Ravenworth. I do not believe he is the villain people have branded him."

"Of course he is not," Aunt Sophie said with no little force. "Why, his father and mother were the very best sort. His younger sister, Margaret, is a delightful young woman."

"I think he behaves as he does because that is the way

people expect him to behave. Secretly he is laughing at them, tweaking their noses. That is what I think."

Aunt Sophie tore away a particularly large chunk of paper. "I wouldn't know about that. I know the earl has been a god-send to us, protecting you from that awful Lord Bascomb. We shall both of us be forever in his debt."

Elizabeth wholly agreed. She couldn't stop thinking of the day he had told her about the shooting, confiding in her, trusting her with his terrible burden. He was telling her the truth, she was sure of it.

As she watched her aunt complete her self-made task and carry the scraps of paper back into her bedchamber, an image appeared of Nicholas in the stable, a long booted leg propped against the stall, watching the little colt as if he were the proud father of the horse instead of Akbar. He had only kissed her once, yet she could remember every touch, every breath, the solid feel of every muscle beneath his shirt.

Sweet God, she was falling in love with him. He drew her with the force of a leaf tossed in a windstorm, a chunk of driftwood in the vortex of a stream.

She couldn't let it happen. The man was married, for heaven's sake—forever out of her reach. She had to be more careful, had to protect herself. Then she thought of Nicholas, of the loneliness she read in his face whenever she looked at him, and wondered if loving him would really be so wrong.

Charlie Barker stood in the darkness along the high stone wall of the house. A few feet away, one of the new men Bascomb had hired slipped quietly through the shadows. Charlie heard a muffled thud, then the sound of a body sliding into the dirt. Two more of Bascomb's men were moving over the grounds, taking out the rest of the guards Ravenworth had placed around the mansion.

"You ready?" Charlie whispered to Nathan, who stood at the base of a ladder they had stolen from the blacksmith's shed and propped against the wall.

"I suppose so."

Charlie went up first, one-handed, the other arm still in a sling, finally reaching the window that led directly into the Woolcot girl's bedchamber. They knew the entire layout of the house; their informant, one of Ravenworth's most trusted servants, had done an excellent job. Bascomb had come through as he always did, or more correctly, Bascomb's money had come through.

Charlie smiled with satisfaction. Ravenworth would hardly be pleased to know he had a spy in his midst.

The window creaked open. That information was also correct—getting in would not be a problem. Charlie stepped over the sill and motioned for Nathan to follow him in. The girl was sleeping, dressed in a prim white night rail, curled in the center of a big canopied bed, a long braid of dark reddish hair nestled against a slender shoulder.

Nathan rounded the bed on one side, Charlie the other. He hated to do it, but he had to keep her quiet. The moment she sensed their presence and her eyes snapped open, Charlie swung a sharp blow with his good arm that struck her on the jaw. She made a little whimper but that was all, just sagged back down on the bed as limp as a rag doll.

Nathan quickly stuffed a handkerchief in her mouth and tied it in place around her head. "Let's roll her up in that fancy silk cover," he suggested.

Charlie eyed the mauve silk folded neatly at the foot of the bed. "Good idea."

Charlie unfurled the cover while Nathan hefted her up and settled her carefully on top, rolling her up inside neat as you please. Even if she did wake up, her arms and legs were pinned, and her cries would be silenced by the gag.

"Come on," Charlie said, "let's get outta here."

Nathan nodded and took a quick peek out the window. "All clear," he said.

With Nathan's help, Charlie slung the unconscious girl over his good shoulder, waited for Nathan to reach the bottom of the ladder, then started down himself. Even with his injured arm, it was easier than he had expected. The girl weighed no more than a feather in a poke, and the men Bascomb had hired were silently efficient. They waited by the horses till Nathan was mounted, the girl draped over the saddle in front of Charlie, then they rode off.

A couple of miles down the road, they split up, the men traveling in one direction while Charlie and Nathan rode off in another. Behind them, no one stirred. Apparently anyone who might have been expecting trouble had been eliminated by the guards. Charlie inwardly winced to think what the men must have done.

He hoped to God they hadn't just up and kilt them.

EIGHT

The pink light of dawn broke over the horizon as Nick strode toward the stables, grim-faced, his blood up and pounding in his ears. Sweet Christ, he could hardly believe it. He had one man still unconscious and five others nursing an assortment of injuries from concussions to broken bones.

"The bastards knew what they were about," Elias said, his long strides keeping pace with Nick's. "Soldiers, maybe. Plenty of 'em around these days, what with the war and all. I figure there was three or four outside, one or two what went into the 'ouse."

"How much of a lead do you figure?" The words came out harsh. He still couldn't believe Bascomb had actually succeeded.

"Accordin' to the men, it was nigh onto midnight when the bastards struck. That gives 'em a little better'n a five-hour 'ead start." Elias didn't need to remind him the men he had hired as guards had all been gagged and trussed up like pigs. They had lain on the cold damp ground until one of the gardeners had come along and found them, then sounded the alarm.

"We'll find 'er, Nick. Don't ye worry."

"I am worried, dammit. I swear if Bascomb has laid a hand on her, I'll see him as dead as his whoreson brother."

"Easy, boy. We'll stop 'em before they ever reach West Clandon."

"We'd better." But he worried just the same. Elizabeth was alone with six hard-edged, obviously well-seasoned men. She was young and she was beautiful. He, more than anyone, knew how strong an urge lust could be.

Nick slung a leather bag over the black stallion's back and swung up into the saddle. Elias mounted a light gray hunter. Silas McCann and Theo Swann were riding a pair of bays. Several others had volunteered—Jackson Fremantle, his coachman, even Edward Pendergass had wanted to come along.

"Let's go." Nick had thanked them all and politely declined. He wanted to travel light, just him and Elias, hoping to make better time. But there were at least four men, possibly as many as six or seven. He wanted Elizabeth returned, but he wanted to be certain she got back unharmed. In the end, taking Silas and Theo was the least he could do.

They rode hard the first couple of miles, Elias slowing now and again to be certain of the track they followed. They almost missed the spot where the group had split up, at the bottom of an incline where a small meandering stream crossed a marshy meadow and hills rose up on each side.

"Looks like four sets of hooves heading off to the west," Silas said. "Two horses continued on north."

"Which group's most likely to have the girl?" Nick asked, but he was already thinking that twice before a pair of men had tried to abduct her. Bascomb wanted Elizabeth, was wildly obsessed with bedding her. He would want to insure she was brought to him a virgin. He would entrust her to men he felt sure he could control.

"'Ard to say," Elias said, scratching his shaggy dark head. "Best we split up just like they done."

Nick barely heard him. "The three of you go after the men who went west. I'm going after the other two. If you catch up with them and they don't have the girl, let them go. I don't want you putting yourselves in danger."

"What about yeself?"

"I have a feeling I can handle these two. If I'm not back at the house in three days, follow me to Bascomb's estate in West Clandon. Bascomb will likely be dead—or I will." He whirled the big black and dug in his heels. The men waved as he rode away.

The day was long and wearing. A dense layer of clouds settled over the landscape and a light rain began to fall. At first the tracks were easy enough to read, the soft ground making deep imprints of the animals' hooves as the men rode along. They were bent on reaching Parkland, Bascomb's palatial estate. Oddly, they seemed unconcerned about who might follow, believing, perhaps, that their five-hour head start would be enough to keep them safe.

The men rode on and so did Nick. He passed a crossroads and the tracks disappeared beneath other sets of hooves and a line of wagon tracks. He studied the ground for nearly half an hour before he picked up the trail again, continuing down a different, even less traveled, mostly overgrown road.

By the end of the day, enough rain had fallen that the tracks became blurred and indistinct. Still, he knew this country and he knew the little-used road they were traveling. He felt certain he was on the right track.

Night fell. He hoped the men would make camp.

Nick slowed the stallion to a walk, letting him rest for a while, then kicked him once more into a gallop. The men might stop, but Nick didn't intend to. Not until he got Elizabeth back.

Elizabeth couldn't remember ever being quite so afraid. Every bone in her body ached, every muscle, every joint, every tendon. For hours she had ridden draped over the saddle, unable to move her arms or legs, choking on the gag stuffed into her mouth. She felt trapped and suffocated, on the edge of panic, when the men had finally relented. At the end of a tether, they had allowed her to relieve herself, then grudgingly agreed to let her ride upright in the saddle in front of the beefy man with the thick red beard.

Elizabeth remembered the men from before, the pair who had attempted to abduct her that night in the garden. Nicholas had saved her. She wondered where the earl was now, wondered if he followed. She glanced toward the men across the clearing. They had ridden far later into the night than she had expected. All day she had worried what might happen when they stopped but they showed little interest in her person, and Elizabeth was grateful. Though she had ridden pressed against the bigger man's chest, he hadn't taken liberties, and though she was embarrassed to be dressed in her nightgown in front of them, the longer she was with them the less she felt threatened in that way.

Apparently Bascomb had made clear his intentions and the men must have known he was a man to be reckoned with when his orders were disobeyed. She stared at the two men now, sitting on a fallen log, each of them gnawing on a hunk of bread and a piece of dried herring. They had offered some to Elizabeth but her stomach rebelled and as hungry as she was, she had been unable to eat.

Elizabeth shivered though she wasn't really cold. Tying her to the base of a tree, they had draped the mauve silk counterpane over her shoulders and she was warm enough, cocooned inside. They were camped in a secluded copse of trees well off the narrow, overgrown path that served as road, isolated and nearly impossible to see. No fire had been built and the horses were tethered some distance away. The men were alternating watches, sleeping then taking up guard duty again.

As tired as she was, Elizabeth could not sleep. Instead her mind kept churning, returning to the day Oliver Hampton had found her alone in her father's study. He had very nearly raped her, though she was certain he wouldn't have seen it that way. It was simply seduction, he would say, pressing her down on the sofa, covering her mouth with slobbery kisses, running his damp palm up her leg as he shoved up her skirt.

Thinking of it now made her mouth go dry and her stomach roll with nausea. He would force her this time. He wouldn't wait, wouldn't chance another escape. He would take her, compromise her virtue, and force her to marry him.

Unless a miracle occurred, by day after the morrow, she would be Mrs. Oliver Hampton, Countess of Bascomb. To another woman it might have been the realization of a dream.

To Elizabeth, it loomed as an unending nightmare.

They set off again well before dawn, Elizabeth still dressed in her nightgown, her legs chafed raw where they rubbed against the stiff leather saddle. Her hair had come loose and with her hands bound in front of her as they were she hadn't been able to rebraid it.

A little after noon, they paused to rest and water the horses, taking time out for something to eat. Elizabeth ate an apple and a little hunk of cheese, but even that threatened to come back up. Her jaw ached where the bearded man had struck her, and her reflection in the stream showed an ugly darkening bruise.

"Time we was off," the skinny man, the one called Nathan, said. He looked at her and grinned. "We wouldn't want to keep his lordship waitin' for his bride."

"I'm not his bride," Elizabeth countered with a show of spirit, one of the few she'd been able to muster on the journey so far. "You men are behaving outside the law. If you are wise, you will release me before I see you thrown into prison."

They broke into gales of laughter, the skinny man slapping his thigh while the red-haired man snorted a chuckle out through his nose.

"If you're wise, you littl' baggage, you'll keep that sharp

tongue in your head—especially when you're in bed with your new husband."

A twig snapped. All three heads swiveled toward the tall man who had just stepped into the clearing. "I believe the lady is correct," Nicholas said in a voice edged with steel. "The two of you are acting outside the law. If you are wise—and you wish to live—you will stand very still and not make any sudden moves." He cocked the pistol he held in each hand aimed directly at the two men's hearts.

Sweet God, Nicholas had come. Her pulse was suddenly raging, roaring in her ears. Where had he come from? How on earth had he found them?

"Bloody hell," Nathan said.

The man called Charlie slowly raised his good arm into the air, but bent his head and spat nastily on the ground.

"You—" Nicholas motioned to the man on the left. "Untie the girl. Do it very carefully, then step away."

She was shaking by the time Nathan approached. He did so gingerly, hauling the counterpane back, pulling the knots free with a hand that was decidedly unsteady. He allowed the rope to slide away then stepped back as the earl had instructed.

"All right," Nicholas said. "Now bring a length of that rope over here and tie up your friend."

The red-bearded man cursed foully, but still didn't move. Nathan did as Nicholas said, tying the rope around Charlie's wrists, binding his hands in front of him, then reaching down to bind his feet.

Nicholas still hadn't looked at her. He glanced at her now, standing barefoot in her thin white nightgown, her hair mussed, a purple bruise on her jaw.

His bold black brows pulled together in an angry frown. "Are you all right?"

"Yes . . . yes, I—I'm fine. A little the worse for wear, but otherwise unharmed."

"Come here," he said gently.

She made her way in that direction, stopped at his side, and was surprised when he slid an arm protectively around her waist. He held her, hugged her briefly. Studied the bruise on her face with a dangerous scowl; his jaw flexed, pulling the muscles taut.

"Do you think you could tie up the other one?"

Elizabeth nodded. "Yes, I believe I could do that." Picking up the other bit of rope from beside the tree, she made her way across the clearing, wincing as an occasional stone cut into the bottom of her foot. As soon as she had finished, Nicholas shoved the pistols into the waistband of his breeches and strode toward her. He checked the knots on both men, tightened them down, then slid an arm beneath her knees and lifted her high against his chest.

"I'm sorry this happened. I wish I could have stopped them."

She clung to his neck and thought how safe she felt. Safe for the first time in days. "You tried. You've always done your best."

He set her sideways across his saddle, then turned and walked back to the tree to fetch the mauve silk counterpane. Wrapping it securely around her, careful to enclose her bare feet, he tucked it in place then swung himself up in the saddle behind her.

"You're certain you're all right? They didn't . . . take liberties?"

She shook her head. "No. I think they were afraid of what Bascomb might do to them if they did."

"I hoped that would be the case." He started to rein the stallion away when a shout erupted behind him.

"Hey! You ain't leavin' us here?" Charlie called out.

Nicholas's smile looked feral. "Only for a while. I intend to send a constable for you at the first opportunity. He'll be happy to untie you and see you safely to jail."

"Now wait a minute, gov'nor," the skinny man whined. "We didn't hurt her. We was real careful with her."

Nicholas stared down at the bruise on her jaw. "Not careful enough, my friend. Not nearly careful enough."

The stallion started off at a gallop and Elizabeth settled herself against Nicholas's chest. Hard-muscled arms wrapped around her. She could feel his heart, beating beneath the lean slabs of sinew across his ribs.

"Thank you for coming," she said, and his hold imperceptibly tightened.

"Which one of them hit you?"

She turned her head to look at him. "Why? Surely it doesn't matter which of them it was."

"It matters."

The harsh tone surprised her. "I was sleeping," she lied. "I don't know which of the men it was." It was Charlie, of course. She would never forget the sight of that big hairy fist crashing down toward her face, but Nicholas had enough trouble in his life already. Taking vengeance against Charlie would only bring him more.

A thin smile curved his lips. "I suppose, then, I shall simply have to horsewhip them both."

Elizabeth shifted in the saddle to face him. "Let the constable handle them. You don't need any more trouble. Please, Nicholas, let someone else take care of this. If not for you, then do it for me."

"There are any number of things I would do for you, sweeting, but letting those men get away with hurting you isn't one of them."

"But—"

"Hush now and get some rest. We've a long ride ahead of us before we can stop for the night."

She did as he said, closing her eyes and absorbing the rhythm of the big black horse, content that she was safe. She snuggled deeper against him, felt the warmth of his body encircling her, the solid, muscular strength of him. Exhaustion took its toll. Before the hour was ended, she had drifted off to sleep.

Nicholas lifted heavy strands of flame dark hair away from Elizabeth's cheek. She was sleeping in his arms, exhausted from her ordeal. Every time he noticed the bruise on her jaw, a wave of fury swept over him. The instant he had seen her tied up in the camp, he had wanted to beat the men into a bloody pulp. Perhaps it was concern for Elizabeth that had kept him on the fine edge of control.

He smoothed her hair and felt the steady rise and fall of her breathing. Her shoulder rubbed against his chest and her bottom pressed against his groin. Exhausted as he was, weary to his very bones, he still wanted her, had from the moment he had seen her in the clearing.

Even now, he was hard inside his breeches, the friction against his arousal a nagging, subtle ache. He knew he could not have her, that in less than two weeks she would be gone.

Sweet God, he would miss her.

He held her close against him, absorbing the scent of her, the pliant feel of her body. He couldn't have her. Elizabeth could never be his. The best he could do was to see her safely married to a good and decent man, protected from Oliver Hampton.

The thought made the weariness settle deeper into his bones.

Elizabeth awoke to the sound of voices. She felt Nicholas's dark hands surrounding her waist, lifting her gently from the horse, her bare feet connecting with the paving stones in the courtyard of an inn.

He handed the stallion's reins to a rosy-cheeked stable boy. "Akbar has worked hard these past two days. Feed him well and rub him down, and there'll be an extra coin for your efforts."

"Aye, milord." The slim lad stroked the stallion's nose then led him off toward the stables behind the inn.

"We'll spend the night here," Nicholas said. "We'll both

feel better after a good night's sleep. With an early start, we'll be back at Ravenworth well before nightfall."

Elizabeth merely nodded. In a way she would be glad to be home. In another way, she wished they could simply keep riding. Waiting where he left her just inside the door, she watched his broad shoulders disappear farther inside the inn to make the necessary arrangements. They had stopped only once, at the outskirts of a hamlet not far from the place where he had left the two men tied up. A constable Nicholas knew lived there, a tall, sallow-faced man named Ragsdale who promised to see the men arrested. Nicholas had vowed to return as soon as he had seen Elizabeth safely home.

Pulling the counterpane tighter around her shoulders, she pressed herself deeper into the shadows, hoping no one would see her. She could hear the sound of voices coming from the taproom and an occasional burst of laughter. Outside the inn, a slight rain had begun to fall and a chill crept into the misty air. Her muscles ached and she was glad they had stopped for the night, but more than that she was grateful for the extra time she would be able to spend with the earl.

It was foolish, she knew. But the moment he had stepped into the clearing, her heart had swelled with joy, and reason seemed to fly out the window. He had come for her, as she had known he would, and the knowledge spun the last silken threads of the web that ensnared her.

It was useless to deny it—she was in love with Nicholas Warring. Desperately, futilely, completely in love with him and there was nothing she could do to change things.

She imagined his dark, handsome features, thought of her hopeless situation, and a memory of her mother, dead these past six years, arose in the eye of her mind. With the same dark auburn hair and slender figure, Elizabeth looked a good deal like her, but there the similarity ended. While Elizabeth loved life and tried to make the most of every day, Isabel had never been happy.

Her marriage to Henry Woolcot had been arranged. She had been forced to marry a man twenty years her senior. Isabel resented the marriage. From the age of sixteen, she'd been in love with another man.

"There is no one else for me," she told Elizabeth once. "I have always loved him. I always will."

Elizabeth remembered that day clearly, a warm summer afternoon on the banks of the small meandering stream behind their big stone house.

"Listen to your heart," her mother had said, staring down at the water with tear-filled eyes. "When you marry, do it for love. Life is not worth living if you cannot share it with the man you love."

It must have been true, at least for Isabel. She killed herself on a cool fall morning, the day she discovered her lover, Captain Eric Blackstone of the Fifth Dragoons, had died in the fighting on the Continent.

Isabel was dead, and Elizabeth alone had mourned her. Her father, feeling angry and betrayed, had died not long after, a lonely, bitter man.

Elizabeth sighed, thinking of the past, thinking that as much as she'd fought against it, she would be following in her mother's painful footsteps. She would have to marry and soon, and the man she would wed would not be Nicholas Warring.

Nick placed a small stack of coins on the counter in front of the innkeeper, a white-whiskered man with a leather apron tied around his waist.

"We'll have ye quarters ready in a thrice, milord." The man scooped up the coins and scurried away to see the task done.

Turning back toward the entry, Nick strode toward the place where Elizabeth's slender figure pressed into the shadows along the wall and a shot of guilt assailed him. She looked like a waif standing there in the darkness. Thanks to that whoreson, Bascomb, she had been dragged from her bed in the middle of the night and forced to endure two days of torture at the hands of Bascomb's men. Damn but he hated the bastard.

Nick ground his jaw. If he had his way, Bascomb would face the same fate as his no-account brother, and Elizabeth would be safe. Perhaps this time the authorities would intercede, he thought, and the earl's pursuit would end. Nick doubted it. As Sydney had said, Oliver Hampton was a force to be reckoned with. Odds were, the local justice would have little power against him.

He glanced to where Elizabeth stood and forced himself to smile. He tried not to think how lovely she looked even with her tousled hair, her cheeks smudged with dirt.

"The innkeeper has given us the last two rooms. Apparently they are above the kitchen. Nothing fancy, I gather, but at least we shall be warm." He caught her answering smile and something squeezed inside his chest.

"I'm sure the rooms will be fine."

The kitchen was in a separate brick building in back of the inn. Still dressed in her wrinkled, dirt-stained nightgown, the counterpane haphazardly wrapped around her shoulders and trailing in the dirt, Elizabeth preceded him up the stairs and he opened the door.

The rooms were adequate, but little more, just two chairs and a rough-hewn table set before a small fire burning in the hearth. A bedside table with a half-melted candle in a scratched pewter holder sat beside a bed fashioned of rope, covered by a lumpy corn-husk mattress, but over it had been placed a deep feather mattress. Clean muslin sheets encased it, topped by a colorful quilt. Apparently, the extra coin he had paid had been worth it.

"I believe the innkeeper has done his best to make us comfortable," he said. "On the morrow I shall find you something more suitable to wear." The counterpane slipped just then, and his gaze followed the path of the pink mauve silk down over Elizabeth's breasts. Outlined by the thin white cotton fabric, two perfectly sculpted mounds pointed upward, the soft peaks forming shadowy circles beneath the cloth.

His throat went dry and he dragged his gaze away, but the size and shape remained etched in his mind.

"I am sick unto death of traipsing around the countryside in my nightgown," she said. "I should be grateful for anything you might be able to find."

Nick nodded. The unwelcome thought occurred that he would like nothing better than to see her out of her blasted night clothes, to have her naked and lying in his bed.

He pushed the thought away. A soft knock sounded and he was grateful for the diversion. "I ordered water for a bath," he said over his shoulder. "Apparently it has arrived." He strode to the door and pulled it open, and four young boys—stable lads and kitchen help—walked in with two steaming tubs filled with water. They trooped through the first room, depositing one tub there, and carried another tub into the second. The bedchambers were tandem, one in back of the other, making the most of the attic space above the kitchen.

Nick glanced uncomfortably toward the door adjoining the two rooms. "I'm sorry there isn't more privacy, but these were the only bedchambers left."

Elizabeth seemed unconcerned. "The rooms are fine, my lord."

The boys headed for the door leading downstairs, and Nick tossed them a coin as they passed. A kitchen maid appeared with a tray of food: cold boiled beef and potatoes, a slice of Wilton cheese, coarse rye bread, and two flagons of wine, which she divided into portions and set on a table in each room.

She gave him a lusty smile as she walked out the door, her hips swaying seductively, but it garnered not the least bit of interest. Instead his eyes strayed again to the door between the bedchambers. "There is a lock, so you needn't be afraid."

Elizabeth turned, smiled at him softly. "I am not afraid of you, my lord. I told you that before."

Nick glanced from the door to the bed, then back to where she stood just a few feet away. His eyes skimmed from her tousled auburn hair to the toes of her bare feet peeping out from beneath the counterpane. He wanted to toss the damn thing away, to tear off her nightgown and stroke those beautiful breasts. He wanted to kiss the arches of her slender bare feet.

"Perhaps you are right," he said gruffly, hating himself for his lustful thoughts. "In truth it is I who am afraid." A last fierce glance and he turned away, his long strides carrying him back through the opening that led to the bedchamber he would occupy for the night.

It would be a long one, he knew. With Elizabeth so very close yet miles out of his reach, odds were he wouldn't get a minute of sleep.

Elizabeth watched Nicholas walk away, tall and lean, and incredibly handsome even in his dusty riding clothes. He disappeared behind the door and her heart felt suddenly leaden, crushed by the weight of her need of him. In a few short hours she had grown used to the feel of his arms around her, the comforting sound of his heartbeat, his solid strength when he held her. She was in love with him, irrationally perhaps, futilely for certain.

She knew her own feelings well, but she wondered—what did Nicholas feel for her?

Ignoring the food on the tray and the rumble in her stomach, Elizabeth turned toward the steaming tub of water. The counterpane fell to the floor, followed by her dirty white nightgown. A clean one sat next to a brush and comb on the bed, she saw, and was grateful for his care of her.

Care. That was something Nicholas felt for her. In some way he cared for her, at least a little.

She thought of his burning gaze in that instant before he

left the room, fierce in its intensity, a scorching glance that seared from the top of her head to the soles of her feet.

Desire was something he felt—he had made that perfectly clear. But the yearning in his eyes when he looked at her said there was a great deal more.

Elizabeth sighed as she sank into the water, allowing the warmth to rush over her, hoping some of her troubles would drift away. Instead she thought of Nicholas, of his lean, hard body and dark, long-fingered hands. She remembered the kiss they had shared, and a soft ache rose inside her. Nicholas wanted her. He did not deny it, yet she knew he would not take her. As Sydney Birdsall had said, Nicholas Warring was a man of honor. He had vowed to protect her and he would do so no matter the cost.

But what of the cost to her?

Elizabeth leaned back in the small leather bathing tub, letting the warmth of the water soothe the aches in her muscles and joints. In a few weeks' time, she would be leaving Ravenworth Hall for good, traveling to London in search of a husband. She would marry a man she barely knew while her heart yearned for another. It was the same fate her mother had suffered.

At least her mother had known love, she thought with a hint of bitterness. Elizabeth had only that one brief kiss, that one brief flare of passion to savor. She would never know what it felt like to lie with a man she desired, to touch him and let him touch her.

Not unless she did something about it.

The notion stayed with her as she washed her hair with a bar of strong lye soap, rinsed it as best she could, then climbed out and dried herself on a thin muslin towel.

Dressing in the clean white night rail on the bed, she sat in a chair before the fire to dry her hair and eat the supper that waited on the table. She poured herself a mug of wine and took a drink, but her mind strained toward the sounds on the opposite side of the wall. She could hear Nicholas moving about, splashing water from the tub as he climbed out and began to dry off. The thought of him naked, all smooth dark skin and hard, unyielding muscle, made her nipples peak beneath her gown.

She closed her eyes and remembered the feel of his mouth over hers, the sweep of his tongue and the pressure of his thigh where it had brushed against her leg. Long minutes passed. A quarter of an hour, then a half. It was quiet in the other room. Nicholas had gone to bed. She wondered if he was already sleeping. Or if perhaps he was thinking of her, as she was thinking of him.

She wondered what he might do if she were to go to him, offer herself to him, ask him to make love to her.

Her heart speeded up at the thought. The desire to go to him was overwhelming, so strong she rose to her feet without thinking. For a moment she stood there undecided, knowing the decision she was about to make would change the course of her life. But the urge was too great, the call too strong, and her bare feet started moving, padding silently toward the door.

Her fingers found the latch, but she didn't lift it. Her heart was thudding, pounding a tattoo much louder than the rain that had started to beat against the window. What would she do if he turned her away?

The thought made her mouth go cotton-dry and her hands start to tremble. How would she deal with his rejection? It would hurt, she knew. But missing this chance at love—perhaps the only one she would ever have—seemed far worse.

Her trembling hand found the latch. It made only a soft muted click as she lifted it and quietly pushed open the door. A single candle burned on the bedside table, dripping wax onto the scarred wooden top. Nicholas was awake, she saw, sitting up in bed, his chest bare, his shoulders propped against the rough-hewn headboard. He had tossed back the quilt, and the sheet rode low on his waist, covering his nakedness. For a moment she just stood there, admiring the incredibly masculine picture he made, her heart beating like a bird trapped in a cage, her breath caught in her throat.

Then those silvery eyes met hers, a muscle flexed in his jaw, and it was all she could do not to run.

NINE

$\mathcal{N}$ick stared at the woman in the open doorway. Long dark auburn hair streamed down to her waist, still damp from the bath she had taken. Backlit by the fire, it glowed with the same fiery hues as the coals in the grate. Through the thin white gown, her figure stood out in shadowy relief: slender, boyish hips, long, coltish legs, an impossibly narrow waist, and high, upthrusting breasts.

His own body tightened painfully even as he swore a silent curse and his mouth thinned to form the words that would send her away.

"Nicholas?"

"You shouldn't be here, Elizabeth. What is it you want?"

She didn't answer, but her tongue slipped out to nervously moisten her lips and her pale hands trembled. "I thought that perhaps . . . I hoped that you would . . ." She swallowed so hard he could see it. "You told me once that you wanted me. You said that you had, almost from the start. Do you want me still?"

He clamped down hard on the surge of desire that rose up with vicious force. "For God's sake, Elizabeth." His fist clenched around a handful of sheet. Surely he was mistaken. Surely he hadn't heard her correctly. "Has something happened? Are you frightened?"

She moved forward into the room, not stopping until she had reached the side of the bed. "I suppose, in a way, I am. I'm terrified that you no longer feel as you did. That instead of making love to me, you will turn me away."

Sweat broke out on his forehead. For a moment he couldn't seem to breathe. "Elizabeth, you don't know what you are saying."

"Yes I do. I know exactly what I am saying. I am asking you to make love to me."

His body clenched harder, but Nick shook his head. "I can't do that, Elizabeth. I'm a married man. I can't wed you and I won't dishonor you by taking your innocence."

She took a single step closer, her nightgown belling out then molding once more around her slender hips. She smelled of soap and a trace of smoke from the fire. It was a clean scent, clean and youthful, and it reminded him of all that he could not have.

"Please, Nicholas—please don't send me away."

He glanced toward the fire, his body throbbing with need. "I want you," he said softly. "I can't remember when I've wanted a woman so much. But the fact remains, I am married to somebody else."

"You are not married," she said fiercely. "Not in the eyes of God. Your wife abandoned you nine years ago." She reached toward him, her hand coming up to caress his cheek. He felt the touch all the way to his heart. "Soon I'll be forced to marry. My husband will be a man I do not know and care nothing about. I want to know what it feels like to be loved by a man I desire. I need you, Nicholas. I want you, and I don't care about anything else."

Nick heard himself groan. He didn't know exactly how it happened, only that one moment he was reaching for her and the next she was there in his arms. His mouth came down over hers, hot and demanding, yet somehow he held himself back. His tongue slid along her trembling bottom lip, coaxing her to open for him. He deepened the kiss, letting her get accustomed to him, careful not to frighten her.

"I know I should send you away," he whispered. "I know it, but I can't. I'm only a man, Elizabeth. Worse than some, better than others. And I need you, too."

She made a small, soft sound in her throat, and he kissed the side of her neck, the softly rounded lobe of an ear. Easing her down on the bed beside him, he smoothed back her thick auburn hair, cupped her face in his hands and kissed her, long and deep, his tongue sweeping in to taste the rich dark cavern of her mouth.

"Nicholas . . ." she whispered. "Nicholas . . ."

His hand stroked over her cheek. He wanted her. Sweet God, how he wanted her. His arousal strengthened, pressing against the rough muslin sheet, making him ache and throb. He tried to tell himself it was wrong, that he could not have her, that Elizabeth could never be his, but his body refused to listen. Instead his hands splayed down her back, over her ribs, then rose to cup each of her breasts. Her nipples were hard beneath the thin cotton nightgown and suddenly he was desperate to see them.

Working the buttons on her gown with unsteady hands, he drew the night rail over her head and tossed it away, leaving her beautifully naked. He saw that she was trembling, but she didn't try to cover herself. Long strands of her fiery hair did that, flowing over her breasts, hiding all but the pale pink tips. They were small and tight, quivering with each of her rapid breaths.

"Lovely," he said, lifting the shiny dark hair away and cupping the rounded weight in the palm of his hand. "I imagined you this way, but I never thought to know for sure."

She whimpered as he lowered his mouth and took the tip between his teeth. Her back arched and her fingers smoothed over the nape of his neck.

"Nicholas . . ." The word came out on a ragged breath of air the instant before he kissed her. He took her mouth as fiercely as he had wanted to do from the start, and Elizabeth kissed him back with the same wild abandon. He could taste her innocence, her trembling desire, and reveled in the passion he awakened in her untried body.

His loins throbbed with heat. He wanted to be inside her, wanted it so badly he hurt. He held himself back by sheer force of will, commanding himself to go slowly. Her fingers splayed through the curly black hair on his chest, testing the muscles beneath, measuring each indentation of his ribs, and a fresh wave of heat rolled over him. She pressed her mouth against the side of his neck, pressed soft kisses across his shoulders, and he thought he might go up in flames.

He eased her down so that she lay beneath him, settled himself between her pale, slender legs. His arousal rode hard against her thigh and a thread of tension seeped into her body.

"Easy, sweeting. I'm not going to hurt you." Nick kissed her deeply, stroked her breasts, kissed her again and felt her begin to relax.

Sliding her arms around his neck, she clung to him as his finger sifted through the curly dark hair at the juncture of her legs and he eased a finger inside her. He heard her sharp indrawn breath, felt the liquid warmth of her, and his arousal went rock-hard.

"You're ready for me, Elizabeth." He stroked her deeply, gently preparing her. "You want me, just as I want you." Her face was flushed, but anxiety darkened her eyes and her bottom lip trembled. His conscience reared up. She was an innocent. He had no right to take her.

Swearing a silent oath, he gently touched her face. "This is wrong, Elizabeth. Tell me to end it. Say it now, before it's too late."

She only shook her head. Dragging his mouth down to hers, she kissed him, long and fiercely. "It is already too late."

It was indeed, he discovered, feeling his hardness slip inside her. Another second had his heavy length pressed firmly against her maidenhead, the last thin barrier he had left to conquer. He hadn't been sure he would find it, had thought perhaps Oliver Hampton had stolen it that day in her father's study. Relief mingled with guilt as he surged forward, claiming the treasure of her womanhood for himself, knowing he didn't deserve it.

Elizabeth cried out at the sharp jolt of pain that tore through her body, but the sound was muffled by a hot, demanding kiss. Clutching Nicholas's shoulders, she lay beneath him, filled by him, her body invaded, breached in a way she hadn't expected. She felt branded, possessed. As if Nicholas had somehow claimed her, as if she belonged to him and always would. It was frightening and yet it was the most incredible sensation she had ever known.

"Sweeting, are you all right?" He held himself rigid above her, his muscles straining with tension, allowing her body to adjust to the size of him, giving her time to accept the feel of having him inside.

Elizabeth wet her lips. "Yes . . . I'm all right." He bent his head and kissed her, a deep, tender kiss that made her forget the pain, made her blood start racing as it had before. The pain subsided. Heat replaced it. She felt hot and cold and tingly all over. He was big and hard. When Nicholas started to move, her body sprang to life.

A soft moan escaped her throat. Elizabeth arched upward, straining toward the feel of him, her body consumed by the heavy thrust and drag that sent shivers across her skin. Instinct parted her legs even wider, taking him deeper, desperate to be closer.

He groaned as he surged forward, filling her again, driving faster and harder, taking all she gave and demanding more. Elizabeth bit her lip at the fire roaring through her, the shivery heat that clouded her thoughts to all but the feel of his powerful body. Her fingers dug into his shoulders. Bands of muscle bunched and his head fell back. Thick black hair curled against the nape of his neck and brushed against the back of her hand. His muscles strained. His jaw clamped down as he fought for control, and suddenly her own body tightened.

Something was happening inside her, something fierce and joyous. Elizabeth cried out at the startling heat that suddenly swept through her, a raging current like a hot wind carrying her upward. A blinding burst of sunlight lay ahead and she exploded inside it. A sound arose, a whimper that came from deep in her throat. Sweetness rolled through her, and pleasure so intense her whole body shuddered out of control.

Above her, Nicholas drove on. Bands of muscle popped out on his neck and shoulders. Two more deep thrusts and he groaned, his body shuddering just as hers had done, his seed spilling hotly inside her. For minutes, he held himself rigid above her. Then he kissed the side of her neck and placed a last soft kiss on her mouth. Slowly he eased himself away, pulling her gently into his arms, cradling her body spoon fashion against him.

Nicholas held her without speaking, his heart pounding so hard she could feel it where his chest pressed into her back. Her own heart seemed filled to overflowing.

She wasn't sure what might have happened if she had simply fallen asleep. But the night was too young for that, too special. Instead, as the minutes lengthened and Nicholas said nothing nor made a move to touch her, she turned and came up on an elbow, leaned over and pressed a soft kiss on his mouth.

"Elizabeth . . ." he whispered, his tone low and rough. "Bess . . ." She turned onto her back, and he rose above her. Then he was kissing her again, her body beneath him, his hardness buried deeply inside. "God, I know this is wrong, but I can't make myself stop. I can't seem to get enough of you." He took her gently this time and afterward they slept for a while.

Just before dawn, she awakened, opening her eyes to find him watching, his expression closed up, his eyes dark and cloudy. She reached for him and his arms went around her. They made love with abandon, Nicholas almost frantic in his need to have her.

It was as if he dreaded the dawn, the rising of a sun that would force their return to a life where their passion could not exist. It made her sad, yet she had known the consequences before she had stepped through the door to his room.

No matter what happens, I will never regret this. Never. How could she regret the most beautiful night of her life? She wouldn't let her feelings destroy her as they had done her mother. In that they were nothing the same. Instead she would savor the hours she had spent in Nicholas Warring's arms— in his bed—lock them away and treasure them forever in her heart.

Nick left Elizabeth sleeping. He rose from the bed, careful not to disturb her, dressed, and went out to the stable. His chest felt leaden. Guilt seemed to pervade his very bones. The stable boy had Akbar groomed and waiting, none the worse for the difficult journey. Nick wished he could say the same for himself.

He glanced back toward the rear of the ivy-covered inn, to the rooms above the kitchen where he had stolen a young woman's virtue. He had known it was wrong, known it deep in his soul, yet the knowledge had not stopped him. He was married to another woman, Elizabeth forever out of his reach. She was a lady and his ward, yet he had taken her to his bed as if she were no better than one of Turner-Wilcox's pretty whores.

He felt sick with disgust at himself. And yet the night with Elizabeth had been so incredible, so intense, it was difficult to be truly sorry.

In truth, Elizabeth affected him as no other woman ever had. She touched him in some way, made him feel things he hadn't felt since before he was sent to prison, before his life had taken such a bitter, irrevocable turn. But his feelings for her didn't change things. The fact was he was married. He had vowed to protect Elizabeth Woolcot and he had failed.

Nick tossed a coin to the stable boy, instructed him to saddle the horse, then set out to find her something to wear. As he walked back through the stable door, he glanced once more toward the windows above the small brick building that served as kitchen and his jaw went tight.

He dreaded the long ride home.

Though she hadn't seen him in nearly a year, Margaret Warring knew something was wrong with her brother the moment he stepped through the front doors of Ravenworth Hall. It had been nine years since she had been there, yet it felt as if only days had passed. She gazed at her brother, but at first he didn't see her, his eyes fixed instead on the woman he led into the entry, a slender auburn-haired figure dressed in the simple brown skirt and white muslin blouse of a servant.

She wasn't one, Maggie knew. The girl was Nick's ward, Elizabeth Woolcot. Maggie had heard the story of the young girl's abduction, having arrived unexpectedly just minutes after her brother had departed in hot pursuit. She had met the girl's aunt, a pleasant if slightly eccentric older woman with a knack for cutting to the heart of whatever was happening around her.

Such as Maggie's unanticipated arrival.

"Why, you're Margaret!" Sophie Crabbe had said, coming upon her in the entry. "Lud, I haven't seen you in years—not since before you went away to the convent. Such a darling young girl you were—the image of your beautiful mother. Have you come home then, dear girl? Your brother will be thrilled—he wasn't at all pleased, you know, with your decision to lock yourself away."

Maggie had been speechless. In a single paragraph, Sophie Crabbe had summed up her life and her current situation. She *had* come home. She had done her penance for the errors she had made and finally realized the life she had chosen wasn't the one she really wanted.

During the years she had spent in the Sacred Heart Convent, she had begun to feel as though life was passing her by. She wanted a chance to discover the world again, to make her own way, to choose which direction she would take and experience the consequences of those choices.

Now as she stood in the entry, studying the tension etched into her brother's handsome face, she realized she wasn't the only one with problems. Poor Nick had done penance as well.

"Nick?" He had suffered for seven long years. She had thought those days were behind him, but the expression on his face said that he was suffering again.

He turned at the sound of her voice, and suddenly his scowl slid away. "Maggie! For God's sake, what the devil are you doing here?" Before she could answer, he had scooped her into his arms and was whirling her around the entry beneath the crystal chandelier. "Damn, but it's good to see you."

"It's wonderful to see you, too, Nick." Dear Lord, was it ever. She had missed him so very much. "I hope you'll still be glad to see me when you find out I've come home for good."

His expression changed to one of concern, then a radiant smile cracked across his face. "You don't mean you're leaving the convent?"

"Yes, I am. I've decided to give the world another chance."

He hugged her, hard. "Thank God." They stood there grinning at each other as if they were ten years old again, then Nick suddenly stopped and turned. "Sweet Jesu, I almost forgot. Lady Margaret, may I present to you my ward, Miss Elizabeth Woolcot."

Elizabeth dropped into a curtsy. "Lady Margaret, it is a pleasure to meet you." She glanced down at her wrinkled brown skirt and simple white blouse and color swept into her cheeks. "Please forgive my appearance, I—"

"I understand completely. Your aunt has given me a rough

idea of what's been going on. Mercy Brown has filled me in on the details."

Elizabeth smiled but Nick frowned. "Bascomb has been giving her fits. He's determined to force her into marriage. Now that you are home, you can help us find her a suitable husband."

Maggie smiled, but Elizabeth's smile slid away. "If the two of you don't mind," she said, "I should like to go upstairs and change. As you might imagine, the journey has been a long one." She was taller than Maggie, with dark auburn hair instead of Maggie's bright golden blond. And her eyes were green instead of a light china-blue.

"Of course you may go. I should have suggested it myself. And please—won't you call me Maggie? I am hoping that we shall be friends."

Elizabeth did smile then. "I would like that very much . . . if you will call me Elizabeth."

Maggie smiled and watched her walk away, noting that whatever was wrong with Nick was also affecting his ward. Her attention swung to her brother. "They didn't hurt her? You were able to get to her in time?"

A muscle worked in Nick's jaw. "Bascomb's men didn't touch her, if that is what you are asking."

She breathed a sigh of relief. "Thank God for that." Her brother made no comment, but a harshness crept into his features that renewed her former concern. She reached out and stroked his cheek, felt the tension thrumming beneath his skin. "Are you all right, Nick? You don't seem quite yourself."

He blew out a heavy breath of air. "I'm fine. I'm just tired, is all. Let me change my clothes and I'll meet you in the study." He smiled but it looked a little forced. "You can tell me all the reasons you've decided to rejoin the living."

Elizabeth let Mercy fuss over her. She was tired to her bones, but more than that, her heart ached unbearably. All the way home from the inn, Nicholas had ignored her. He'd been polite, but distant, as if the night they had shared had never happened. And because he was, it seemed as though it never had.

"Come on now, luv, into the tub with ye." Mercy prodded her gently in that direction, pulling the light silk wrapper she wore off her shoulders. "Ye look limp as day-old puddin'."

Elizabeth climbed into the sudsy water and the unwelcome thought arose—last night a bath had been the prelude to hours of making love.

"Now then, ain't that better?"

Elizabeth sank down beneath layers of rose-scented bubbles. She nodded, the best she could muster. "Thank you, Mercy." The water soothed her aching body, but her heart still hurt. She wished she could let herself cry.

"Lady Margaret's 'ere—did ye know?"

"Yes, we met briefly before I came upstairs."

"'Is lordship'll be 'appy to know she's 'ome for good. Cook says they was two peas in a pod when they was litt'l. Says the earl was always crazy about 'is baby sister."

Elizabeth thought of Stephen Hampton, dead at Nicholas's hand. "So I gathered."

Mercy's eyes fell to the bruise on Elizabeth's jaw. "That bleedin', no-good Bascomb. Those men of 'is—they did that to ye?"

"They were trying to keep me quiet. Other than that they acquitted themselves quite well, considering the circumstances."

"Good thing they did. The earl would 'ave give 'em the same what 'e gave to that blighter who 'urt his sister."

Elizabeth's eyes went round. "Sweet God, you know about Lady Margaret?"

Mercy laughed. "I know just about everything that's 'appened in this place—even if I weren't 'ere when it 'appened."

"If that is so, then you also know his lordship shot Lord Stephen in self-defense."

"'Course I do . . . not that it matters a whit. Our Nick would 'ave kilt the whoreson anyway for what 'e did." Mercy said it with pride, as if killing Stephen Hampton was a godsend instead of a crime. Elizabeth thought of Oliver and wondered if perhaps she was right.

"I hope you won't say anything. I'm sure Lady Margaret would be hurt very badly if she knew her past was the subject of gossip."

Mercy's lips flattened out. "I'm not the kind to do that. Besides, it's nothin' but old news by now."

"Yes, it is, and I'm sure his lordship would like to keep it that way." Mercy said nothing more. She left a few minutes later, leaving Elizabeth to enjoy her bath alone. She might have, except that every time she looked down at her body, she saw an image of Nicholas's dark hands skimming over her flesh. She remembered the way he had kissed her, the way his hardness had felt inside her.

In some strange way, she belonged to him now, and the fact that he had so coldly rejected her sent a sharp sting of pain to her heart. Their strained journey home had been a nightmare. Nicholas had said almost nothing, and the taut silence kept Elizabeth's nerves on edge. She had known there would be consequences to pay for her night of wicked abandon, but the earl's brooding silence hadn't been among them.

She wondered at the cause. Perhaps a night in his bed had satisfied his desire for her. Perhaps he was repulsed by her brazenness. Perhaps he simply felt guilty.

Elizabeth did not know.

And she was afraid to find out.

"So, big brother, you are not upset that I have barged into your life unannounced?"

Nick smiled at the young woman who perched on the sofa, her back perfectly straight, her head held high. Before she had left home she would have sat with her legs curled up beneath. She was the proper convent miss, now, and it saddened him to think of the years of her youth she had missed.

"A few months back, I might have hoped for a bit more

notice, but even then I would have been grateful to have you home."

"A few months back," Maggie repeated. "You mean before the arrival of your ward?"

"Actually, I've only begun to reform my wicked ways in the past several weeks, but yes, in a manner of speaking, I suppose Elizabeth was the cause." He lifted his glass of brandy and took a slow, burning drink. "Having her here made me realize just how jaded I had become."

"She's a beautiful girl." Maggie watched him from beneath her fine gold lashes, studying him in that way she had always had of seeing past his defenses. He strengthened them by forcing himself to relax.

"Elizabeth is lovely and intelligent," he said, trying not to remember how beautiful she had looked lying naked in his bed. "Sydney Birdsall is working to find her a husband. Once she is married, Bascomb will have to resign himself." He said the words without the slightest indication that the notion brought a bitter taste to his mouth. "He'll have no choice but to leave her alone."

Maggie leaned over the marble-topped table in front of the sofa, picked up her gold-rimmed teacup and took a delicate sip. "How is Rachael?" she asked in a swift change of subject, gleaning more of his thoughts, perhaps, than he had imagined.

"I wouldn't know. I've seen her only once since my return to England and that was to work out an arrangement for her to continue her residence at Castle Colomb."

Maggie sighed. She was as pretty as ever, he thought, with her heart-shaped face and wavy gold-blond hair, cut short now that she had been living in the convent. Nick couldn't help wondering how he could have been such a fool not to see the tempting lure she posed to Stephen Bascomb.

"I don't suppose your wife would consider returning home. The least she could do is give you an heir."

The words still held the power to hurt him. His sister was

one of the few people on earth who knew how badly he had wanted a son. "That time is past. I feel nothing for Rachael and she feels less than nothing for me."

"It isn't fair, Nicky. You wanted a family so much. I think about it often. So much of what has happened is my fault. If only I hadn't let Stephen—"

"Stop it. None of this was your fault. Not a bit of it. Stephen was a grown man and you were a child. Besides, it is all in the past."

Maggie shook her head. "Perhaps it is, but there is still poor Elizabeth. I pray to God Bascomb doesn't find a way to hurt her the way his brother hurt me."

Nick said nothing, but his stomach knotted painfully. Bascomb hadn't stolen Elizabeth's innocence—Nick had. It never once occurred to him he would ever think of himself in the same low terms he thought of Stephen Hampton.

TEN

ercy Brown came bearing the news of Sydney Birdsall's arrival three days later. Elizabeth was summoned to Nicholas's study late in the afternoon. He was sitting behind his desk when she walked in, immaculately dressed in a burgundy tailcoat over a striped dove-gray waistcoat. A frilled shirt and lacy cravat stood out against his dark skin. He rose to his feet as the butler closed the door, and she didn't miss the tension that made his jaw look tight. It matched the unsteady pulse that was thrumming in her ears.

"Good afternoon, Elizabeth. I'm glad you were able to join us."

As if I had a choice, she thought. *As if you were really glad I'm here.* He looked incredibly handsome, and so distant her heart twisted painfully inside her. She lifted her chin a notch. "Good afternoon, my lord."

Sydney crossed the room to where she stood, reached out and clasped both of her hands. "Elizabeth, my dear, it's delightful to see you." He bent and kissed her cheek and she gave him a halfhearted smile.

"It's good to see you, too, Sydney." It *was* good. She had missed Sydney's comforting presence, particularly these past few days. A glance at Nicholas, whose stern features hadn't remotely softened, gave her the sudden urge to cry against Sydney's fatherly shoulder.

"I gather you have had quite an adventure," he said, his silver hair gleaming in the light of the whale-oil lantern on the desk.

"Yes, I suppose I did." Elizabeth thought her greatest adventure wasn't her abduction but the night she had spent making love. "Fortunately, Lord Ravenworth arrived before Bascomb's men were able to reach the earl's estate in West Clandon."

"So I heard. I knew you could count on Nicholas."

A slight flush rose beneath the dark skin over his cheeks.

"He was quite brave," Elizabeth said, her eyes pinning him where he stood just a few feet away. "I was grateful for his timely arrival."

Ravenworth cleared his throat. "Sydney is here because I sent him a letter. I told him what happened with Bascomb's men, and he came straightaway from London."

"Dreadful." Sydney gave a disgusted shake of his head. "The man is an outrage. But perhaps between the four of us—I gather Lady Margaret has also offered her services—we can manage to foil his efforts for good."

"What Sydney is trying to say," Nicholas put in, "is that the Season has begun and he believes it is time for you to begin your introduction into Society."

"That's right, my dear. I've already spoken to several very well-thought-of young men and they are eager to meet you. Once you have chosen your future husband and the two of you are wed, you will be safe from that scoundrel Bascomb."

Nausea clutched her stomach. She had known this time was coming but still she wasn't prepared. She tried not to look at Nicholas, but her glance strayed there of its own accord. His features were immobile, as stiff and unreadable as if he were made of wood. "I hadn't . . . I hadn't thought you would be ready so soon."

"Fortunately, I was prepared for something like this," Sydney said. "I imagined Bascomb might be breathing down our necks. He must have been trying to circumvent our endeavors, get to you before you reached the city."

She flicked a glance at Nicholas, but he simply looked away. "How . . . how long before we leave?"

"I thought perhaps you and Lord Ravenworth could be ready to travel by the end of the week."

Nicholas's head snapped up. "What did you say?"

"I said I hoped that you and Elizabeth—"

"Bloody hell, Sydney—you aren't suggesting I go with her?"

"But of course I am. Surely you understood? You can't simply send her away, Nick. You'll have to go with her. Elizabeth won't be safe for a moment until she is married. In the meantime, without you there to offer your support and protection, Bascomb is bound to find a way to compromise her virtue and force her into marriage."

Tension seemed to shimmer the length of Nicholas's tall frame. "That is ridiculous. I cannot possibly go. Surely it is apparent that my presence in London would ruin any chance of Elizabeth's success in Society."

Sydney shook his head. "That isn't necessarily true. You may be somewhat of an outcast, my friend, but you are still rich as Croesus and you wield a tremendous amount of power. Most of Society is afraid to incur your wrath, and shunning your ward would certainly do so."

Nicholas turned from Sydney to Elizabeth. His eyes met hers, saw the turbulence she worked so hard to hide, and for a moment his hard look softened. *I'm sorry,* his gaze seemed to say. *I can't do this. Don't ask it of me.* Then the harshness returned and she thought that she must be wrong.

"It's out of the question. There must be some other way."

"There is no other way," Sydney argued. "You must go to

London. You must lend Elizabeth your support. Fortunately, once you arrive, we will have an ally in our camp."

"An ally? What do you mean?"

"The Duke of Beldon has agreed to sponsor Elizabeth." He eyed Nicholas with a lift of his snowy brow. "You may remember him," he said with sarcasm. "Before you went to prison, the two of you were friends."

Nicholas stared off toward the fire. "I haven't thought of Rand Clayton in years."

"Perhaps not, but your friend has never forgotten you. As I recall, he made a number of efforts to contact you upon your return, but you quite purposely ignored him."

Nicholas's eyes swung to Elizabeth. "Before the shooting, Rand Clayton was my best friend. He wasn't a duke back then, merely the Marquess of Glennon. By the time I returned to England, he had inherited the dukedom and I didn't want to embarrass him by forcing him to acknowledge a friendship with a man who had been convicted of murder."

"That was very noble," Sydney said, "but apparently the duke sees the matter in quite a different manner. He has offered us his support and, for Elizabeth's sake as well as your own, I am imploring you to accept it."

Nicholas said nothing for the longest time, but his eyes remained locked with hers. She wondered what thoughts were reflected in those silvery depths, but nothing in his bearing gave him away.

"And there is your sister to think of," Sydney pressed. "Now that she has left the convent, she will be facing an uncertain future, unless she is able to overcome the problems of the past. His Grace's help would be invaluable."

Nicholas worked a muscle in his jaw. Tension tightened the skin across his finely carved cheekbones. Then a sigh of resignation whispered past his lips. "All right, Sydney. Once again, you leave me no choice."

The older man seemed to sag with relief. "Capital. When shall I expect you?"

"There is the matter of the men involved in Elizabeth's abduction. I plan to leave for Dorking on the morrow. As soon as the situation is handled to my satisfaction, I shall return." He swung his gaze once more to Elizabeth. "You and your aunt should be prepared to leave three days hence."

"As you wish, my lord. We can be ready to travel whenever you say."

He nodded, then turned to Sydney. "As you so artfully pointed out, my sister will be coming as well. I believe if all goes as planned, you may look for us before the end of the week."

Sydney smiled and relaxed even more. "Very good. In the meanwhile, I shall order your town house opened and readied, inform His Grace of your pending arrival, and make whatever other arrangements are necessary for our plan to proceed."

"Thank you, Sydney." Nicholas turned a last cool look in Elizabeth's direction. It hurt to be on the receiving end of that expression when there was a time she had garnered such tender looks instead. "Inform your aunt of our plans and tell Mercy that she is to accompany you."

"Yes, my lord." She turned and smiled at Sydney, and hoped he couldn't see her pain. "Will you be staying for supper?"

"I'm afraid not, my dear. Too much to do." He reached for her hand, raised it to his lips. "I shall look forward to seeing you soon."

"And you, Sydney. You are the dearest of friends."

Nick watched Elizabeth leave and, once the door was soundly closed, found that he was again able to breathe.

Sydney continued to speak. "I know this is hard for you, Nicholas. These people have turned their backs on you for the past two years. They won't be kind, I'm sure, but in time they will be forced to accept you. I hope it helps to know you are doing the right thing."

He supposed it was. Sydney was right. Even with his notorious past and his rakehell reputation, he was still a powerful man. He might be an outcast, but with Beldon's support, they wouldn't shun him completely. His sister would have a chance to overcome her painful past and Elizabeth would be allowed sufficient movement within upper-class circles to insure she would find a suitable husband.

The thought sat heavy on his chest.

Nick said his farewells to Sydney, who left a few minutes later, and he was finally left alone. He poured himself a brandy and sat down in front of the fire, still seeing Elizabeth as she had looked standing there in his study, proud and defiant, and utterly enchanting. He had hurt her, he knew, yet there seemed no other choice. Their night of loving had been a terrible mistake. By ignoring her, he was making the fact more than clear.

Perhaps there was a better way to go about it. Perhaps he should simply tell her how sorry he was, but in truth he was afraid to.

He was weak when it came to Elizabeth Woolcot. If he allowed her even a glimpse of that weakness, he was afraid she would see how much he still wanted her. If she made the slightest overture, sweet God, he wasn't sure he could resist.

He certainly hadn't been able to that night at the inn.

Nick slept little during the long hours of the night, his dreams haunted by Elizabeth Woolcot, filled with erotic images of her naked and arching beneath him. When he wasn't thinking of her, he was dreaming of his parents, of the happy days before his mother had died, of the close bond he had shared with his father until he was sent to prison. He dreamed of Elizabeth cradling a black-haired child in her arms, a boy who carried his image. He heard her laughing, telling the child to call him Papa.

He awoke to the night sounds, crickets grating, the eerie hoot of an owl. The dream had felt so real. Without its glowing warmth he felt desperately alone.

By the time he got out of bed, dressed and made ready to leave, he felt ill-tempered and out of sorts. Akbar was saddled and waiting when he reached the stable, as well as a tall bay hunter for Elias, who was traveling with him to Dorking. They were headed for the gaol in nearby Niber Castle and his meeting with the local justice of the peace.

"Constable Ragsdale agreed to take them there," he told his friend. "He said he would see the men were held until I could return to press charges." He smiled grimly. "A good long stretch in Newgate ought to teach them the folly of their ways."

Elias scoffed. "Newgate! The bastards will be lucky if they don't 'ang."

A muscle tightened in his cheek. If that was the sentence, so be it. They had threatened a woman he had sworn to protect. If the law didn't deal with them, Nick would.

Or at least that was his plan until he arrived at the castle at the outskirts of Dorking only to discover Cyrus Dunwitty, the justice of the peace, had turned them loose.

"You are telling me they are gone? That Bascomb simply strolled in here and demanded their release?"

Dunwitty swallowed hard. "It wasn't exactly that way. But yes, the men are gone." The son of a wealthy squire, he was a pale-skinned man, dish-faced and grossly overweight with thinning mouse-brown hair. "Lord Bascomb said there had been a terrible mistake. He said the men were merely escorting his fiancée to his home for a visit, as they had been instructed to do. Since neither you nor the girl were here to naysay his claim, I was forced to release the men into his lordship's care."

Nick reached across the walnut desk and grabbed the man by the lapels of his expensive velvet-trimmed coat. "You simpering fool. You wanted to curry Bascomb's favor—that's why you released them. That was all you cared about."

Dunwitty strained against Nick's hold. "For God's sake— the man wants to marry the chit. He'll make her his bloody countess! The little baggage ought to be down on her knees giving thanks."

Nick jerked him up on his toes. "Listen to me, you odious little toad, and you had better listen good. That girl is my ward. She has refused Bascomb's suit. Those men took her from my home against her will." Nick dragged him higher. "The next time I tell you someone has broken the law, you had better believe it. If you don't, it won't be Bascomb you'll be answering to—it will be me!"

Dunwitty sputtered and nodded, his face turning a fierce, purply red. Elias stood grinning as Nick lowered him back to his feet.

"Give your father my regards, Cyrus," Nick said dryly. Turning away, he and Elias walked out the door.

"Bloody bastard," Elias grumbled, pulling his horse's reins from the stable boy who stood out front and tossing the lad a coin.

"I should have known Bascomb would get wind of what happened. His estate is less than a day's ride away. Christ, he was probably here before nightfall."

Elias clapped him on the shoulder. "Not to worry, Nick me boy. Odds are, 'is bleedin' lordship will be headin' to London, soon as 'e finds out that's where Miss Woolcot's gone. Those boys will likely go with 'im. We'll get our chance at them yet."

Nick's hands unconsciously fisted. He wanted a chance to even the score all right. But he wanted a go at Oliver Hampton even more.

The night before their journey to London, Elizabeth went for a last walk in the garden. The violets were in bloom alongside bluebells. Clematis climbed trellises along the gravel paths. Earlier in the day, she had spotted a beautiful citrine wagtail, a rare sight with its canary-yellow head and jet-black collar, a sight she would carry with her all the way to London.

A sigh whispered into the darkness. She had grown to love

it here at Ravenworth. Now she would be forced to leave it forever, to make a new home for herself in a place she had never been, with a man she did not know and did not love.

"Elizabeth?" His voice floated toward her across the hedgerows and her stomach instantly tightened.

"Over here, my lord."

He walked in that direction, his footfalls crunching on the gravel path, yet he moved with such grace there wasn't all that much sound. "My sister said I would find you out here."

He was dressed in a dark blue tailcoat over a white frilled shirt. She tried not to notice the way the moonlight fell on his hair, the way it cast his cheekbones into shadow and outlined his jaw.

"I wanted to remember how lovely it is." *I wanted to remember the place where you first kissed me.* "It's beautiful out here, especially this time of the evening."

He gazed toward the men who patrolled the walls, checking to be sure it was safe.

"I won't stay long, I promise."

His mouth curved faintly. His eyes moved over her face, his expression growing intense. "I've been meaning to talk to you. I should have done it sooner. I tried to tell myself it was better to leave the matter alone, but the truth is I was a coward." He stared off into the shadows then back again. A muscle ticked in his cheek. "I want you to know that I'm sorry. What happened between us was a mistake, a terrible, costly mistake I'll regret for the rest of my life."

Elizabeth's heart twisted up inside her. "Please . . . please don't say that."

"Why not? It's the truth. You were a virgin, for God's sake. I'm supposed to be your guardian."

Elizabeth's spine went rigid. "You are a man, nothing more. You told me that yourself. I was the one who came to you. I begged you not to send me away. If anyone should regret what happened, it is I. I am not sorry, my lord. My only regret is that you are."

Nicholas said nothing, just stared at her as if he tried to see inside her. Tension thrummed through his long, lean body. His shoulders seemed honed in steel. Then his head came up and he took a step away.

"We leave for London at seven o'clock in the morning. It would be a good idea for you to get some sleep."

Elizabeth made no reply, just stood there watching as he turned and disappeared into the darkness. Her heart beat painfully. Something burned at the back of her eyes. She didn't regret what she had done. She didn't believe she ever would.

She only wished that Nicholas did not regret it. And that she could forget his hurtful words.

Maggie leaned back against the carriage seat, feeling a sense of unreality. It had been nine years since she had traveled to London. It was the year of her coming out, a young girl of sixteen, making her debut in Society. Her father had been so proud. Dozens of young men had vied for her hand, but she was young yet, and having far too much fun to think of marriage.

Then fall had come and the end of the Season, and they had returned to Ravenworth Hall. Nine years later, she couldn't imagine what it was about Stephen Bascomb that had made her fall head over heels in love with him. In truth, he had simply seduced her, and in her innocence she had believed it was love.

Maggie looked out the window as the carriage bowled along. Great fields of green slipped past, gently rolling hills bordered by low stone walls. Occasionally they passed through a hamlet or village where children and dogs rushed out to greet them, but mostly they simply rolled on toward the city.

It was quiet inside the carriage. Elizabeth sat across from her, next to her plump aunt Sophie, while Nicholas rode up on top with Jackson Fremantle, the coachman. Mercy Brown, Edward Pendergass, and Elias Moody rode in the coach behind that transported their baggage.

Maggie looked down at the nine-year-old gown she wore, one of dozens still hanging in the rosewood armoire in her bedchamber. With its overfull watered-silk skirt and rows of pink ruching around the hem, it was hardly the height of fashion. It reminded her of all the years that had passed, of the shame that had turned her life upside down.

In one way or another, the days ahead would be painful for all of them. She and Nick were social pariahs, though in fact, few people knew the truth of what Stephen had done. Elizabeth, she guessed, would rather be marrying for love than simply accepting a match that her brother and Sydney arranged.

But all of them were survivors, and all of them were determined. Nick wanted his ward safely wed. Elizabeth wanted to be free of Oliver Hampton, and Maggie wanted a chance to discover life again.

At least they wouldn't be alone, she thought, and for the first time that day, she smiled. She remembered Rand Clayton from when she was a girl, tall, broad-shouldered, dark-haired, and imposing. If the Duke of Beldon was the same man he had been when she had last seen him, there was every chance their plan would succeed.

Constructed of sturdy red brick, Nick's town house in Berkeley Square stood three stories high and was built in the classic mode. His mother had furnished it lavishly in the neo-Grecian style, using elegant Sheraton sofas, Wedgwood urns, and Hepplewhite tables. Just walking through the halls made him think of her, made him a little bit wistful and also made him smile.

They had arrived late yesterday afternoon in a flurry of baggage and servants, but everyone had quickly settled in. The house was so inviting it had a way of doing that, making people comfortable even in their unfamiliar surroundings. This morning he had received a message from the Duke of Beldon requesting a meeting. As he descended the spiral staircase,

Nick checked the time on the tall gilded clock in the entry. The duke would be arriving any minute.

Rand Clayton, Duke of Beldon. Nick hadn't allowed himself to think of his friend since his return to England, had ignored any overtures Rand had made, certain they came only from a sense of obligation. That Rand had stepped forward again, making it clear he still valued their friendship, made a knot of emotion rise in his chest.

Nick made his way into his study and had almost reached his desk when Pendergass tapped lightly on the door.

"My lord?"

"Yes?"

"I am sorry to disturb you, my lord, but His Grace, the Duke of Beldon, has just arrived. I have shown him into the Green Drawing Room."

"Thank you, Edward. Tell him I'll be right there." Nick took a steadying breath. He owed his friend an apology. It seemed lately he'd been doing a lot of that.

He walked down the hall and into the drawing room, an elegant affair with moss-green walls and ornate white-painted moldings. Heavy green draperies hung at the windows, a sienna marble fireplace stood at each end, and his mother's small gilt harpsichord sat along one wall.

Rand stood up from a long moss-green velvet sofa as Nick came through the door and started walking toward him. He was a big man, thick chested and hard muscled, with coffee-brown hair and gold-flecked brown eyes. He was smiling such a warm, familiar smile, some of the tension Nick was feeling drained away.

"Your Grace—it's good to see you."

Rand grinned, gouging a dimple in his left cheek. "Your Grace, my arse. I'm still Rand to you and always will be."

Nick grinned back. He couldn't remember when he had last done that. He gripped Rand's big hand and Rand gripped his shoulder. "I feel like a fool," Nick said. "I just didn't want to embarrass you."

"You didn't do anything I wouldn't have done, under the same set of circumstances. The rot of it was they sent you to prison."

Nick smiled. "I fooled them though—I lived." He turned and started walking toward the carved oak sideboard along the wall. "How about a brandy? I could certainly use one."

Rand nodded. "Sounds like a winning idea."

Nick couldn't seem to stop smiling. "God, it's good to see you." He had seen his friend only once since his return to England, just weeks after his arrival. Rand had insisted Nick come to the house for a visit but he had declined, worried his past would cause problems for his best friend's family. Until today, Nick hadn't realized how badly he had missed him.

Rand joined him at the sideboard. "I started to come to Ravenworth a dozen times, but something always seemed to crop up. And I wasn't really sure of my reception."

Nick poured the amber liquid into two crystal snifters. "As I said, I was a fool. But you would have been more than welcome." Nick handed the glass to his friend and they carried their drinks across the deep Turkish carpet. They sat down facing each other on a pair of sofas in front of the hearth.

"I have to tell you," Rand said, "there were times these past few years, I wondered if you would ever make it home. I heard stories about the treatment of indentured prisoners. It must have been a nightmare."

"At times it was worse than that." Because he valued Rand's friendship, Nick told him a little about the life he had lived in Jamaica, about the scorching days and the backbreaking labor, about the dysentery, the discipline, and the bugs. It sounded like hell, but in truth there was nothing he could say to describe how bad it really was.

"I'm glad you're back," Rand said, "but I gather your troubles haven't quite ended."

"If you mean Bascomb, you couldn't be more than right. I really appreciate what you're doing for us, Rand."

"Sydney tells me your ward is quite charming. Apparently Oliver thinks so."

Nick felt a niggle of guilt, then the usual surge of anger. Briefly, he told Rand the lengths to which Bascomb had gone in his efforts to force Elizabeth to his will.

"In a way it doesn't surprise me," Rand said. "The man was always obsessive when it came to the women he wanted. There was that actress from Drury Lane—what was her name?"

"Maryann Wilson."

"Yes. Every time she refused him, he bought her another expensive piece of jewelry. In the end, he paid a bloody fortune to set her up as his mistress."

"I remember."

"There were others while you were away. Last summer there was a pretty young widow. Her name was Cynthia Crammer. Apparently money couldn't sway her. Rumor went round—Oliver threatened her children."

"Tell me you aren't serious."

"I wish I could."

Nick swore an oath beneath his breath. "God's blood, the man is a menace."

Rand took a sip of his brandy. "Elizabeth Woolcot is the only woman he has ever offered marriage. I don't imagine her refusal sat lightly."

"That is to say the least."

"I've set my secretary to work planning the first step in our campaign—a ball scheduled for Saturday next. I believe he could use some help, though. Perhaps your Elizabeth would be willing to assist him."

Your Elizabeth. Guilt rose again, mingled with a shot of desire. Every time he thought of her, he remembered the night she had spent in his bed. "I'm sure she'll be happy to do whatever she can. I don't know if Sydney told you—my sister is here as well."

"Little Maggie is here?"

He nodded. "She's left the convent for good. You wouldn't recognize her, Rand. She's no little girl anymore. She's grown into a beautiful woman."

Rand's mouth curved into a smile. "She was pretty when she was sixteen."

Too pretty. And far too naïve. Easy prey for a bastard like Stephen. "Maggie's as much an outcast as I am. You're sticking your neck out for us, Rand, and this time I won't forget it."

Rand leaned back against the sofa. "I don't like Bascomb any more than you do. I'm happy to do what I can."

They finished their brandy, relaxed now, laughing over old times as if the years had never come between them. Stories of their years together at Oxford, pranks they had played as boys, women they had known. The hour slid past and all too soon it was time for Rand to leave. Nick walked him out into the hall.

"I imagine you've heard about the dinner party Sydney has arranged on Friday evening. He's invited David Endicott, Lord Tricklewood, one of the men on his list of prospective suitors. He hasn't yet said whether or not you are planning to attend."

Rand smiled. "It's already marked on my calendar. I can't think of anything that I should like better. It will give me a chance to renew my acquaintance with Maggie and finally meet your ward."

Nick smiled, but an unwanted thought occurred: Rand Clayton was a bachelor, a handsome and powerful man. He wasn't in the market for a wife, he had told Sydney. But he had yet to meet Nick's lovely, fiery-haired ward.

Irrationally, he worried his friend might change his mind.

Nick lounged against his chair in the breakfast room, enjoying the familiar sight of his sister standing next to the window. She looked no more than twenty, blond and attractive, in the first blush of womanhood. The convent had helped do that, shielding her against the harshness of life these past nine years. At five and twenty, Maggie had regained the strength to return to the world and still possessed the vitality to enjoy it. Some of the loneliness he lived with seemed to fade whenever he looked at her. God, he was glad she was home.

She stared down at the gown she was wearing and frowned in disgust. "These clothes of mine are dreadful, Nick. I need a whole new wardrobe and Elizabeth needs a few things, as well. Mercy says you have forbidden her to leave the house, but she must come, Nicky. Please say you'll let her."

He only shook his head. "Bascomb is in town. I've had a Bow Street runner keeping tabs on him ever since Elizabeth's abduction. The earl arrived this morning and I'm not about to take any chances."

"Fine, then you can come with us." Maggie smiled the endearing smile he had missed for so long. "Elizabeth will be safe as long as you are there to protect her."

Nick glanced to where Elizabeth sat silently watching, and steeled himself. He knew how persuasive his sister could be. "No."

"Come on, Nick. Look at me. Do you really want me gadding about all over London looking like a sixteen-year-old girl?"

He studied the out-of-date clothing that made her look so young and smiled with a hint of amusement. "I didn't say *you* couldn't go, Maggie."

"But Elizabeth must go, too. You want her to find a proper husband, don't you?"

His smile disappeared and a knot tightened in his stomach. He glanced at Elizabeth and then looked away. "Of course I do."

"Then she must be properly clothed. Come with us, Nick. We shall have a grand time, the three of us. Once we are done with our shopping, we can explore a bit of the city."

Nick stared in Elizabeth's direction. She was sitting across the table, her expression carefully guarded as they bantered back and forth. She was lovely in her mint-green muslin gown, her hair swept into fiery ringlets on top of her head. Looking at her made the knot in his stomach clench harder. The gown outlined the roundness of her breasts and he felt another tightening lower down.

Dammit, he wanted her. No matter how he fought it, no matter how hard he tried to convince himself she wasn't for him, his body would not listen.

There were times he hated her for stepping through the door of his room that night at the inn.

He felt her eyes on his face, deep green and probing, seeing things he did not want her to see. Bloody hell. The sooner she was married, the better. He wanted to stop feeling guilty. He wanted to stop feeling this constant, tormenting desire for her.

He wanted her gone and his life back to normal.

Grudgingly he turned in her direction. "You probably do need some clothes," he said gruffly. "Get your bonnet. I'll have the carriage brought round."

ELEVEN

Elizabeth sat next to Margaret Warring, across from Nicholas in the sleek black Ravenworth carriage. The tension inside seemed to eat up the very air, but little by little, Maggie's soft banter, her excitement at seeing the city again after so many years, helped ease the mood.

They drove along Piccadilly to St. James's, passing into an area of elegant shops and restaurants. The streets were crowded with carriages and vendors: newsboys, coal merchants, bellmen, cherry-sellers, shoeblacks. There seemed to be no end to them. Along the paving stones, ladies and gentlemen hurried past, elegantly dressed, their arms piled high with brightly wrapped packages and boxes.

Maggie chatted pleasantly, but Elizabeth only kept wishing that she wasn't there.

"Look, Nick!" Maggie pointed toward a cluster of children standing in a circle outside L. T. Piver's, a perfume and glove shop. "It's a puppet show. I haven't seen one since I was a girl."

Nicholas caught the heightened color in his sister's cheeks, and for an instant, Elizabeth thought he might actually smile.

He didn't, of course, simply instructed the driver to pull over, drawing the carriage to a halt in front of Madame Boudreau's, the city's most fashionable modiste.

With brusque efficiency, he helped them down from the carriage and Elias Moody joined them, a guard of sorts, she suspected, jumping down from the top where he had been riding with the coachman.

While Elias stood out front and Nicholas waited patiently on an elegant settee, lending his opinion now and then on fabric, design, or color, Elizabeth and Margaret were fitted for gowns.

Elizabeth finished first, needing only a few new dresses to supplement her wardrobe. When the last gown was fitted, she had no choice but to join the earl where he sat on the small settee, their legs nearly brushing, her skirt trailing over the top of his polished black shoe.

He flicked her a glance, a row of thick black lashes coming down to veil the silver-blue of his eyes.

"You chose well," he said. "The emerald and gold is perfect for the ball the duke has planned."

"I'm glad you like it."

"'Tis not a matter of what I like but of what will show you off to your best advantage, as the emerald and gold will surely do."

She stared into his handsome face and a fine thread of anger slid through her. "I am not a piece of merchandise, my lord, to be packaged and put on display. If my suitors do not approve of the way I look, they can find someone else to marry."

Nicholas's black brows pulled into a frown. "And what of Oliver Hampton? Need I remind you the man means to force you into his bed?"

Color burned up her neck and infused her cheeks. "I assure you I haven't forgotten."

He leaned closer, his eyes dark gray and intense. "Listen to me, Elizabeth. I know how you feel about Bascomb. I know things have grown even more . . . complicated over the past few weeks. But in truth, I only want what is best for you." He turned her cheek with his hand, forcing her to look at him. "I want you to be happy. You deserve a man who will care for you and treat you with respect."

He was staring at her with such sincerity, her bottom lip began to tremble. "Do I?"

"Yes, you do."

"And what of love, my lord?"

His turbulent gaze slid away. "Love is a fairy tale, Elizabeth. Perhaps for some it is real, but for the rest of us, it is only a fantasy. It doesn't really exist."

Elizabeth said nothing, but she ached inside. Ached for the love she felt for Nicholas that he would never return, ached for the love that Nicholas had never known.

The afternoon crept by, tense, and often strained. Even Maggie's lighthearted banter couldn't penetrate the brittle atmosphere in the carriage as they finished the last of their shopping. When they were done, at Maggie's insistence, they stopped for an orange ice in a small confectioner's shop. Elizabeth managed to spill some down the front of her dress and, for the first time that day, Nicholas smiled. Then Maggie handed her a damp cloth to wipe away the stain and the wetness made her nipple peak beneath the fabric. Elizabeth flushed and Nicholas scowled. He turned and stalked away.

Nicholas remained curt and withdrawn all the way back to the town house. She didn't see him again until the end of the week, not until time for the dinner party Sydney Birdsall had arranged for Friday night. He was avoiding her, she knew, but Elizabeth preferred it that way. He had made it painfully clear he had nothing to say to her and she certainly had nothing to say to him.

Choosing a high-waisted sapphire-blue silk gown shot with silver and tied with a silver ribbon beneath her breasts, Elizabeth prepared herself to face the evening ahead. All day she had dreaded the encounter with the first of her prospective suitors, but no amount of wishful thinking could postpone the inevitable for long.

Pasting on a smile, she made her way downstairs, stopping at the bottom to join Aunt Sophie, who walked with her into the drawing room. Sydney was waiting. She greeted him with a kiss on his wrinkled cheek, then made the appropriate greeting to Ravenworth. He was equally formal, presenting her as his ward to the rest of their guests, including the Duke of Beldon.

"My dear Miss Woolcot," the duke said with a smile, taking her gloved hand as she rose from a curtsy. "It is indeed a pleasure to meet you." He grinned and a tiny dimple appeared in his cheek. "Praise from your admirers has been lavish, but I can certainly see it was not undeserved."

She had to admit she was impressed. Beldon's presence was magnetic. For a moment she was actually able to forget the equally powerful presence of Nicholas Warring. She smiled into the duke's handsome face. "Thank you, Your Grace."

She flashed an assessing glance at the earl, wondering what he might have said about her. They spoke a few moments more, then she excused herself and returned to stand beside Sydney, feeling safer, somehow, in his company.

"I believe you have already met Lord Tricklewood." Sydney turned to the attractive young viscount—the first of her potential suitors—who had just joined them.

"Yes. Lord Ravenworth introduced us earlier in the evening." David Endicott, Lord Tricklewood, was lean and sandy-haired with a boyish smile and wide-set blue eyes. He was a little shy at first and she liked that about him, that he was as far the opposite of Oliver Hampton as any two men could get.

Maggie arrived just then, elegant and lovely in a gown of yellow silk that set off the gold of her hair. She paused for a moment, just inside the drawing room doors.

"Good God, is that little Maggie?" Beldon's deep voice boomed across the Oriental carpet.

Nicholas's deep laughter joined in. "I told you she wasn't so little anymore."

"Yes, you did." Beldon approached her, reached out and took both of her hands. "Welcome back, Lady Margaret. You have been away far too long."

Maggie smiled. "Thank you, Your Grace. There are times it seems I was gone forever. Now that I have returned, I can hardly believe I was ever away."

"You've grown into a lovely young woman. I know your father and mother would be proud."

A flicker of emotion, then Maggie smiled. "Thank you, Your Grace."

The evening went passably well. Aunt Sophie, in her usual good humor, was seated next to Sydney, and several times during the course of the meal, Elizabeth could hear his soft laughter at something Aunt Sophie said. There were other guests as well: the Marquess of Denby and his petite wife, Eleanor; Sir Wilfred Manning and a widow named Emily Chester whom Sir Wilfred was courting, all of them friends of Beldon's. They were present to begin Elizabeth's introduction into Society, along with the return of the disgraced Ravenworth siblings, a task far easier tonight than it would be in the future.

Elizabeth sat next to Lord Tricklewood, who grew less and less shy as the evening wore on.

"Mr. Birdsall tells me you quite like to read."

"Yes, I find it very relaxing. Currently I am reading one of Mrs. Radcliffe's Gothic novels, *The Mysteries of Udolpho*, though I am sure a number of people would not approve."

Tricklewood smiled. "Actually, I just finished reading it myself, and in truth, I liked it very much." Thus began a discussion of books, which turned to a discussion of gardens, which ended in of all things a lively discussion of birds.

"My last day at Ravenworth," Elizabeth said, "I spotted a

citrine wagtail. As I had never seen one before, it was really quite a thrill."

Tricklewood seemed impressed. "I can imagine. I have never had the good fortune to see one, myself. I know that they are quite rare."

They continued conversing in a pleasant vein until Elizabeth felt Nicholas's hard gaze boring into her. When she glanced to where he sat at the far end of the table, she saw that his jaw was set, and his delicious plate of veal stuffed with woodcock sat nearly untouched in front of him. Apparently he didn't approve of David Endicott as a potential husband.

Which meant, in Elizabeth's book, he was an even more likely candidate.

"Well, what did you think?" Sydney Birdsall sat next to Rand Clayton in Nick's study the following morning. "I thought it went off rather well for a first attempt."

"Elizabeth and the young viscount definitely seemed to get along," Rand said. "From what I've heard, Tricklewood is quite a decent fellow. What did you think, Nick?"

He leaned back in his chair. "David is a boy. Elizabeth needs a man."

Beldon frowned while Sydney pursed his lips. "He is nearly three and twenty, three years Elizabeth's senior. Old enough, I should think. He has money enough, but a modest fortune, so her dowry will still be of interest."

"Elizabeth seemed to like him," Beldon put in.

"Elizabeth likes everyone," Nick grumbled.

"Except for Oliver Hampton."

His jaw tightened. "I stand corrected," he said darkly.

Rand smiled. "Cheer up, old man. We've only made the first foray into the field of battle. Elizabeth is lovely in the extreme. She won't want for suitors. You'll be able to pick and choose."

Pick and choose, yes. Except that because of me she is

no longer a virgin. But he would deal with that problem when the time came.

"The ball at your house is next," he said to Rand. "That should be a crucial move in the game. With you as Elizabeth's sponsor, they'll be hard-pressed to ignore her, but of course we can't be sure."

"Leave that to me," the duke said with no little authority. "If they know what is good for them, your ward will be welcomed with open arms."

Nick glanced up. One look at his friend's stern features and he could almost believe it. Still, it wouldn't be easy. Not for him. Not for Maggie, and especially not for Elizabeth.

Elizabeth dressed with care for what would be her official debut into London Society. She was wearing the gold and emerald gown Nicholas had insisted she purchase in Madame Boudreau's dress shop. It was actually a soft cream silk, trimmed beneath the bodice, down the sides, and along the hem with bands of emerald and gold in an Egyptian motif. The low-cut bodice displayed a good bit of her bosom. The color, he had said, brought out the deep green of her eyes.

Standing in front of the mirror, she grudgingly admitted the earl was right. With her auburn hair and fair complexion, the gown set off her features better than any dress she had ever worn.

Elizabeth smiled bitterly. Ravenworth would surely be pleased. He wanted to be rid of her, to see her married and out of his hair. He had satisfied his desire for her and now he wanted to dismiss her, just as he had done Miriam Beechcroft. God, she had been a fool to believe a man like the earl could change.

"Are you ready?" Maggie stuck her head through the open door to her bedchamber.

"I suppose so, though I must say I'm hardly looking forward to the evening."

Maggie stepped into the room and quietly closed the door.

"Believe me, I quite agree. God only knows what reception we shall receive." She was gowned in ice-blue silk, a shade lighter than her eyes. With her fair skin and golden blond hair, she looked stunning. "Poor Nick is likely to get the brunt of it. He should be used to it by now, but Sydney says he isn't."

Elizabeth made no reply. She didn't want to think about Nicholas Warring. She certainly didn't want to feel sorry for him.

Maggie studied her from beneath a row of gold lashes as thick as Nicholas's black ones. "On the surface, my brother seems hard, but in truth, he is more sensitive than you might believe. He cares for people—cares very deeply. If he thinks of you as a friend, he'll do anything in his power to protect you—no matter the pain it might cause him."

Elizabeth pondered that. Was Maggie trying to tell her something? As far as she knew, Margaret Warring knew nothing of her feelings for her brother, or had any idea what had transpired between them. She studied the toes of her gold satin slippers, carefully choosing her words.

"Lord Ravenworth has been very generous to my aunt and to me. Both of us are greatly indebted."

Maggie's expression turned intense. "He cares for you, Elizabeth. I can see it in his face whenever he looks at you. I hope you don't hurt him. Nick's been hurt enough already."

Elizabeth just stood there, her eyes wide with astonishment. "You think *I* might pose some sort of threat to your brother?"

Maggie smoothed a lock of her short blond hair, tucking it neatly behind an ear. "Nick is lonely. His wife has abandoned him. He doesn't know it, but he is desperately in need of a woman who will love him. Unfortunately, he is married, which means that woman can't be you."

No one knew that better than she. Elizabeth walked over to the window, stared down at the street lamps below. A watchman reached the corner, stopped and turned, walked back to the small wooden shed in which he was housed.

"You've been gone a long time, Maggie. People change. From what I've seen, your brother is quite adept at assuaging whatever loneliness he might feel. He has any number of women at his beck and call, and he doesn't shy away from taking what is offered." That wasn't exactly true. He had tried more than once to avoid what Elizabeth had practically forced on him. It was her fault, not his, that he had failed.

"Nick has always been handsome and sought after. He is a dangerous, capable man when he has to be, and that holds some special appeal to women. Since Stephen's death, they have pursued him perhaps more than ever. But the fact is, Nick is lonely. You may not see it, but I do."

Elizabeth said nothing. She had thought that same thing on more than one occasion. She wondered now, as she hadn't before, if perhaps the distance he put between them was not an effort to rid himself of her, but an attempt to protect them both.

Lounging against the wall below the spiral staircase, Nick glanced up to see Elizabeth approaching the top of the stairs. In the gold and emerald silk gown he had insisted she purchase, she looked so lovely his breath caught, began a slow burn in his chest. He pushed away from the wall with careful nonchalance as Maggie joined her, and the women descended the stairs.

"You both look lovely," he said to them, but his eyes remained on Elizabeth. "Every man in the place will be falling at your feet."

Maggie smiled. "I hope you are right." She looked more nervous than he had expected, her shoulders rigid with tension. "I shall deem the evening a success if we receive the cut direct from less than half the people in the room."

Nick reached out and cupped her cheek. "It won't be so bad. Rand will be with us, and his mother, the dowager duchess. Together, we'll be quite a formidable force."

A slight shiver moved over Elizabeth's slender frame. Nick

saw it and his chest went tight. This was his fault, all of it. And yet there was nothing he could do.

"I'm sorry, Elizabeth, that it has come to this. If there were any way to make this easier for you, I would. Your father would never have allied himself with my family if he had known the trouble it would cause. But that, I'm afraid, is spilt milk, and it is all in the past. Just remember, whatever happens tonight, keep your chin up and your emotions in check. If God is with us, when we return home, my sister will be one step closer to putting the past behind her, and Elizabeth Woolcot will be on her way to a new life."

Elizabeth simply nodded. He could feel her nervousness, though she did her best to disguise it. He wanted to hold her, comfort her, tell her everything would be all right. Instead, he remained where he was, wearing a look of cool indifference, afraid the least amount of sympathy would only make things worse.

Her aunt appeared a few minutes later, smiling and cheerful as always, and he urged his little party toward the door. Descending the front-porch steps, he helped the ladies climb into the carriage, then climbed in himself, settling back against the plush velvet squabs. Up on the driver's seat, Jackson Fremantle slapped the reins, the carriage lurched forward, and in seconds they were bowling along the crowded streets toward the Duke of Beldon's town mansion on Grosvenor Square.

As they had planned, the ball was well under way by the time they arrived. Stylish phaetons and curricles, elegant calèches, and gilded black coaches formed a long line out in front. Instead, Nick ordered the driver to head for the side door, as Rand had arranged. Inside the house, they were ushered into an elegant drawing room where the duke and dowager duchess joined them a few moments later.

"Maggie, you're looking splendid," Rand said, striding forward, then bowing with great formality over her hand. He turned a warm smile on the slender, auburn-haired woman who stood beside her. "Elizabeth, you are a vision. Your beaux will be lining up for places on your dance card." He flashed a second smile. "And you, Nick, as usual, will have the women fighting like cats to garner a moment of your attention."

"I daresay, Nicholas," the duchess put in, "all that hard work didn't seem to hurt you a lick. If anything, you are even more handsome than you were nine years ago." She smiled. "It's good to see you, my boy."

"Thank you, Your Grace." She was a small woman, slightly stooped at the shoulder, silver haired, with deep-set blue eyes and the same formidable nature as her son. She had always been outspoken, and even the subject of Nick's imprisonment was not taboo.

He watched as she turned her attention to his sister, granting her the same warm welcome that he had received. "It's been too long, dear child. It is delightful to see you again."

Some of Maggie's nervousness eased at the duchess's warm welcome. He had forgotten how gracious the Clayton family could be. More than ever, he regretted the years he had missed seeing his friend.

Then Rand presented Elizabeth to his mother, whose discerning eyes studied her from head to foot. Elizabeth made a deep, graceful curtsy. "I am delighted to meet you, Your Grace. I shall never be able to repay your kindness."

"Nonsense. Helping Lord Ravenworth has been good for my son. He grows jaded and bored. He hasn't been challenged by anything in years."

Elizabeth smiled and he thought she seemed to relax. It was imperative she make a good impression if she were to find a suitable husband. Nick watched her and reminded himself it was the only choice she had, that it was the best thing for Elizabeth, the best thing for both of them. But an ache crept into his chest and his insides felt leaden. The small group talked a few minutes longer, but guests were still arriving and the duke's and the dowager's presence would soon be missed.

The moment was at hand—time to face the dragon.

"Chin up, all of you," Rand said, ushering the small group toward the door. "Never show them mercy, nor the slightest trace of fear—they'll go for blood if you do."

He was grinning when he said it, but Nick inwardly shuddered, certain the statement was true.

WELVE

$\mathcal{T}$he gold and emerald gown
swayed with each of her nervous steps. Elizabeth made her
way down the wide, marble-floored hall on the Duke of Beldon's arm, while Ravenworth escorted the dowager duchess,
Aunt Sophie and Maggie trailing along in his wake. The
mansion was bursting with guests, crowding into each ornate
doorway and passage.

Elizabeth pasted on a bright, carefree smile as they shouldered their way through the mob and entered the huge gilded
ballroom. It shimmered with tall beeswax candles and glittered with silver urns filled to overflowing with dozens of
alabaster roses, their soft scent mingling with the heavier
perfume worn by the women.

Walking toward the orchestra at the far end of the ballroom, Elizabeth clutched the duke's thick-muscled arm and
continued to smile. So far, things had gone smoothly. She had
liked the duchess immediately and she liked Rand Clayton
more and more. His hand covered hers, sure and strong, and
she thought how lucky they were to have him stand as friend.

Several heads turned, a dozen eyes found them, then fifty,

then a hundred. The hubbub in the room lowered to a low boiling simmer. Seconds passed. Watching their progress, the room fell silent, then the whispering began. They were staring at Nicholas, scandalized at his appearance at such a gathering, and Elizabeth's heart went out to him. Her spine prickled as if each person's gaze held a razor-sharp edge, and pity welled inside her. He had done this for her and for Maggie. He had done it because he cared.

"Good Lord—that isn't Ravenworth," someone muttered from a few feet away. "Why, the man is a criminal. Surely he wouldn't have the gall."

"I daresay it is," confirmed a rotund matron in an out-of-fashion powdered wig. "And that little blond tart is his sister."

Beneath her hand, the duke's arm tensed, but he kept on walking. The voices continued as they passed through the crowd and Elizabeth felt sick to her stomach.

"Who's the red-haired gel?" a nattily dressed young man asked. "She is certainly a prime bit of baggage."

"That, old chap, is Sir Henry Woolcot's daughter. Ravenworth is her guardian." He chuckled softly. "Rather like a wolf guarding the sheep, wouldn't you say?" Both men laughed—until Beldon stopped and turned. One look from those cool brown eyes and all merriment immediately ceased.

They continued across the ballroom, Elizabeth's knees quaking beneath her skirt, until they reached the edge of the dance floor. The duke made a slight inclination of his head and the orchestra began to play. As custom demanded, he began the dancing, partnering his mother first, the highest-ranking woman in the room. The second dance he saved for her.

"Smile, my dear, you look positively ravishing. You haven't a thing to worry about." He cast a quick glance at Ravenworth, who stood beside the dowager duchess just a few feet away. Nicholas's expression was intense, but Elizabeth couldn't read his thoughts.

The music swelled. Beldon took his position across from her on the black and white marble floor. "He is worried about, you," Rand said as the line of dancers came forward. "You are fortunate to have made such a friend."

There was little she could say to that. Friendship with Nicholas Warring was the last thing she wanted. She wanted him to love her and that he would not do.

The duke smiled and Elizabeth did the same. As Beldon had said, it was imperative the ton believe that nothing was amiss, that they were exactly where they belonged, that their presence should be readily accepted.

He danced with Maggie next, wrapping them both in the protective cloak of his authority, and from that moment on, the tone of the evening began to change. Men appeared at her side as if they had stepped through the mirrored walls, and several women, she noticed, had the courage to seek Nicholas out.

She steeled herself from the shaft of jealousy that speared through her. She knew what the earl was like. He was a rake and a rogue, no matter what sacrifices he might be making in her behalf.

She forced her eyes away, brightened her pasted-on smile, and accepted an offer to dance with a young lord introduced by the dowager duchess. He was handsome and charming, but not one of the four potential suitors Sydney Birdsall had in mind.

Besides Lord Tricklewood, the list included Lord Addington Leech, second son of the Earl of Dryden; Sir Robert Tinsley; and William Rutherford, Baron Talmadge. All of their reputations were impeccable, as Sydney demanded, and their need for a wife well known. Each of them had been invited to the ball, but aside from Lord Tricklewood, only Lord Talmadge had come.

Sydney, who had arrived less than an hour ago, introduced Talmadge with a smile of approval.

"You should be flattered, my dear. His lordship came specifically to make your acquaintance."

She gave him the best smile she could muster. "How kind
of you, my lord."

"Not at all. I was quite happy to come. Sydney has told me
a good deal about you and I can already see that we shall get
on admirably well." He was a man in his late thirties, graying
at the temples, tall and spare, and well-spoken. He was a wid-
ower with two small children, a boy and a girl. The idea of
mothering his offspring held an unexpected appeal, but aside
from that she found the man a bit stiff and oddly forbidding.

As they partnered in a contra dance, she tried not to com-
pare him to Ravenworth, tried not to see Nicholas's tender
smile against the stern set of Talmadge's features. She tried
not to think of the night she had spent in Nicholas's bed, in
his arms, tried not to remember how it had felt when he was
inside her.

That road was madness, yet she couldn't stop thinking
about it. Or that marriage to Talmadge would surely be a joy-
less existence not far removed from an alliance with Oliver
Hampton.

Nick strode to the sideboard in his study and poured a generous amount of gin into his glass. He took a long, comforting swallow, felt the fiery liquid burn its way into his stomach.
He had drunk only a moderate amount all evening, had been
on his very best behavior in an effort to counter his wicked
reputation.

Now that his ladies were home and safe, there was nothing he wanted more than to get blindly, stupidly drunk and
forget the whole bloody affair.

He raised the glass and took another deep draw on his
drink. He had guessed the welcome he would receive and he
hadn't been wrong. He had only prayed Maggie and Elizabeth would be able to overcome their association with him,

and as it had turned out, Rand made the difficult task far easier than he had imagined.

By the end of the evening, the whispers had dulled to a few muttered words, and both his sister and Elizabeth, lovely as they were, had garnered a stream of male admirers. No, strangely enough, as difficult as he had perceived the task of returning to the ton, in the end that wasn't the problem.

Nick took another dulling drink of his gin. With a weary sigh, he sat down on the tufted leather sofa in front of the hearth and rested his head against the back, trying not to remember the smile on Elizabeth's face every time she had danced with another man. In truth, his distress came not from the tension of the evening, but from its success. In his wildest imaginings, he hadn't considered Elizabeth's triumph would hit him so damnably hard.

A soft curse slipped off his tongue. Every time he saw her dancing, it was all he could do not to storm across the room and drag her away from her partner. He couldn't stand to see another man's hand touching that lovely white skin, couldn't stand to watch another man's leering gaze drift down to the swell of her breast.

He didn't want them smiling at her. He didn't want them laughing with her. Bloody hell, he didn't want them anywhere near her.

Nick downed the rest of his drink, but it did little to deaden the sharp prongs of jealousy that pierced his insides. He had no right to feel them—no right at all, yet the hot shafts of anger would not abate.

"Good Christ," he muttered, rising to refill his glass, determined to take the edge off his turbulent emotions. What the devil was wrong with him? He had been with other women—dozens of them. What was it about the fiery little redhead that made him half crazy with lust? Lust and something more. A need to simply touch her. To hold her. To protect her. It was a feeling he had never experienced, not with his wife nor in any of his many affairs.

Seated once more on the sofa, Nick drained his glass, rose to pour another, and this time returned with the half-full decanter. He had promised to reform, but he was no saint. Besides, with her high full breasts, silky dark auburn hair, and sweetly enchanting smile, Elizabeth Woolcot was enough to make any sane man turn to drink.

Elizabeth perched on a seat in the small informal garden behind the town house. It wasn't nearly as elaborate as the gardens at Ravenworth Hall and few birds braved the smoky air of the city, but it was green and cool, a place of refuge that soothed her dismal mood.

A week had passed since the duke's lavish ball, deemed a resounding success, though not everyone in the ton welcomed their return with open arms. A start had been made, however, and several invitations arrived the following morning, several more the day after that. They attended each affair, and by the end of the week, Elizabeth was over her nerves and determined to make the best of her situation.

Maggie was struggling a bit, out of her element for certain after nine long years in a convent. But she was lovely and gracious and any number of men had made their interest clear.

On the opposite hand, Nicholas seemed more and more reticent each evening, his manner withdrawn, often brooding, at times even harsh.

It didn't deter the women. In truth, they seemed drawn to the dark side of his nature, excited by the dangerous quality that surrounded him. He was, after all, the Wicked Earl, and they wanted to taste the deep, seething passions they sensed were inside him, to touch those flaring black brows, kiss the hard set of his mouth.

Jealousy burned away the last of the hurt Elizabeth had been feeling, turning it instead to anger, a slow simmering boil that made her want to lash out at him, made her want to hurt him as he had hurt her.

"I am sick unto death of your brother's foul disposition,"

she said to Maggie upon their return home late one night. "He was rude to Lord Tricklewood and barely civil even to the duke."

To say nothing of the fact that Miriam Beechcroft, Lady Dandridge, was there at the ball and flashing him seductive glances through the entire miserable evening. "I realize, as my guardian, he feels obligated to see this matter through, but I am beginning to think it would be better for us all if he simply returned to Ravenworth Hall."

Maggie pulled her cashmere shawl off her shoulders and tossed it over a chair. "You know he can't do that. That could be precisely what Bascomb is waiting for." She sighed. "I realize Nicholas can be surly at times, at times a bit brooding, but it isn't like him to be purposely rude. I cannot imagine what is wrong with him."

Neither could Elizabeth. Perhaps a woman was involved, someone he wished to pursue as his next mistress. Perhaps he was simply weary of the task of finding his ward a husband. Whatever it was, Elizabeth vowed to ignore him, vowed that from now on Nicholas Warring could go straight to Hades.

Unfortunately, ignoring him wasn't that easy. Wherever she went, whomever she spoke to, she could feel the silver glint of his eyes on her. They made her insides flutter and her mouth go dry, reminded her what it had felt like when he touched her, made love to her that night at the inn.

Her anger swelled. Jealousy warred with desire, burning like a hot coal in her belly. She wanted him to suffer as she did, wanted to make him jealous, too, wanted to make him burn for her as one glance from those hot silver eyes could make her burn for him.

Elizabeth left the garden infused with a new determination. She was tired of being ignored, tired of Ravenworth's constant disapproval. Choosing a seductively low-cut gown in shades of black and topaz, she pulled the pins from her hair and began to brush it with swift, firm strokes, her mind awhirl with plans for the evening.

A smile of purpose settled over her lips. Two could play games of seduction. She might not be as skillful as Nicholas, but she was a very quick study. Ravenworth had held the winning hand long enough. Tonight she meant to even the score.

Standing at the edge of the drawing room, a lavish salon done in pale pink and cream, Sydney Birdsall clasped Elizabeth's hand and tucked it into the crook of his arm.

"My dear, you look splendid. Every head in the room turned your way as you walked in."

Elizabeth smiled, unconsciously smoothing the bodice of her low-cut silk gown. "Thank you, Sydney." They were attending a soirée hosted by Lord and Lady Denby, the marquess and his wife she had met at the dinner party Sydney had arranged when they first arrived in London.

"Two more of your suitors are here. Lord Addington and Sir Robert Tinsley. Both are eager to meet you."

Elizabeth glanced at Nicholas, who stood just a few feet away. His mouth seemed to thin, but he made no remark. She flashed a wide, sunny smile. "As I am eager to meet them. The duchess has a particular fondness for Sir Robert, and Lord Addington is rumored to be handsome in the extreme."

"He is also quite wealthy." Sydney glanced toward the door, lifted the monocle he wore to one eye. "Ah, there he is now. I believe he is making his way in our direction." Most certainly he was, Elizabeth saw.

"If the two of you will excuse me . . ." Nicholas turned and walked away. He hadn't gone far when a supple blond woman with an elegant figure stepped into his path and said something Elizabeth couldn't hear. She caught his low murmured response, then the rough sound of his laughter as the pair conversed.

Fury enveloped her. How dare he! He was cordial enough to the blond, but to Elizabeth he remained rude and surly.

When Lord Addington appeared, she turned all of the charm she could muster, every ounce of her feminine wiles in his direction, laughing at his inane banter, smiling at his efforts to impress her with his wit. He was handsome enough, in a dandified way, and she flattered him until his chest puffed out.

His eyes slid down to where her breasts swelled over the top of her bodice. "Would you care to dance, Miss Woolcot?"

She flashed him an overbright smile. "Why, yes, that would be lovely. I have heard, my lord, that you are an exquisite dancer."

His mouth curved in approval. "Actually, I believe I am rather adept. Shall we?"

She gave him a lighthearted laugh, turned, and felt a shot of satisfaction to see that Nicholas was standing there scowling.

The night wore on, endlessly it seemed to Elizabeth. Sir Robert was a pleasant surprise, a studious man with light brown hair and an attractive smile. It embarrassed her to flirt overly with such a man, even to make Nicholas jealous, so she opted instead for a brief walk in the garden.

When they returned to the house, Nicholas was waiting on the terrace beside the door, the grim set of his features worth every effort she had put forth that evening so far. Sir Robert's voice drew her eyes from his tall, imposing figure.

"Might I call on you, Miss Woolcot?" He was slighter of build and several inches shorter than the earl, but an attractive man just the same. "Perhaps we could go for a drive in the park on the morrow."

"I should like that." She smiled, hoping she looked more enthused by the notion than she felt. Of the four men Sydney had chosen as suitable husbands, only David Endicott and Robert Tinsley held the slightest appeal. Perhaps if she knew them better she could come to care for one of them. Perhaps in time . . . for in truth she had no other choice.

Nicholas started forward, his long legs closing the distance between them, the hard planes of his face still etched into a scowl.

"Lord Ravenworth," Sir Robert said. "Your ward is enchanting."

"Isn't she?" Nicholas said dryly, his eyes gray and glinting like storm clouds on the horizon.

"Why . . . why, yes she is. She has graciously agreed to my escort on the morrow."

A sleek black brow arched up. "Has she, indeed? In that case, I'm certain you won't mind granting us a moment of privacy. There are a few things we need to discuss."

A flush rose into Sir Robert's cheeks. "No . . . I mean yes, yes, of course." He turned an uncertain smile on Elizabeth. "Until the morrow, Miss Woolcot."

Elizabeth nodded and forced her lips to curve up as he walked away. Then her furious gaze swung to Nicholas.

"What in the world is the matter with you? Must you be rude to every man I speak to?"

His features tightened. "Must you flaunt yourself like a trollop in front of every man you meet?"

"What! How dare you insult—"

His hard grip on her arm cut her off. Tugging her forward, he urged her down the steps of the porch, leading her deeper into the dense green foliage of the garden. In the shadows behind the gazebo, well beyond the house, he turned her to face him.

"What the devil are you playing at? You've been flirting outrageously ever since we arrived tonight. You've got half the men in the ton thinking of ways they might bed you." His mouth curved harshly. "Or perhaps that is your game. Watching you, one would certainly think so."

Her hand itched to slap him. She tossed her head instead.

"I haven't done anything wrong. You wanted me to find a husband. You insisted, in fact. I am merely complying with your wishes. If you don't like the way I am going about it, that is simply too bad."

His jaw clenched, the muscles bunching, his eyes like shards of glass. "Don't push me, Elizabeth. I'm still your guardian, and I'm not about to stand by and let you make a spectacle of yourself."

Fury swept through her, making it difficult to think. "A spectacle? You are the one who has been eyeing every woman in the place as if she were a juicy piece of meat."

A dark eyebrow went up. "Have I?"

"Well . . . they have certainly been eyeing you! On top of that, ever since the duke's party, you've been vile-tempered and mean-spirited. You've been boorish and rude, even to your friends." She clamped her hands on her hips and tilted her head back, looking him straight in the eye. "You know what I think, Nicholas Warring? I think you are angry with me because you are jealous. That is what I think." It was a stupid thing to say and for an instant his furious expression made her wish she could call back the words.

A muscle twitched in his cheek. His eyes were so gray and flat they looked opaque. "Jealous?" he repeated.

"That is what I said."

Nicholas swore a savage oath. "Of course I am jealous! What the devil did you expect? Every time I see one of those dandies whispering in your ear I want to wring his damnable neck!"

Elizabeth just stared at him, unable to believe she had heard him correctly. "What . . . what about all of those women? Why would you be jealous of me, when you can have any one of them?"

His anger seemed to fade. "Sweet God, Bess. Don't you understand?" His hand came up to her cheek. "I am jealous because they are not you."

Her fury drained away like water seeping through sand.

She was in his arms in a heartbeat, clinging to his neck, her cheek pressed hard against his. "Oh, Nicholas, I've missed you. I've missed you so much."

He groaned as she rose on her toes and kissed him, then pressed soft, feathery kisses at the corners of his mouth.

"Elizabeth," he whispered, his voice deep and rough, a plea or a sound of surrender.

She only kissed him again, parting her lips, encouraging the invasion of his tongue. Nicholas complied, dragging her against him, tasting her deeply, wrapping her tightly in his arms. She could feel the hardness of his arousal and a tremor of heat ran through her.

"God, I want you," he whispered against her ear. "It's all I can think about. At night, it's all I can dream."

Elizabeth kissed him again, pressed her breasts against his chest, felt her nipples tighten into firm, throbbing peaks.

"We shouldn't," he said. "Ah, God, we shouldn't." But already he was easing down the top of her gown, taking her breast into his mouth and suckling deeply. Her legs felt weak and she clutched him tighter. Heat roared into her stomach, began to pulse through her limbs.

"I need you, Nicholas. I need you so badly."

He took her mouth again and his tongue delved deeply, stroking along the walls, tasting her even as his hands reached down to hike up her skirts. His kiss was hot and hungry, and wildly, fiercely possessive. She kissed him back with the same hot need and heard him groan. She could feel his long fingers moving up her thigh, little tongues of fire licking wherever he touched. His hands slid under the hem of her chemise and she sucked in a breath at the feel of them skimming over her bottom, then urging her legs apart and deftly probing her sex.

She was wet and ready, on fire for him, desperate to feel him inside her. "Please . . ." she whispered as his finger slipped in and he gently began to stroke her. All the while his mouth moved over hers, kissing her deeply, taking what he wanted, making her want it, too.

Rational thought disappeared. She couldn't think, could only feel, burned with heat and need and uncontrollable desire for him. She writhed against his hand, arched into each of his touches, and softly moaned.

Nicholas kissed her fiercely, his mouth claiming hers, his tongue sweeping in. He moved down to the swell of her breasts and began a hot manipulation of her nipple.

"Dear God . . ." Elizabeth clutched his shoulders, felt the bands of muscle bunch, felt the scorching heat of passion burning over her skin. Then he was working the buttons on his breeches, popping them free one by one, his shaft springing forward, demanding to be inside her.

Lifting her up, he ravaged her mouth as he lowered her down his body, sinking himself deep inside, filling her with his hardness,

"Wrap your legs around my waist," he commanded, and Elizabeth complied, her body shaking, tongues of fire swirling around her.

He pressed her back against a wall of the gazebo, his hands gripping her bottom, lifted her and thrust deep inside her again. He was thick and hard and each of his thrusts sent a spasm of heat roaring through her. Again and again, he drove into her, as if he couldn't get enough, as if each stroke claimed another part of her.

"Nicholas . . ." Moaning softly, she clung to his shoulders, feeling powerless and powerful at the very same time. The heat at her core began to expand, yet with each of his hard-driving thrusts, her body coiled tighter. Just when she thought she couldn't stand a moment more, Nicholas drove into her again, and the coil of heat broke free inside her. She cried out his name and dug her nails into his flesh, holding on for dear life, afraid if she let go, she would fly apart. The heady sweetness of release washed over her, the pleasure so intense for a moment she forgot to breathe.

Then she was drifting down, floating back to awareness,

clinging to Nicholas and feeling his lips against her cheek, the lobe of an ear, the side of her neck. He pressed a soft kiss on her lips.

"Are you all right?" he asked gently, easing her the length of his body until her gold satin slippers came to rest once more on the ground.

Elizabeth smiled, but inside she still trembled. Nicholas was holding her. He had made love to her. "I am fine." But she wasn't really fine. She wasn't sure at all what she was feeling. Strains of the music began to filter in, the sound of distant voices. She turned her head toward the house, but all she saw was the glimmer of candlelit windows through the trees, and the dense green darkness of the garden. She smoothed down her skirts, tucked in loose strands of her hair. "What . . . what do we do now?"

Nicholas did not falter. Instead he took her hand and brought it to his lips. "We're going home." He started toward the gate at the side of the garden, tugging Elizabeth along behind him, but she drew back, forcing him to stop and turn.

"Nicholas?"

"Yes, love?"

"When we get back, don't you dare say you are sorry."

His mouth curved up. His smile was warm and tender, filled with feelings she could not begin to guess. "I am tired of being sorry. When I think of you and the way we are together, it is impossible for me to be sorry."

Elizabeth threw herself into his arms, and he kissed her, swift and hard. "We have to go," he said gently. "It wouldn't do for someone to see us."

"No . . . it surely would not do." For the first time it occurred to her the bold step she had just taken. She wondered if Nicholas had realized it, too, for all the way back to the town house he grew more and more silent.

Fear began to gnaw at her. Perhaps she had misread his feelings, made more of his desire for her than what it truly was. Perhaps she had simply been a convenience of the moment. He was, after all, the Wicked Earl and he was still a married man. There was no future for them.

She didn't know what to believe, and as long as Nicholas said nothing to reassure her, there was no way to be certain. She felt as if she had come full circle from the first time they had made love.

And she was even more confused than she was before.

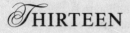

THIRTEEN

*R*achael Warring, Countess of Ravenworth, rolled onto her back in the deep feather mattress in her lavishly furnished bedchamber at Castle Colomb. It was done in shades of mauve silk, the bed hangings a lighter hue than the curtains. An elegant gilded armoire sat in one corner, beside a tall, ornate cheval glass she had purposely tilted to reflect what was happening on the bed.

"I'm sorry, my darling, but it's time for you to go." She glanced at the hands of the ormolu clock on the black marble mantel. "It's a quarter to twelve." She gave him a feline smile. "My beloved *husband* is due to arrive in less than an hour and I am hardly ready to make an appearance." She trailed a finger along her lover's spine. "Unless you wish me to entertain him naked."

Greville Townsend, Viscount Kendall, came up on an elbow. With his light brown hair and hazel eyes, he was a handsome, virile man, taller than average, well built, and two years younger than Rachael.

"That is the last thing I want and you know it. The less you have to do with your damnable husband, the better I like it." He pulled her down beside him and began to kiss the side of her neck, taking little nibbling bites out of her flesh. Rachael laughed and struggled to push him away.

"Be a good boy, Grey, and let me get dressed. Nicholas may no longer play the role of husband, but I doubt he would appreciate a blatant reminder that other men share his wife's bed."

Greville frowned. "Other men? Perhaps in the past, my love, but from now on there had better only be me."

She patted him on the cheek. "Of course, my darling. You know that isn't what I meant."

But Grey did not look appeased as he climbed up off the mattress, the youthful muscles rippling across his strong back. She would have to do something special for him tonight when they made love—punish him a little, perhaps—he always liked that.

"Be a dear now, will you, and stay out of the way for a while. As I said, I shouldn't want Nicholas to see you."

Grey frowned. "I don't give a damn if he does. The man is a villain. He should have been hanged nine years ago when he murdered Stephen Bascomb. If he had, you would be free to do as you please."

Rachael didn't tell him that as far as she was concerned, she was free. Free to spend Nick Warring's money. Free to live on his lavish estate. Free to take a younger man as her lover for as long as he pleased her.

Drawing on a mauve satin wrapper, she leaned over and tugged on the bellpull, summoning her maid. "I'll join you as soon as we're finished," she said to Grey. "The sun is out. Perhaps we shall go riding."

But Grey continued to frown. "I wonder what he wants."

"I'm sure I haven't the slightest idea." But the thought made her a little uneasy. As Rachael knew—and Stephen Bascomb had learned—Nick Warring could be a dangerous man when there was something he wanted.

Nick sat forward in his seat, waiting impatiently as his driver pulled the carriage to a halt at the entrance to Castle Colomb. It was only a half day's ride north of London, yet he hadn't been there in over nine years. His last meeting with Rachael on his return home from prison had been on neutral ground—Sydney Birdsall's office in London near the Stock Exchange on Threadneedle Street.

Through the open carriage window, he stared up at the tall ivy-covered towers, the tops crenellated for firing arrows, the rounded walls repelling intruders since the late medieval days. Inside, of course, the vast stone fortress had been modernized, its salons—at Rachael's insistence and Nick's expense—decorated in the height of fashion.

As the carriage rolled through the gates and into the bailey, Nick studied the timeless gray stone, the carpet of daffodils planted where the moat had once been. In the years he had been gone, he had forgotten how lovely the old place was, a family inheritance on his mother's side dating back to the days of Edward III.

The hand he rested on the windowsill began to tighten, his long fingers balling into a fist. His mother would hardly be pleased to know the home she had loved as a girl had fallen into the hands of his recalcitrant wife, a woman who had abandoned him, denying him even his right to an heir. A woman who now stood between him and the chance to make a life with Elizabeth Woolcot.

The coach rolled to a stop in front of the massive wooden doors to what was once the great hall. Nick took a steadying breath, knowing how important this was, knowing how carefully he must tread if he were to succeed.

"The kitchen is round back," he called up to Jackson Fremantle, the driver, a friend of Theo Swann's, a convict who had come to him a little over a year ago searching for work. "Have one of the stable lads water the horses and find yourself something to eat. I don't know how long this will take."

However long it was, he wouldn't be staying the night. Spending a moment longer than necessary under Rachael's roof was a notion he couldn't conceive.

The butler ushered him into the drawing room, which, he noticed, had been redecorated in the years that he had been gone. Minutes ticked past, but instead of taking a seat on the brocade sofa, he found himself pacing in front of the empty hearth.

The drawing room doors slid soundlessly open. "Nicholas, my love, it's good to see you." Rachael floated into the room looking like a black-haired goddess, her hands extended, a warm smile of welcome on her lips.

Nick accepted her greeting, bent and kissed her cheek. "Rachael. You're looking as lovely as ever." Better even than he remembered, her thick black hair clustered in glossy curls at the side of her neck, her skin perfect shades of rose petals and cream.

Her heart as cold as the high stone towers she lived in.

"And you, my love, are looking extremely handsome." Her eyes ran over his face, taking in the tight lines of worry, the signs of frustration and fatigue he tried to disguise. "Though I must say you seem a bit tense. I hope whatever has brought you here is not the cause."

Nick sighed. "Actually, it is." He pointed toward the sofa. "Why don't we have a seat?"

Rachael complied, her composure perfectly in place. A servant arrived with tea and cakes, then the doors were closed and he was left to explain his mission. He did so briefly and to the point, telling her he had met someone, though he didn't say who it was. He told her he wished to remarry, carefully laid out all of the advantages of giving him his freedom—being rid of his scandal-laden name, the thousands of pounds he offered, the properties he would concede, the pension he would bestow on her for the balance of her life.

"I would be more than fair, Rachael. You could have everything you've ever wanted. And of course, you would be free to marry again."

Through it all, Rachael had been strangely silent. Now she leaned forward and a slow smile lifted her ruby lips. "And for all of this bounty I would simply have to grant you a divorce—is that right, Nicholas?"

"Yes. Sydney could arrange it. With your acquiescence, it would not be difficult to achieve."

An unexpected peal of laughter erupted. She shook her head as if he had said something outrageously funny. "My dear Nicholas, for a man as worldly as you undoubtedly are, sometimes I am amazed at your naïveté."

He stiffened. "Meaning?"

"A divorce—good God, how rich." She laughed again. "I think this girl—your latest mistress, I presume—must have somehow addled your brain."

Anger slipped through him. He fought to control it. "There is nothing wrong with my brain. I am tired of living alone and I want an heir. You know how much having a son would mean to me. Until now, it never occurred to me that there might yet be a way to accomplish it. I need a divorce, Rachael. I have offered you a veritable fortune to grant me one."

She pondered that, looked up at him from beneath a black sweep of lashes. "An heir, is it? Well, in that regard I suppose you do have a point." She moved from her end of the sofa, sliding closer, until their feet touched and her hand reached out to caress his thigh.

"Perhaps . . . for some of the concessions you have mentioned, I might be persuaded to return to Ravenworth for a while . . . long enough to bear you a son. After that, of course, I would expect a return of my freedom. I would want to move back in here."

Nick bit down hard on his temper, trying to control the rage that bubbled inside him. His mouth thinned harshly. "And of course you would be willing to leave the child in my care."

"Of course."

He wanted to strangle her. He wanted to wrap his hands around her pretty neck and squeeze some of the selfishness out of her. "There was a time, Rachael, when I might actually have agreed to such a proposal. Now I can think of nothing worse than siring a child with a woman like you for its mother, a woman who could walk away from her own flesh and blood with the same amount of effort it takes to leave the table after a particularly filling meal."

Her hand snaked out, slapped him hard across the cheek. The sharp sting only helped to focus his attention and calm his raging nerves.

Rachael sprang off the sofa to her feet. "Whatever your reasons, I haven't the least intention of granting you a divorce. I happen to like the life I lead. I enjoy being the Countess of Ravenworth. I like living at Castle Colomb. I like the money and the freedom. I am not about to endure the censure of divorce, nor the stigma that accompanies it—not for you or anyone else." Her smile looked tight and thin. "You may have your little whore, Nicky dear. You may get her with a dozen bastard children. But you will never marry her—I will personally see to that."

His control went right out the window. Rage made it hard to think. A fog of anger seemed to envelop him. "You'll pay for this, Rachael. I swear by all that is holy, someday—God help you—you will pay!"

Turning, he strode from the room, his body shaking with barely suppressed fury, his hands balled tightly into fists. He should have known better than to come here. He should have known she would never agree.

Thoughts of Elizabeth had driven him to it. He wanted her. He had ruthlessly stolen her innocence and marriage was the proper course. Divorce would have solved the problem. It would have made him an outcast again, but he thought that perhaps it would not matter. Not if he could have Elizabeth and the son he had always wanted.

He'd been a fool, and because he had started to believe he might actually have some sort of future, he had hurt Elizabeth again. Sweet God, what could he say to her?

Worse than that, what could he do?

There was only one solution. The answer he had fought since the moment he had met her. Marry her to somebody else.

The thought made him sick to his stomach.

A tall grandfather clock chimed the hour. Greville Townsend shoved open the doors between the grand salon and the petit salon that adjoined it at the rear of the room. Rachael rose in surprise as he strode in, her hand unconsciously rising to the slim white column of her throat.

Good, he thought. She deserved to be afraid. After the way she had behaved, she deserved far more than that.

He didn't stop until he reached her. When he did, he gripped her shoulders, dragged her up on her toes, and shook her—hard.

"I can't believe what I just heard. What did you think you were doing? Were you actually contemplating a return to that bastard's bed?"

She broke away from him, cast him a slightly disapproving smile. Already she had regained her composure. It was difficult if not impossible to unnerve Rachael Warring.

"You were eavesdropping, you naughty boy. That is a very bad thing to do. I shall have to punish you. Yes, I believe I will do so tonight."

His loins tightened; the coppery taste of desire washed over his tongue, but his anger did not fade. "We are talking about your husband, Rachael. He came here asking you for a divorce. It was perfect—the solution to all of our problems—and you turned him down."

Rachael shook her head. In the light streaming in through the mullioned windows, her hair was as shiny as onyx. He knew what it felt like skimming over his flesh, knew the seductive way she used it when they made love, and lust made his shaft grow hard.

"Poor Grey," she said, walking over to the sideboard, pouring herself a glass of sherry. "Haven't you realized yet, I don't want a divorce? You heard what I told my husband. I like being the Countess of Ravenworth. I like the freedom I have."

His chest tightened. He was in love with Rachael Warring. He thought that she loved him. "And returning to his bed? Were you willing to do that in order to keep your freedom—or was it simply a matter of money?" He took a step toward her, fighting the jealousy that curled into his bones. "Or was it because part of you still lusts for Nicholas Warring?"

Her ripe red lips went thin, then curved unpleasantly. "I was baiting him, that is all. I simply wished to understand his intentions."

"You wanted him. I could see it in your eyes."

She shrugged indifferently. "Nicholas was always a skillful lover. A little variety—"

In two long strides he reached her, his hands snaking out to wrap around her throat. "You don't need variety—not any longer. You belong to me now, Countess, and I do not share."

She pried his fingers loose from her throat, gasping for air and massaging the bruises. "Have you gone mad?"

"I don't think so. I think, where you are concerned, my senses are finally returning. You and I, Rachael, we are a pair. I understand you, perhaps as no other man ever has. I love you, Rachael. I want you for my wife. If you refuse to divorce your husband, I will have to live with that, but if I can't have you, neither will he—and neither will anyone else."

He smiled bitterly and with warning. "There'll be no other men, Rachael. Not now, not ever again."

Rachael said nothing. Still rubbing the bruises on her throat, she turned and left the room.

He wished he knew what she was thinking.

* * *

For three of the longest days of her life, Elizabeth thought of Nicholas, worried where he could have gone, and tried to act normal.

She had entertained Sir Robert Tinsley, though their ride in the park had been quelled by Elias Moody, who, along with Theophilus Swann, had been set to the task of protecting her while Nicholas was away. David Endicott had practically taken up residence in the departed earl's absence. As much as Elizabeth liked him, she wished he would simply go home.

Now, as she sat in the drawing room, she pondered Nicholas's return. He had arrived at the town house late last night, his clothes wrinkled and smelling of liquor, his face unshaven, his features haggard and drawn. He had said not a word, had gone upstairs and locked himself in his bedchamber. She hadn't seen him since.

"You look tired, my dear." Aunt Sophie twined another piece of string around the dirty ball of odds and ends she held in her lap. They were seated in front of the fire, Elizabeth fidgeting, gazing toward the stairs, wishing she could somehow make Nicholas appear. "Worrying about his lordship will not do a single ounce of good."

Elizabeth flushed. Was she really so easy to read? "I was just . . . perhaps I am a bit tired." That was a lie. She wasn't the least bit weary, but certainly tired of whatever cat and mouse game the Earl of Ravenworth continued to play.

"Why don't you go on upstairs and get some sleep? Lord Tricklewood will be here again on the morrow. You did say that he would be taking us to do a bit of shopping?"

"Yes . . . yes, I did." David was the only one she had told about Bascomb. He had been outraged, of course, and agreed to whatever precautions Elias and Theo might make in order to keep her safe. Seeing himself as her protector had increased his ardor, as well as his determination to win her hand, but Elizabeth wasn't ready to make so grave a decision. Not yet. Not until she had spoken to Nicholas.

Not until he told her the truth about the way he felt.

He made an appearance the following afternoon. With a polite but brusque greeting, he ordered a light lunch served to him in his study and closed himself in.

At least he had shaved, she thought with a bitter pang, and the clothes he wore were presentable, but deep lines gouged his forehead and fatigue marred his harshly elegant face.

She stared at the door closed against her and an ache rose deep in her chest. Tears burned the backs of her eyes and she blinked to push them away. She refused to cry for Nicholas. She had suffered for him long enough.

For an hour, Elizabeth nervously paced the floor of the drawing room, waiting for him to appear, trying to work up the courage to confront him. By the time the clock struck four, her nerves were strung taut and anger formed twin spots of color in her cheeks.

Sweet God, he was as much to blame as she for what had happened. Whatever he was thinking, she deserved better treatment than this! Her hand slammed hard against the wall. Right or wrong, nervous or not, she had waited long enough!

Lifting the narrow skirt of her mint-green muslin day dress, Elizabeth stormed toward the drawing room door and out into the hallway. Her footsteps echoed along the marble passage, announcing her arrival long before she knocked on the study door.

"What is it?" The familiar cadence of his voice evoked a sharp sting of longing. Elizabeth didn't answer, just opened the door and walked in.

Nicholas's head snapped up. "Elizabeth . . ."

"That is correct, my lord. I am surprised you remember my name, since my presence here seems to have slipped your mind these past few days."

He came to his feet behind the desk, but made no other move in her direction. "I've been meaning to talk to you. I thought perhaps later in the day—"

"Not later, Nicholas. Now. This very minute."

Ravenworth said nothing, but a muscle jumped in his

cheek. There was something in his eyes, something dark and forbidding, something of regret or defeat. The sight somehow moved her, made the ache rise again in her chest, yet it did not weaken her resolve. She could not let it. The pain of not knowing was simply too great.

She forced up her chin. "You've been gone for three days. You left without a word. After . . . what happened . . . how do you think that makes me feel? You can't just simply ignore me. You cannot pretend that I am not here."

"I didn't mean to. It's just that . . ." He broke off, glanced away.

"It's just what, Nicholas? I have to know. I have to understand what is going on in your head." A thick lump formed in her throat. She swallowed hard to get past it. "Whatever you are thinking, I can handle it. I'm a strong woman, Nicholas. Since my mother and father died, I have had to be." Unwelcome tears burned her eyes. She tried to blink them away, but they welled and began to slide down her cheeks. "I can deal with whatever it is you have to say." Her voice cracked. "All I ask is that you tell me the truth."

"Elizabeth . . . ah, God, love." He rounded the desk and walked toward her, and a painful ache throbbed in her chest. His hands came to rest on her shoulders, elegant hands, strong yet gentle. "I'm sorry," he whispered, trying to draw her close, but Elizabeth would not let him.

"Don't you dare say you are sorry. Don't you ever say that to me again."

Nicholas shook his head, his eyes dark with frustration. He raked a hand through his hair. "You don't understand. I'm not sorry that we made love, only that I've hurt you again. I'm sorry I didn't speak to you sooner, tell you the truth."

She brushed at the tears on her cheeks, feeling pitiful and lost and hating herself for it. "What truth?"

Tension crept into his shoulders, and Elizabeth felt a dull pang of dread. "I went to see Rachael. I asked her to give me a divorce."

"What?" Surely she hadn't heard him correctly. "You asked for a divorce? But why would you—"

"You know why, Bess. So that I could marry you."

Elizabeth said nothing, just let the incredible words sink in. *You know why, Bess. So that I could marry you.* Her heart began pounding, battering frantically against her ribs.

"Rachael said no," he went on. "She said she liked being the Countess of Ravenworth. She said she would make certain we were never able to marry."

"Oh, Nicholas." She went into his arms and he drew her close, cradling her head against his shoulder. "I never expected you to do something so wonderful, so terribly courageous." *I only wanted you to love me.*

His muscles went rigid again. Nicholas stepped away. "Didn't you hear me? She said no, Bess. There is nothing more we can do."

"I don't care what she said. It doesn't matter. All that matters is that you wanted to marry me, that you cared enough to risk yourself that way." She cupped his face between her hands. "I know the sort of scandal a divorce would cause. I know the kind of courage it took for you to go there. Can't you see? I don't care that you are married. I only want to be with you—any way that I can."

Nicholas shook his head, a thick black curl falling over his forehead. "You don't know what you're saying, what it would mean."

"I do know. Other men have mistresses. You have had any number of them. That I become one of them doesn't matter in the least."

"It does matter. I'm your guardian. You're an innocent young woman in my care. Once the ton discovers what we are about—and sooner or later they will—we'll be ostracized forever. This time there will be no return."

"I don't care. I don't care about anything but you."

"What about Bascomb? You need a husband to keep you safe."

Elizabeth shook her head. "I don't need a husband. At least I won't after Bascomb finds out you are sleeping in my bed. He wanted to marry me. I doubt he will want me after he discovers that I am a fallen woman."

Nicholas said nothing for the longest time. "That may be true, but there are other things to consider . . . more important things even than Bascomb." His troubled gaze searched her face. "What if there are children, Elizabeth? You realize they will be bastards? Can you tell me in good conscience you would wish that on a child?"

Pain settled into her chest and she turned away. Having a child out of wedlock. She could barely imagine such a thing. "There are ways to avoid conception, if that is what you want."

He gripped her shoulders, turning her to face him. "That is not what I want! I want sons. I want a family of my own. I have wanted it every day of my life for the past nine years. But the children we would have would be shunned by Society. They would suffer for our indiscretions and an illegitimate birth that is not of their choosing. I would not want that for my sons."

Fresh tears burned, formed a hot path down her cheeks. "If we had children, we would love them, Nicholas. We would love them and somehow we would protect them."

Nicholas reached for her, gathered her into his arms and buried his face in her hair. "Are you sure, Elizabeth? Are you sure that is what you want?"

She nodded against his chest, her hands clutching his shoulders. "I'm sure." She turned her face up to his and saw him through a film of tears. "I love you, Nicholas Warring. I didn't want to. God knows I tried not to—but the fact is I do. I don't want to marry Robert Tinsley or David Endicott. There is no one else I want but you."

He crushed her against him, held her for long, achingly tender moments. When he stepped away, the haunted look had faded from his face, the hollow, bone-weary expression was gone. "It won't be easy," he said. "We'll have to plan very carefully."

"Perhaps it would be best to return to Ravenworth Hall. My aunt and I could find a cottage nearby—"

Nicholas shook his head. "We can't leave London, not yet. We still have Maggie to consider. She has only just begun to make a new life. We cannot destroy what she has only just started to build."

Lady Margaret. How could she have forgotten? "No, of course not. I was being selfish. I hadn't thought of Maggie."

His hand gently brushed her cheek. "Already she is beleaguered with suitors. If we are careful, perhaps for a time— long enough to see my sister settled—we can manage to avoid being caught. The first thing we must do is get you out of here. I'll arrange to let a town house for you and your aunt somewhere near." He frowned. "It may be difficult to keep your aunt from finding out."

Elizabeth flicked a glance at the door, thinking of the woman who had come to mean so much to her in the years since her mother had died. "I'll speak to Aunt Sophie. I know my aunt may be odd, but she is the most giving, warmhearted woman I have ever known. Aunt Sophie might have wished for a different sort of life for me, but I know she will understand. I believe she knew even before I did, the way I felt about you. She has always just wanted me to be happy."

The tension eased from Nicholas's broad shoulders. "There is still the problem of Bascomb, but whether you are here or somewhere else will not change the threat he poses. The servants in my town house are all handpicked. They have long ago learned the value of discretion. The ones I brought from Ravenworth Hall would never do anything to betray me. You'll have Theo and Elias, Mercy, of course, and I'll be there as much as I can. Once Maggie's future is settled, we can return to the country. As soon as we do, we'll allow Bascomb's spies to discover the truth about us, and you will finally be safe. We will both be ruined, but perhaps that is not such a high price to pay."

Something tightened in her chest. She would be his mistress, another of Nick Warring's women. It was a frightening step and yet she felt she had no other choice.

Reaching up, she cupped his cheek. "No . . ." she agreed. "If we can be together, no price is too high to pay." The silver of his eyes turned a hot, sultry blue. He lowered his head and kissed her, a long, hard, deeply erotic kiss that left both of them groaning, wishing they were somewhere—anywhere—besides his study.

"We'll work things out," he whispered. "You won't be sorry, Elizabeth. I'll take care of you. You'll have everything you ever wanted."

A chill slid through her. Elizabeth pressed her face into his shoulder to hide a sudden feeling of doubt. She would be with him and he would take care of her, but Nicholas would never really be hers. He belonged to another woman. She told herself it didn't matter. All that mattered was Nicholas and that they would finally be together. But the niggling doubt remained.

If only he had told me he loved me. Surely he did, she thought. He had wanted her enough to marry her.

Still, the tiny flicker of doubt refused to go away.

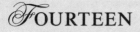OURTEEN

$\mathcal{O}$liver Hampton sat at the desk in the study of his Mayfair town house across from a scrawny little man with greasy brown hair named Wendel Cheek, a former Bow Street runner, a man with an unscrupulous past he had hired to keep track of Elizabeth Woolcot.

"Go on," Oliver prompted, leaning back in his deep red leather chair.

The little man scratched his balding head then looked up. "Like I was sayin', gov'nor. Until last week, she was making the social rounds, just like you said. Had at least half a dozen suitors—though me money was on Tricklewood or Sir Robert Tinsley. Then three days ago, the gel and her aunt moved out of his lordship's town house. Rumor was, it was better for the lady's reputation, him bein' the Wicked Earl and all."

Oliver suppressed a smile of satisfaction. So Ravenworth thought it was safe for her to leave, that Oliver had finally given up his pursuit. If the earl thought Elizabeth's suitors and the prospect of her marriage posed an obstacle he couldn't overcome, the man was a bigger fool than he had believed.

"How many men does Ravenworth have guarding her?"

The little man pursed his lips. "Near as I can tell, he's got men posted outside round the clock—the same who was guarding his town house. Inside there's his valet, Elias Moody, and a footman name of Swann."

"Yes . . . Ravenworth's convicts. He values their services highly."

"And rightfully so, the way I hear. Word round abouts is that Moody is as tough as boot leather, and one of the best men with his fists ever to come down the pike."

Oliver pondered that. He had known getting to the girl, especially here in London, wouldn't be all that easy. "I gave you the name of my man on the inside, the one who sold us information before. For enough money, I think he would sell his own mother. Did you have a chance to speak to him?"

Wendel nodded. "Talked to him first thing this mornin'. Didn't seem all that eager to help, but as you said, a bit of coin seemed to loosen his tongue."

"What did he say?"

"Not much. Said I'd heard right about Moody, and that Swann was a whole lot tougher than he looked. Said he'd keep his eyes open, let us know if there was anything he thought we oughtta know."

Oliver shoved a small leather pouch across his desk. It clinked pleasantly as the little man picked it up, hefting the weight of the coins in his hand.

"Keep up the good work," Oliver told him. "There'll be more where that came from as long as you keep me informed."

Wendel Cheek rose from his chair and slipped from the room as slickly as he did everything else. Oliver pondered this latest information. As soon as things settled down, he would send for the rest of his men. Charlie Barker and Nathan Peel had failed him before, but after he had saved them from a stint in prison—perhaps even a trip to the gallows—they were eager to make amends.

Oliver glanced down at the calendar that sat open on his desk. An invitation had been received for a costume ball tonight at the Duke of Chester's mansion, one of *the* social events of the season. Husband-hunting as she was, Elizabeth was bound to attend.

Oliver smiled thinly. He had stayed in the background long enough. He had missed seeing Elizabeth's lovely face, missed touching that silky auburn hair. In public, there was little he could do in the way of seduction, yet there was always the chance he might get her alone long enough to blacken her name and force her into marriage. In lieu of that, a bit of dancing, perhaps a little conversation, would have to do.

As wealthy and powerful as he was, if she wished to remain the darling of the ton, he knew she couldn't refuse.

The Duke of Chester's mansion on the outskirts of the city was nearly as impressive as Beldon's. He had spared no expense on the lavish costume ball that was his favorite event of the year and had become a sort of tradition. His third-floor ballroom glittered with thousands of candles, so many there were footmen with water cans at the doors in case of an accidental fire.

So far there had been no such mishaps. The mirrored walls shimmered with light and glinted off the gold and silver sequins, pearls, and brilliants that studded the lavish costumes each guest wore. Women gowned as Cleopatra, Joan of Arc, and Aphrodite; milkmaids, mermaids, butterflies, and angels. Men dressed as sixteenth-century courtiers, knights in armor, sailors, soldiers—any and every sort of costume one could imagine.

With her future still so nebulous, Elizabeth hadn't really wanted to attend, but Nicholas had insisted.

"We have to go on with our lives as if nothing has changed. We have to think of Maggie."

In a way nothing really had changed. Though she and Aunt Sophie now had a town house in Maddox Street just a few blocks north of Berkeley Square, Nicholas had yet to make an appearance. She wasn't quite sure why. She knew he was concerned for his sister, hoping one of the men paying court to her would make an offer for her hand.

Not that he felt any of them were good enough. Not for his Maggie. Still, in the past his sister had wanted a husband and family. Now that she had left the convent, he wanted her to have the chance. Time was what she needed. Nicholas intended to see that she got it.

Elizabeth glanced around the lavish ballroom, wondering where he was. She had arrived with Aunt Sophie, Maggie, the Duke of Beldon, and the dowager duchess, an odd little assembly with Aunt Sophie dressed as a medieval matron in tunic and tall, cone-shaped hennin; the duke in a Roman toga that bared one powerfully muscled shoulder; Maggie as the lady Rapunzel; and the dowager as Madame du Barry.

"I loathe costume balls," the older woman grumbled. "I shall hold you in my debt for this, Elizabeth." But she winked as she said it, smiled, and held out a hand to her handsome son, who bowed extravagantly and guided her onto the inlaid parquet dance floor.

Alone for a moment, Elizabeth searched the crowded room for Nicholas, hoping to spot his tall, dark figure somewhere in the milling throng. *Nicholas.* At times, she couldn't believe she had agreed to become his mistress, a life so different from the one she had planned, a future that would have included a husband and family. But the die had been cast and she would not change things.

She had cooled the ardor of her four potential suitors by hinting to each of them her favor lay with one of the other three.

"I'm sorry, my lord," she had said to David Endicott, "but the heart is incredibly fickle. One never seems to know which way it will turn." The implication was that her favor would be cast to Sir Robert Tinsley, but of course to Tinsley she hinted of Tricklewood. All four had received the same subtle news, and though each continued his pursuit to a certain degree, only Tricklewood remained dogged in his efforts.

"I shall win you," David vowed. "In time you will see how perfectly suited we are."

Elizabeth had merely smiled, wishing she could tell him the truth. She liked David Endicott, and she was worried about him. She was afraid he was falling in love with her and she knew only too well the heartache that could bring. She was glad that tonight Lord Tricklewood was not there.

Elizabeth studied her reflection on the mirrored ballroom walls. Aunt Sophie had helped with her costume, donating feathers from her bizarre, somewhat bedraggled collection, helping her dye them a lovely dark green then sewing them onto a clingy white lawn gown. Tonight she was a female Icarus, determined to fly to the heavens, but in the end soaring too close to the sun.

Behind a forest-green feathered and sequined mask, she waited nervously for Nicholas to appear, trying in vain as she spoke to Maggie to keep her mind from wandering. She wondered what costume he would wear and hoped that tonight, disguised as they were, they might dance, as they had never dared.

He appeared an hour before midnight, and even with the red and black satin loo mask he wore, she knew in an instant who it was. He was dressed—appropriately, she thought—as the Knave of Hearts, his long, sleekly muscled legs encased in tight red and black satin breeches. She watched him cross the floor, admiring his broad-shouldered build and narrow waist, noticing the way the costume gloved the considerable bulge of his sex. Behind her feathered mask, her cheeks began to burn.

He paused directly in front of her, his eyes taking a long, appreciative sweep of her body, returning to where the bodice of her gown dipped low and dark green feathers teased the upthrusting swell of her breasts.

A corner of his mouth curved up. "Perhaps my memory deceives me, but I thought Icarus was a man."

Pleasure poured through her that he had guessed whom

she portrayed. "Perhaps he was, perhaps not. It is a legend, after all, and as such there is the chance that the story is wrong."

His smile went broader. "That there is. At any rate, you make a beautiful Icarus"—he bent close to her ear—"and I should like nothing better than to strip away those feathers one by one." The heat in her cheeks burned hotter. Nicholas bowed elaborately over her hand. "Would you care to dance, my lady Icarus?"

"I should like that above all things, my lord."

A silvery glint came into his eyes. "All things, my lady? I should think perhaps there is something else, something more . . . intimate . . . that might please you even better."

Desire rolled through her. *Dear sweet God.* She could feel that hot silver-blue gaze burning as if he touched her. He was flirting with her, playing games of seduction he had never allowed himself to play in his role as her guardian. He felt safe behind the mask, permitting her to see a side of him she had never seen before. Seduction was a game the Earl of Ravenworth played without equal. It made her feel womanly and warm.

She lowered her lashes. Perhaps two could play the game. "You are far too bold, Knave of Hearts. But in truth, there is something about you I find pleasing. Perhaps a kiss would help me discover what it is. A long, very deep, very hot kiss with your body pressed to mine. Perhaps that would—"

Nicholas's groan cut her off. "Vixen. I thought you were new at this game."

"I am a very quick study, my lord. And you are a very good teacher."

"There is much I wish to teach you, my lovely Bess. We've had so little time together. A night of guilty pleasures, a hasty coupling in the garden. Tonight, I will come to the town house. We'll take our time, begin your lessons in earnest. 'Twill be my privilege to teach you the art of making love."

Elizabeth's mouth went dry. Heat swirled in her stomach

and moisture collected lower down. *Tonight.* Nicholas would come to her tonight.

"In the meantime, I would still like that dance."

He danced as he moved, with elegance and grace, his steps flawless and completely instinctive, yet there was purpose in his eyes, and whenever he touched her hand or his arm went around her waist, heat shimmered over her skin. Dressed as he was in black and scarlet, he looked dangerous and seductive. An air of sensuality seeped from his very pores.

For the first time it occurred to her the will it had taken to hide this side of himself for so long. He had done it for her, done it because she was his ward and he had given his word. She admired him for it—and she was glad that the tight control he had bound himself with was finally gone—or at least it was gone for tonight.

Tomorrow they would resume their respective roles, but now Elizabeth had glimpsed the dangerously attractive, wicked side of his nature, and in the long hours of the night he would show her more. The promise in his eyes said tonight he would take her as he never had before.

Her hands trembled and she pressed them into the folds of her skirt. Her heart hammered and her breasts felt deliciously swollen. She would enjoy the ball with Nicholas for as long as she dared, then make her excuses and leave. Elias Moody and Theo Swann had accompanied the duke and his party. She would be safe with them on the journey home.

Nicholas had chosen the town house with care; it had windows that could be shuttered and locked—and a separate outside entrance that led directly upstairs. She glanced in his direction, felt the heat of his gaze, caught the faint curve of his lips. There was promise there, too, sweet and erotic.

He left her with her aunt while he danced with his sister, who, costumed in a gown of blue silk and a long blond wig that nearly touched the floor, had been dancing all evening with one man after another. The ballroom was crowded.

Someone jostled her from behind. She turned and gripped a pair of wide shoulders to keep herself from falling.

"I beg your pardon. I—I didn't see you—"

"My, my, St. George, look at the lovely little bird who has flown into our midst."

She knew that voice. The sandy-brown hair above the gray silk mask belonged to the Viscount Harding, and beside him, Nigel Wicker, Baron St. George. Even his disguise as an overweight sultan couldn't hide his familiar girth.

"I'm afraid you will have to excuse me, my lords. I was just on my way to the ladies' retiring room."

"Were you now?" Harding moved closer. "I shall be happy to walk you, my dear Miss Woolcot. We wouldn't want you getting lost before you get there."

She glanced up. "How . . . how did you know it was I?"

Harding smiled. "The feathers, I suspect. Or perhaps it was all that glorious auburn hair."

"Gel's a beauty, all right." St. George eyed her lewdly from head to foot. "Had to be to snag Ravenworth in her claws. Must be a veritable tigress in bed."

Elizabeth's face turned a bright shade of pink. She was glad for the dimly lit room and the cover of her mask. "His lordship would not appreciate your crude insinuations and neither do I. If you will excuse me—"

Harding didn't try to stop her, just laughed as she walked on by, and St. George's booming laughter chimed in. For the first time she realized just what being Nicholas's mistress would truly entail. She shuddered to think of it and continued out of the ballroom and down the stairs to the room set aside for the ladies' use on the second floor.

She had just rounded a corner of the long carpeted hall, when she heard the echo of heavy footsteps behind her. Certain that Nicholas had followed, she turned with a smile and stopped dead still at the sight of Oliver Hampton bearing down on her.

Bascomb! With a plumed hat perched on his head and a musketeer's cape billowing out behind him, he was only a few steps away. He caught her wrist before she could escape, pulled her into an alcove, and pressed her up against the wall.

"Let me go or I promise you I shall scream."

His full lips curved. "I wish you would, my dear, I truly do. I'm sure the ladies down the hall would be quite aghast at my boldness." He was as tall as Nicholas, two years older and more thickly built, with dark brown hair and deep blue eyes, a handsome man, most would say. Elizabeth did not think so. "Of course, I would merely explain that my heart has completely addled my brain where you are concerned, that I have asked you to marry and was doing my best to convince you to say yes."

Her mouth thinned. "Whereupon I would simply tell them I am not interested in marriage to you—not now, nor at any time in the future."

"You could do that—but screaming would certainly make them believe there was a great deal more going on than a man merely trying to woo you into marriage. You would be ruined. You would no longer be welcomed in the ton, and neither would Ravenworth nor his sister."

Elizabeth tensed. Nicholas wouldn't care what the ton thought about him, but Maggie—Maggie was a far different story.

"What is it you want?"

He made no response, just hauled her close and dragged her mouth up to his for a wet, sticky kiss, his fleshy lips almost swallowing her whole before she could jerk free and slap him.

The sharp sting brought a moment of stunned disbelief. She pulled free of his hold and darted away, gone before he could stop her, almost running down the hall toward the stairs. She was shaking all over, her pulse so fast she felt a little dizzy. If ever she had doubted how much she despised Oliver Hampton, one of his rancid, sloppy kisses, one touch of his damp, clammy hands was enough to remind her.

She returned to the ballroom, still a little shaken, pondering her unfortunate encounter with Bascomb. She shoved the memory away, her mind turning instead to thoughts of Nicholas and the night ahead.

A tremor of anticipation ran through her. It was tempered with a hint of uncertainty. Tonight she would become his mistress in truth. She wondered what particular lesson he might have in mind for the hours ahead.

Gowned in blue silk, a shade lighter than her eyes, Maggie Warring stood next to Rand Clayton, who stood beside the Marquess of Trent. Even though he wore a fifteenth-century doublet, she remembered Andrew Sutton, a good-looking, brown-haired man of medium height and build, a friend of Nick's from Oxford. He and Andrew had been close before her brother went to prison, but as Nicholas had done with the rest of his former acquaintances, he had reasoned, as a convicted criminal and outcast of Society, that his friendship with the marquess was at an end.

Maggie hadn't seen him since the scandal and didn't think her brother had. She remembered his teasing, lighthearted banter when she was a girl. She hadn't paid attention to him then, her head full of foolish fantasies about Stephen Hampton.

As a woman, she felt the marquess's presence as she hadn't before, felt those assessing brown eyes and the power of his smile, and an odd little shiver raced over her skin.

"That was your brother, was it not—dressed as the Knave of Hearts?"

Maggie smiled. "I'm surprised you recognized him. I helped him with the costume. I thought it a good disguise."

"For most perhaps, but I have known him far too long." His mouth curved faintly. "The costume was appropriate, I think. Nick has always had a way with the ladies and tonight is no exception. The way he was looking at that lovely creature in the feathered gown, there was little doubt what he was thinking—nor that the lady returned his interest."

Surprise was followed by a trickle of unease. In the beginning, she had been worried about Elizabeth and Nick, but she had convinced herself she was wrong. Tonight she had been having such fun, been so engrossed in the evening, she had paid little attention to Elizabeth or her brother. They had danced together, was all. Nick was fond of her, might even be attracted to her, but he would never actually pursue her. And she didn't believe Elizabeth would encourage him even if he did. The marquess must be wrong.

"At any rate," he continued, "I'm glad to see he's decided to make his return. I know his past has made things difficult, but whatever happened with Hampton that night—and there are those of us who have our doubts—he has paid for his sins, and I for one am happy to see him here."

Maggie smiled, relieved the subject had taken a different turn. "That is kind of you, my lord. Perhaps Nick has more friends than he believes. It would please him to know the way you feel."

He gave her a long assessing glance and the odd little shiver returned. "Then I hope that you will tell him." He smiled. "Or perhaps, with your permission, I shall call upon you both and tell him myself."

Her stomach fluttered strangely. Surely he wasn't implying he would be making a call on her? No matter what her brother might want for her, she wasn't ready to entertain suitors—she had been locked away far too long. And yet this particular man intrigued her.

"That would be very thoughtful, my lord. I'm sure it would mean a lot to Nick." His gaze lingered, a warm velvet brown, and finally she glanced away.

"Perhaps, Lady Margaret, you would care to dance?"

Maggie smiled with a bit of uncertainty. It was one thing to dance with men she thought of as friends and another thing altogether to dance with a man who made her insides turn to mush.

"My lady?" he pressed.

She placed her hand in his but made no effort to move forward. That first night at the ball, she had been terrified to step out on the dance floor. She'd been petrified of what people would say, but in the end, with Rand's protection and gentle encouragement, the evening had been a success.

There had been a few lewd remarks, of course, but the dowager had squelched most of the gossip. The story was told that she had entered the convent because of the scandal her brother had caused. The why of Stephen Bascomb's death remained shrouded in mystery, and the blame for Maggie's departure dumped squarely on poor Nick's shoulders, but they were broad, and he didn't seem to mind.

The Duke of Beldon appeared beside her. "Go on, Maggie. You'll be as safe with Andrew as you are with me."

He was right, of course. The marquess was a friend of Nick's and the perfect escort, a man nearly as powerful as the duke. She smiled into Andrew Sutton's handsome face.

"All right, but I warn you, my lord—I am still a little rusty. I pray you will have patience."

He returned the smile and her heart beat faster. "I was born with patience, my lady." He extended his arm and she rested her hand on the heavy velvet sleeve of his doublet.

On the way to the dance floor, a few sly comments were made as they usually were, but the wagging tongues stilled when they realized her escort was the wealthy Marquess of Trent. It was a long dance and she thoroughly enjoyed it.

"Thank you, my lord," she said to him when the music ended.

A thick brown eyebrow went up. "What for?"

"For helping me remember some of the pleasures of life."

The brown of his eyes went indigo dark. He bowed over her hand. "Perhaps there is more I can show you, my lady."

His breath felt warm through her glove and a tingle ran up her arm. "Perhaps there is, my lord."

FIFTEEN

$\mathcal{N}$icholas left the ball first, before the party-goers were unmasked, yet Elizabeth glimpsed his tall frame outside the mansion half an hour later, waiting until she was safely ensconced with her aunt in Beldon's carriage, Elias and Theo, dressed in the duke's gold livery, riding as footmen at the rear.

When she reached the town house, she said good night to her aunt and went straight to her room, growing even more nervous and uncertain. Nicholas would be arriving any minute. He expected her to play the role of mistress as she had agreed. He would kiss her, touch her, make love to her. Her stomach swirled and her mouth felt parchment dry. It was one thing to make love to him in an instant of unbridled passion, another thing entirely to set out on a course of action that would change the balance of her life.

It is already changed, she told herself. *It was altered the instant you fell in love with him.* From that moment on, her happiness was forever entwined with his, her future enmeshed with that of the Earl of Ravenworth.

Mercy was waiting in Elizabeth's bedchamber to help

her undress. She allowed the girl to dispense with the buttons and tabs fastening her costume together and help her out of the green-feathered tunic. Her maid hadn't yet guessed her relationship with the earl. As perceptive as Mercy was, Elizabeth was certain it wouldn't take her long to figure it out.

Mercy would know, and soon the other servants in the house would begin to suspect, yet Elizabeth felt as Nicholas did that their staff was loyal and at least for a time their secret would be safe. Still, it bothered her what each of them might be thinking.

The buxom little maid pulled the last of the pins from her hair and brushed out the tangles.

"Thank you, Mercy. I can do the rest myself. Go ahead and get some sleep."

"Are ye sure?"

"I'll be fine."

"All right, then. Good night, miss."

"Good night, Mercy."

She waited till the girl left the room, then, still wearing her chemise, lit the candle that sat on a table in front of the window. Shadows flickered against the walls and a soft yellow glow seeped into the corners. Elizabeth glanced toward the door, nervous yet strangely excited. She had made her choice. Nicholas would come. The night ahead should be special. What to do?

Then her eyes came to rest on the green-feathered mask she had tossed onto her dresser. Slowly she reached for it, settled the mask over her eyes, and tied the string around her head. In the mirror, dark green sequins glittered. Through the holes in the mask, her eyes seemed to glitter as well. For a moment she hesitated, then daringly, she slipped off the straps of her chemise and let it slide down her body. Naked she crossed the room and climbed up into the big four-poster bed, propping herself up against the pillows.

Minutes ticked past. An ember snapped in the fire, hissed

against the grate. When she glanced back to the door, Nicholas stood framed in the opening. His costume was replaced by snug black breeches tucked into high black boots. A full-sleeved white lawn shirt stretched over his powerful chest. The door closed softly behind him, but he did not move, just stood there, the silvery blue of his eyes running over her naked body.

"I see you have dressed for your lesson," he said in a voice rough with seduction.

"I hoped to please you."

He strode toward the bed with his easy grace, his gaze meeting hers through the mask. "Then you have—and most exquisitely. But tonight, my love, it is I who intend to please you."

Heat rolled from the top of her head to the bottoms of her feet. Her heart thumped madly. Nervously, she moistened her lips. "Is there . . . is there something you wish me to do?"

His hot gaze raked her. "Aye, my love. There is a good deal you will do before this night is done." He crossed to the bed, sat down beside her, and pulled her into his arms. "But first, I would simply like to kiss you."

She closed her eyes, felt the softness of his lips over hers, then the warm, probing pressure of his tongue. He tasted of brandy and his shirt smelled faintly of bay rum cologne. He kissed her deeply, erotically, pressing her down in the mattress, letting her feel the hard length of his arousal, sparing none of her maidenly sensibilities. That time was past. She was his woman now and he meant to show her exactly what that meant.

Tilting his head, he took her mouth again, his tongue sweeping in with expert skill, tasting her thoroughly, firing hot sensations that pulsed through her body. Elizabeth kissed him back with the same fierce passion, returning what he gave, encouraging him to take more.

"Put your arms around my neck," he softly commanded, and she did so, her breasts pressing into his chest. He groaned and deepened the kiss, then trailed his mouth along the side of her neck, kissing his way along her throat and shoulders. When he reached the swell of a breast, he pebbled the end with his tongue then took the roundness into his mouth and began to suckle the end.

Intense heat poured through her, hot and sultry, flaring out to the ends of her limbs, coiling deep in the pit of her stomach.

"Nicholas . . ." Clinging to his shoulders, she arched upward, desperate to absorb the heat of his mouth over her skin. He teased the second breast, taunting the little tip until it ached and distended, then laved and suckled until she writhed beneath him.

He pressed her back down on the bed, his face harsh with need in the light of the candles, a thick curl of jet-black hair tipping over his forehead. His arousal pressed hard against his breeches. She could feel the heavy weight of him against her thigh, feel his rigid length, and the promise it spoke made her tremble. Nicholas kissed her breasts again, slowly and with purpose, then began to move down her body. He paused to ring her navel, feathered soft kisses across the flat plane beneath.

"Nicholas . . ." Her body was on fire, desperate with the need to feel him inside her. "I want to touch you, too. I want to see you naked."

His eyes seemed to smolder. "Soon, my love. For now there are things I wish to show you, lessons I wish you to learn."

The words sent a fresh wave of heat rippling through her. He kissed her again, deeply, fiercely. His hands found her wrists and he lifted them above the headboard. It was ornately carved and fashioned of dark, polished wood. He laced her hands through a bouquet of intricately carved wooden flowers, making certain each finger found purchase.

"Don't let go," he softly commanded. "No matter what happens, don't let go until I tell you."

She was shaking now, the rough-edged cadence of his

voice rolling over her flesh, the touch of his hands, setting a torch to her blood. Reaching behind her, he pulled the string on her mask and drew it away.

"I would see you when you find your pleasure." His eyes fixed on hers with such intensity they seemed to glow. He spread her auburn hair out around her shoulders, then he was kissing her breasts again, her navel, moving lower, his fingers sifting through the soft reddish hair above her womanly core.

"Spread your legs for me, Bess."

A soft cry escaped. She trembled.

"Do it, sweeting. Do as I tell you."

She bit down on her lip to control the fire scorching through her. Tentatively, she opened for him, exposing her most secret place.

"Wider. Give yourself to me, Bess. Trust me with your body as you have trusted me with your heart."

It took a shot of courage, but she did as he asked, allowing him access to that which he sought, ignoring the flash of embarrassment that made her even hotter than before. Her body was trembling, her hands gripping the headboard so hard her nails were white.

Bracing himself on his elbows, Nicholas settled himself between her legs and slid his hands beneath her bottom to lift her against his mouth. She nearly swooned when his tongue found her flesh, then the pulsing, rigid bud at the center. He began to lave it, to stroke it with tender care, and her body arched up off the mattress.

"Nicholas!" She twisted, tried to draw away, but he held her fast. And as he had commanded, she didn't let go of the headboard. Instead, she closed her eyes and absorbed the feel of his soft, erotic kisses, of his tongue tasting and probing until thin ropes of fire began to tighten inside her. "I can't," she whispered. "I can't stand a moment more."

He glanced up, the bands of muscle across his shoulders hard as steel. "You can. You can and you will." He took her again with his mouth, and this time, the taut ropes flared and burst. They snapped like filmy threads, flinging her into space, into the heat of the sun. Fire roared through her, scorching splinters that sucked away her breath and impaled her on sweet shards of pleasure.

Limp and sated, she didn't notice when Nicholas left her, only knew that he had returned, that he was naked, his hard, dark body looming above her. Gently he reached for the fingers still clutching the headboard and carefully unwound each one.

"You can let go now, my love," he said with a tender smile. "I should rather feel your hands on my body."

She only stared, barely able to think. "That was so . . . I never could have imagined—"

"And this?" he asked, surging into her hard and deep. "Surely you imagined that?"

Her body arched upward, taking him fully. Fresh heat boiled through her. Elizabeth moistened her lips. "Yes, my lord. I well imagined that."

Nicholas laughed softly and began to move. Every stroke brought her new heights of pleasure, every deep thrust heightened her desire for him. He took her with skill and exquisite demand, his hardness filling her completely. In minutes, her body was trembling, her response matching his, and she was soaring once more into climax.

Nicholas followed, his muscles rigid above her, every tendon straining, every sinew taut. His tall frame shuddered then went still, finally slumping against her, a sheen of perspiration mingling with the dampness on her own skin.

Eventually, he eased himself away, pulling her into the circle of his arms, holding her spoon fashion against him. He kissed the side of her neck. "There is more to teach you—so much more. And now that you are mine, there will be time enough for you to learn."

Time enough? Unease filtered through her. She wondered how much time she would really have. The future was so nebulous, so fraught with peril. He was married. And he had never said that he loved her. Elizabeth closed her eyes, vowing tonight she would not think of it. Tonight she would love him and let him love her.

Tonight she would pretend that the future did not exist.

Nick made love to Elizabeth two more times that night, then awoke with the first dim rays of sunlight, the grayness creeping over the sill, invading his peaceful slumber. Beside him, Elizabeth curled against his side, her glorious dark auburn hair fanned out across his chest. For a moment, he simply watched her, thinking of the hours they had spent making love.

The game of seduction he had started had turned to something deeper as the hours wore on. Something indefinably tender. It was odd how it happened whenever he was with her. The loneliness he had lived with for so many years seemed to fade and disappear.

Nick ran a hand through his hair, knowing it was time to leave, reluctant to do so, disturbed in some way. It was the guilt, he suspected. The guilt he had hoped he would not feel. It wasn't right, what he was taking from Elizabeth, her warmth, her beauty, her innocence. Those things came with a price and that price was marriage, the protection of his name, the security of a home, the love of a family. He had none of those things to give and yet he took the gifts she offered just the same.

It bothered him, yet the decision had been made, and he was too selfish to alter the course he had taken.

With a sigh of reluctance, he eased himself from the warmth of her body and drew on his clothes. He meant to leave before she awakened, but when he turned, he found her watching, a hint of uncertainty etched into her face. Nicholas reached for her hand and brought it to his lips.

"What is it, sweeting? What's wrong? If you are worried about last night—"

She fiercely shook her head. "Last night was beautiful. Perfect. I'm not worried about what happened between us. It's just that . . . it's about something that happened at the costume ball, something that I didn't tell you."

He stiffened, wariness sifting through him like dirt through a threadbare rug. "You lied to me?"

"No! Of course not. I just . . . I just didn't tell you last night at the ball and I probably should have."

His temper began to rise, warming the back of his neck. "Tell me now."

Elizabeth flushed guiltily. "Last night Bascomb was there. He accosted me outside the ladies' retiring room. I didn't want to cause trouble. I didn't think—"

"You didn't think? No, you didn't. You didn't think at all." He caught her shoulders and dragged her up from the bed. "Dammit, Elizabeth, I am trying to protect you. If Bascomb was there, you should have told me. Something could have happened. *Anything* could have happened. God in heaven— don't ever—ever—do something that foolish again." He saw her wince, realized how tightly he held her, and eased his hold.

He drew in a steadying breath. "I'm sorry, I didn't mean to hurt you. It's just that—" Just that he couldn't stand the thought of Bascomb being anywhere near her. His breath came out on a sigh of frustration. "What exactly did the whoreson do?"

Elizabeth glanced away, her cheeks a soft shade of pink above the sheet she held over her breasts. "He kissed me. The foulest, most repulsive kiss I have ever been forced to endure."

Nick clamped hard on his jaw. "What else?"

"Nothing. I slapped his face and ran away. That was all that happened."

"You slapped him?"

She nodded, then grinned. "As hard as I could. I'm surprised you couldn't hear it all the way into the ballroom."

He found himself returning the grin. "I wish I had." The smile slowly faded. "Listen to me, Elizabeth. Bascomb is a dangerous opponent. We have to be careful. *You* have to be careful. Promise me, if that bastard comes anywhere near you again, you'll tell me."

"I would have. I just didn't want you to get into trouble."

He reached out and caught her chin. "Promise me."

She sighed. "All right, I promise."

Leaning down, he gave her a quick, hard kiss. "Good girl." Nick turned away, his body responding, growing hard inside, his clothes. He wished he could make love to her again but the sun was rapidly rising. "I have to go," he said a bit gruffly. "I'll see you tonight."

"Tonight? You're coming back tonight?"

His body tightened just to think of it. "Yes, love. I hardly think your study is complete after only a single lesson."

"No . . . no, indeed it isn't." Elizabeth smiled sweetly, and lust pulled low in his groin. She leaned back against the pillow with a dreamy smile. "Until tonight then, my lord."

Nick felt a tug of amusement. "Until tonight," he agreed, wondering why it was she had such a powerful effect on him—and how the hell he could possibly wait that long.

Oliver Hampton pulled open the door and motioned for Nathan Peel and Charlie Barker to step inside his wood-paneled study.

"We come as soon as we got your message," Nathan said, a battered felt hat gripped between his long, bony fingers. Charlie walked beside him, scratching his burly red beard.

"Yes, and it's a damned good thing you did." Oliver moved behind his heavy walnut desk and sat down in a black leather chair. "Some . . . complications have arisen. I should like the two of you to take care of them for me."

"Complications?" Barker repeated warily. "What complications? More trouble with that black-haired devil, Ravenworth?"

"Undoubtedly there is that. The man is my nemesis, appearing like a cloud of doom in the middle of all I do. In this case, however, it is merely Miss Woolcot's suitors I wish you to dispense with."

"You want we should kill 'em?" Nathan asked, the peak of his brow arching upward.

Oliver shook his head. "Nothing quite so permanent—at least not yet. I simply want you to discourage them from their courtship." He lifted the lid off the humidor on the top of his desk and pulled out a fat cigar. Running it slowly beneath his nose, he savored the rich tobacco scent.

"Let us say, for example, that footpads were to set upon the men. Their purses would, of course, be stolen, perhaps a blow or two delivered in the scuffle—along with a warning to stay away from Elizabeth Woolcot—if they wish to insure the incident doesn't occur again."

"What are the names of these men?" Charlie asked.

"From what Mr. Cheek has been able to discover, there were four men that Sydney Birdsall originally interviewed in regard to a match. Only two appear to remain in the running, David Endicott, Viscount Tricklewood, and Sir Robert Tinsley. While you have your little chat with them, I shall subtly pass the word that Miss Woolcot is spoken for. A gentle hint here, a little pressure there, and Miss Woolcot's suitors will disappear like coins in a drunken sailor's purse."

"Tricklewood and Tinsley," Charlie repeated. "How do we find 'em?"

"Mr. Cheek has been keeping an eye on them. He has written down the places they usually frequent. Get a look at them, make certain you know which men they are, then simply deliver my message."

"We'll take care of it," Charlie said with authority.

"See that you do. And this time don't get caught."

Nathan's face turned red. Charlie stroked his beard. "What about the girl?" he asked. "Appears you still mean to have her."

Oliver clipped the end off the cigar with a pair of silver nippers. He studied the neatness of his work. "Things are a bit more difficult, here in the city. It may take a little more time, but in the end, it will all work out exactly the way I've planned."

Barker and Peel said nothing more, just stood waiting for the information they needed. Oliver gave them Cheek's address and dismissed them. In unison, they turned and started for the door.

Oliver watched them leave, thinking of the men who had been courting Elizabeth and feeling a smug sense of satisfaction. Whatever the bastards got, they deserved. Elizabeth belonged to him. The sooner they realized that the better.

The sooner *she* realized it the better. He remembered the slap she had delivered and his mouth turned hard. He liked a woman with spirit but Elizabeth carried the notion too far. She would have to learn her place, and soon. He would tolerate her defiance for only so long.

Oliver held the cigar beneath his nose a second time. Instead of the scent of tobacco, he imagined the fragrance of Elizabeth's soft perfume.

A storm set in, dense gray clouds and a thick damp mist. Elizabeth hardly noticed. Her thoughts were too filled with Nicholas. He had come to the town house every night that week, staying until the first faint rays of dawn, making passionate love to her. It was sinful, she knew, yet it was powerfully addicting. And each time they were together, her attraction to him grew.

He liked the same books she did, could quote her favorite poems. He liked to walk in the garden. When she spoke of her beloved birds, he didn't seem bored but actually interested, asking her to describe them, suggesting that perhaps she make sketches of the birds she had seen.

And yet there was something missing, a link of sorts, a connection found only between a husband and wife. Perhaps it was the fact that he didn't really love her. He cared for her, yes. But love? Elizabeth no longer tried to convince herself that love was what he felt. It was enough, she believed, that she loved him.

She ignored the inner voice that reminded her he was married, that called her a fool and a sinner. She ignored the haunting fear of what friends like Sydney Birdsall, the duke and the dowager duchess, even Mercy and Elias, would say once they found out.

Making her way along the paving stones in front of the town house, her heart suddenly heavy, Elizabeth climbed the steep stone steps to her front door, Elias Moody on one side, Theophilus Swann on the other.

She stopped beneath the crystal chandelier in the entry. "Thank you, gentlemen. It looks as though the weather may continue to improve. If it does, perhaps we might go out again on the morrow."

Elias made a slight inclination of his silver-flecked dark head. "As you wish, miss." If he thought it unusual she had begun to visit the church each afternoon, he didn't say so. And she felt better for the journey.

"Ah, there you are." Aunt Sophie waddled up on her way to the drawing room. "I thought you'd be home before this." Her girth seemed to have increased by several inches since their arrival in the city. She needed more exercise, Elizabeth thought. At Ravenworth, her aunt spent a good deal of time out of doors. Perhaps Aunt Sophie missed the place as much as Elizabeth did.

"I had a bit of shopping to do," Elizabeth told her, continuing beside her into the drawing room, "then I stopped at St. Mary's Church. It is always so peaceful there."

Aunt Sophie frowned. "You were there yesterday and the day before that. I've never known you to be quite so pious."

Elizabeth glanced away. "I suppose until now I never had reason to be."

A thin gray eyebrow arched up. "I didn't realize you felt

that way. If I had, I might have tried harder to dissuade you from the course you have taken. It isn't like you to do something you are ashamed of, Elizabeth."

"I'm not ashamed—not exactly. I don't know how to explain it. I love Nicholas. I know in my heart there is no one else for me, but—"

"But no matter what you feel or even what his lordship might feel, he isn't your husband. In truth, he is married to another woman."

Something burned at the back of her eyes. "Yes." She shook her head. "I told myself it didn't matter. Rachael Warring abandoned her husband nine years ago. As far as I am concerned, she has no claim on him now. She cares nothing for him and he cares nothing for her."

"If all of that is true then why are you spending half the afternoon down on your knees in church?"

A painful knot rose in Elizabeth's throat. "I don't know." The tears she had been fighting began to slip down her cheeks. She sank down on the sofa and Aunt Sophie sat down beside her.

"I believe I do," her aunt said gently. "I believe the answer is that as much as you love Lord Ravenworth, you were never raised to be the sort of woman you must become in order to keep him."

"You mean being his mistress." She hated even saying the word.

"That, my dear, is exactly what I mean. You were raised to be a wife and mother, to make a home for your husband and his children. True, your mother had her own odd set of values, but they were never truly yours. You were always more like your father, a man of dignity and honor. He would never have done something that went against the principles he believed in, and under most circumstances, neither would you."

A painful ache rose in Elizabeth's chest. She wiped at the tears on her cheeks. "But these aren't most circumstances. I'm in love with a man who is carrying a burden he shouldn't have to carry. He is desperately lonely, Aunt Sophie. He has suffered for nine long years. Whether or not I am his wife, Nicholas needs me. No matter what my conscience says, I cannot abandon him."

Aunt Sophie patted her hand, gave it a gentle squeeze. "I know you can't. I wish I could tell you what to do, my dear, but in this I simply cannot. You must do what your heart and your conscience dictate. That is the only way you will ever be happy."

Elizabeth said nothing. What her aunt prescribed was impossible. Her heart and her conscience were at odds on this particular issue. Even the hours she spent in church couldn't seem to help her find a way to bring them together.

Yet equally powerful was the feeling that she couldn't abandon Nicholas, no matter that the church and society both saw their union as wrong.

"I believe I could use a cup of tea," she said, feeling suddenly weary. "Would you care to join me?"

"I don't think so, if you don't mind. Our neighbor down the block, Mr. Whitfield, passed away last month, and some of the items from his home are being put up for sale. I thought perhaps I would see if I might find something useful."

For the first time that day, Elizabeth smiled. "You always find something useful, Aunt Sophie. That is the reason there isn't an inch of space left upstairs in your room."

Her aunt had the good grace to flush. "Yes, well, you needed my feathers, did you not? In these uncertain times, one never knows what might come in handy."

Elizabeth sighed. "I suppose that is true." One certainly never knew which path her life might take. Elizabeth had learned that stark fact better than anyone of her acquaintance.

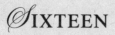SIXTEEN

Maggie Warring stepped
down from the Duke of Beldon's carriage, which was returning her to the town house. Rand and his mother, the dowager
duchess, had been her escorts for an evening at Vauxhall Gardens. Rand had been handsome and entertaining as always
and his mother had been charming. Then the Marquess of
Trent had joined them at their table in the garden and the balance of the evening had passed in a nervous blur.

How could he do that? Make her stomach flutter and her
heart beat like a schoolgirl at her first recital when no other
man had the slightest effect. Until tonight he had played the
role of gentleman, at least in front of the others. But tonight,
the moment they chanced to be alone, his eyes found hers
and they seemed to burn.

"You're looking radiant, my lady," he had said, pressing
the back of her hand against his lips. "A man could fall headlong into trouble just looking into those blue, blue eyes."

Maggie stiffened in surprise, flushed, and made some
inane response, unnerved and at the same time oddly excited.
Later, her nerves still on edge, she broke away from the others

to walk, for a moment, alone in the garden. She was staring up at the moon, studying the shadows and valleys, when Trent appeared out of the darkness.

"I saw you slip away. I hope you don't mind if I join you." He was impeccably dressed and though he was only of average height and build, there was something about him that gave him the appearance of being much larger.

"No, I . . . I simply needed a moment to myself."

"Then you do mind." But he made no effort to leave and suddenly she didn't want him to. He moved closer, his gaze following hers up to the starlit night, then returning to her face. The air seemed to thicken and expand around them.

"Breathtaking," he said, and she knew that he didn't mean the sky. His hand reached out to brush her cheek. He cupped her face between his palms and his mouth came down over hers.

Heat filtered through her, warming her in ways she hadn't imagined. His shoulders were broad. She could feel the fabric of his coat beneath her hands. His mouth was warm and masterfully skillful as it moved over hers. For a moment she allowed herself to enjoy the delicious sensation, a coaxing, a tasting so different from the harsh, almost brutal kisses Stephen Bascomb had taken from her.

Then reality began to filter in, the knowledge that someone might come upon them. The marquess pulled away at the same moment she did, but his warm brown eyes remained on her face. Her hands were shaking as they unconsciously reached up to touch her lips, slightly swollen from his kiss.

"I am sorry if I have offended you. I have been wanting to do that since the moment I met you."

Maggie said nothing. Her mind felt muddled, confused.

"Come, my lady." Gently, he took her arm. "I believe it is time we returned. The others will begin to worry."

Indeed they would. In truth, she never should have left them. But she had and he had kissed her.

And now it was morning. As the first rays of dawn slipped

over the sill and into her bedchamber, she thought of that kiss, thought of Trent and her night of restless slumber, and dragged herself up out of bed.

What was happening to her? Was Andrew merely toying with her, trying to seduce her, as Stephen Bascomb had done? Or were his intentions more serious—which, considering the fact she was no longer a virgin, that she had just broken free of a nine-year confinement and entertained not the slightest interest in marriage, would, in Maggie's estimation, be far worse.

She desperately needed to talk to someone. Someone who would try to understand and might be able to help her. Maggie rang for her maid, who stumbled in half asleep, her mob-cap askew and her mouse-brown hair falling down.

"You called, my lady?"

"Yes, Clarice. I want you to help me get dressed."

"Now, my lady?" She studied the purple morning sky. "'Tis barely past daybreak."

"Now, Clarice. There is something I must do." It didn't take long. In minutes Maggie was dressed in a warm gray serge gown and bowling along in the Ravenworth carriage on her way to Elizabeth's town house.

It was hardly the thing, to appear on one's doorstep at this ungodly hour of the morning, but Elizabeth had always been an early riser. They were friends, after all, and considering her sleepless night, Maggie needed a friend very badly.

When she reached the rented brick house in Maddox Street, a lamp was burning in Elizabeth's upstairs bedchamber, and seeing it, relief filtered through her. Thank God her friend was at least out of bed—she could see a woman's shadow outlined clearly on the wall. She started toward the house, feeling a little better about her intrusion, then paused as a second shadow appeared. A man's shadow, lean and broad-shouldered, standing nearly a head taller than the woman's.

Maggie froze. Holy Mother of God—Elizabeth was upstairs with a man! Shock tore through her. Then worry. Good heavens—what if it were Bascomb or one of his men? Maggie raced up the steep stone steps and pounded on the door until the sleepy-eyed butler pulled it open.

"My lady? For heaven's sake, what is it?"

She started to blurt out her fears—but what if she were wrong? Elizabeth was a woman. Maggie knew only too well how easily a woman could fall prey to the wrong sort of man. "I—I have urgent business with Miss Woolcot. It can't wait until later. Don't worry, I shall show myself upstairs."

"But my lady—"

Maggie never heard the rest. Instead, she hurried upstairs and started pounding on the door. "Elizabeth! Elizabeth, are you all right?"

Elias Moody appeared in an instant, Theo Swann close at his heels. "What the devil's goin' on?"

Maggie ignored them. "Elizabeth, please open the door."

It swung open a few moments later and Elizabeth stood in the opening dressed in a blue velvet wrapper, her dark hair unbound and tumbling around her shoulders. "Maggie—what in the world is the matter?"

Margaret Warring looked up at the lovely, slender woman who was her friend and knew in an instant the man in the room wasn't Oliver Hampton. "It's all right, Elias," she said to the man hovering tensely beside her. "I wanted to talk to Elizabeth, is all. I know she rises quite early."

Elias stalked away with a disapproving scowl, a disgruntled sigh, and a yawn. Theo shuffled back to his quarters, and Maggie turned to Elizabeth, careful to keep her voice just above a whisper.

"I know I am hardly the one to criticize your behavior, but the fact is, my brother has gone to a great deal of trouble to insure your future, and I hardly think this is a proper way to repay him."

Elizabeth looked confused. "I'm afraid I don't understand. What are you talking about?"

"I am talking about the man you have hiding in your

bedchamber. I saw him in silhouette when I drove up in the carriage."

Elizabeth's face went pale. "It—it must have been a shadow."

"It wasn't a shadow and both of us know it—dear God, I wish it were." Maggie reached out and took her hand, felt it faintly trembling. "Elizabeth, do you have any idea what you are doing to yourself? Believe me, I do. No one knows better than I what a fall from grace can do."

Elizabeth's trembling increased. "But I'm not . . . it isn't . . ." She turned away then, tears streaming into her eyes, beginning to roll down her cheeks.

"Come inside, Maggie," came the cool, deep voice she knew only too well, a voice that sent a wave of dread down her spine. "Come in and close the door."

Nick studied the two women he cared most for in the world. Elizabeth's face was as pale as a sheet. Beneath her short blond hair, his sister looked tortured.

"I can't believe it," Maggie said to him. "I just can't believe it. I thought you cared for her. I thought you wanted to protect her. Instead, you've ruined her—just as Stephen ruined me."

Nick said nothing, but every word stung like the sharp edge of a saber.

"It isn't his fault." Elizabeth brushed at the wetness on her cheeks. "He tried to warn me. He tried to protect me. I am the one at fault. I love him, Maggie. I wanted to be with him."

"You were an innocent. Nick knew better. He should have—"

"I should have stayed away from her," Nick finished harshly. "I should have kept my word. Is that what you were about to say, little sister?"

Maggie's chin went up. "You've changed, Nick. There was a time your honor meant more to you than seducing an innocent young girl."

Nick lunged away from the wall where he had been leaning. "Is that what you think? That all I care about is seduction? That the only thing I want from Elizabeth is the pleasure of her body? If that is what you think of me then you are the one who has changed."

Maggie's eyes searched his face. He wondered if she could read his pain, could see the ache of regret that made his features look hard.

"You are right," she said, her gaze locked with his. "There was a time I believed you would never do such a thing."

"And now?" He had brought this trouble to Elizabeth— he deserved his sister's scorn, yet it stabbed at his heart like a blade.

Maggie's eyes filled with tears. "Now I am older, not able to see things nearly so clearly." She reached out a shaky hand, rested it against his cheek. "If I were younger, I would have seen from the start how much you care for her, how much you need her. That this is hurting you, even more than it is hurting Elizabeth."

Nick's throat constricted. Of course she could see. She had always been able to see inside him. The ache remained, yet it was tempered with the knowledge that the bond between them remained.

"Oh, Nick." Maggie went into his arms and he held her close, wishing somehow he could have spared her.

"I'm sorry. I don't know what else I can say."

She brushed a tear from her cheek. "I am the one who is sorry. It was wrong of me to condemn you—either of you. I suppose my past has made me expect the worst of people."

"You weren't wrong." Nick looked over his sister's shoulder to the pale-faced woman who stood a few feet away. "Everything you said is true. I've ruined Elizabeth's future. I've put your future in jeopardy, as well. I wanted Elizabeth so much I was willing to risk anything—everything—to have her. In truth, I'm no better than Bascomb."

"No!" Elizabeth turned and walked toward them. "That isn't true. You are nothing like Oliver Hampton—nothing!

You are generous and good. You are kind and you are caring. You deserve a measure of happiness—no matter the risk you must take."

Nick shook his head, but Maggie gripped his arm. "Elizabeth is right. You deserve to be happy, Nick. If Elizabeth is willing to accept things as they are, then nothing else matters."

But of course it did matter. Elizabeth trusted him to take care of her. His sister trusted him to protect her and see to her future. So far he had done a poor job of both of those things.

He closed his eyes against a feeling of failure. Surely there was something he could do to make things right. Surely there was something.

Nick vowed in that moment that he would find a way.

"Good Lord, isn't that Lord Tricklewood?" Maggie peered over Elizabeth's shoulder out the window of the town house. Now that she knew the truth of the relationship Elizabeth shared with her brother, an even stronger bond had formed between them. Both of them loved Nicholas Warring. Both of them wanted him to be happy.

"Tricklewood?" Elizabeth's eyes swung to the man limping slowly up the path. "Why, yes, and it looks as though he has been injured."

"I can scarcely believe it—surely he and Sir Robert didn't both encounter footpads." Maggie had arrived just after breakfast, bearing news that Sir Robert Tinsley had received a broken arm in a skirmish two days ago with thieves.

"Surely not," Elizabeth said, hurrying to open the door before the butler could reach it. "David, what on earth has happened?"

He stood on the front porch, a grim look on his face. His knuckles were scraped, one eye blackened, his lip cut and swollen. "It's a long story, Elizabeth. May I please come in?"

"Oh, of course. Forgive me. Let's go into the drawing room. You'll be more comfortable there. I'll have the butler bring us tea."

Assisting the viscount into an overstuffed chair, Elizabeth sat down on a blue silk sofa next to Maggie. "David, please—you must tell us what has happened."

He gave up a long-suffering sigh. "It is incredible, really. As evidenced by the bruises on my face, I was set upon by ruffians—last night—on my way home from the club."

"You mean Boodles? You said you were a member."

"Yes. I always go there of a Friday evening for a bit of gaming. Last night was no exception, other than that after I departed, a few blocks from the club, my carriage was waylaid. Two men attacked me, one tall and thin, the other more heavily built, with a thick red beard and red hair."

Elizabeth felt a prickle of alarm. "Please, go on."

"They coshed my driver on the head then came after me. They stole my purse, which was rather lighter than usual, since my evening at the tables had been exceedingly grim, then they started to beat me. I fought back, of course, and I believe I acquitted myself rather well, considering. With two of them against me, they won out in the end, left me in the gutter nearly unconscious, but before they departed, they delivered a message."

"A message? What was it?" She was almost afraid to ask.

"They said that I was to give up any thought of marriage to Elizabeth Woolcot. They said she was already spoken for. They said if I continued to court you, the next time I would receive far worse than a beating."

"Oh, my God," Maggie said.

"Bascomb," Elizabeth whispered, cold chills racing down her spine.

"They warned me to say nothing. They threatened to kill me if I didn't keep my silence." He smiled endearingly. "That I am here, dear Elizabeth, is proof of the feelings I hold for you."

A hard lump rose in Elizabeth's throat. Still another person had suffered at Bascomb's hands, suffered because of her. She came up off the sofa and crossed to his side. "Bascomb is obsessed and there is no telling why. You were brave and loyal in coming here, and I shall never forget you for it." She reached out and took his hand. "But I'm afraid, my lord, there are things you don't understand."

"I understand completely. I realize Oliver Hampton is a power unto himself and he will do anything to have you." He smiled, his blackened eye and puffy lip making him look like a little boy. "In a way I don't blame him."

Her chest ached. The lump in her throat grew more fierce. "Listen to me, David. I care for you a great deal. You have become a dear, dear friend and I shall never forget the courage you have shown in coming here today. But the truth is, my lord—I'm in love with another man."

For a moment he said nothing, just sat there looking grim. When he started to protest, Elizabeth shook her head. "This isn't an infatuation, if that is what you are going to say. It isn't something that will go away. I love him deeply and forever. I want to be with him for the rest of my life."

Tricklewood resumed his silence. With a sigh, he came to his feet. "Then marry him, Elizabeth, and soon. Bascomb is an unscrupulous bastard. It is obvious he will stop at nothing to have you. There ought to be some way to stop him, but in truth there is little the authorities can do. With the power of his shipping concerns, he is nearly an unstoppable force, and you have no proof of his crimes, or his intentions. Marry this man you love, Elizabeth—and pray he is strong enough to deal with Oliver Hampton."

Marry this man you love. If only she could. Her chest squeezed and a sharp ache rose beneath her breastbone. "Thank you, my lord, for your friendship—and your concern."

"Be careful, Elizabeth. God only knows what that bastard will do."

"I will, David, I promise." She took his arm and guided him out of the drawing room to the front door. When they reached it, she went up on her tiptoes and kissed his cheek. "Take care of yourself, my lord."

He nodded. His battered face looked suddenly forlorn.

"And you, Miss Woolcot. If for some reason you should ever change your mind, you know where to find me."

She watched him walk away, her heart an icy lump in her chest. If Bascomb was dangerous before, he was doubly so now. His obsession seemed to be growing. Until he knew that she was Nicholas's mistress—until he no longer wanted her for his wife—she would never be safe.

The thought made her even more depressed. Bascomb would have to know, and once he did, so would everyone else. She would be shunned as a woman of low virtue, no longer welcome in polite society.

Her shoulders sagged as she returned to the drawing room and sat down beside Maggie to a cold cup of tea. *I will simply have to deal with it,* she thought, *as women have done for thousands of years.* She was strong enough and Nicholas was worth whatever she might have to endure.

The notion should have been a comfort. She discovered that it was not.

Nick took a sip of the Madeira Elizabeth had poured into his goblet and watched as she picked at the food on her plate but didn't really eat it. He had been there over an hour, had arrived a little early so that they might share a late supper. He'd noticed that something was wrong the moment he stepped through the door, but so far she had not told him what it was.

He had tried to be patient, had allowed them both to enjoy the delicious meal of venison roasted with gooseberries that her cook had prepared, but still she said nothing. She had evaded each of his efforts to draw her out and his patience was wearing thin.

He tossed his napkin down on the table. "All right, Elizabeth, let's have it. Something is obviously bothering you. I hoped you would tell me on your own. Since you have not done so, I am asking you now what it is."

The spoonful of dessert she had taken paused halfway to her lips. She rested the spoon back down on her plate and smoothed the skirt of her blue silk wrapper. "I do not believe I like the fact that you can read me so easily."

His mouth curved thinly. "And I do not like the fact that you are keeping something from me. Now . . . tell me what it is."

She wet those pretty pink lips and Nick felt a tug at his groin. Across the way, the bed had been turned back and a dozen times throughout the meal, he had imagined what he would do to her once they had finished.

"David Endicott came to see me today."

A thread of jealousy filtered through him. "Tricklewood? I thought you had persuaded him you wished merely to be friends."

"I tried to persuade him. He is rather a persistent fellow."

"I'm sure he is."

"Yes, well, actually, David is no longer a problem. Neither is Sir Robert Tinsley. Apparently Lord Bascomb has dissuaded them for me."

Nick sat up straighter in his chair. "Bascomb? What the devil does Bascomb have to do with you and Tricklewood?"

Elizabeth told him about the men who had waylaid Tricklewood's carriage, about the beatings the two men had received—and the warning Lord Bascomb had delivered.

"I knew you would want to know, but I . . . I was worried about what you might do once you did."

Nick came out of his chair. Leaning his hands on the table, he loomed above her. "You had better be concerned, my lovely Elizabeth, for what I shall do if you continue to ignore my dictates is resume the role of your guardian—and put you over my knee!"

Elizabeth lifted her chin, tilting her head back to look up at him. "I no longer play the part of your ward, Lord Ravenworth. In case you have forgotten, I am currently your mistress. As long as you wish me to continue in that vein, you will save your threats for someone else."

A muscle ticked in his cheek. "Dammit, I am trying to protect you!"

"As I am trying to protect *you,* my lord!"

He hadn't thought of it quite that way. He took a steadying breath, some of his anger draining away. She was worried about him. It felt good to know she cared so much. "Bascomb has to be stopped—one way or another. I'm going to call him out."

Elizabeth jumped up so fast her chair toppled over on the carpet. "Are you insane? Even if you killed him, you are the one who would suffer. After what happened to his brother, there isn't a court in the land that wouldn't hang you for murder, no matter the reason you had for shooting him."

Nick sighed. She was right of course, but it didn't change the fact that he was sick unto death of Bascomb. Sick of his threats and his bullying tactics, sick of the jeopardy he put Elizabeth in every day since he had made her his obsession.

"Perhaps, then, instead of a duel, I shall simply have to kill him. If I am careful, they will never discover who was behind the deed."

Elizabeth stared at him in horror. "You can't do that!"

"Why not? It is what the bastard deserves."

"Because, no matter what people think, you are not a killer." Elizabeth rounded the table and gripped his arm. "We have a plan, Nicholas, remember? As soon as Maggie is settled, we will retire to the country. We'll let Bascomb discover that I am your mistress. He will scarcely want me for a wife after that. His obsession will come to a swift and decisive end, and we can go on with our lives."

Nick stared at her for long, silent moments. Turning, he left the table, weighing her words, trying to convince himself that Elizabeth was right. He paced to the wall, then crossed the room toward the bed. He felt tied in knots, a puppet being pulled by Bascomb's strings. He was angry at Elizabeth for refusing to trust him with her secrets and angry at himself for being helpless in the face of Bascomb's threats.

"Come here, Elizabeth."

Her head came up. She caught the tone of command in his voice and flashed him a look of uncertainty. "My lord?"

"I said for you to come here."

She walked to the place in front of him, her expression a little bit wary.

"Remove your wrapper."

She hesitated, bit down on her lush bottom lip. "Why?"

"Why do you think? You play at being my mistress. If you are, then do as I say and remove your clothes."

"Are you still angry?"

Amusement brought a faint curve to his lips. "Some. But you will learn there are times when anger can be a means to heighten one's pleasure."

Interest flickered in her eyes and the pulse at the base of her throat increased its tempo. Seeing it, his own pulse picked up, started to throb in his groin.

"I'm sorry if I have upset you." She pulled the strings holding her silk brocade wrapper in place and let it pool at her feet. Beneath it she wore a lacy chemise that ended just below her bottom.

His arousal surged, pressing hard against the front of his breeches. "It's all right. Trust takes time."

"But still you are angry."

Angry, yes. And hungry to have her, more so by the moment. "You are about to soothe my anger. Climb up on the bed. I want you on your hands and knees."

A little tremor went through her. He watched as she weighed his words and the hunger she read in his eyes, then climbed up on the bed, looking back at him over one shoulder. "Like this?"

Heat tugged low in his belly. Blood rushed into his loins, making him harder than he was already. "That will do very nicely." He undressed without haste, letting the tension build, enjoying the sight she made and the sweet anticipation. Her fiery hair hung loose, draped over one shoulder, nearly brushing the sheet. Through the lacy chemise that outlined her hips, he caught glimpses of her smooth, pale skin. Desire pounded through him and his shaft throbbed with impatience to be inside her.

He clamped hard on his need, removed the last of his clothes and strode to the bed. Climbing up on the mattress, he took a place behind her, lifted her long auburn hair away from her nape, kissed her there, slid the straps of her chemise off her shoulders and filled his hands with her breasts. They were smooth and heavy in his palms, the nipples already distended. He pinched the ends, not hard, just enough for a quick shot of pleasure/pain.

He felt her trembling, felt the heat of her bottom nestled against his groin, knew she could feel his hardness throbbing there. He massaged her breasts then moved lower, his hands skimming over her body. He raised the chemise, baring her to the waist, and heard her quick intake of breath. He nibbled the lobe of an ear, kissed the side of her neck.

"Part your legs for me, Bess."

She made a little sound in her throat but did as he asked, and his fingers slid inside her. She was wet and ready, hot and slick and tight. He tarried only a moment, stroking her deeply, feeling the moisture collect, hearing her soft little whimpers of passion, fighting the surge of heat that forced him to fight for control.

He entered her in a single hard stroke, impaling her completely, their hips locked tightly together. God, she fit him so perfectly, took him so eagerly. He eased himself out and thrust in even more deeply. Elizabeth responded with a sweet-sounding moan that made him go rock hard. Out and then in, gripping her hips, plunging harder, faster, deeper.

What anger was left slid away, replaced by something else, something that rose deep inside him. It swelled and expanded, changing form, growing into a terrible yearning, a need so powerful it frightened him. A well of longing rose up. He was suddenly desperate to look into her eyes, to watch her face as he gave her pleasure. He wanted to taste her, smell her, fill himself with the essence of her.

Drawing himself out, he urged her onto her back, covered her, and filled her again. He kissed her passionately, erotically, stroking the walls of her mouth with his tongue, claiming her lips with the same fierce possession as he took her body. Feelings for Elizabeth rose up, emotions that erased the dark hollows where loneliness had lived for so long. The shadowy depths inside him flared with a bright glow of warmth.

"Elizabeth . . ." Sliding his hands beneath her hips, he sank into her farther, desperate to claim her, to make her a part of him. Elizabeth moaned and her body tightened around him, nearing the point of release. He felt the power of her climax when it came, soft rippling spasms that flexed around his shaft and drove him nearly to madness. He pounded into her, allowing his release to come, allowing her little whimpers of pleasure to warm him as she milked him of his seed.

When he was finished, he collapsed on the bed beside her, carrying her with him, keeping himself locked inside. They lay quietly for a while, his mind filled with thoughts of her, swirling emotions, questions that haunted his mind. He had wanted to marry her. He had wanted a home, a family, sons to carry his name.

But there was something more, something deep and unsettling. Each time he was with her, his feelings for her grew. He had never felt such powerful emotions, never felt so intensely connected. He wanted her as he had never wanted a woman; he felt incomplete, less than whole, when she wasn't with him.

It wasn't like him to react this way and he found it greatly disturbing. He was a hard man, used to a life of emotional isolation. During the years of his indenture, he had learned to bury his feelings behind an iron control, to cut them out of his mind and heart. In the past few months, his emotions had begun to return. When it came to Elizabeth Woolcot they were fiercely powerful and undeniably frightening.

He wasn't sure exactly what he felt for Elizabeth Woolcot. He only knew she belonged to him, and he would do anything in his power to keep her with him.

Nick closed his eyes, steering his mind to less intense probings. He felt Elizabeth's fingers tracing patterns on his chest, cracked open an eye, and saw that she was smiling.

"You aren't mad anymore."

He couldn't help a smile in return. "Not a bit."

Elizabeth flashed a seductive, mischievous grin. "Perhaps, in the future, I shall anger you once in a while, just to see what will happen."

He tried to frown, but laughed instead. "Minx. I would be careful if I were you. There is always the chance I will beat you."

She gave a funny little shake of her head against the embroidered pillow. "I don't think so."

"There are always other, more subtle forms of punishment."

She pursed her lips. "True. I shall have to walk a very fine line."

He cupped her face and kissed her, deeply, thoroughly, felt himself begin to grow hard again. It bothered him, this powerful hunger she made him feel. For the moment he ignored it. "You must learn to trust me. I realize you have your own set of fears but in this you must do as I say."

Elizabeth sighed with resignation. "All right, from now on, I shall endeavor to obey your wishes." A single reddish brow arched above green eyes dancing with mirth. "Unless, of course, I wish to make you angry."

Nick growled low in his throat. "Wench." He kissed her hungrily, the light in her eyes making him want her again. Settling himself between her legs, he filled her in a single deep thrust. Troubling thoughts slid away, worries about the future, fears of his disturbing emotions. He would deal with his problems on the morrow, deal with Bascomb and whatever else he must face.

For now, Elizabeth was his and the night was young. He had far more pleasant endeavors.

$\mathscr{S}$EVENTEEN

$\mathscr{A}$ wave of heat settled in, thick and sticky, the air so heavy it was difficult to breathe. Even with the high molded ceilings and the windows open, it was warm in the study. Oliver peeled off his blue broadcloth jacket and hung it over the wooden valet behind his desk, pulled the bow on his wide white stock and let it hang loose around his neck. His meeting with Wendel Cheek was hardly a formal occasion.

The little man appeared a few minutes later, dressed in a frayed brown tailcoat, his hair slicked back from a sloping forehead. Oliver motioned him toward the desk where he was seated, but made no indication that Cheek should sit down.

"Your message said you had uncovered some new information."

"Right ya are, gov'nor, I surely did."

Oliver leaned back in his chair. "What sort of information?"

"A very interesting sort."

"Go on."

"Just like you said, I set a man to watchin' the lady's house, keepin' an eye on her durin' the day and stayin' outta sight near the town house till after she had gone to bed. A few nights back, she went to the opera with Ravenworth's sister and that big bloke, the Duke of Beldon. My man followed her home, but he fell asleep before she went to bed, didn't wake up till nearly dawn."

"I hope you didn't pay the bloody fool."

He laughed, an odd, crowing sound. "Thing of it is, when he did wake up, he seen a man comin' outta her town house."

The hackles went up on the back of Oliver's neck. He leaned forward in his chair. "What man?" he asked softly.

"That's just it. Man was walkin'. He slipped between some buildin's and got away."

"You are telling me a man spent the night in Elizabeth Woolcot's room?" he scoffed. "I don't believe it."

"Weren't just any man, as it turned out. The next night I decided to have a look meself. When Miss Woolcot come home, I didn't leave, just waited there in the shadows. A little after midnight, a man showed up, tall he was, with hair as black as the devil's own. Climbed the back stairs quiet as you please—didn't come out till dawn the next mornin'." Cheek grinned. "Plain truth is, it's Ravenworth what's been paying the lady visits. Midnight visits . . . if you see what I mean. He's bein' real careful about it, walkin' sometimes, sometimes travelin' in a plain rented carriage. Don't go home till just before sunup."

On the top of his desk, Oliver's hand fisted around the pouch of coins that was the man's pay. Red seemed to swirl before his eyes. The walls of the room pressed in, forcing the anger down his throat.

"If you're wrong about this, I will personally kill you."

Cheek's olive skin turned an ashen shade of gray. "I ain't wrong, gov'nor. You got me word on it."

Oliver tossed the bag of coins so hard Cheek caught it with an audible grunt. "Get out," he said, leaning over the desk. "Get back to doing your job and don't come here again until I send for you."

"Right ya are, gov'nor. It's gone, I am. Have a pleasant day."

Oliver made no reply. The haze of anger was nearly blinding. All the time he had been worrying about Elizabeth's suitors, Ravenworth had been in her bed. Nicholas Warring had stolen the prize of her innocence that should have been his, and there was no way to replace it.

Rage seared through him, so hot it made him dizzy. Images of Nicholas Warring rose up, naked and buried between Elizabeth's lovely pale thighs. His fist slammed down on the desk, once, twice, thrice. The earl would pay. Elizabeth would pay.

As much as it galled him to take Ravenworth's leavings, Oliver still intended to have her. He wouldn't marry her—not now—not if she was the last woman on earth. He would simply do as his predecessor had done and make Elizabeth his whore.

But first there was the earl to dispense with—one way or another—and long overdue.

Oliver intended that justice would be done.

Nick paced the floor of his study, waiting for the hours to pass, waiting for darkness to descend so that he could return to Elizabeth. He was sick unto death of this hiding, this skulking around in the night, as if they were committing some heinous crime.

To make matters worse, he had learned today where Elizabeth had been spending her afternoons—in prayer at St. Mary's Church—begging God to forgive her, he presumed, for sins that were his, not hers.

Heartache, guilt, grief—all of them suffered simply because his beloved *wife* wished to continue her life of unhindered pleasures.

Nick slammed his fist against the wall, welcoming the blunt edge of pain. Dammit, Rachael was the key to this whole bloody affair. If she would only give him a divorce as he had begged her to do, he could marry Elizabeth. Society might frown on them, but Elizabeth could walk with her head held high, content in the knowledge that she was the Countess of Ravenworth. She would be free of Bascomb, safe beyond the earl's reach.

And Nick could have a family, legitimate sons to carry on the Warring name.

If Rachael would only agree.

Nick sighed, turned and leaned against the wall, his head falling back, his eyes sliding closed against the obstacles that seemed so insurmountable. When he opened them again, his gaze came to rest on a picture of Rachael that hung above the mantel.

He rarely noticed it anymore, had meant to see it removed, but so far simply hadn't got round to it. At the moment, he was glad he hadn't. Staring at the painting, he saw something he hadn't thought of before, something unutterably important. He studied the picture, feeling his hopes rise for the first time in weeks, assessing the exquisitely beautiful raven-haired woman gowned in ruby-red silk. But it wasn't her features that drew him, nor the ripe swell of her breasts. It was the long, slender column of her throat, pale and gracefully arched.

And nestled at the base sat the shimmering Ravenworth rubies.

Nick's heart picked up its pace, making the blood pound at his temple. He had offered his wife a fortune for his freedom, offered her everything he could think of to induce her—everything but the single thing she wanted most in the world: the priceless, exquisite Ravenworth rubies.

In truth, they were a goodly portion of the reason she had married him, a lure a woman like Rachael could scarcely resist. A necklace of huge bloodred rubies, each intricately ringed by a cluster of perfectly matched, brilliantly faceted diamonds. Except for England's Crown Jewels, the necklace and matching earrings were the most extravagant pieces of jewelry in the realm.

A gift from his great-grandfather, the first Earl of Raven-worth, to his beloved wife, Sarah, they were protected by a covenant that gave each successive earl full control. They were the one thing that belonged to Nick that Rachael could not have, a legacy so dear to the Warring family she knew he would never give them up—and she coveted them with every ounce of her villainous soul.

Nick strode to the door and jerked it open, strode out and went down the stairs.

"Pendergass!" He headed straight for his study, the tall, gaunt butler hot on his heels.

"Yes, my lord?"

"I've a note I wish you to carry. It's imperative it reach Sydney Birdsall today." Seating himself behind his desk, he plucked a quill pen out of the inkwell, lifted a sheet of foolscap, and began to inscribe on the page. When he had finished, he signed it simply "Ravenworth," waited for the ink to dry, then folded it and handed it to the butler.

"Tell him I need the items I've requested as soon as I can get them. Ask Jackson to drive you. You'll make better time."

"Yes, my lord." Edward accepted the note, made a stiff bow, and left the study.

Nicholas breathed a heavy sigh and sank down in a deep leather chair. His heart was still pounding, his hopes even higher than they were before. He wasn't simply going to offer the jewels.

He was going to take them to her.

He could imagine the look of rapture on Rachael's face when he spread them out on the table, a brilliant array of deep red fire more irresistible than the devil's own words. She would take them. He could feel it deep in his bones.

Once he had made her the offer, there was no way in hell she could simply stand by and watch him carry them away.

Rachael Warring stared down at the glittering array of jewels spread before her on top of the gilt-edged table. The Ravenworth rubies. She could remember every time she had ever worn them, each occasion sweeter for the sharp looks of envy from the women, the appreciative glances from the men.

She studied them now, each bloodred stone perfectly faceted, each diamond flawless, clusters of clear white fire that formed the perfect setting. Her hand shook as she reached out to touch them, aching to feel their coolness against the heat of her skin.

Across the way, Nick said nothing, his expression carefully controlled, but she knew he had guessed how badly she wanted them. Oh, yes, he knew!

She glanced up at him from beneath her lashes. "Divorce is a high price to pay for a mere set of baubles, my darling."

Nick rose languidly to his feet. "I am sorry you feel that way. I had hoped . . . considering the balance of my offer was far beyond generous . . . that the rubies might sway you." He released a sigh. "But perhaps it is just as well. The Ravenworth rubies have been in the Warring family for generations. Perhaps it is too much to sacrifice for the sake of bedding a woman." He started toward the jewels, leaned down to gather them up, but Rachael gripped his arm before he could reach them.

"Perhaps I *am* being selfish. After all, you do need a legitimate heir and it is unfair of me to stand in the way of your getting one. The jewels would be small consolation for the scandal of a divorce, but if it would make you happy, Nicky dear, I suppose I shall be forced to agree."

She caught a brief flash of triumph, but he quickly subdued it, schooling his features behind a mask of control.

"Well, then, I suppose, since I have already made the offer, 'tis too late to entertain second thoughts. The rubies are yours. I shall leave them in your care and have Sydney draw up the ownership papers with the documents of divorce. I'm sure it will take a while, but with your agreement, eventually, it shall be done."

He left the rubies lying on the table, wickedly seductive,

astoundingly beautiful. He wasn't afraid she would sell them or try in some way to steal them. She wanted to wear them, he knew, and to do that, she would have to own them. He was leaving them because the divorce would take time and he didn't want her to change her mind.

He knew her well, knew that every time she looked at the rubies, every minute they were in her possession, would make it harder for her to give them back. In truth, it was already impossible.

Rachael forced herself to smile. "Well, beloved, it appears that in the end you have won."

Nick actually smiled. "I believe in time you will see that both of us have won."

She arched a brow. Perhaps there would be some interesting ramifications to the fact that she would be back in the marriage market again. One never knew what rewards a clever woman might reap. She watched her tall, handsome husband walking toward the door and felt an unexpected pang of longing.

"You must love her very much."

His brows pulled into a frown. "Love? Love is a fantasy. You of all people ought to know that."

Rachael didn't answer, just watched as he turned and walked out the door. She looked back down at the jewels, mesmerized by the glittering sight. Behind her, the doors at the rear of the drawing room slid open and Greville Townsend walked in, his handsome face brightened by a smile of satisfaction.

"You've done it, my sweet. I can scarcely believe it. You'll have your freedom again."

"True. I was a bit hasty, perhaps, but the deed is done and I do not wish it undone."

He drew her to her feet, swept her into his arms. "No, indeed. Why should you? You'll be free of Ravenworth and as soon as the divorce is final we can be married. I'm a wealthy man in my own right and you'll be my wife, the Viscountess

Kendall. In time, the scandal will die down and we'll be accepted back into the fold."

Rachael shoved at his chest, carefully extricating herself and pushing him away. "I thought I made myself clear, Grey. I do not wish to marry you. I do not wish to marry anyone."

"Nonsense. Of course we will marry. 'Tis the only sensible thing to do."

"Sensible for you, perhaps, but not for me. I have no wish to be tied down to a husband—not you or anyone else."

Grey's face turned a mottled shade of red. "I warned you, Rachael. I told you before—you're mine. You belong to me and I keep what is mine."

"And I told you, I belong to no one but myself!"

The viscount gripped her shoulders. "Dammit, Rachael—"

"Stop it, Grey. I grow weary of your high-handedness, your constant demands for attention. Even your prowess in bed is beginning to bore me. I think it is time for you to leave."

"Leave? What the devil are you talking about?"

"I'm telling you it's over, Grey." She flicked a glance at the jewels. They seemed to be calling her name. She couldn't wait to put them on and wear them. "I'm telling you we are finished. Our affair is ended, Grey. Over and done."

For a moment he gaped at her as if she had lost her senses. Then his face turned an even darker red and he took a threatening step toward her. "This isn't finished, Rachael. It isn't over between us until I say so." His hand balled into a fist and he lifted it toward her face. "Do you hear me, Rachael? Do you hear what I am saying?"

Some of her bravado faded. Still, she was tired of him pushing her around. "I hear you. And I still want you to leave. If you don't, I shall call for a footman and have him see you out."

He scoffed at that. "Do you really believe one of your damnable footmen is going to keep me away from you? If you do, you are quite mistaken." Still, he headed for the door, his strides long and angry. "This isn't finished, Rachael. I promise you, this is not over!"

She watched him leave and a shiver of unease ran down her spine. Grey was young and unpredictable. Still, she had always been able to handle him.

She looked down at the rubies and smiled.

It was dark when the Duke of Beldon climbed the stairs to Nick Warring's town house. Unfortunately, his friend wasn't home.

"When is he expected?" he asked the butler as they stood in the entry.

"I believe he should have been back several hours ago, Your Grace. Perhaps a problem arose. Would you care to wait until his return?"

"No," Rand snapped. "I would, however, appreciate your leaving him a message. Tell him the Duke of Beldon was here on a matter of grave importance and that I should like to see him at his earliest convenience."

"Of course, Your Grace."

Rand started for the door but before he reached it, the silver knob turned and Nick walked in.

"Well, look who's here," Rand said darkly.

"Beldon! Good to see you. I didn't expect—" Then he frowned. It wasn't like Rand to arrive without notice and certainly not this late at night. "What is it? Has something happened?" His lean frame went tense. "Bloody hell, it isn't Elizabeth? Bascomb hasn't—"

"For God's sake, no, it's nothing like that. As far as I know, Elizabeth is safe . . . at least from Bascomb."

Nick relaxed and the smile returned to his face. Rand couldn't remember when he had ever seen his friend look so happy. It made his own foul mood grow even worse.

"There is, however, a matter concerning Elizabeth—a matter of some importance—I have come here to discuss."

Nick's smile slid away. A wary look came over his features. "Why don't we go into my study?" Ravenworth led the way and Rand followed, closing the door behind them. "I hope you haven't been waiting. I would have been here earlier but one of the carriage wheels broke while we were on the road and it took my driver several hours to fix it."

"Actually, I just arrived. I've been meaning to come for the past several days but I wasn't quite sure what I wanted to say."

"How about a drink?" Nick asked, making his way to the sideboard. "From the tone of your voice, I think I may need one."

"Perhaps you will."

Nick poured the drinks, a brandy for Rand and a glass of gin for himself. He lifted his glass. "To better days."

Rand didn't drink. "I can't imagine your days could get too much better—not if you are bedding your lovely ward as I strongly suspect."

A muscle went tight in Nick's jaw. He set his barely touched glass down on top of a piecrust table near the hearth. "What makes you think I am bedding her?"

"I saw you the night of the costume ball. You left before the unmasking, but I knew it was you." Rand had recognized his friend's tall frame, black hair, and unmistakably lean, graceful movements. He had wondered why Nick had not come forward, then he had seen him dancing with Elizabeth Woolcot and instantly he had known. "Knave of Hearts, I believe. I am afraid we have known each other far too long for your disguise to fool me."

"What does the costume ball have to do with any of this?"

"Nothing, except watching you that night confirmed my suspicions. I'm not a fool, Nick. God's blood, the way you look at her—the way she looks at you. I know the signs of physical involvement when I see them. Good Christ, man—you have sworn to protect her!"

Nick lifted his glass and took a deep drink of his gin. "I know what you must think, and you are right." He sighed into the silence. "I should have stayed away from her. She would have been better off without me. I can only tell you I tried. God knows how hard I tried. For reasons I still can't completely comprehend, Elizabeth believed we should be together." Nick looked up and his mouth curved into a smile. "I'm going to marry her, Rand. I went to Castle Colomb today. Rachael has agreed to a divorce."

Rand stood there, thunderstruck. Of all the scenarios he had imagined this was not among them. "A divorce? You can't be serious."

"I'm deadly serious."

"And Rachael agreed? I can scarcely credit that."

"She didn't at first. I offered her a considerable fortune, but she refused. Today I offered her the Ravenworth rubies."

"Good God—you must be insane—or in love."

Nick's smile faltered a moment, then his mouth curved up again. "I don't know about love. I know Elizabeth means a great deal to me. I don't deserve her, but I'm damned grateful to have her."

Rand walked over and clapped him on the back. He felt as if a great weight had been lifted from his shoulders. "Congratulations, my friend. And you're wrong. You do deserve her. You're a good man, Nick. You always have been."

"Thank you, Rand. I hope you know how much I value your friendship."

Rand just nodded. The path his friends had chosen wouldn't be easy, the taint of divorce would always be with them, but if Nick Warring cared that much for a woman, she was a lucky woman, indeed.

"Have you told Elizabeth yet?"

Nick shook his head. "As a matter of fact, I only came home to change, then I was going over to see her. It's funny, you know. I can hardly remember the day I asked Rachael to marry me. Our parents had arranged things. Asking her was only a formality. I never thought I would be doing it again. This time I am actually nervous."

Rand grinned. "Hopefully, you will storm the battlements and capture the prize before your damsel in distress has time to flee."

Nick laughed, then the smile on his face slid away. "I hope the divorce doesn't take too long. I want Elizabeth safe from Bascomb, and once we are married, she will be."

Rand sighed. "Things like that take time. I realize her reputation would suffer if Bascomb should discover that Elizabeth is your mistress, but at least he would leave her alone."

"Actually, that was our plan. We were only waiting out the Season, hoping my sister might have a chance to get settled."

"Maggie . . . yes. That does pose a problem. She is a charming woman, your sister. Were I in the market, she would make an excellent wife."

"She is out tonight. I wonder where she went."

"Out with friends, I imagine. She has made quite a number these past few weeks."

"You are a friend of sorts. Is there anyone special, anyone she might be considering as a possible husband? According to Elizabeth, Maggie had no such plans. She says she is enjoying her newfound freedom. While I approve of the concept, I want her future secure. Deep down, she has always wanted a husband and family. I won't be satisfied until she is safely wed."

Rand sighed. "She is enjoying herself, I think. Can you blame her? Nine years is a very long time." He took a sip of his brandy. "As to her suitors, as far as I know there is no one special. The scandal of your divorce will pose her some problems, but in time the gossip will die down."

"I hope so. I want her to be happy."

"As I am sure she will be, once she hears the news of your upcoming marriage." Rand extended a hand. "Good luck to you, Nick. I hope you know you may count on me for anything you might need." He set his glass down on the table. "Now, I believe there is a matter of some importance you were planning to take care of this evening."

Nick grinned broadly. "Yes, I believe there is."

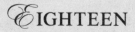IGHTEEN

$\mathcal{E}$lizabeth paced the floor of her bedchamber, her silk skirts rustling with every turn. Nicholas had vowed to come early, had asked that she stay home for the evening, retire to her room so that they might spend the extra time together. Cook had prepared a special meal but that was hours ago. The food sat cold and congealed on a table in the corner. The smell of roasted quail had begun to make Elizabeth's stomach churn.

A dinner prepared for two, served upstairs in her room. She knew the household had begun to guess she was involved in an intimate affair. There were whispers from the servants of the "sinful goings-on" in their domain, but out of loyalty to their employer, so far none of them had quit.

Mercy, Elias, and Theo had guessed the man she was seeing was Nicholas Warring, but instead of receiving looks of condemnation for succumbing to the wages of sin, Elizabeth merely garnered looks of pity. Everyone knew what little regard the Wicked Earl held for women. That Elizabeth had fallen among the endless number who had gone before only told them how foolish she was.

She didn't try to argue. Only Nick himself could convince them she meant more to him than that and so far he had kept silent. Elizabeth prayed they were wrong, that Nicholas cared for her above all others, perhaps even loved her. He rarely spoke of the future, but when he did, she sensed that she was included.

She paced back toward the hearth, then turned and walked over to the window. The evening air was cool and the scent of blossoms rose up from the garden. She smoothed an unseen wrinkle from her gown, a high-waisted green silk trimmed in black Belgian lace she had chosen especially for the evening. Now the ruffle at her breast was beginning to chafe and the ends of her slippers pinched her toes.

Nicholas, where are you? He had never been late before, and as the minutes ticked past, her annoyance turned to worry. Had Bascomb done something terrible to Nick, hurt him in some way, as he had done Lord Tricklewood and Sir Robert Tinsley? But Nicholas wasn't David or Sir Robert. He was tough and he was strong, and he would be on guard.

Other thoughts crept in, darker, more disturbing. What if the others were right and she was wrong? Certainly they had known Nick Warring far longer than she had. Perhaps he had done tonight as they had believed in time he assuredly would. Perhaps he'd grown bored and gone off with another woman.

The thought sent a soul-deep chill down her spine and worry throbbed behind her breastbone. She believed in Nicholas Warring, believed that what they shared was special, more than just another liaison, yet a wall of icy fear began to collect around her heart. The minutes ticked past, setting her nerves on edge, making her angry and worried and fearful all at once.

Then the sound of familiar footsteps bounding up the back stairs reached her ears, a key sounded in the lock, and relief swept through her. Uncertainty followed in its wake as she hurried toward the door. What had he been doing? Why hadn't he sent word that he would be late?

She opened the door before his hand reached the latch, stepping back with a sweep of her skirts to allow him in. He was smiling, she saw, holding a huge bouquet of red roses. Her anger withered and began to fade, as he must have known it would.

"They're beautiful." Accepting the roses, she buried her nose in the petals of a dozen perfect blossoms, gaining time to recover her composure.

"I had the devil of a time finding them. It made me later than I was already."

The reminder pricked like a thorn. "You might have sent word," she said, but there wasn't much sting in her voice. How could she be angry when he had obviously gone to so much trouble? She watched him cross the room, pluck up a silver vase and remove the day-old flowers inside, bringing the container over for the roses.

He seemed different tonight, his mood hard to read, and there was an underlying tension that made her own tension build. He was dressed elegantly, not in the simple white shirt and dark breeches he usually wore, but in a navy blue tail-coat that fit perfectly over his broad shoulders, a crisp white ruffled shirt and lacy cravat. Snug gray breeches outlined the muscles in his legs, flexing with each of his purposeful moves.

"I'm sorry. I should have sent a note, I suppose, once I got home. I had an errand to run out of town. On the way back, the carriage broke down."

Curiosity smothered the last of her pique. "What sort of errand?" For the first time she noticed the expensive bottle of champagne he had placed on the table in front of the sofa.

"Why don't we have a glass of champagne and I'll tell you about it?" He reached for her, pulled her into his arms. "But first I'm in need of a kiss."

It wasn't the kiss she expected, a hungry kiss full of impatient desire, a ravenous kiss that spoke of the night ahead. This kiss was different, special. It was hot and seductive, all of the things it should have been and infinitely more. It was fiercely possessive, wildly passionate, and unspeakably tender. She was breathless by the time he released her, clinging to him, her heart drumming wildly in her chest.

"I missed you," she said softly. "I'd begun to worry that something might have happened."

"Something has happened, my love. Something quite unbelievable." He smiled at her, kissed her again, then drew her over to the sofa against the wall and urged her to take a seat. Walking to a small marble-topped table, he snatched two crystal glasses off a silver tray, returned and opened the bottle of champagne, pouring two frothy glasses of the sparkling liquid and handing one to her.

Her nervousness increased, though she couldn't say why. Something was happening, something important, but she couldn't imagine what it was.

Nicholas lifted his glass and Elizabeth followed his lead. "To us," he said, his eyes soft on her face, glinting with a silvery light that seemed to reach inside her.

She sipped the bubbly liquid, felt it stealing softly through her limbs, but still couldn't seem to relax. Her pulse was pounding, her hands faintly trembling. What was different? What was happening? Then Nicholas took her glass and set it down beside his on the table.

"There are two very special nights between a man and a woman. The night a man makes a woman his mistress—and the night he ends the affair."

"Ends the affair?" she echoed hollowly. Surely she hadn't heard him correctly. Surely what he said wasn't what he meant. But her stomach started churning and she couldn't seem to think.

He smiled. "That's right, my love. If you agree to what I'm about to say, this will be the last night you will ever be my mistress."

Dear, sweet God! Tears burned the backs of her eyes. Elizabeth fought to blink them away. They had all tried to warn her. Her knees felt suddenly weak and she was grateful to be sitting down. "Is that . . . is that the reason you were so late tonight?"

"Yes, my love, it is."

"Is there . . . is there someone else?"

"Someone else?" For the first time he noticed the glitter of tears in her eyes. "Dear God, Elizabeth—sweeting, please don't cry. Of course there is no one else." He set his glass down on the table and raked a hand through his hair, disturbing the wavy black strands. "For God's sake, I knew I would make a muddle of this. I am asking you to marry me. From this night forward, you would no longer be my mistress—we would be engaged to be married and you would soon be my wife."

A flood of tears rushed into her eyes. With it came a tide of relief so fierce she felt light-headed. In an instant she was wrapped in his arms, her head against his shoulder.

Nicholas stroked her hair. "I'm sorry, sweeting. I wanted this to be perfect, but I was just so nervous. I should have known I would say the wrong thing."

"Oh, Nicholas." She sniffed as he handed her his handkerchief. "I don't understand. How could we possibly wed?"

Nicholas clasped her hand. Briefly summarizing, he explained his trip to see Rachael and the bargain he had made. "I should have thought of the rubies before, since she has always wanted them so badly. The divorce won't happen quickly, but as soon as Sydney can arrange things—if you will have me—we can be wed." He kissed the top of her head, eased away from her, went down on one knee.

"It would be my greatest honor, Elizabeth Woolcot, if you would consent to be my wife."

Her heart expanded with love for him. She knuckled away a tear. "You gave her the rubies? But surely the rubies—"

"Elizabeth, I am asking, begging on my hands and knees, for you to marry me."

She mustered a teary smile, her heart nearly bursting. "I would be honored to marry you, my lord."

He came to his feet and drew her into his arms.

"Elizabeth . . . love . . ." He kissed her again, gently this time, then he was lifting her up, carrying her off toward the bed.

"I love you," she whispered, clinging to his neck, bubbling with happiness more heady than any champagne. Nicholas kissed her briefly and she waited, silently praying he would tell her that he loved her, too. She told herself that perhaps he had whispered the words, but if he did, she did not hear them.

Elizabeth awakened beside him, cocooned in his warmth. He was turned away from her, lying on his side, his long, hard frame stretched out naked beneath the covers. She studied the faint white marks on his shoulder, a contrast to his smooth dark skin. Bending her head, she pressed her lips against one of the narrow lines, inhaling the scent of him, tasting the warmth of his flesh on her tongue.

Beside her, Nicholas stirred and rolled onto his back, his thick black lashes coming open. "You were kissing me. I could feel your mouth on my skin. I believe you have the most voracious appetite of any woman I have ever met." He was smiling, his hand reaching out to tangle in her hair, but Elizabeth didn't smile in return.

Her finger traced one of the thin white lines. "They beat you, didn't they? When you were in Jamaica—they beat you."

His hand fell away. Absently, he shrugged his shoulders. "I was there because I killed a man. I learned quickly what it took to survive, to avoid the guards' displeasure. It happened only a very few times."

"It bothers me to think of what you must have endured."

Nicholas sighed, propped his arms behind his head on the pillow. "It was difficult, yes, but I survived. The hardest part was the loneliness. Sometimes it was nearly unbearable. I missed my home, my family. My mother had died before I left, but my father and I were close. I worried I would never see him or my sister again. In the end, my father was dead by the time I returned, my sister shut away in a convent. I'll never forgive myself for the pain I caused them, and yet if the same thing happened, I would do it all over again."

Elizabeth brushed a kiss against the side of his neck. "You deserve to be happy. You have been alone too long." She smiled at him softly. "I want to give you a son, Nicholas. I want to give you the family you've always wanted."

He came up over her, forcing her onto her back, his eyes glinting with a mixture of hunger and tenderness as he looked down into her face. "Then perhaps we should start right now, this very minute. It might not be as easy as one would think."

She studied his face, reached up and touched him. He had asked her to marry him. She wanted to ask him if he loved her. She prayed each day that he did. Instead she reached up and kissed him. She knew he should have gone before this, as he usually did, but Nicholas seemed reluctant to leave and she didn't really want him to. Parting her legs with his knee, he slid himself inside her. They had just begun to make love when a knock sounded loudly at the door.

Nicholas groaned and Elizabeth's cheeks turned red. Easing herself away from him, she snatched her wrapper from behind the dressing screen, tossed back her tumbled hair, and headed for the door. A second knock sounded before she could reach it. When she lifted the latch, Mercy stood framed in the opening, a worried look on her face.

"Sorry to bother ye, miss, but there's a couple of men downstairs—constables, they say. They're lookin' for 'is lordship."

"Good Christ, what the devil could they want?" Nicholas came up behind Elizabeth. "And why would they look for me here?"

"Tell them I'll be down in a moment," Elizabeth said to Mercy, who nodded, turned, and bustled away toward the stairs.

Hurriedly, Elizabeth drew a brush through her hair, tied it back with a ribbon, then stepped into a simple beige morning dress. Her hands trembled slightly as Nicholas did up the buttons.

"I'll wait here. Tell them you have no idea where I might be—you presume that I am home."

"Why do you think they are here?"

"I haven't the slightest idea, but I don't like it."

Elizabeth said nothing else, but her stomach tightened with nerves. At the top of the stairs she paused, taking a deep breath to steady herself. The men were waiting in the drawing room, a robust man named Evans with thick brown hair and a curly mustache, and his dour-faced companion, a Mr. Whitehead, who stood glaring at her from a few feet away. Both of them were there in search of Nicholas Warring.

"Why are you looking for him?" Elizabeth asked carefully, trying to appear nonchalant.

The man named Evans slowly surveyed the drawing room, noting the elegance of the furnishings, taking inventory, it seemed. "I'm afraid, Miss Woolcot, there has been an unfortunate occurrence. A woman has been murdered."

Elizabeth sucked in a breath. "Murdered?" Dread moved through her, a sudden premonition of doom.

"That's right. Sometime yesterday afternoon. The woman who was killed was Rachael Warring. The servants said her husband was among the last few people to see her while she still lived."

Elizabeth took a couple of unsteady steps and sank down on the sofa. Rachael Warring was dead. And Nicholas had gone to see her. "I'm afraid I—I don't know what to say. This is . . . this is very upsetting news."

"I'm certain it is." Constable Evans stood in front of her, his heavy dark eyebrows drawn together. "I realize, Miss Woolcot, what I am about to say is of a rather delicate nature, but the fact remains we have reason to believe Lord Ravenworth is here in your town house. If that is the case, it would be in both of your best interests if you would ask him to join us."

Elizabeth straightened on the sofa, each movement a struggle, as if her muscles refused to obey. She moistened her trembling lips. "What . . . what makes you think Lord Ravenworth is here?"

The shorter man, Mr. Whitehead, pierced her with a glare. "Since Lord Ravenworth is currently not in residence at his town house—and it would seem that *you* are his current mistress—we believe that he is here."

Elizabeth said nothing. The words refused to leave her throat.

"There is no way for him to escape without being seen," Constable Evans put in, "so you may as well go and get him."

Elizabeth's nails dug into the palm of her hand. "But I . . . but he . . ."

"It's all right, Elizabeth," Nicholas said gently, stepping through the door of the drawing room in the same dark blue coat he had worn the night before. "I am certain these two . . . *gentlemen* . . . are the height of discretion." There was infinite warning in his voice and murder in the icy glint of his eyes.

Murder, Elizabeth thought, and fought hard not to swoon.

"Lord Ravenworth, I'm Constable Alfred Evans. This is my associate, Constable Whitehead. I gather you were listening to our conversation."

"Yes. You are here because my wife is dead."

"That is correct. The countess has been most foully murdered, strangled, in fact. Since that is the case, there are some questions we would like to ask. I'm afraid you will have to come with us, down to the police magistrate's office." Evans, the taller of the pair, thick-chested with a hard-edged smile and cool, perceptive eyes, tipped his head meaningfully toward the door.

Nick ignored him. "I'd prefer to speak here, unless I am officially a suspect. If that is the case, I should like to summon my attorney, Sydney Birdsall."

Evans smiled coldly. "Perhaps, then, it would be best if you did."

Nick clamped down on a growing sense of alarm. Across the way, Elizabeth made a small sound in her throat and came up off the sofa, crossing the room to his side.

"It's all right, love. Under the circumstances, there are bound to be unanswered questions."

"I'll send Elias for Sydney. He can meet us at the magistrate's office."

Nick took her hand, felt it trembling. "Go with Elias. Tell Sydney what has occurred. I want you and Elias to wait for me at Sydney's office."

Elizabeth's eyes flew to his face. "But I'm coming with you! There might be some way I can help."

He squeezed her hand but shook his head. "Get Sydney. It's the most important thing you can do." He didn't want her involved in this. He didn't want her dragged through the mud of an investigation. He remembered the way it had been before, what it had done to Maggie, and his stomach knotted.

Elizabeth looked as if she might argue, but instead she nodded. "If that is your wish, my lord."

He left with the men, but said nothing on the way to the magistrate's office, worried he might somehow make things worse. He was clearly a suspect. His past would be a factor. Innocent or not, he had to be careful.

Murder, he thought, his mind in turmoil. Images arose, gruesome scenes of Rachael lying dead on the floor, haunting memories of Stephen Hampton, of the seven long years he had spent in prison, of heat and loneliness and despair.

He thought of Elizabeth, of the beautiful night they had spent making love, of the plans they had made for their marriage, uncertain now, until the matter of Rachael's death was resolved.

Who had killed her? Why had they done it? And what would Elizabeth believe? Surely she wouldn't think he was the one who had killed her.

Nick stared out the window, fighting his growing fears, his awful memories of the past, trying to harness his desperate need for answers.

Elizabeth reached the magistrate's office, Sydney Birdsall in tow, half an hour later, the traffic being heavy through the crowded London streets. Nicholas was waiting in a small windowless, airless room, his coat off and hanging over a ladder-back chair. He came to his feet the moment they walked in.

"Sydney, thank God—" He broke off when he saw the woman who entered behind him. "Elizabeth, what the devil? I thought I told you to wait for me in Sydney's office."

Elizabeth straightened. "I can hardly help you if I am there."

"I don't want your help. I don't want you mixed up in any part of this sordid affair."

"I'm sorry, my lord, but I am already mixed up in it. I am here to help and I intend to stay—whether you wish it or not."

His jaw clamped. A muscle jumped in his cheek. Then he sighed. "Little hoyden. Someone needs to take you firmly in hand."

She smiled for the first time that morning. "You may have the privilege, my lord, as soon as we put all of this behind us."

Something flickered in his eyes, then it was gone. He turned his attention to Sydney. "I'm afraid I'm in a bit of a bind, my friend. Perhaps it is not as bad as it seems, but I didn't want to take any chances."

Sydney set his leather portfolio on the seat of a second wooden chair. Except for a battered oak desk and a dented whale oil lamp, it was the only furniture in the room. The walls needed painting, Elizabeth noted, and the place smelled of rancid tobacco.

Sydney snapped open the latch on the satchel. "You did just the right thing in calling me. I am not adept at criminal matters, but I believe I can help with the basics. If it comes to it, we shall find the best barrister in the city to defend you. For now, tell me exactly what happened when you went to see Lady Ravenworth."

Nicholas did, simply and completely, explaining that he left the rubies with Rachael to be certain that she would not have second thoughts.

"I wonder if they know why you were there," Sydney pondered, placing his monocle in his eye to peer down at the notes he had just taken. "If they've guessed you were after a divorce, that gives you a motive for murder."

"But Rachael had already agreed. I had no reason to kill her. If the rubies are still there—"

"If?" Sydney glanced up. "You are thinking that perhaps the rubies were stolen, that perhaps they were the motive for the murder?"

"It seems a good possibility."

Sydney let the monocle fall from his eye. "Yes, well, the first thing we must do is ascertain exactly how much the authorities know. From there we can begin to formulate a defense."

Nicolas's face looked grim. A muscle throbbed in his cheek. Elizabeth's heart went out to him. Dear God, this couldn't be happening!

He raked a hand through his hair. "They know about Elizabeth and me. It is not too great a leap to see the benefit Rachael's death would have been to me."

Sydney tossed a glance to where Elizabeth sat on the wooden chair. "Yes, Elizabeth has informed me of your . . . relationship."

"I'm sorry," Nicholas said. "I know how disappointed you must be. I can only tell you I never meant for it to happen. Neither of us did. Now you can see why a divorce was so important."

Sydney sighed. "I have to be honest, my boy, this doesn't look good. We shall have to proceed very carefully. We'll begin by telling them only the facts. You were there to see your wife on a matter of personal business. You were there—how long?"

"Less than an hour."

"Once your business was concluded you returned immediately to London. There wasn't time to go back and commit murder."

The lines of Nicholas's face went hard. "Unfortunately, that isn't quite true. There was a delay of several hours when a wheel broke on my carriage."

Sydney frowned. "Several hours, you say? Who can vouch for your whereabouts during that time?"

"My coachman, Jackson Fremantle."

Sydney arched a brow. "But I thought . . . is he not one of the men you knew in prison? Is he not a convicted criminal?"

"Jackson is a convict. That doesn't make him—"

Elizabeth's hand on his arm cut him off. She could feel the tension running through him. "Sydney is not attacking your friend's character, Nick, merely considering his suitability as a witness. Surely you can see the difficulty it might pose for you."

Nicholas sighed, rubbed a hand wearily over his eyes. "Yes . . . I see what you mean. Unfortunately, Fremantle's word is all I have. No one saw us. He pulled the carriage some distance off the road into a copse of trees to work on the broken wheel."

Sydney replaced his monocle, scribbled a few more notes. "I'll speak to the authorities, see what they know. For now we shall simply lay out the barest facts and see where it leads."

Nicholas turned to Elizabeth. "I didn't kill her," he said. "You must believe me, Elizabeth. She was alive when I left the house."

Elizabeth went into his arms, tortured by the bleakness in his eyes. "Of course I believe you." Time and again she had doubted him, wondered at his motives, let her own insecurities make her believe the worst. In this, she hadn't the slightest doubt. "You are innocent. In time, they will discover the truth."

Nicholas lifted her chin with his fingers. "Thank you," he said softly. He stared into her eyes a moment more, then gently set her away. "I'm ready when you are," he said to Sydney, who nodded gravely and led him out of the room.

Elizabeth did not follow, fearful her presence might make matters worse. All she could think of was Nicholas, the pain he was suffering, and the future they might never have.

NINETEEN

$\mathcal{N}$ick paced the floor of the drawing room in his town house. Across the Aubusson carpet, Elizabeth sat on the sofa next to Maggie, both of them pale-faced and worried, holding each other's hands. Just watching them made his insides twist with regret.

He forced his gaze beyond them to the end of the sofa where a tall, stately man, gray at the temples, stood with his notebook in hand, Sir Reginald Towers, one of the foremost barristers in England. Rand had insisted Nick hire him or someone of equal reputation. Rand, who now stood at the sideboard.

"Would anyone care for a drink?" Beldon drawled in that deep voice of his. "I certainly need one, and Nick, old boy, you look as though you could use one, too."

"No . . . no, thank you, Rand, not right now."

Sir Reginald studied his notes. "All right. In our favor, there is now another suspect. Viscount Kendall has come forward. He has admitted his presence at Castle Colomb the afternoon of the murder. Unfortunately, he claims to have left while the countess was still living. Lady Ravenworth's servants confirmed the fact, and he was later seen at a tavern some distance away."

"And Kendall knew I wanted a divorce," Nick said darkly.

"Yes. As her 'great and good friend' he was privy to all sorts of information."

"She was obviously his mistress," Maggie said bitterly. "Rachael was discreet but extremely self-indulgent."

Beldon took a drink of the brandy he had poured. "The fact that Kendall came forward of his own accord lends credence to his tale." His gaze swung to Nick. "He is certain you killed Rachael and he is screaming for your head."

Elizabeth's face went pale. "How could he possibly believe that? If he knows Nick asked for a divorce, he must know about the rubies. Why would he think Nicholas killed her?"

"Apparently because the rubies are gone," Rand said. "He believes Nick had second thoughts about giving them up, that he came back, killed her, and reclaimed the gems."

"Time is the only problem." Sir Reginald turned to Nick. "So far they haven't discovered the missing block of time while your carriage was broken down. Once they do and they have had a chance to pull the evidence together, they are bound to arrest you."

Elizabeth's eyes darkened with pain, and guilt assailed Nicholas. He had hurt her from the moment he had met her. Good Christ, he should have left her alone.

"We won't let them arrest you," she said, her eyes fiercely intent. "We'll find a way to prove your innocence before that can occur." Coming up off the sofa, she crossed to where he stood, stopping just in front of him. "You don't have the rubies. Rachael's murderer is obviously someone else."

"There is only his lordship's word that they are not in his possession," Sir Reginald gently reminded her, "and only the word of a convicted criminal to support his alibi. Coupled with the fact he has been convicted of murder before—"

"He killed Stephen Hampton in self-defense," Elizabeth broke in, and Nick felt a tug at his heart. He reached out and took her hand but resisted the urge to hold her. He had no real claim on Elizabeth. She was his mistress, nothing more. It occurred to him how very much he had wanted that to change.

"It's all right, love. As you said, I am innocent. There has to be a way to prove it."

"There is a way." Beldon strode forward with his usual magnetic force. "We shall simply have to discover who the real villain is."

Hope lightened Elizabeth's features. "How? Where do we start?"

"The task is at hand as we speak," Beldon said. "I imagined this affair might be a bit more serious than Lord Ravenworth at first wished to admit. I've hired a Bow Street runner—several, in fact." Beldon sipped his drink, glanced at Nick and smiled. "And Lord Ravenworth has posted a substantial reward for information leading to the apprehension of the countess's murderer."

Nick smiled faintly. "Thank you. I should have done that myself. I'm afraid I haven't been thinking very clearly."

"Understandable, under the circumstances."

"So what do we do now?" Elizabeth asked. It bothered him to see her so upset, bothered him more, even, than his uncertain future.

"We wait," he said softly. "For now that is all that we can do."

Sir Reginald spoke up from a few feet away. "You have all been extremely diligent in your efforts, but there is something I must ask of Lord Ravenworth and Miss Woolcot."

Unease filtered through him. "What is it?"

"I must insist that you and Miss Woolcot refrain from any further contact until this matter is resolved."

"B-but surely—"

"No," Nick said flatly. "I won't agree to that."

"You must. The headlines you saw in the *London Chronicle* may have seemed brutal—" Indeed they had. COUNTESS OF RAVENWORTH DEAD—HUSBAND, FORMER CONVICTED

KILLER, SUSPECT. "I assure you that will be child's play should they learn you had a motive—that you are currently involved with the young woman who is legally your ward. So far the authorities have been circumspect in their dealings with the press. Should the information leak out, public opinion will turn completely against you. People will be certain that you murdered your wife to marry Elizabeth Woolcot. You must not see each other—not until this matter is ended."

Elizabeth closed her eyes and he felt her sway against him. "Sir Reginald is right," she said. "We must not be seen together, not even by the servants. It is simply too dangerous."

His chest squeezed painfully. His stomach felt tied in knots. He didn't give a damn what the public thought—it was Elizabeth he was worried about. The scandal she would face as the mistress of a suspected killer would be unbearable. He felt like a selfish fool for wanting her with him when the consequences could be so devastating to her.

And Maggie. God's blood, his sister's life would be mired in scandal—again. This time she would be completely ruined. No decent man would have her.

"You're right, of course," he said to the attorney. "It wouldn't be fair to Elizabeth. I'll stay away from her until this is over."

Sir Reginald nodded. "That will be all for now. The best thing each of you can do is try to get some rest. The days ahead will be taxing." He glanced sidelong at Nick. "And Lord Ravenworth is going to need your strength."

The invitations stopped arriving. Callers failed to show up at the house. The days of basking in the ton's acceptance had come to a crashing end. Maggie hadn't thought she would miss it, but she did. And though she was loath to admit it, even more than she missed the presence of people she had begun to think of as friends, she missed Andrew Sutton, Marquess of Trent.

In the drawing room as the evening wore on and darkness

masked the late summer light, Maggie sat down at the piano-forte, lifted the lid, and settled her fingers over the keys. It had been years since she had practiced, not since before she went into the convent. She used to love to play, had spent hours learning new music, listening to the entrancing rhythm of the chords.

Now her fingers felt stiff and disjointed as they tried to form the notes; the once graceful movement of her hands now seemed clumsy and inept. Still, she forced herself to continue, needing the distraction, craving the solace from thoughts of her brother, the terrible fear for him that drowned her in despair.

He had gone out for the evening—she didn't know where. He wasn't with Elizabeth. He was determined not to see her, not to hurt her any more than he already had.

Maggie looked down at the keys, trying her best to concentrate. A sour note collided with a brisk knock at the door. With a sigh of frustration, uncertain whether to feel angry at the interruption or relieved she wouldn't be forced to continue, Maggie made her way to the drawing room door.

Pendergass stood just outside. "Beg pardon, my lady, but His Grace, the Duke of Beldon has arrived. He asks if he might have a private word with you."

Beldon was here. Her heart beat uneasily. Had something happened to Nick? "Show him in, Pendergass, if you please."

"Of course, my lady."

Rand strode through the doors with his usual brusque efficiency, his long, muscular legs moving with power and precision.

"Your Grace? Rand—what is it? It isn't Nicholas? Something hasn't happened?"

He captured her hands, felt them shaking, bent and kissed her cheek. "No, my dear, it is nothing of the sort. I have come to see you, that is all. Nick mentioned you would be in residence this evening. I know I should have sent word, but I hoped that you would indulge me, since the reason I've come is important to us both."

"Of course, Your Grace. You know you are always welcome here."

"Rand," he gently corrected. "That is what you usually call me. There is even less reason for you to be formal tonight."

Her unease was rising again. "Shall I ring for tea, Your—Rand—or would you prefer something stronger?"

"Something stronger, I believe. A glass of brandy, perhaps a sherry for you?"

He didn't wait for an answer, just moved to the sideboard and prepared them both a drink. Maggie hid a smile at the way he always took charge.

He handed her a sherry and she inhaled the nutty aroma. Rand took a sip of brandy from the snifter he cradled in one of his big hands.

"Why don't we sit down?" He seated her on the sofa, then took a place beside her. His glance strayed a moment, to the marble-topped table in front of the couch. Bending forward, he plucked up a copy of the *Whitehall Evening Post* that sat atop a stack of several other papers. The headline read, SEARCH CONTINUES. HAS RAVENWORTH KILLED AGAIN?

"The papers have not been kind," Rand said, tossing the newsprint back on the table with a disgusted flick of his wrist.

"No . . . no, they haven't been kind at all. In truth, they have all but crucified my brother." She didn't say they had also rehashed every cruel detail of Stephen Hampton's so-called murder nine years ago, including speculation as to why the act was committed. Which meant Margaret Warring's name had also been dragged through the mud.

"The papers are part of the reason I am here—the gossip, the damnable scandalmongers and their bloody vicious tongues."

Maggie glanced away. It hurt just to think of it. It hurt to hear the words people whispered behind her back, to feel the burning looks as she walked past them down the street. For the first time, she remembered why she had gone into the convent. The thick walls kept the burning hatred away.

Rand smiled gently and the slight indentation of a dimple formed in his cheek. "But gossip is only part of the reason I am here. The second part is purely selfish. I am in need of a wife and I have come to believe that you would make a very good one. I am hoping you will marry me."

If the ceiling had opened up and the stars had fallen down, Maggie couldn't have been more stunned. "Good heavens, Rand, what on earth are you talking about?"

"I am asking you, in my own indelicate way, if you will be my wife, Lady Margaret, the next Duchess of Beldon."

For a moment she was too astonished to speak. She looked into his dear, handsome face and knew in an instant exactly why he was there. In that moment she almost wished she could say yes, that she was in love with him, and he was in love with her.

She wasn't, of course, and neither was he.

She reached out and took his hand, felt the strength, tempered with gentleness. "Randall Clayton, you are truly the dearest man. No one could ask for a better, more loyal friend. My brother and I are the luckiest people in the world."

"Then we are agreed. Very good. I shall see the banns posted on the morrow."

Maggie actually laughed. "You are also the most arrogant, domineering, overbearing man I have ever met—worse even than my brother."

He dragged her hand over his heart. "Maggie, my sweet—you wound me."

She chuckled softly. "You know it is the truth. And the answer is no—I will not marry you. I wouldn't do such a thing to so dear and wonderful a friend."

Rand simply frowned. "I came to you first before I spoke to your brother. I realized that you have a mind of your own, that you make your own decisions. Perhaps if I speak to Nick he can convince you—"

"No. The answer is no and it shall remain so. I care for you greatly, Your Grace. I know you are doing this in an effort to protect me and I will always love you for it. But I will not marry you."

"Maggie—"

"No, Rand. You deserve a woman who will love you as Elizabeth loves Nick. I love you as a dear and trusted friend."

Rand grumbled something she could not hear. "Are you certain, Maggie? Sometimes love between friends can grow."

Maggie smiled. Without warning, Andrew Sutton's handsome face rose into her mind. They had spent a good deal of time together in the days before the murder, always with friends, never alone, and yet, she had thought in some way he was coming to care for her. She closed her eyes against an unexpected feeling of loss.

"I'm sure, Your Grace, very sure." She rested her hand over his. "I'll make it through this, Rand. As long as I have friends like you, I shall certainly be all right."

But Rand's expression said he wasn't so sure.

And in truth, neither was Maggie.

The headline read: DID HE STRANGLE HER TO MARRY HIS MISTRESS? NEW FACTS UNEARTHED.

Elizabeth crumpled the newspaper and tossed it into the fireplace. She sank down on the sofa, fighting not to cry. Someone had leaked the story. Lord Kendall? Someone in the constables' office? Or was it someone else?

At least I can see him, she thought, wiping the wetness from her cheeks. *It will make not the least difference now.* She had missed him desperately. And she had been so afraid.

"My dear, what has happened? I can tell it is something untoward by the look on your face." Aunt Sophie waddled into the drawing room, clutching a tapestry bag that contained her embroidery.

Elizabeth absently rubbed her temple, where a headache was beginning to build. "The newspapers have discovered my involvement with Lord Ravenworth. It gives him a motive for the murder. They are clamoring for his arrest."

Aunt Sophie sat down heavily in an overstuffed chair, reached over and took the paper. "That poor, dear boy. Surely he has suffered enough without this."

Elizabeth ached to think of it. "I just keep thinking over and over, who could have done it? Why did it have to happen just then? Nicholas believes it was a thief, but I am not so certain."

A shuffling sounded at the door. The butler stood with a calling card captured in a white-gloved hand. "A gentleman has arrived, Miss Woolcot. The Earl of Bascomb. He wishes to see you."

Elizabeth's face went pale. "Bascomb? Bascomb is here?"

"Yes, miss, waiting in the foyer."

Elias Moody stepped through the door of the drawing room. "Not to worry, miss. Theo's out there with 'im. Say the word and Bascomb is out of 'ere—on 'is bloody 'ead if that's what ye want."

Oh, how she wished she could say yes. She would like nothing better than to see the mighty Oliver Hampton thrown out of the house on his ear. But good sense prevailed. They certainly didn't need more trouble.

"I shall speak to him, Elias. However, I should like you to come with me."

Elias flashed her a look that said there was no doubt of that. "Right ye are, miss."

They found his lordship waiting beneath the crystal chandelier, wearing an expression that could only be described as smug, enjoying, she imagined, all of Nicholas's woes.

"I am surprised to see you here, my lord. I thought I had made my dislike of you clear when you accosted me at the costume ball."

His mouth tightened a fraction. He forced himself to smile, but there was no mistaking the anger that lay beneath it. It was obvious he had read the papers, that he had discovered her relationship with Nicholas. A thread of fear trickled down her spine and she was glad that Elias was there.

"A moment of your time is all I ask, nothing more. Considering the scandal in which you are currently immersed, I thought perhaps you might be in need a friend."

She scoffed. "You are hardly that, my lord. And if the 'scandal,' as you put it, has ended your ridiculous attempts to force me into marriage, then at least some good has come of it."

"You may rest assured, my dear, your dirty little affair with Ravenworth has indeed ended any thought of marriage. Still, there is a matter I wish to discuss and it would behoove you to listen."

She eyed him from top to bottom, disliking him more each time they met. Standing as tall as Nicholas but more heavily built, Oliver was not unattractive. Dressed in a dark brown tailcoat, white piqué waistcoat, and buckskin breeches, he looked every bit the gentleman. She knew only too well he was not.

"We may speak for a moment in the drawing room—as long as the doors are left open."

"But of course, my dear." He gave her a leering half-smile. "We wouldn't want to ruin your sterling reputation."

Elizabeth clamped down on her temper. She led him into the drawing room, but didn't offer him a seat, merely turned to face him. "All right, tell me why it is you have come."

Oliver smiled but the anger remained, simmering just beneath the surface, adding a ruddy tint to his complexion. "I was worried about you, of course. As a friend of your father's, I came to offer you my friendship and protection."

"Protection? The only protection I am in need of is protection from you."

"That is not quite the case and you know it. It is becoming quite clear that Ravenworth will soon be arrested. He'll be tried for murder, and quite frankly, there is every likelihood that he'll be found guilty. Your reputation is in shreds, the chance for a decent marriage long past. Every rake and rogue in the city will be trying to toss your skirts and Ravenworth won't be there to protect you. I, on the other hand, will be able to keep you safely sheltered from overzealous swains and vicious wagging tongues."

Her hands unconsciously fisted. "As your mistress." Sweet Jesu, she couldn't imagine anything worse.

"You are offended?" Bascomb's face turned hard. "There was a time not long ago that I wanted you for my wife. You chose the bed of a murderer instead."

"Lord Ravenworth did not kill Rachael Warring."

"'Tis certain the courts will not agree. Warring will hang and you will be left a ruined woman." His lips curled unpleasantly. "I can protect you from that. As my mistress, you'll be sheltered, live a life of luxury, and be safe from any man who might treat you with less than respect. You'll have everything you ever wanted and you will be safe."

"You—offering me protection. I find that most amusing." She turned her back to him, fighting to remain in control. Much of what the earl had said was true. She was now a woman of infamy. As the Wicked Earl's mistress, every man in the city would be trying to seduce her. "You know I will not agree." Even with her back turned, she could feel his smoldering rage, feel his eyes burning into her.

"Not today, perhaps. But in time you will have no choice. You belong to me, Elizabeth. Your dalliance with Ravenworth hasn't changed that. It has simply altered your future status from wife to mistress." He moved toward her, gripped her shoulders and turned her to face him. "You may as well resign yourself. In a very short time, Ravenworth will be swinging from the gallows and I will be the man in your bed."

Elizabeth jerked away, too angry to speak. And frightened. She tried to tell herself she had no reason to be, that she was in no danger, but she couldn't quite make herself believe it.

At the silence, Elias stepped through the door, his stance filled with warning.

"Don't bother seeing me out," Bascomb said. "I believe I know the way."

She watched his controlled, purposeful strides, heard his footfalls in the foyer then the front door closing behind him, and still she did not move. For the first time since Rachael's murder, Oliver Hampton had returned to her thoughts. It occurred to her as it had before that he was a dangerous, ruthless man.

Ugly thoughts swirled in, frightening thoughts. She had believed that she would be safe from him once he discovered she was Nicholas's mistress. Instead, she found herself in even more danger. In truth, he was as wildly, insanely determined to have her as he had been before.

She thought of what he had done to Lord Tricklewood and Sir Robert Tinsley. Would he go as far as murder?

A shiver ran through her. Fear for herself meshed with a terrifying suspicion. It settled like a frozen lump in the pit of her stomach.

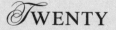

TWENTY

It rained all that day and on into the night. The sky opened up and sheets of cold gray water poured down. Flat black clouds smothered the stars, and the wind blew dirt and bits of paper over the cobbled streets.

Wrapping her cloak around her, Elizabeth grasped Elias's hand and let him help her down from the carriage.

"Ye shouldna' come, miss. 'Is lordship will 'ave me 'ead for bringin' ye."

"If you hadn't, I would have come without you."

Elias sighed. "Aye. Do ye think I don't know it?"

Holding her hood up against the wind, Elizabeth waited while Elias lifted the heavy brass lion's head knocker on the front door of the Ravenworth town house and rapped it loudly against the plate.

The door came open. Though the papers had blatantly revealed the scandal and there was little doubt that Edward Pendergass had read them, his face revealed nothing, except perhaps a trace of pity.

"I'm sorry. I know I should have sent word, but I wasn't sure I was coming until it was too late." She had told herself to stay away, that it was best for Nicholas if she did, best for both of them, and she knew it was what he wanted. But the gossips knew the truth of their involvement now, and she wanted to see him. Had to. She had missed him desperately these past few days.

The butler cleared his throat. He glanced toward the stairs and his expression became uncertain. "I'm afraid, Miss Woolcot, Lord Ravenworth isn't up to greeting visitors. He's a bit . . . under the weather, you see. Perhaps on the morrow—"

"Nicholas is ill? Where is he?"

"In his bedchamber, miss, already retired for the evening."

She pulled the string on her cloak and handed it over. "I'll just check on him, then, see if there is anything he needs." She started for the stairs, Pendergass close on her heels.

"Please, miss. He has asked that he not be disturbed. If you could just come back in the morning . . ."

Suspicion filtered through her. Something was wrong. "I'm here now and I wish to see him. You needn't bother to show me up. I believe I know the way." Whirling toward the stairs, she climbed them swiftly, ignoring the disgruntled sighs of the men she had left below in the foyer. Her heart beat uncomfortably. Worry made her footsteps unsteady.

She knocked on the door to his suite, lifted the latch without waiting for permission, and stepped into the elaborately furnished drawing room. The smell of alcohol and tobacco hit her with the force of a blow.

"Good heavens." It was nearly dark in the room, just the glow of a low-burning fire and the flame of a single candle lit the interior. Nicholas leaned back in a gold brocade chair before the fire, his hair slightly mussed, his shirt unbuttoned and open to the waist, a decanter of gin in one hand, a thin black cigar clamped between his straight white teeth.

He took the cigar out of his mouth, let a lazy column of smoke drift into the air. "Well, look who's here. A vision has appeared straight out of my dreams. Are you real, Elizabeth, or am I still dreaming?" In the glow of the fire, his silver eyes raked her, a slow perusal that did nothing to veil the heat of his thoughts.

"I'm quite real, my lord. I came to see how you were feeling. The butler said you were ill."

White teeth flashed. "Do I look ill, sweeting?"

"You look drunk, my lord. I believe you are well and truly foxed."

He came up out of the chair, staggering slightly, bringing the gin decanter with him, tossing the cigar into the flames. Bands of muscle tightened across his chest, a dark golden bronze in the glow of the fire, lightly furred with curly black hair. "Not too drunk for a little diversion. Come here, Elizabeth. I've got something for you."

Her heart beat faster even as her temper inched up a notch. She could see that he did. It was pressing hard against the front of his breeches. "I'm certain you do."

He staggered closer, steadied himself against a small Sheraton table. His eyes moved over her, lazily, sensuously, an erotic voyage that sent heat sliding into her stomach.

"Do you know how much I want you? I've thought of nothing but you for days." Those hot silver eyes came slowly to the swell of her breasts. "I'm hard for you, Elizabeth. I have been since the moment you walked through the door. Can you imagine how incredibly desirable you look? Can you possibly guess the hours I've spent thinking of you in my bed?"

"Nicholas . . . please . . ."

"I know I'm drunk. I don't care. It doesn't make me want you any less. Why don't you kiss me? We can start with that. Then I'm going to strip off those clothes you are wearing." He swayed a bit. Lifted the crystal stopper off the gin and took a long pull straight from the bottle. "Too many clothes . . . only get in the way. Get them off, then I'm going to take you . . . do what I've been dreaming about . . . bury myself inside you."

Elizabeth flushed. He was definitely the Wicked Earl tonight, and though part of her was annoyed to find him in such a condition, those hot looks and sinful words were doing strange things to her insides.

"You need to be in bed."

A corner of his mouth curved roguishly. "That's exactly what I was saying." He set the gin decanter down and moved toward her, stumbling slightly, stopping just inches away. Leaning precariously forward, he reached out and cupped one of her breasts, his touch surprisingly gentle.

"So lovely. I've been dreaming about them. I've been thinking of the way the pretty pink tips get hard when my tongue slides over them." His words were enough to make it happen. Her nipples peaked beneath her gown as if he had actually touched them.

Sweet God, she hadn't come here for this! She might be Nicholas's mistress, but there were limits to what she would put up with.

He reached for her, staggered and nearly fell. Elizabeth caught his arm, steadied him against her.

"I had better get Elias. He can help you undress."

Hot gray-blue eyes slid down to her breasts. "Oh, no. Not Elias. You, Bess."

Elizabeth rolled her eyes. He was beginning to get to her, the cross between a helpless little boy and an excitingly virile man. It did nothing for her rapidly beating heart, or her fast eroding temper. "All right, fine. I'll help you undress."

"And I'll help you." A long dark finger found a button at the nape of her neck. He tugged on it once, twice; she heard the fabric rip, turned, and slapped the marauding hand away.

"All right, Nicholas Warring, I've had just about enough. Now, we are going into your bedchamber. You are going to sit down on the edge of the bed and I am going to help you undress. If you don't behave while I'm doing it, I'll have to call Elias."

A lock of black hair fell into one eye. He looked suddenly contrite. "All right, I'm sorry. Let's just go to bed."

She wasn't about to tell him she had no intention of

joining him there—not when he was as drunk as a sailor on leave. And damnably heavy, she thought as the two of them lurched toward the door of his bedchamber, one of his arms slung casually over her shoulder.

Once they reached the bed, he sank down heavily, and Elizabeth went to work. She removed his shoes and stockings, stripped off his jacket and shirt, then eased him onto his back to work the buttons on his fly. She could feel his arousal and her hand started shaking. Nicholas groaned and Elizabeth's fingers went still.

"I won't . . . I won't be a moment more."

"Take your time, sweeting." The words came out rough, seductive. A corner of his mouth curved up, and scalding heat washed through her.

Damn you, Nicholas Warring. But she wasn't really angry anymore, or even disappointed in him. Along with the desire he had managed to arouse, what she truly felt was pity. He had needed escape from his troubles. He had found it, at least for tonight.

With cool efficiency, she stripped away his breeches, determined not to notice the hard slabs of muscle across his ribs, the sinews in his thighs that traveled the length of his long lean legs. Easing him back on the bed, she pulled the sheet up to his waist.

"Now you," he said softly, drowsiness creeping into his voice.

"Not tonight. I can't stay with you tonight. Maggie is here. The servants would gossip." But in truth, she wished she could. Tonight he played the Wicked Earl, but drunk or sober, he was the most exciting man she had ever met. Her body ached for his touch, her heart ached just to be near him. He didn't love her, but he needed her tonight and she wanted to be with him. She wished she could climb into bed beside him, give his body the comfort the liquor had given his troubled thoughts.

"Shouldn't have gotten drunk," he said groggily. "Wanted to forget. Do you forgive me?"

She bent and kissed his forehead. "My lord, I would forgive you almost anything."

She started to turn away, but he caught her wrist. "Stay for a while." His eyes drifted closed, thick black lashes against the hard, carved planes of his face. "Just for a while . . . even if we can't make love."

How could she argue? "All right, just for a while."

Half an hour later, he had drifted off to sleep. Elizabeth's eyes filled with tears just to watch him. He didn't deserve this. He deserved the home and family she had wanted so badly to give him.

But what about her? She couldn't walk down the street without people whispering her name. They jeered at her and turned away as if she had some sort of plague. It hurt to be treated that way. Dear God, it hurt so badly. She couldn't have imagined how awful it would be to be shunned completely from Society.

Elizabeth sighed and wearily rose to her feet. When she stepped out into the hall, Elias Moody was waiting, sitting on a bench beneath a gilded sconce in the corridor.

"He all right?"

"He'll have a pounding headache in the morning, but yes. For now he is all right." She glanced back to the room. "He wanted me to stay."

"And you wanted to?"

"Yes, wrong as it is, I wanted to."

Elias's weathered face held a world of understanding. "Stay, then. Before it gets light, I'll come for ye, see ye get home. No one will ever be the wiser."

Elizabeth bit her lip. It was a dangerous, scandalous thing to do. There was Maggie to consider, the gossip was already unbearable. Thinking of Nicholas alone in his big bed, it didn't seem to matter.

Elizabeth reached out and caught Elias's hand. "Thank you, Elias. You're a very good man."

"Our Nick—he's the one. Ye be good to 'im, lass. 'E needs a woman to love 'im."

She blinked but her eyes swam with tears. "I do love him, Elias. More than anything in the world."

"Go, then. Make 'im forget his problems for a while."

Elizabeth nodded. Returning to his room, she silently removed her clothes and slipped into the big bed beside him. Still fast asleep, Nicholas enfolded her against his naked body, wrapping her tightly in his arms.

Tears burned the backs of her eyes. She would be there if he needed her. It occurred to her how badly she had come to need him.

As promised, just before dawn of the following morning, Elias arrived with the carriage to take her home. It was late in the afternoon of that same day that Elizabeth changed into a simple gray silk gown trimmed with small seed pearls for her return to Nicholas's town house. She was determined to have the conversation with him she had intended to have the night before.

Elizabeth flushed to think of it, of the hours in the night when Nicholas had awakened and begun to make slow, sensual love to her. She had felt his need, and in some way he had sensed her own. They had come to a crashing peak, their bodies locked together, then drifted back to sleep, still as one. She had left him shortly before sunrise, returning home then sleeping later than usual, allowing Nicholas to sleep as well.

He would need it, she thought with a hint of amusement. By now he would be paying for his folly of the night before.

She arrived at the town house, Elias again in tow, as the sun broke free of the clouds, the steep stone steps leading up to the door still glistening with the last of the rain.

Pendergass showed her into the drawing room. "I shall tell

his lordship you are here," he said, slipping silently down the hall.

Nicholas appeared a few moments later. "Elizabeth . . ." He said her name softly, his expression unreadable, but his long strides never faltered and in seconds she was wrapped in his arms. "You shouldn't be here," he whispered against her ear. "You shouldn't be anywhere near me. You shouldn't have come last night—I should have sent you home."

Elizabeth looked into his dear, handsome face. "I don't see what difference it makes anymore. The papers know the truth about us. By now, so does everyone in London."

He sighed. "Unfortunately, that is true." He pulled her into the drawing room, bent his head and kissed her. "God, you've only been gone for hours and it seems as if it's been days." He kissed her again, deeply, thoroughly. "Already I want you again." He nuzzled the side of her neck, his mouth warm against the pulse racing there. "Rand is here," he said between soft, feathery kisses. "He and Sir Reginald. They are waiting in my study."

Elizabeth broke free and a flush rose into her cheeks. "You have a house full of visitors and we are in here kissing?"

The corners of his mouth edged up. "I suppose I should have told you. I was enjoying myself too much."

"You *are* wicked. It is one of the things I love most about you."

His smile seemed to falter. The knowledge that she loved him always seemed to make him uncomfortable. *In time it will be different*, she told herself, but it bothered her nonetheless. Taking her hand, he led her back through the drawing room door, and Elizabeth forced her thoughts in that direction.

"If Beldon is here," she said, "something must have happened."

Nicholas nodded. "A report has come in from one of the Bow Street runners. Apparently Viscount Kendall is not so lily-white in all of this as he would like us to believe." He shoved open the door to the study and the men inside came swiftly to their feet.

"Elizabeth," the duke said with a smile. "It's good to see you."

Sir Reginald greeted her with warmth, bowing over her hand. "A pleasure, Miss Woolcot."

"I didn't mean to interrupt. Nicholas was telling me one of the runners may have uncovered something of importance concerning the Viscount Kendall."

"That is correct," said the duke. "It appears Lady Ravenworth and Greville Townsend had been having trouble of late. As a matter of fact, according to the servants, the day of the murder they had quite a row, and it wasn't the first time."

"Yes," Sir Reginald agreed. "One of the footmen heard him making threats the day of the murder."

Elizabeth's heart leapt with hope. "Then Kendall may very well be the man who killed her."

"He may, indeed," Nicholas said. "Unfortunately, the man has a very tight alibi. He was seen by the tavern owner of the Swan and Sword and was supposedly there for several hours. Unless we can discover how he might have convinced the man to falsify the truth, we aren't much better off than we were before."

Elizabeth bit down on her bottom lip. It seemed every ray of hope had a dark cloud hovering above it. She looked at Nicholas. She had come to see him because she was determined to voice her suspicions about Oliver Hampton. Every possibility was important, but what would the other men think?

"You're frowning," Nicholas said to her gently. "If there is something you wish to say, Elizabeth, you certainly have leave to say it."

She studied his face, noting the weariness beneath his eyes, the lines of tension across his forehead. "Lord Bascomb came to see me."

"Bascomb? That whoreson had the nerve to accost you in your own home!"

"I didn't mean to upset you. I only mentioned it because . . . I know this may be hard for you to believe, but . . ."

"Go on—what has Bascomb done now?"

"Perhaps he has murdered the countess."

"What!"

Rand leaned forward in his chair. "I realize this is highly upsetting, Elizabeth. We are all of us desperate for answers, but accusing a man of murder—"

"I know it sounds incredible. It was something he said." She frowned, shook her head. "No, not exactly what he said, not in so many words. Perhaps it was the way he said it. Whatever it was, it got me thinking."

Her gaze swung to Nicholas. "Nothing he has discovered about us has ended his obsession, my lord. If anything, he seems more determined than ever. He had poor Tricklewood beaten. His men broke Sir Robert's arm." She shifted her scrutiny to Rand. "Lord Ravenworth has always been the biggest obstacle in Oliver's path. I started to wonder how far he would actually go in order to get what he wanted. Perhaps murder isn't out of the question."

"He did that to your suitors?" the duke said, his expression incredulous.

"Yes. He told them I was already spoken for and they were to give no further thought to marriage."

"The man is a bloody outrage!" Rand thundered. He shook his head. "Still, murdering Rachael—it wouldn't make sense. He would have to have known Nick was going to see her and the purpose of his visit. There is no way he could have known that."

Nicholas frowned. "Actually, there is. He knew which room Elizabeth was staying in at Ravenworth Hall and exactly how to get his men inside the house. I thought his spy was one of the servants I left behind, but if it is someone I trusted, someone who traveled with us to London, it's possible Bascomb could have known."

"Good God, surely he wouldn't have killed the woman simply to get you out of the way."

"You're forgetting about his brother. Bascomb and I go a long way back. He hates me for killing Stephen. If killing Rachael would give him Elizabeth and see me dead, he just might do it."

Silence fell. Sir Reginald's voice broke into the quiet. "So now we have three possibilities. A thief who might have killed her for the rubies. Lord Kendall, who could have murdered her in a jealous rage. Or Oliver Hampton, who may have killed her with cold, calculating purpose."

Elizabeth said nothing, but a shiver ran down her spine. Nicholas reached out and drew her into his arms. "We'll discover the truth," he said gently. "We're learning more every day. We just need a little more time."

But time was running out and both of them knew it. Dear God, she was so afraid!

WENTY-ONE

I am sorry, my lord, but it is my unfortunate duty to place you under arrest—in the name of the Crown—for the murder of your wife, the Countess of Ravenworth."

Nick stood frozen. Once before in his life he had heard those chilling words. He had tried to prepare himself, but in truth, he had never thought to hear them again. "I presume you have a good deal more evidence than you had when last we spoke."

Constable Evans moved farther into the entry, allowing the watchmen who had come with him to step inside as well. "It appears there is a gap of several hours in the time sequence you gave us, my lord." He lifted a busy eyebrow. "Perhaps you wish to clarify that error now."

Nick took a steadying breath. He had known this was coming, known yet prayed it would not. "The hours you are missing occurred when a wheel broke on my carriage. It took my coachman several hours to repair it. He, of course, can vouch for my whereabouts during that time."

"Your coachman. By that you are referring to one Jackson

'Light-fingered Jack' Fremantle—a convicted thief who has also been arrested on several counts of assault. I'm sorry, my lord, but Fremantle is hardly a viable witness. Along with that, there is also the matter of the argument you had with your wife on a previous visit. You neglected to mention that as well, or the threats that you made at the time."

Nick's stomach tightened. He had forgotten about the fight they'd had. Damn, he had tried so bloody hard to hang on to his temper. "I was angry. I said things out of hand. I didn't—"

"I'm sorry. That is a matter for the courts to decide. Now if you will please come with me—"

"Dammit, she had already agreed to the divorce! I had no reason to kill her!" The constable merely stood there. Nick closed his eyes, fighting for control. He released a shaky breath. "I'll need a moment to collect my hat and gloves, leave word for my sister and my attorney." *Get a message to Elizabeth.* He would have to find someone to tell her. What could he possibly say?

"Sir Reginald has already been informed," the constable was saying. "He will meet you at the prison."

Nick's stomach rolled. *Prison.* The word weighed him down like a heavy stone, and a chill sank into his bones. He had spent weeks in a cold cell in Newgate before he had been transported. Now he would face those dank, unforgiving walls again.

And this time he might not leave.

It took all of his considerable will to return to the foyer when instinct told him to run—to get as far away from London as he possibly could. Under different circumstances, he might have.

Elizabeth's lovely face rose into his mind. Elizabeth laughing at something he had said. Elizabeth holding him as he lay sleeping, her fingers stroking gently through his hair. He had wanted a life with her, wanted the children she could give him.

"Are you ready, my lord?"

Nick simply nodded. The constable's carriage waited out in front. He climbed in and settled himself against the cracked leather seat, fighting not to think of the grim days ahead, of the trial and its possible outcome. Instead he focused his thoughts on Elizabeth, on the way she had come to him that night in his bedchamber, the refuge he had taken in her arms, in her body. She had given herself to him totally and completely, and with such tender sweetness that for a few short hours there was no room in his heart for the worry that consumed him.

She was everything he wanted in a woman, sensuality tempered with innocence, softness infused with an underlying strength.

Elizabeth! he silently called out to her. She was safe for the moment, tucked away inside the walls of her town house. But she couldn't stay there forever.

Was Bascomb behind Rachael's murder? If he was, who among those Nick trusted had betrayed him? And if Bascomb had killed her, what grave danger might Elizabeth be facing?

He thought of Maggie, saw her battered face, her torn and bloody clothes. In his mind's eye he saw Oliver in Stephen's place, his black rages and destructive need for possession. God's blood, what might a man like that do to a woman he was so wildly obsessed with?

On the carriage seat, Nick's hands unconsciously fisted. The fear he felt for himself suddenly paled in the face of the terror he felt for Elizabeth.

With a shaky hand, Maggie accepted the glass of sherry Elizabeth handed her then sank down on the sofa. "Thank you." She had arrived at her friend's house in Maddox Street, the carriage streaking up in front, Maggie in tears as she climbed the front steps.

She took a sip of the sherry, hoping it would steady her nerves, somehow help to ease her fears. "I still can't make myself believe it."

Elizabeth sat down on the edge of a chair, her face as white as the lace on her navy blue gown. "Where . . . where have they taken him?" Her voice sounded strained, the words thin and distant, as if they came from far away.

"Newgate, I suppose. Marshalsea and King's Bench are debtor's prisons. They took him to Newgate before." Maggie took another sip of sherry, holding on to its fortifying warmth, brushing the tears from her cheeks. Crying wouldn't help Nick. She wasn't certain what would.

"When did they come for him?"

"Early this morning. I wasn't yet out of bed. He was gone by the time I dressed and arrived downstairs."

Elizabeth stared off toward the window. "We have to go to him. We have to make certain that he is all right."

Maggie pulled a handkerchief from the pocket of her pale peach morning gown, dabbed at her eyes and blew her nose. "Sir Reginald was to meet him. He'll pay the garnish, see that Nick is given a cell on the master's side of the prison."

Elizabeth's eyes swung to hers. Maggie noticed how hollow they looked, yet deep inside, the light of determination seemed to burn. "I'm going to see him. Then I'm going to find a way to prove that he is innocent."

"How? What can you possibly do that my brother and Rand aren't already doing?"

"I'm not sure but there has to be something."

Maggie shook her head. "I don't know, Elizabeth . . . I just feel so useless. I'm terribly worried about him. And the gossip . . . it's been so awful. I don't . . . I'm not certain how much more I can stand."

The green of Elizabeth's eyes seemed to sharpen as they focused on Maggie's face. "You're not saying what I think you are? You're not thinking of returning to the convent?"

Maggie glanced away. Andrew Sutton's image appeared in her mind. It faded away as he had faded from her life and a sharp ache rose in its place. "I'm not certain what I am thinking. My thoughts are so muddled, I hardly know what day it is."

Elizabeth strode toward her, reached out and gripped her shoulders. "You listen to me, Margaret Warring. I don't believe for a moment you belong locked away in a convent. You have too much to offer, too much to give. Nicholas said you wanted children. You can still have them, Maggie. The right man won't care about the scandal. The right man will care only for you." Gently, she shook her. "And you have your brother to think of. Nicholas needs you. You can't just abandon him."

Maggie shivered as a tremor ran through her, accompanied by a flicker of shame. "I know. It's just that sometimes . . ."

"Sometimes it just seems so hard."

She nodded. "Yes. Sometimes it just seems so hard."

"You can't run away, Maggie. You can't give up your dreams a second time."

Maggie stared out the window, caught a glimpse of blue sky, heard the call of a newsboy hawking the morning paper, the laughter of children playing on the porch next door. Elizabeth was right. Maggie had run from her troubles before but the cost had been higher than she could have imagined. This time she would stay and fight for a life in the world outside, even if it meant living that life alone.

Setting the glass of sherry down on a marble-topped table, she rose slowly from the sofa. "My carriage is still out in front. I shall inform Elias and Theo that we are in need of their escort to the prison."

Some of the tension eased from Elizabeth's slim shoulders. "I won't be a moment. I'll get my wrap and meet you in the foyer."

Maggie watched her leave and wearily turned to the door. For weeks she had reveled in her newfound freedom, so caught up in the excitement of the social whirl she had missed as a girl she hadn't understood her own heart and what it was she really wanted. A home of her own. A husband and family to love. Now that she had lost the chance for those things, she realized just how important they were.

It was too late for that, but as Elizabeth said, there was her brother to think of. Nicholas needed her as he never had before. Maggie straightened her shoulders and started to the door. No matter the cost, this time she would stay and face the dragon.

Nick leaned back against the rough gray walls of his cell in Newgate prison. Outside the sun was shining, yet it was icy cold inside the damp, thick-walled chamber. He was quartered in the master's side of the prison—being an earl and a man of considerable wealth did, after all, have its advantages.

But the threadbare rug did little to warm the cold stone floor. The battered wooden chairs and scarred oak table hardly equaled the comforts of home. The lumpy corn-husk mattress on its woven hemp frame had provided little solace against his restless slumber of the night before.

Still, it was better than the others got, the thieves and murderers, pickpockets and whores, who made up the bulk of the population, better than he had received in the early days of his imprisonment nine years ago.

Those memories formed a cold knot in his stomach. Hammocks on board the transport ship stacked so close together he could barely draw in the fetid humid air, weevily gruel, maggoty meat, and the smell of unwashed men. Backbreaking labor from sunrise to sunset in the sugarcane fields, bugs, and dampness, and heat. But those days were past and he refused to think of them. No matter what happened, he wouldn't suffer that fate again.

If they found him guilty, this time he would hang.

Nick paced away from the wall toward the small barred opening that served as a window. In winter it would be plugged with rags, but for now it let in air and gave him a glimpse of the world outside, the spires and towers of London, the gabled roofs and mullioned windows, rising above Newgate's walls.

He couldn't see Elizabeth's town house on Maddox Street, yet if he closed his eyes, he could pretend that he was there. That he was lying beside her in the big feather bed, that he was touching her, that she was smiling, leaning over to kiss him. He could imagine far more if he allowed himself, but it would only make the pain of her absence far worse.

Instead he stared through the bars of the window. In the courtyard below, prisoners in filthy, ragged garments, disease-ridden and half-starved, fought for scraps of food and bits of clothing to secret away for the cold months ahead.

He wondered where he would be then, still confined within these bleak walls, waiting for another trial, another appeal to his sentence, or outside in the world again.

Or if he would be dead.

A knock at the door drew him from his morbid thoughts. A guard turned the rusty iron lock and the door swung open on creaky hinges. "A visitor, milord."

A tall, weathered man with silver-tipped black hair stood in the opening. Nicholas smiled. "Elias—thank you for coming, my friend."

"'Tis good to see ye, Nick, me boy." The men shook hands, Elias trying to be cheerful. "I was 'ere yesterday, but they wouldn't let me in. I brung yer lady and yer sister. They said we couldn't see ye until ye were settled in."

Guilt clawed its way into his chest. "Elizabeth and Maggie were here?" God's breath, that was the last thing he wanted.

Elias shrugged. "There's no holdin' the two of 'em back, once their minds is set. Mad as hornets they were, but the guards said no women, leastwise not yet. Even money couldn't sway 'em. Just bein' obstinate, I suspect, throwin' their weight around."

"I'm glad they were turned away. I don't want them here." Especially not Elizabeth. Not yet. Not until he was ready.

"They'll come. There'll be no stoppin' em."

"I'll stop them. I'll tell the guards not to let them in. I'll—"

Elias gripped his shoulder. "They need to see ye, lad. 'Specially yer lady. She loves ye. She won't rest till she knows yer safe."

Nick's insides clenched. *She loves you.* Each time he heard the words, something tightened inside him. He didn't want her to love him—not now—not when the cost was so dear.

"I suppose you're right. Once they're reassured, I'll forbid them to come." Elias looked askance at that, but Nicholas ignored him. "I presume Elizabeth is somewhere safe?"

"Took 'em both to 'Is Grace's. Man's got an army of footmen, if 'e needed 'em—which, like as not, 'e wouldn't."

Nick felt the pull of a smile. The women were safe with Rand—that was certain. He was strong as an ox, a champion boxer at Oxford, and stubborn enough not to quit, even when he was down.

"In the past several days, I've had time to do some thinking. Elizabeth believes Oliver Hampton may be behind Rachael's murder. There is a chance she may be right."

Elias just nodded. "'Twould make an odd sort of sense."

"If it's true, then there must be a spy and it is one of the people I trusted, one of those who accompanied us to London: Edward Pendergass, Theo Swann, Mercy Brown, or Jackson Fremantle."

"It could be me, ye know."

Nick just smiled. "But we both know it isn't."

"Nay, lad, 'tisn't me. You're like a brother to me, Nick. Ye stood by me in prison, took a floggin' for me when I was too sick with the fever to survive it. A man don't forget a friend like that. I'd sooner cut me 'eart out than do aught to 'urt ye."

"What about the others? I consider all of them friends. It's hard to believe any of them would betray me."

"'Tis Jackson, I'm thinkin'. 'E were a friend of Theo's, come to ye lookin' for work, but 'e ain't really one of us. And 'e's got a weakness for the coin in a man's purse."

Nick nodded, having thought that same thing. "Jackson drove me to Rachael's. He knew I was going to see her again the following day. He could have told Bascomb. As a matter of fact, he could have done something to the wheel on the carriage. Perhaps the reason he pulled so far off the road was so that no one could verify my story."

"'Tis Jackson," Elias said coldly. "The bloody bastard's turned traitor. When I get me bleedin' 'ands on 'im, I'm gonna pound the life from 'is worthless 'ide."

Nick squeezed his friend's shoulder. "No, Elias—if we're right about this, the last thing we want is for Bascomb to know we're on to him."

Elias's mouth thinned in grudging agreement. "All right, we'll leave 'im be—for now. And don't ye worry about yer lady. Ye can trust she'll be safe with me."

"I know she will." Nick gripped his friend's hand a final time. Elias left the cell and the door slammed shut with a hollow ring. It was the echo of the years ahead, he thought, the echo of scandal and whispered accusation—even if he were lucky enough to escape the hangman.

Another day passed. Nick sank down on the hard wooden chair, ignoring the cold in the cell. Sir Reginald had sent a number of books, but his mind was not on reading. Instead, he stared up at the small barred window, yearning to feel the sunlight, missing Elizabeth, knowing he would miss her for as long as he lived.

In the last few solitary days of his confinement, he had faced a painful truth. The dream he'd had of marriage to Elizabeth was exactly that—a fantasy that could never be real.

Rachael's murder had destroyed whatever slim chance they'd had of being together. Ironic, he thought. By dying, she had freed him and at the same time shattered any chance he'd had of making a life with Elizabeth.

At least not the sort of life she deserved.

Nick rose and began to pace the cell, thinking about her,

knowing that even if he were acquitted, the scandal would remain. His conscience said he was destroying her life for his own selfish purpose. He wanted her. Needed her, he admitted. But now he was suspected of murder. He could no longer think of himself. He had to do what was best for Elizabeth.

What kind of a life would she have married to a man twice accused of murder? In truth, Elizabeth was lost to him now far more than she ever was before.

Rachael was probably laughing from the grave.

He glanced at his dismal surroundings and thought of the painful decision he had made. It was time to put his selfishness to an end, time to do what he should have done from the start. No matter how much it hurt to lose her, he was going to set her free and at the same time see her safe from Bascomb.

Nick dragged in a lungful of cold, musty air. He felt hollow inside, numb in a way he couldn't have imagined. *Let her go,* the voice inside him demanded as it had a dozen times.

This time he was determined to listen.

Elizabeth stood beneath a high brick wall of the garden at the rear of her town house. Unlike the flowers and shrubs at Ravenworth, these were slightly neglected, the gravel paths overgrown, the ivy gone wild and haphazardly climbing the worn red brick.

The place needed care, and since her arrival, she had begun its resurrection, trimming and replanting a little at a time, refusing to hire a gardener since the area was so small, more a high-walled cubicle that boxed her in than a place of escape, as the gardens were at Ravenworth Hall.

And yet it was the only refuge she had. With the papers full of Rachael's murder and the scandal of the earl and his mistress, she rarely left the house anymore. She saw only Maggie and Rand, her aunt, and the guards and servants who surrounded her.

Dear God, how she missed the freedom she had taken for

granted, the happy days before Oliver Hampton, before her parents had died, when her life had truly been her own.

Elizabeth sighed and glanced around. Pulling on a pair of old leather gloves, she brushed dirt and leaves from a rusty iron bench that sat next to the garden wall, then wearily sank down. She hadn't slept in the past three nights, not since the morning Maggie arrived with news of Nicholas's arrest, and her body ached with fatigue and the endless hours of worrying about him. Her head throbbed dully and a slight buzzing filled her ears. She was tired to the bone yet she couldn't stand another moment indoors.

She gazed toward the garden wall, saw Theo discreetly standing guard, felt a mutinous shot of rebellion. She was a prisoner in her very own home, a prisoner . . .

The thought died away, doused by a wave of guilt. Nicholas was the one in prison. Nicholas. How could she complain when it was he who suffered, he who had been so terribly wronged? An image of filthy stone passages and the stench of urine and unwashed bodies arose, so powerful that bile rose into her throat.

She had gone to the prison each day since Nicholas's arrest, seen the filth and the neglect, smelled the foul odors of disease, seen men chained together like animals, their wrists and ankles crusty with old dried blood. He was there yet they wouldn't let her see him. He was there and he was alone.

Elizabeth's eyes suddenly burned, but no tears came. She hadn't cried. She wished she could. Instead, her tears had frozen like a block of ice trapped painfully inside her. She hadn't cried because tears would be useless and because it would mean that there was a chance that Nicholas would hang.

She didn't want to believe it, fought it with every ounce of her will, but the effort had drained the last of her strength and she felt strangely askew, and so brittle she thought she might break at any moment.

She stared at the walls of the garden, thought of the ugly stone walls of Newgate prison, thought of Nicholas, and purpose arose from the ashes of her strength. She had to see him, rules or no. She had to find a way to help him.

Turning toward the house, she pulled off her gloves and tossed them down on the rusty iron bench.

"Elias!" she called out, knowing he would be somewhere near, her legs weak from fatigue, but her steps surprisingly strong.

He appeared in the doorway like a tall dark shadow. "Yes, miss?"

"I'll need you and Theo. We're going back to the prison— and this time they are going to let us in."

"But I thought—"

"That was before." She smiled with grim determination. "Today is another day and we shall be stopping on our journey, inviting a friend to join us." She lifted her skirt, stepping over the threshold into the house. "We'll be making a call on His Grace, the Duke of Beldon."

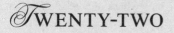WENTY-TWO

$\mathcal{N}$ick paced his cell. He had been there little more than a week, yet it seemed like a lifetime. He had forgotten how he hated the confinement, how he loathed the suffocating closeness of the damp stone walls even more than the filth and the fetid smells, the worry about disease, and the brutal treatment of the guards.

He had forgotten the loneliness, the hours that seemed to have no end.

He turned back again, heading toward the tiny barred window, his boot heels thudding on the rough plank floors, thudding, thudding, a hollow, empty sound that mirrored the way he felt inside. So far only Elias, Sir Reginald, Rand, and Sydney had been allowed inside his cell. It was Sydney's return he awaited.

The guards were bringing him up now. Nick could hear footsteps and several men's voices, echoing in the thick-walled corridor outside. A key grated in the rusty lock and the door swung open.

White hair neatly groomed, Sydney walked in, his features carefully schooled against whatever it was he was thinking.

"I've done as you asked," he said without preamble. "I like it no better now than I did then." His face looked grim as he removed his cloak, tossed it over the back of a rickety wooden chair.

"I take it you've been to see Tricklewood."

Sydney's thick white brows pulled together. He sank down on the hard wooden chair. "I saw him."

"Did you mention Elizabeth's dowry? Did you tell him it would be doubled should they wed? That is quite a sizable amount of money. Enough to keep him in style for a good many years."

His features tightened. "I mentioned it, but there was no need. The boy is in love with her. He has been eaten up with worry since the murder. He has read the papers, of course. He is appalled at the terrible things being written about her. If Elizabeth will agree, he'll marry her by special license as soon as it can be arranged."

Something sharp knifed into his chest. Jealousy, he knew, the thought of Elizabeth in David Endicott's bed. "He's a good man," he said gruffly. "He'll make her a very fine husband."

Sydney said nothing for the longest time. "I don't like this, Nicholas, not one bit. There is yet the chance you may be acquitted. The two of you could marry as you once planned."

"The odds of my acquittal are slender at best and you know it. Besides, even should I be released, the doubt would still remain. What kind of a life would Elizabeth have married to a convicted killer with the taint of a second murder hanging over his head?"

Sydney fell silent; Nick's words were heavy with the ring of truth. Shoving back his chair, he rose from the table and walked to the window. "How will you convince her to marry him?"

The pain in Nick's chest stabbed deeper. She would marry the viscount. He would see to it. He would do whatever it took to convince her. "Have no doubt, Sydney. Elizabeth will marry him—and soon."

"But surely—"

A knock at the door interrupted them. Swearing at the intrusion, Nick crossed to the heavy wooden door, heard the jangle of keys and the sound of the lock grating open. Rushing past Rand Clayton and a slightly overweight guard, Elizabeth entered the cell and flew straight into his arms.

"Nicholas—thank God." Unconsciously his arms tightened around her, pressing her close against his chest. She looked pale and shaken. Purple smudges darkened the skin beneath her eyes. A pang of guilt speared through him, and the ragged ache of regret.

"I've missed you," she whispered. "I've been so worried—and I've missed you so much." She closed her eyes, but tears squeezed past her lashes. She turned her face into his shoulder and held on to him with all of her strength.

Nick smoothed a hand over her dark auburn hair. He realized it was shaking. "It's all right, love. Please don't cry."

She looked up at him, her eyes bright with moisture. "I'm sorry. I didn't mean to." She scrubbed at the tears on her cheeks. "I haven't cried once. I told myself I wouldn't cry here."

He breathed in the scent of her hair, the soft rose of her perfume. "Sometimes it's good to cry." He forced himself to smile, used the pad of his thumb to wipe away a drop of wetness.

Elizabeth sniffed again, accepted the handkerchief he offered. "Are you all right?"

He wasn't all right. He felt as though the heavy gray walls were closing in, crushing him with their weight, squeezing the air from his lungs. Loneliness ate at him like a living, breathing thing. His heart was battered by thoughts of Elizabeth, of what he must do, his mind tormented with grief at losing her.

He forced another smile. "I'm fine. This may not be as grand as Ravenworth Hall, but it's really not so bad. Those poor devils below—now they have something to complain about." He glanced over her head to Rand, who simply shrugged his shoulders.

"She needed to come," his friend said. "She was beside herself with worry. She wasn't eating. She hasn't been able to sleep. I thought it would be better if she saw for herself that you were all right."

Her fingers rested lightly on his chest. Her touch seemed to burn straight into his heart.

"I can't stand it," she said, looking up at him. "I can't stand to think of you locked up in here. It isn't right that you should suffer like this again."

He caught a loose curl of fiery dark hair, tucked it gently behind an ear. Perhaps it was better it happened like this, with Rand and Sydney to take care of her. "I won't be here long. Soon all of this will be over and I'll be returning to Ravenworth Hall."

There was something in the way he said it, something Elizabeth picked up on, as he had known she would. "You? Do you not mean *we*?"

His false smile slid away. "No, Elizabeth. I mean *me*. Since I've been locked away in here, I've had time to do some thinking."

"Thinking?" A note of alarm rose into her voice. "What . . . what sort of thinking?"

Nick studied her face, saw the fatigue she fought to hide, and his heart squeezed hard inside him. He turned her a bit, allowing her to see the white-haired man who had come to his feet the moment she entered the cell.

"Sydney is here. We were just talking about you."

She mustered a smile, but it looked faint and grave. Blotting the last of her tears, she went over and kissed Sydney's cheek. "I'm sorry. It's just that I've been so worried. Is he really all right?"

"As good as can be expected, under the circumstances."

Nick walked toward them. "Sydney was just telling me that

he has recently spoken to a friend of yours—David Endicott.
Apparently Lord Tricklewood has been worried about you."

"The viscount has always been kind to me. I hope you will
tell him, Sydney, how much I appreciate his concern."

Nick moved closer. "Lord Tricklewood wishes to marry
you."

Her eyes swung to his face. She bit down on her bottom
lip. He noticed it had started to tremble. "I am betrothed to
another—or perhaps, my lord, you have forgotten."

It was suddenly hard to breathe. *How could he possibly
forget?* "I'm sorry, Elizabeth, but a marriage between us is
no longer possible."

"What . . . what are you talking about?"

"I am talking about being in prison. I am talking about a
trial, about the fact that I may hang."

"But you are innocent. You said yourself all of this would
soon be behind you."

Tension moved through his body. His features turned hard.
He reached out and gripped her shoulders. "Don't you see?
Even if I am acquitted, there will always be speculation. What
kind of life would you have? What kind of life would your
children have with a father twice accused of murder?"

Her eyes welled once more with tears. "They'll find the
man who did it! They'll know it wasn't you!"

He shook her. Hard. "Listen to me, dammit. Think of yourself for once. I care for you, Elizabeth—you know how much
I care. I asked you to marry me. I wanted a family. I wanted
you to give me sons. But I am not in love with you. I'm not
the kind of man for that. I don't even know what love is."

Elizabeth stared at him, tears streaming down her cheeks.
She glanced at Rand, whose jaw was clamped, then to Sydney. Something flickered in the older man's eyes, concern, or
perhaps it was pity. Nick's own eyes betrayed nothing of what
he was feeling inside. He felt as if he were dying.

"Perhaps his lordship is right," Sydney said gently. "There

comes a time when a person must look after his own wellbe-ing. Young Endicott is very much in love with you. He can protect you from Bascomb and he will make you a very fine husband. He'll be a good father for the children you will have."

Her eyes swung back to Nick's face. They were filled with so much anguish, so much pain, his insides twisted up inside him. He wanted to take back the words that had hurt her so badly. He knew that he could not.

"Is that . . . is that what you want, Nicholas? For me to marry David Endicott?"

Regret clawed its way into his chest. It was the very last thing he wanted. It was painful just to breathe. "Under the circumstances, yes—that is exactly what I want. I believe it would the best thing for both of us."

Her eyes held his for long, agonizing moments, then she looked away. "I will . . . I will consider what you have said, but at present—"

Nick gripped her shoulders, turned her to face him. "You have to marry him, Bess. Has it never occurred to you that even now you might be carrying my babe? What will you do if you discover that you are with child?"

Elizabeth swallowed hard. She looked suddenly pale and achingly vulnerable. His chest rose harshly. He hated him-self for what he was doing, yet he knew he had no choice.

"We don't . . . we don't know if that has occurred. There is no reason to believe it is so."

He gave her a mocking half-smile. "No reason? What do you call what happened in my bed the last time we were to-gether? If I remember correctly—"

"Nicholas! I beg you, please . . . I can't . . . I don't—" Her voice broke on the last. He fisted his hands to keep from reach-ing out, from dragging her into his arms. There was too much at stake. She had suffered enough already.

"I am merely reminding you there is every reason to be-lieve it could be so."

Her eyes locked with his, wounded eyes, dark with a soul-deep pain. "And if it were? You are saying you would want your child to be raised by another man?"

God, no. The thought made him sick to his stomach. "I would wish him to have a father. There is every chance that I will be dead."

"Don't say that!"

"I am only speaking the truth. Marry Tricklewood. Make a life for yourself that does not include me."

Her chin edged up, but the bleakness remained in her face. "If we . . . if I should discover that I am . . . that I carry your babe, there will still be time to decide what to do."

Nick turned away, pacing toward the tiny window, staring out but not really seeing. The pressure in his chest was excruciating. He returned to the place in front of her. "You know the way I feel. I want you to think of yourself, do what is best for you."

Elizabeth's trembling hand reached out to cup his cheek. "I love you, Nicholas. Whatever happens, that won't change. If you no longer want me, there is nothing I can do about that." The hand fell away, leaving a chill in its wake. "As for the rest, I will govern my own life as I see fit. I have managed to survive thus far. I will do so in the future."

The tightness in his chest fanned out, an ache, raw and intense. He didn't know exactly how it happened, but suddenly she was there in his arms. "You must think of yourself," he whispered, pressing her tightly against him. "You must go on with your life."

Tears slipped down her cheeks. Her arms slid around his neck and she pulled his mouth down to hers for a kiss. Her soft lips trembled and he could feel the wetness of her tears on his face. Nicholas kissed her back with every ounce of his soul, knowing it was the last time he would touch her. Knowing he had to let her go, that he had to send her away.

It was Elizabeth who ended the kiss. She swayed a bit unsteadily and Rand caught her arm. "Take care of yourself, my lord."

He glanced off in the distance. "And you, Bess. You take care of yourself as well."

"Yes . . ." she whispered. "I shall."

Several seconds passed. When he turned, he saw Elizabeth standing next to Sydney, her face turned into his shoulder. Together with Rand, they walked out of the room.

As soon as the door was closed, Nick sank down in the chair, his heart beating dully, a bitter ache throbbing beneath his breastbone. Something burned at the back of his eyes. *It's over,* he told himself. *You've done what you had to do.* Elizabeth would marry Endicott and she would be safe. In a few years, the scandal would be forgotten. Her youthful indiscretion with the Wicked Earl could be passed off as little more than gossip.

Whether he lived or died would not matter.

For once, you did the right thing, he told himself. He just wished it didn't hurt so damned badly.

Elizabeth sat alone in the drawing room of her town house. Her hands were so cold. Her skin was cool and clammy and nothing could warm her.

Nicholas didn't love her. He wanted her to marry another man. Even if he won his freedom, he didn't want her with him. Her chest ached. Her lungs burned. She felt as if a hole had been gouged in her heart.

It was dark inside the drawing room. The curtains were pulled, not a hint of sunlight crept in. She didn't want to see the sun. She didn't understand how there could possibly be any warmth on such a terrible day.

Oh, God, Nicholas. She thought of him, imagined his sinfully beautiful face, and wondered how she could have been such a fool. In truth, she had no one to blame but herself. She had known what he was like from the moment she had met him. A heartless rogue with little regard for the women he took to his bed. That he had been kind to her, that he had so very often been tender, didn't change his nature. He didn't love her. She should have known he never would.

Pain throbbed in her chest. Over and over the voice in her head repeated the words he had spoken in his cell. *I care for you Elizabeth, but I don't love you.* It hurt more every time she heard them. *I care for you, but I don't love you.*

He cared for her. He also cared for his beautiful horses, for Elias Moody and the convicts he had hired at Ravenworth Hall.

Had he also cared for Miriam Beechcroft? She imagined that in some small way he probably had.

Oh, God, oh, God, it hurt so badly. She had known the risk she was taking when she gave her heart to the Wicked Earl. She never could have guessed the awful, terrible grief she would feel to discover she had lost what small part of him that she had ever had.

Elizabeth leaned back against the sofa, giving in to a hot round of tears. She had instructed the servants not to disturb her and so far none of them had intruded. Aunt Sophie had taken leave to visit a friend in the country. She wouldn't be back for several days, and Elizabeth was glad.

She needed time to pull herself together, time to decide what course she should take. They could no longer stay in her town house—Nicholas's town house, she corrected—the place she had come to think of as their home.

Her throat constricted. She couldn't stay here, yet with Bascomb still a threat, she couldn't leave. Perhaps Nicholas was right and she should simply marry the viscount, get on with her life as best she could.

Elizabeth suffered a fresh jolt of pain. For now she didn't want to think about the future. She simply wanted to sit alone in the darkness and try to deal with her grief.

Oliver Hampton strode up the wide stone steps of his West End town house. In truth, it wasn't exactly his, or at least he didn't live there. He simply paid the rent. It was occupied by his mistress, an opera singer named Chartrice Mills, a saucy little chit of two and twenty with overblown aspirations. She wanted to sing center stage instead of being happy in the chorus.

He had seen her some months back, a girl with a pretty face and incredible auburn hair. She was slender and willowy, taller than average, with fair skin and a passable figure, even if her breasts were a bit too small.

After six months of having her in his bed, he still knew nothing about her and didn't really care. He rarely listened to her monotonous conversations, usually just walked in and dragged her off to bed. He had wooed her for one simple reason.

With her fair complexion, slender stature, and long dark auburn hair, she reminded him of Elizabeth Warring.

Oliver opened the door without knocking, climbed the stairs, and went into her bedchamber. Sitting on a small petit-point stool in front of the mirror, she gave a start at the sight of him appearing in her room so unexpectedly. Still, she came to her feet with a smile.

"My lord. You should have sent word. I would have been better prepared." She indicated her dishabille, that she was dressed simply in her chemise and stockings, her hair free of its pins, a loose cloud of burnished auburn around her narrow shoulders.

Oliver felt a tug at his groin. He had come for a purpose—the time had arrived to end the affair and he wanted it over and done. Still . . . she did look fetching sitting there half-naked.

She rose from the stool, the simple chemise molding to her slender curves. "You seem tense, my lord. Is something the matter?"

He smiled. "Nothing a go at you won't cure. Come here, my dear."

She flushed a bit. He liked that about her, that she hadn't

had many lovers. For a whore, she was relatively innocent—
just like Elizabeth. The thought made his mood a little darker,
but his shaft went stiff as a stick.

"I told you to come here."

"Yes, my lord."

She was surprisingly well trained. He had seen to that himself. It was amazing what a bit of discipline could do, a cuff
here and there, the back of his hand now and again. She hadn't
complained. She needed the money. She liked the trinkets he
brought, and he was more than generous. And there was always the promise he had made, that in time she would sing
at the center of the stage. She wanted to be a star and she believed he had the power to see it done.

Perhaps he did, but not for her.

She came to him as he demanded, pressed a soft kiss on
his lips. "My lord?"

He thought of Elizabeth, imagined her responding to his
commands, imagined her naked and standing in front of him.
"Remove your chemise."

She did so without complaint, allowing the soft embroidered fabric to pool at her feet. When she was left in only
her white silk stockings, her tiny nipples erect from the slight
chill in the room, he rested his hands on her shoulders and
urged her down, telling her without words what he wanted.

She complied, of course, opening the front of his breeches,
filling her hands with his stiff member, taking him into her
mouth. He imagined Elizabeth's warm lips caressing him, her
hands cupping his heated flesh. He imagined her obeying each
of his commands without question, and filled his hands with
thick auburn hair. Chartrice's clever little tongue darted out.
She used it to tease him, used her fingers to stroke him and
make him even harder than he was already.

Yes, he had trained her well, as he would train Elizabeth.

Her mouth opened wider, took more of him, and he knew
his release was near. He imagined Elizabeth on her knees
in front of him, imagined plunging himself between her

willing lips, and a hot climax rolled through him. He gripped the little whore's shoulders, hissed out a sound of pleasure, and swayed on unsteady legs as the final spasms of release subsided.

Chartrice simply smiled. Reaching for a towel, she wiped him clean of the remnants of his seed, tucked him back inside his breeches, and refastened the buttons. For a moment he said nothing, enjoying the satisfaction, the moments of contentment, the last vestiges of a memory that didn't really exist.

He straightened as she retrieved a thin silk robe and drew it over her slim white body. Smoothing a wrinkle from the front of his coat, he reached into the pocket of his waistcoat and retrieved a small bag of coins.

"Thank you, Chartrice, you did very well. I have no doubt your next protector will find you quite accomplished. He'll have me, of course, to thank for that. And you . . . you will have learned a few things that should make you a valuable commodity." He handed her the bag of coins.

She looked at them strangely. "What are these? What are you talking about?"

"I am bidding you farewell, Chartrice. 'Tis time for our affair to end. There is money enough in the pouch to see you through the next few months, until you are able to find another protector."

The girl stared down at the bag, then back into his face. "You came in here intending to get rid of me? You used me like a whore and now you wish to discard me?"

Oliver frowned. He didn't like that tone of voice. He had warned her of that before. "I told you, I no longer require your services. You are free to choose someone else."

Her auburn brows flared up. Anger heated her face to a mottled red. "Someone else? I don't want someone else. I want you to do the things you promised. You said you would make me famous. You said—"

"I know exactly what I said. Now I am saying something

altogether different, and I am warning you, m'dear, that you had better listen."

Instead she threw the bag of coins at him with all of her strength, the weighty pouch just clipping the side of his head. "You aren't getting rid of me that easy. You are going to do what you promised!"

His hands fisted. He stepped toward her. "I thought I taught you to obey your betters. I believed you had learned to do as you were told." He reached out and slapped her, sent her reeling toward the bed. "Apparently, you have not."

Her face went from rosy to pale. "Don't touch me. Leave me alone."

"You don't give orders here—I do." He reached for her, grabbed the front of her robe and jerked her toward him, slapped her hard, once, twice, hit her again and watched the blood spring into the corner of her mouth. With a grunt of satisfaction, he tossed her backward onto the bed.

"All right, you win," she whispered. "Don't hurt me anymore. Just leave the money and go."

But it was too late. The anger pumping through him had aroused him again and he had decided to have her one last time. He gripped her wrist and twisted it up behind her, rolled her over and forced her facedown on the bed. "I thought you were smarter than this, my dear."

She whimpered, tried to speak, but he wrenched the arm higher and the pain forced her into a trembling silence. With his free hand, he unbuttoned his breeches and freed himself, spread her legs with his knee. He fondled her, felt her tightening against his intrusion, and drove himself roughly inside her. She whimpered again and he knew he was hurting her. Somehow that added to the pleasure.

"Little fool," he taunted, grunting over her, ramming into her again and again. "When the next man tells you something, you will know enough to do as he says." He surged deeply once more, allowed his release to come, then withdrew and casually rebuttoned his breeches.

He could hear her weeping as he crossed the room toward the door. "I want you gone by tomorrow." With a last glance over his shoulder at the pitiful lump she made on the bed, he turned and walked away, stopping only long enough to pluck up the pouch of coins and tuck it back into his waistcoat.

Elizabeth retired to her bedchamber early. Aunt Sophie would be home tonight and she wasn't ready to face her. She had no idea what she would say to her when she did.

After hours of tossing and turning, she finally fell asleep, only to awaken in the hours before dawn. Unconsciously, she reached toward the place beside her, searching for Nicholas, desperate to feel his warmth. The cold sheet was empty, bringing her brutally awake, reminding her he was gone, that he would never sleep beside her again.

Her throat closed up and she started to cry, deep wracking sobs that tore at her heart and shook her slender frame. She cried for what seemed hours, until her throat hurt and tears soaked her pillow.

In the darkness, it took a moment to realize her aunt had come into the room and was sitting in the chair beside the bed.

"What is it, child? It isn't like you to cry this way. What terrible thing has happened while I have been gone?"

Elizabeth sat up slowly, dragging in a painful breath of air. Leaning over, she went into her aunt's pudgy arms. "Oh, Aunt Sophie—I just want to die." For the next few minutes, it was as though her heart had been lanced wide open. All of the hurt spilled out, all of the anger and the sadness.

"He doesn't love me, Aunt Sophie. He doesn't want me anymore. Oh, God, I should have known this would happen."

A plump hand gently patted her back. "He is a hard man, your Nicholas. And very brave, I think."

"I hate him."

"You love him."

Her throat constricted. "Yes. I love him so much."

Her aunt's hand smoothed back her hair. "So your Nicholas says he doesn't love you, that you should marry someone else. For a man who cares so little, it was quite a noble thing for him to do."

Elizabeth straightened, sniffed in a shaky breath. "Noble? What do you mean?"

"I mean that Lord Ravenworth is facing the gallows. His friends are few and he is in dire need of the ones he has left. He is locked behind prison bars yet he has driven away the only woman who can give him comfort. He has done it so that you will be free of the scandal, so that you will be spared the pain he believes he will bring you if you stand at his side."

She only shook her head. "He doesn't love me. He told me he doesn't even know what love is."

Aunt Sophie brushed tears from Elizabeth's cheeks. "Perhaps that is the problem. Perhaps Lord Ravenworth is unable to recognize love as among the things he is feeling."

Her heart ached. She sniffed, blew her nose on the handkerchief her aunt gave her. "What are you saying, Aunt Sophie?"

"I am merely pointing out that before all this occurred, his lordship went to great extremes to offer you the protection of his name. He gave up his priceless family jewels. He was willing to suffer the stigma of divorce. He did those things for you, my dear. He made grave sacrifices—all of them for you. Perhaps he is making such a sacrifice again."

Something started throbbing, burning inside her chest. It was hope this time, desperate, aching hope. "You don't . . . you don't really believe he would lie about such a thing?"

"I believe he is trying to protect you. For a man like his lordship, love may be a difficult thing. It may take time for him to realize what exactly he is feeling. Whatever it is, his concern for you runs deep, and I do not believe he wishes you to marry anyone else but him."

Elizabeth blinked and fresh tears rolled down her cheeks. Was it possible? And yet it would be so like him. He believed himself so hard, so unfeeling, when the opposite was true.

"I don't want to marry David Endicott."

"Then I suggest you find a way to help free his lordship so that the two of you might have a chance to work things out."

Hope mushroomed, began to sweep through her. Her heart started pounding, no longer dull and hurting, but beating with a new well of strength. Nicholas had always cared for her. He had always done his best to protect her. Was it possible he loved her? There was no way to know for certain, yet what if it were true?

Elizabeth dragged in a shaky breath. She loved him. She would cling to the hope for as long as she dared. She wouldn't give up until she knew for certain what was true.

"You are right, Aunt Sophie. Nicholas needs my help. That is exactly what I must do." Drawing back the covers, she got up from the bed. Dawn had not yet grayed the windows. The household was still abed, and yet she was too keyed up to sleep.

"I need to think, Aunt Sophie. I've got to work this out."

"That is a very good notion. In the meantime, I shall go down to the kitchen, light the stove, and make us a pot of tea."

A feeling of gratitude moved through her. Elizabeth smiled at her aunt and blotted the last of her tears. Aunt Sophie was always there when she needed her. She always had been. Turning, Elizabeth reached for her wrapper, her mind already spinning, churning over the words Nicholas had said. Mostly she was remembering the look on his face when he said them, the anguish he had worked so hard to hide. There was pain there, too. At the time, she thought she had imagined it.

It was there, she was now certain. Aunt Sophie was correct. Nicholas might not love her, not yet. But he cared for her greatly and he needed her.

She wasn't about to abandon him.

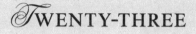WENTY-THREE

$\mathcal{E}$lizabeth sat on the sofa in the drawing room, reading the latest edition of the *London Chronicle*. Her hands shook as she scanned the words and the letters began to blur.

She squeezed her eyes closed and took a steadying breath, resting the paper back on top of the stack of newsprint that sat in front of her. The *Public Advertiser,* the *Whitehall Evening Post,* the *Daily Gazetteer*—even the *North Briton*—all were full of the brutal murder of the Countess of Ravenworth and all were slanted the same—the killer was none other than the lady's husband—former convicted murderer Nicholas Warring.

She wiped away a trace of wetness, hoping her aunt hadn't noticed. Lately, it seemed, she had been crying far too often.

"They're going to hang him, Aunt Sophie. They're going to find him guilty on their skimpy bit of evidence and they are going to hang him."

Her aunt's plump hand reached out to cover hers where it trembled slightly in her lap. "You mustn't lose hope, my dear. You can't be certain what will happen. Sir Reginald holds a great deal of hope, and you have yet to hear from Mr. Moody and Mr. Swann. Perhaps in their foray last night they found something that might be useful."

She had asked for their help two nights ago and, as she had known they would, they had agreed.

"We have to find out who killed Rachael Warring," she had told them as they enjoyed a glass of Nick's expensive French brandy she had insisted they drink. "Most likely it is Oliver Hampton or the Viscount Kendall. If it is, he is very likely in possession of the Ravenworth rubies."

"Aye," Elias said. "Whatever blighter took 'em must be the one what kilt 'er."

Theo grinned. "If you're askin' me to have a look-see in the gentlemen's town houses, I'll be more than happy to oblige. Been a while since I used me skills, but 'tisn't somethin' a man forgets."

"It's dangerous. If they catch you, you'll wind up in prison along with Nick. I wouldn't ask if I could think of any other way."

"Ye mustn't worry," Elias said. "For a time, me and Theo was the best there was—even better than Light-fingered Jack. We only made the one mistake. Cost us seven years, but we learnt our lesson. Wouldn't be thievin' again if it weren't for our Nick."

Our Nick. They had done it for Nicholas, risked themselves and still turned up nothing.

Elizabeth drew in a shuddering breath and turned back to her aunt. "They searched both men's houses but they didn't find a thing. At least not anything that could help prove Nicholas's innocence."

Aunt Sophie wrapped the last piece of string she had collected around the thick ball in her lap and set it away. "Are they certain they overlooked nothing?"

"They were able to open the safe in Lord Bascomb's town house. They found jewelry and a great deal of money, but the rubies weren't there. Nothing at Lord Kendall's, either."

Elizabeth's hands dug into her skirt. "I know it's Bascomb. In my heart, I know it is he." She stood up from the sofa, walked over to the hearth and stared down into the flames, her mind turning to thoughts of Nicholas. *I care for you, but I don't love you. Marry Endicott.* Though she tried to convince herself he hadn't really meant what he had said, there was no way to be certain. An ember hissed against the grate. The sound made her shiver.

"Bascomb has done this to get Nicholas out of the way," she said, "and to avenge the death of his brother."

"I vow I have grown to hate that man," Sophie said.

"He is obsessed with power, determined to have anything that is forbidden him."

Aunt Sophie frowned. "Surely there is something we can do."

A light knock sounded and Elizabeth marched toward the drawing room doors. "There is something we can do— something we must do—if we are to keep Lord Ravenworth from hanging." She slid open the heavy wooden panels and Elias and Theo walked in.

"Evenin', miss."

She smiled, nervous yet filled with determination. "Thank you both for coming. As a matter of fact, thank you for risking yourselves as you have these past two nights, even if it did no good."

"Nick would 'ave done the same," Elias said. "I owe 'im me life and I ain't likely to forget it."

"He give me a job when no one else would," Theo added. "I'd be back to thievin' if it hadn't been for him."

Another voice sounded from behind them, a woman's voice, clear and strong. "Our Nick, 'e took me and the others in, give us all a 'ome. We'd do anything to 'elp 'im."

It appeared that Mercy Brown had also arrived in the drawing room. It heartened her, the loyalty of Nicholas's friends. She wondered if he still counted her among them.

She motioned to Elias, who firmly closed the door. "All

right, then." Crossing to the sofa, she reached down to the table and picked up one of the papers. "I know none of you can read, so I'll tell you what these say. They say that the Earl of Ravenworth has murdered his wife. They state it as if it is fact. They encourage that belief because it sells papers. Because it is in print, the public will believe it, too. Lord Ravenworth will be tried in the House of Lords, and he'll be convicted. His peers will believe he is guilty, just like everyone else."

"What about that fancy barrister?" Mercy asked. "Why can't 'e do somethin' to 'elp?"

"I'm sure Sir Reginald is doing his best. But the fact remains the evidence is completely against Lord Ravenworth. The public believes he is guilty. There isn't the slightest doubt that Nicholas will hang." She forced herself to say it out loud, though it made her stomach roll.

Silence fell over the room. Elizabeth searched each downcast face. The only person notably missing was Lady Margaret. Maggie wasn't up to this. She was barely able to cope with the gossip. What Elizabeth had in mind was going to make the gossip far worse, but there was no other choice—not if Nicholas were to live.

"Ye brung us 'ere for a reason." Elias's voice broke into the silence. "Get to it."

Elizabeth took a calming breath, searching for just the right words. "The way I see it there is only one way to save Nick. We have to find the real killer and prove Lord Ravenworth's innocence, or Nicholas must flee the country. Nick hates being in prison. I don't think he'll allow Sir Reginald to delay the trial. That means—"

"You're sayin' we ain't got much time," Elias cut in.

"I'm saying the trial may start as early as next week. Once it begins, they'll tighten security around Nick's cell. There'll be no way for him to escape."

Theo's blond head came up. "Escape? Are ye sayin' what I think ye are, miss?"

Elizabeth steeled herself. It was asking so much and yet she believed it was the only chance Nicholas had. "I'm saying we have to get his lordship out of Newgate prison."

The group fell silent. Aunt Sophie fanned herself with her fat ball of string.

Theo was frowning. His eyes fixed on her face. "I been there, miss. Gettin' outta a place like that won't be easy."

"No, it won't. But I have a plan I think might work. The problem is I'll need your help."

Elias's grin was slow in coming, but in time it bloomed full force. "The lass's right. We gotta bust 'im outta there. Shoulda' thought of it meself."

Theo laughed. "Right ye are, Elias. Count me in."

"And me," Mercy said. "'E'll need a place to stay once ye 'ave 'im safe. I've a cousin what's got 'imself a tavern right 'ere in the city. We can 'ide 'im right under their noses."

Hope swelled inside her. Elizabeth felt a pang of affection for the small, loyal group of Nicholas's friends. "Thank you. You'll never know how much I appreciate your help."

She wondered what Nicholas would say when they appeared inside his cell. Her heart squeezed to think what he might do when he saw her. What if he truly wanted her to marry someone else? What if he had tired of her as he had a dozen other women? What if the simple fact was he wanted her gone from his life as he had said?

Elizabeth forced the painful thoughts away. In truth, it didn't really matter. She loved Nicholas Warring and she meant to help him. The rest would be up to him.

Lying on the corn-husk mattress in his cell, Nick stared up at the heavy oak planks that formed the floor of the cell above him. It was early in the evening, barely dark outside. Yet he was so very tired. He slept only a few short hours each night. The relief of blessed unconsciousness, of a deep relaxing slumber, remained elusive as it did now.

Instead, he stared at the ceiling, feeling the weight of the stones closing in, the unbearable loneliness pressing into his chest, wearing at his soul.

He shifted on the pallet, trying in vain to get comfortable, thinking of Elizabeth, missing her with each beat of his heart. He remembered the peaceful days they had shared in the garden, the moments of laughter, the nights of incredible passion. If he closed his eyes, he could imagine the taste of her lips, the fragrance of her hair, the smoothness of her skin. He remembered the glint of mischief that sometimes entered her eyes and wished he could coax that look from her again.

Instead, he lay on his cold, hard pallet, aching for her, knowing he might never see her again, and cursing himself for a fool.

He should have known this would happen. He should have known he'd be blamed for Rachael's murder. His last bitter taste of English justice had lasted seven long years. The instant he had learned of his wife's death, he should have known he would be the one to pay—whether he was guilty or not.

He should have guessed this would happen—and he should have run.

Nick closed his eyes, fighting to overcome the feeling of hopeless that swept over him, the crushing sense of despair. He was a rich man, his money well protected. He could have left England at the first sign of trouble. He could have taken Elizabeth with him, married her, and started a new life somewhere else. Instead he had waited, succumbing to his resurrected sense of honor, believing his name would be cleared.

His fantasy had cost him Elizabeth. She was lost to him forever—pushed by his own machinations into the arms of another man. In truth it didn't matter if they hanged him. He no longer cared if he lived or died.

Nick leaned his head against the wall, ignoring the feel of the hard, rough stone, the cold that seeped into his bones. Weariness invaded him, made him lethargic. His need for Elizabeth grew like a living thing, blossoming inside him. *Elizabeth.* He wondered where she was. He wondered if she

ached for him as he ached for her, or if his callous treatment
had turned her love to hate.

He wondered if she was with David Endicott, and prayed
that wherever she was she was safe.

Two days passed before the plan was actually completed. Elizabeth's original idea still formed the core, but parts of it had
been discarded, plucked full of holes by Elias and the others, who'd had far more experience in places like Newgate
Prison.

One detail remained—which of them would stay behind
in the cell, allowing Nicholas to take that person's place and
escape.

"I tell you it should be me," Elizabeth argued. "If he's
dressed as a woman, they'll never suspect it is he."

"That's right," Elias agreed, "and they won't believe for a
minute ye didn't 'elp 'im escape. They'll lock ye up in Nick's
place and ye won't be gettin' out."

"Well, we certainly can't leave you or Theo behind and
we can't leave Mercy there, either. You've all been arrested
before—besides, you've your own parts to play."

A heavy sigh whispered into the room, and all four heads
swiveled toward the sound. "Well, then, I suspect that leaves
only me." Aunt Sophie hauled herself up from the sofa. "They
will certainly not suspect that I am involved in planning his
lordship's escape—I'm nothing but a dotty old lady. Lord Ravenworth may look a bit silly, posing as an overweight old
woman, but aside from that, 'tis the only solution that makes
any sense to me."

Elizabeth stared in stunned disbelief. She had debated
whether to tell her aunt their plans but she trusted Aunt Sophie, and she thought, since the attempt would undoubtedly
be dangerous, it was only fair her closest relative know what
was going to occur.

This, however, she had not expected. "I appreciate your
offer of assistance, Aunt Sophie—we all do. It is a very

courageous thing for you to do. Unfortunately, I couldn't possibly allow you to help us. If something went wrong, I would never forgive myself."

Elizabeth glanced at Elias, looking for agreement, but his face remained carefully blank. She looked at Theo, who seemed to be digesting the notion, then at Mercy, whose lips curved into a smile.

"'Twould work," Mercy said. "They'd never believe Mrs. Crabbe would be part of somethin' like this."

Elizabeth clamped down on her fear. "But we can't possibly involve my aunt in this! What if something went wrong? What if—"

"If something goes wrong," Aunt Sophie broke in, "we shall all of us be in a great deal of trouble. Instead, we shall simply have to make certain that it does not."

"God's eyes," Theo said. "I'm beginnin' to believe we can do it."

"Of course we can," Mercy said. "And far better if Mrs. Crabbe is willing to 'elp."

"Then it's settled." Aunt Sophie's round face lit with satisfaction. Elizabeth wasn't quite certain how she had been so easily maneuvered but it was obvious she had been.

"Do we send 'is lordship word?" Mercy asked.

Elizabeth pondered the notion. On the surface it would seem the logical course. Instead she shook her head. "If we do, there is every chance Nicholas will try to stop us. Once we are there, he'll have no choice but to come with us or jeopardize all of our lives."

"So be it," Elias said, a determined glint in his eyes.

"So be it," the rest of them said, nearly in unison. Elizabeth hoped they worked half so well together when they broke into the prison.

Maggie sat alone in front of the fire in the drawing room of her brother's town house. The crackle of embers cut through the silence in the house. Summer had waned. A chill wind swept down from the cold North Sea and a slight fog had begun to creep in. The polished wooden floor creaked in the hall.

Pendergass, no doubt. The butler was the only member of the household still up at this hour of the night. Maggie sighed and leaned back in her chair. It was so empty in the house without Nick. So empty. And she felt so alone.

Maggie picked up the book she had been trying to read, *Fugitive of the Forest,* but the pages seemed to blur and she found herself rereading the words. Through the walls of the town house next door, the faint sound of music drifted in. A small soirée was in progress. Maggie, of course, had not been invited. She would never be invited into the world of the ton again.

She sighed again, fighting a painful swell of emotion. She hadn't thought she would miss it—the crowds and the pretty clothes, the flattery and the attention—but she had been wrong. The laughter and the dancing, the music and gaiety, had nurtured something long closed up inside her. Being out in the world, she had begun to blossom, to experience life for the very first time.

And there was something more, something she had refused to admit. She had fallen in love with Andrew Sutton. He was handsome and he had been charming, but it was more than that. There was something about him, a solidness she could count on. An honesty she had thought that she could trust.

She had been wrong, of course. Andrew had disappeared from her life at the first sign of scandal, disappeared just like all her other fair-weather friends, and now that he was gone, she'd discovered how much their time together had meant. She had wanted to know more of him, to uncover the depth of her feelings, to explore the possibilities of a future together.

She would never have the chance. Not now. Andrew's feelings had been as shallow as the others' and the fact made a soft ache throb in her heart.

A shadow appeared at the door to the drawing room. "My

lady?" Pendergass stood in the opening. "I am sorry to bother you at this late hour, but there is a gentleman to see you. I told him it was entirely inappropriate at this time of night, but—"

"But I told him it was urgent," said the handsome man who appeared beside him. "I told him I would not leave until I saw you."

The blood drained from her cheeks. Andrew Sutton stood in the doorway. Andrew had come. Her heart strained, started beating with frantic emotion. It was ridiculous, insane, that one glimpse of him should make her feel this way.

She dragged in a breath, battled for composure, turned and started walking toward the fire.

"I am surprised to see you, my lord, considering the taint your reputation may suffer at these few moments in my presence. Why is it you have come?"

His footsteps were muffled as he approached her from behind. She felt his hands on her shoulders, turning her to face him. The light touch made her tremble. She felt hurt and betrayed, yet her pulse raced at the sight of him.

"I know what you must think, what you must surely believe, but I have come to tell you it isn't the truth. I didn't know a thing about any of this—the murder—the scandal. The day before the countess was killed, I left the country. I didn't discover what had happened until my return this afternoon."

She looked up at him, into those arresting brown eyes. "My brother did not kill Rachael Warring. He is innocent. You probably don't believe that, but it is the truth."

"I am sorry for Nick. I pray that indeed he is innocent of the crime, but that is not why I am here."

She swallowed hard, tried to look away, but his gaze seemed to hold her immobile. "Why, then? Why did you come? What is it you want?"

His features softened. His eyes ran gently over her face. She remembered the night he had kissed her at Vauxhall Gardens.

"I came because of you, Lady Margaret. I've read the papers. I've heard the gossip, the insinuations. They've dredged up the past, and you as well as your brother are being made to suffer. I can only imagine what a nightmare you must be living."

She glanced away, a thick lump rising in her throat. "The scandal has not been pleasant, but I suppose I shall survive."

He lifted her chin with his fingers. "Will you, Margaret? Or will it break you, as it nearly did before?"

She didn't reply. She didn't know the answer. Instead her eyes filled with tears. His hand felt gentle as he brushed the wetness from her cheeks with the tip of a finger.

"I was a fool to leave you. I did it on purpose, you know. I had business on the Continent. I thought that a few weeks away would give me a chance to think things through, to see if what I felt for you was genuine. I didn't want to make a mistake."

Her heart squeezed. What was he saying? That he cared for her in some way? "You left because of me? I'm afraid I don't understand."

"Such an innocent. I left because I was falling in love with you. The moment I saw you, I wanted you. Everywhere you went, I watched you. I heard you laugh and I wanted to kiss you. I saw you smile and I wanted that smile to belong only to me. I wanted to make love to you, but it was more than that. What I felt went deeper than desire, and it frightened me to death. I left to sort things out. I regret now that I did. If I had stayed, you wouldn't have had to suffer the way you have."

She was trying to comprehend, trying to listen to his words over the fierce pounding of her heart. "Your staying wouldn't have changed things. The countess would still be dead and the scandal would be the same."

"If I had stayed, they wouldn't have dared to malign you as they have. I could have offered you my protection, Margaret, as I have come to do. I am asking you to marry me."

Maggie bit down on her bottom lip. The world seemed to tilt crazily. Stumbling away from him, she sank down on the sofa, her legs suddenly too weak to hold her. Andrew knelt in front of her, reached up and took her hand.

"I know you were not expecting this. If there were time, I would court you as I should. But there isn't time, Maggie. I can only hope that the days we've been apart have allowed you to examine your own feelings. If you care for me half as much as I care for you, I pray you will accept my offer of marriage."

Maggie wet her trembling lips. It was all so confusing, so unexpected. She blinked back a fresh film of tears. "I thought you felt nothing at all for me. I thought that the gossip had driven you away."

"The gossip—I don't give a damn what the scandalmongers say. I'm in love with you, Maggie. I want you to be my wife."

Her heart squeezed inside her. She looked into his strong, handsome face, and the uncertainty began to melt away. She was in love with him. She had known it for some time, perhaps since the moment he had asked her to dance at the costume ball. She had tried to deny it, to tell herself it wasn't so, but the truth was there in her heart. She loved him, deeply and sincerely, and far more than she had allowed herself to believe.

And because she did, she would have to refuse him.

Fresh tears burned. Her throat closed up, ached so badly it was hard to speak. "I can't marry you, Andrew. Forgive me, but I simply cannot."

Andrew stiffened, coming to his feet, the muscles in his shoulders rigid beneath his perfectly tailored dark brown coat. "Then I was wrong. I thought you had feelings for me. I thought . . ."

Maggie watched the set of his jaw and wildly shook her head, more miserable than she had ever been before. She stood up from the sofa. "No, my lord, you don't understand. I love you, Andrew. I realized that in the days you were gone. But I am not the woman you believe me to be and I love you too much to ever deceive you."

He scowled, paced away from her, then returned. With his thick brown hair and intense brown eyes, his hard, sculpted jaw, and patrician nose, he was incredibly handsome. There was power in each of his movements, purpose and determination. He was, in every way, the Marquess of Trent.

"Now it is I who do not understand."

"I can't marry you. The scandal in my past makes marriage to you or anyone else impossible for me now."

He made a rude sound in his throat. "I know all about 'the scandal in your past' and I don't give a fig about it."

Her chin went up but inside her heart was breaking. "You know? What exactly, my lord, do you think you know?"

"I know that you were young and innocent. I know your brother killed Stephen Hampton because he was a married man who attempted to seduce you. If you had been my sister, I might have done the same thing myself."

"My brother killed Lord Stephen in self-defense. Oliver Hampton covered up the truth. But Nicholas didn't kill him because he *tried* to seduce me. Stephen managed very well to accomplish the task. Even that was not the cause of his death. Nick killed him because when I went to Stephen about the child I carried, he beat me so badly I lost the babe."

The color drained from Andrew's face, and in that moment she wished with all her heart that she had already returned to the convent. She watched the way his hands shook, then fisted, the way his mouth went thin and a muscle jerked in his cheek, and knew in that moment that she *would* go back. Without Andrew Sutton, there was nothing left for her in the world outside.

Now that she had discovered what it was she really wanted, she had also learned she could not have it.

She swallowed past the lump in her throat, squared her shoulders, and walked toward the door. "Thank you for coming, my lord. Your kindness is appreciated and will not be forgotten." She fought not to cry, but a tear rolled down her cheek. "Good-bye . . . Andrew." She had to say his name one last time, to feel the warmth of it on her tongue. She vowed she wouldn't allow herself to say it ever again.

His gaze found hers and did not move away. "I am glad your brother killed him. If Hampton were still living, I would kill him myself."

Maggie said nothing. There was nothing left to say. She stared at him, memorizing each of his features, her heart aching, tearing itself in two. She thought he would turn and walk away, that she would never see his handsome face again. Instead he reached out to her, cupped her cheek in his hand.

"Do you think so little of me, Maggie? Do you believe I would value the maidenhead of your youth above the woman that you have become?" He bent and brushed her mouth with a feather-soft kiss. "I don't give a damn what happened nine years ago. I love you, Margaret Warring, and if you will have me, there is nothing I want more in this world than to make you my wife."

Tears spilled over, traced a path down her cheeks. "Andrew . . ." She didn't recall the moment she went into his arms, only found herself pressed against him, clinging to his neck and absorbing his strength. She was shaking all over. A faint tremor ran through Andrew's solid frame as well.

"I love you," she whispered. "I didn't know exactly how much till I saw you walk through that door. I love you, and if you are sure that is what you want, I would be honored to be your wife."

His arms tightened around her. He buried his face in her hair. "We'll be married by special license as soon as I can arrange it. Once we are wed, you'll be safe from the gossip."

She looked up at him, her heart filled with love. "Andrew, are you certain?"

He bent his head and kissed her. "More certain every moment. It's what I want and I believe it is what your brother would want as well."

It was true. Nick had wanted her to wed and he would surely approve her choice of husband. Her brother would be grateful that her future was secure and she was protected. She tightened her hold around Andrew's neck, feeling safe as she hadn't since she had left the convent.

A pang of guilt slid through her. She was safe, but what of Nick and Elizabeth? She only wished her brother was safe as well.

$\mathscr{T}$WENTY-FOUR

$\mathscr{I}$t was early evening. Darkness had just settled in, denser, more encompassing, since there was no moon above the city. A pale fog crept through the mist-slick cobbled streets outside the prison. It would thicken as the night wore on, helping to mask their way.

Pulling her cloak more closely around her, Elizabeth walked silently beside Aunt Sophie, wearing a smile of reassurance she didn't really feel. She had to help Nicholas escape—of that she had no doubt. Yet her heart squeezed to think what he might say.

I care for you, but I'm not in love with you. She forced the words away, forced away the pain that went with them. Clasping her aunt's pudgy hand, she crossed the high, walled courtyard of the prison, Elias following in their wake.

They had bribed the guards to let them in, not a difficult task since visitors were often allowed and the earl's mistress, an aging fat woman, and Ravenworth's valet hardly posed a threat.

And there were other visitors in the prison. The hour wasn't late and any number of people milled about, the inmates' wives and children, vendors hawking their wares to the slight few with coin enough to buy them. Elizabeth was counting on the hustle and bustle around them to serve as a distraction.

She steeled herself as the small group entered a long stone wing of the prison, the master's side, where those with money enough could serve their term in some minor amount of comfort. In silence, they climbed two flights of stairs and passed down a dank, dimly lit passage toward the cell at the end that belonged to the Earl of Ravenworth.

Elizabeth shivered at the dampness that seeped through her clothes, pressed a handkerchief over her nose against the fetid smell that clung to the walls. Her heart ached to think of Nicholas locked up in here, cold and alone, and her determination grew to see him freed of his terrible surroundings. No matter what feelings he held for her, he didn't deserve to be locked up in here. He deserved to be free, and once he was, he'd be able to leave the country.

Emotion made a lump rise in her throat. Nicholas would leave and most likely she would not be going with him.

The guard urged them on. "'Urry up, now—don't be dawdlin'." The beefy man swaggered ahead of them, his sword clanking against his boots, the sound of his footsteps a harsh echo in the shadowy darkness.

He turned when he reached the heavy wooden door, set his lantern down on the filthy plank floor, and inserted the big metal key.

He leered at Elizabeth. "Are ye sure ye want these other two beggars in there with ye, gel? 'Tis certain his bloody lordship would rather tup ye than talk to ye, whatever 'tis ye've got to say."

Elias stiffened beside her, but Elizabeth caught his arm. "Just let us in, please."

He gave her a long, lecherous perusal that sent a shiver running down her spine. "As ye wish." The key turned in the lock and a thin blade of light from inside the cell sliced into the passage. Through the widening crack in the door, she could see Nicholas approaching, his face drawn and haggard, and a fierce stab of pity knifed into her heart.

"Elizabeth! For God's sake, what are you doing here?"

She forced herself to smile, to appear as if things were completely normal. That he hadn't wanted her to marry someone else.

"I needed to see you, that is all. I convinced my aunt and Elias to accompany me. It's important. Please don't be angry." She glanced toward the guard, who was smirking.

"Be back at half past," he said as he closed the door. "Ye want to stay longer, it'll cost ye more." He chuckled lewdly. "Ye don't have money, there's other ways ye can pay."

Nicholas's jaw went tight. He started to say something to the guard, but Elizabeth raised a finger to her lips and he fell silent. The beefy man's footsteps fell away down the passage, and she turned to look at Nicholas. For a moment his features looked taut. Then whatever displeasure he felt at her presence seemed to slowly drain away.

His eyes clung to hers, ran over her from head to foot, then returned to her face. There was something dark in their depths, something fierce and painfully disturbing.

He drew himself up, turned away. "What has happened? Why have you come?"

It took all of her will not to go to him, not to beg him to hold her again. *Tell me you still want me,* she silently pleaded. But she didn't say the words.

"They're going to hang you, Nicholas. You know it and so do I. We aren't going to let that happen." Turning, she pulled several tightly folded pillowcases from the deep pockets of her cloak and handed them to the man beside her. "Elias?"

"Right ye are, miss." Nicholas looked grim, but Elias merely drew out the long slender blade concealed in his boot and walked over to the corn-husk mattress in the corner.

"What the devil . . . ?" Nicholas watched him split open

the mattress and begin to fill the pillowcases with the dry, rustling husks.

Elizabeth turned to the woman beside her. "Aunt Sophie?" But already her aunt was busily removing her cloak and draping it over a chair.

Nicholas glanced from one of them to the other. "Would someone mind telling me what exactly is going on?"

Elizabeth pasted on an airy smile. "'Tis quite simple, my lord." She began unfastening the buttons at the back of Aunt Sophie's gown and Nicholas was forced to turn his back as she lifted the fabric carefully over her aunt's gray-haired head. "We're helping you escape."

"What!" He spun to face her, undaunted by the sight of Sophie Crabbe's bulky frame in a long cotton chemise and thin white stockings.

"There isn't time to protest." Elizabeth spun him back around. "We have a plan that will work if you will simply do as we say."

He turned to her once more. "Are you mad? Have you all gone completely insane? You can't possibly do this—if they catch you trying to help me escape, they'll throw the lot of you in here right along with me."

This time her smile was sincere. "Then you had better cooperate so that doesn't happen." She accepted the frayed woolen blanket Elias had plucked from Nicholas's pallet and draped it around her aunt's thick shoulders.

Nicholas aimed his appeal in that direction. "Aunt Sophie—surely you have enough sense to see how dangerous this is. The whole idea is crazy."

"We haven't much time, my lord," her aunt simply said. "'Twould be better for us all if you stopped talking and let Elias strap those sacks around your waist."

"But you can't possibly—" He whirled once more toward Elizabeth. "What about Maggie? If you do this—"

"Your sister has someone else to look after her. She is marrying the Marquess of Trent."

His black brows shot up. "Maggie is marrying Trent?"

"That is correct. Apparently, they are both very much in love."

Some of the fight went out of him. "Thank God."

"Nicholas, I don't mean to hurry you, but we have to get going. We don't have all that much time."

"She's right, lad. Ye better get movin' or we'll all be facin' the three-legged mare."

He stared at her, his silver-blue eyes intense. Reaching out, he gripped her shoulders. "You can't possibly do this, Elizabeth. What about Tricklewood? He wants to marry you. He wants—"

"I'm not marrying David Endicott so you may as well forget it. I love you, Nicholas. Whatever you feel for me is not important. What's important is that we get you out of here."

Something flickered in his eyes. Pain? Hope? Longing? For a moment he just stood there. A shudder rippled through his tall frame, and then she was in his arms. He pressed her against him, holding on to her fiercely. "Ah, God, Elizabeth."

She clung to him with all of her strength. Wanting him. Needing him. Loving him. Praying he felt at least some of those things for her.

"I've missed you," he said, burying his face in her hair. "God, I've missed you so much."

She held him tighter, hope, love for him, and fierce determination throbbing in her breast. "I've missed you, Nicholas. I've missed you every minute, every second." She hugged him hard once more, then drew away. "But right now we have to leave."

His hand came up to her cheek. "Do you know what you are doing? Do you realize the consequences? If we cannot prove my innocence, you'll be a fugitive the same as I am. We'll have to leave the country. We'll have to—"

"We, Nicholas?"

A look of yearning swept over his features. "If we do this

thing, there is no way I'll let you out of my sight again. You'll be stuck with me for the rest of your life."

Her eyes burned. A sweet flood of longing washed over her. "Don't you understand? As long as you are with me, I don't care where we have to live."

He hesitated only a heartbeat, gave her a last hard kiss and the most beautiful smile she had ever seen. "All right, then, let's do it. By God, I must be as crazy as the rest of you."

Elias chuckled. "Lift ye arms so I can tie these around ye." Pulling a length of rope from his pocket, he used it to secure the hastily fashioned pillows around Nicholas's narrow waist. Once the task was completed, Aunt Sophie's gown went over his head to hide his full-sleeved shirt and black breeches and the husk-filled sacks tied around his waist.

Since Nicholas was a good head taller than her aunt, Elias dropped to one knee and cut the thread that held up the false hem of the gown they had fashioned for exactly that purpose. It fell to its proper length, hiding his boots beneath it. Fighting a grin, Elias draped Sophie's cloak over the entire bizarre ensemble, adjusted the hem in the same fashion, and drew up the hood, hiding Nicholas's face in the shadowy folds.

Elizabeth stifled a grin but it wasn't easy. Not when Nicholas looked like a walking, oversized tent and crackled every time he moved.

"I can't believe I'm doing this," he grumbled.

"'Twill be time soon." A smile curved Elias's lips. "Are ye ready . . . Mrs. Crabbe?"

Nicholas scowled. "I don't think I'll ever be ready for this."

"Hunch down a bit when you walk," Elizabeth instructed. "Hopefully, they won't notice how tall Aunt Sophie has grown in the past few minutes." In the meantime, her aunt sat down in a chair while Elias carefully bound her hands behind her and placed a gag in her mouth.

"Are ye all right, Mrs. Crabbe?"

She nodded and Elizabeth didn't miss the sparkle of

merriment that flickered in her watery blue eyes. Aunt Sophie was actually enjoying herself. If she had ever doubted her aunt's kinship she didn't doubt it now.

"Guard's comin'," Elias said softly. Silently, they took their places behind the door. The lock turned. The heavy plank door swung wide. The guard stared into the room, frowned at the silence, and stepped inside.

And Elias swung a neat, crushing blow to the side of the beefy man's head. With a soft grunt of pain, the guard sank to his knees, his eyes rolling up as he collapsed to the rough wooden floor.

"Let's go." Nicholas stepped through the door and out into the dimly lit passage, his wide girth swaying with each of his moves. "He won't be unconscious long. We had better be gone by the time he awakens."

They nodded in silent agreement. Moving stealthily, Nicholas stooping slightly forward, they made their way down the passage and descended the first flight of stairs. A guard stood watch at the bottom. Elias moved silently up behind him, dispatching him with the same skillful ease he had taken care of the man upstairs.

Another flight down and they entered the courtyard, passing several guards in conversation, slowing their pace to a leisurely stroll. It seemed to take forever to cross the distance to the front gates of the prison. Elizabeth's heart was slamming like a hammer and her palms were slick with sweat. She walked slightly in front of the men, reaching the guard an instant before the others, smiling into his ruddy face.

"Thank you for letting us see him. You've been very helpful."

He flicked her an assessing glance and she smiled again, hoping she could keep him from looking too closely at Nicholas.

"Be better, miss, if ye came in the daytime. Place like this can be dangerous at night."

"Thank you for the warning," she said sweetly. "Perhaps if I do come again, you could show me upstairs yourself."

His chest expanded. He gave her a hopeful smile. It wasn't lecherous, as the other guard's had been, but it was definitely male and decidedly interested. "Mayhap I could, miss. You and your aunt take care now." But he didn't even look in that direction—thank God.

"Thank you, we will." With a last warm smile, she turned and walked away, her aunt's stooped, rotund figure swaying and crackling beside her.

She was trembling and weak in the knees by the time she reached the corner outside the prison. Theo was waiting, his body tense and alert, prepared in case they encountered any sort of trouble. He said not a word, just opened the carriage door and motioned them in, then climbed up on the driver's seat. A quick slap of the reins and the vehicle lurched into motion.

Nicholas settled himself beside her, his eyes a dark silver-blue and fixed on her face. "I still can't believe I am here. You are incredible." Leaning over, he kissed her, hard and thoroughly. Then, safe behind the closed carriage windows, he pulled the hood of Aunt Sophie's cloak back, untied it and tossed it away, and began to work on his bulky clothes.

Elizabeth smiled at him softly. "Mostly it was your friends. They've been wonderful, Nick."

He glanced at Elias. "Thank you, my friend."

"'Twas only repayment fer what ye done fer me."

Nicholas only smiled. It took some effort in the tight confines of the carriage, but with Elizabeth and Elias's help, they eventually had the oversized gown unfastened and removed, the sacks untied, and Nicholas free of his corn-husk burden.

"I don't believe I shall ever be fat," he grumbled, and Elizabeth grinned.

"No, my lord. I don't imagine you will."

He gazed at her and the harsh planes of his face softened

into a look of incredible tenderness. "I meant what I said. I won't let you leave me again."

She reached up and cupped his cheek. "Are you certain, Nicholas?"

"Seeing you married to Tricklewood was the last thing I wanted." He looked as though he would kiss her again, glanced at Elias and instead leaned back against the seat. "Since you have planned this so well thus far, I assume you have also arranged a place for us to hide."

"Yes. Mercy took care of that small problem."

"Aye, milord," Elias put in. "We'll be staying in rooms above the Pig and Fiddle. 'Tis a place at the edge of the city. Odds are, the watch will be expectin' the two of ye to be running, 'opin' to get outta the country. They'll not think to look so close at hand. And Mercy swears 'er cousin can be trusted."

Elizabeth toyed with the folds of her skirt. "I just hope Aunt Sophie doesn't encounter a problem."

Elias grunted. "I wouldn't be worryin' about yer aunt. Best be worryin' about those guards if they give 'er any trouble."

"What have you planned?" Nicholas asked.

"If Aunt Sophie isn't home in a couple of hours, Mercy's to contact Sir Reginald and tell him the three of us went to the prison and never returned. Hopefully, he can handle things from there."

Nicholas leaned back against the deep leather squabs of the carriage. Clasping Elizabeth's fingers, he brought them to his lips. "It would seem, my love, you have matters well in hand. Since that is the case, I shall entrust myself into your care for the balance of the journey."

Ignoring the rumble of the wheels and the rapid clop of hooves, he closed his eyes and in seconds his dark head eased down against her shoulder. Elizabeth's heart went out to him. The smudges beneath his eyes and his too-gaunt features said he was deeply fatigued. She ached for what he had suffered. Dear God, she loved him so much.

He had said he would take her with him. He hadn't said

he loved her, but perhaps as her aunt had said, he didn't yet know what loving someone meant. Hope rose inside her. She brushed the raven-black hair from his face and pressed a soft kiss to his forehead.

For what was surely the first time in days, Nicholas was fast asleep.

Rand Clayton accepted the latest copy of the *London Chronicle* from one of the two men who had just arrived in his study.

He eyed the Bow Street runner, whose expression looked grim, then turned his attention to the headline on the front page of the paper: RAVENWORTH ESCAPES WITH MISTRESS. In smaller print below it read, *Assaulting an elderly woman and several of the guards, the Earl of Ravenworth escaped from Newgate Prison in the early hours of the evening by disguising himself in women's clothing.*

Rand finished reading the article then crumpled up the paper and tossed it across the room. "Bloody hell."

"I'm sorry to be the bearer of bad news, Your Grace." Bromwell Small, a runner in his forties, spare and ruddy complected, was honest and hardworking, and extremely good at his job.

"'Tis hardly your fault, Brom."

"'Twill certainly complicate matters."

"I'm certain it will." Rand's hard gaze swung toward the second man in the room, this one tall and thick-chested, with a coarse black beard and curly black hair. Still, he spoke to Brom. "My friends are in a considerable amount of danger."

"True, but you can't really blame them. He would have hanged for certain."

"Yes," Rand said, still staring at the tall, black-haired man. "But Mr. Gibbs is going to change all of that—aren't you, my friend?"

Tanner Gibbs, the tavern keep at the Swan and Sword Inn, shrugged a pair of massive shoulders. "If telling the watch that Kendall weren't really at the pub all the time he claimed, then I suppose I am."

"They'll want to know why you lied. They won't be happy about it. They may want to press charges."

"Small said you could fix that. He said you could see they let me go, long as I told 'em the truth."

Rand fixed him with a hard, dark glare. "And you're quite certain that's what it is."

Another slight shrug. "Kendall paid me a goodly sum to lie. You're payin' me a whole lot more to tell the truth."

"Which is . . . ?"

"His bleedin' lordship come to the tavern, drank enough ale to get hisself drunk, and left about half an hour later."

"Leaving plenty of time to return to Castle Colomb and strangle the Countess of Ravenworth."

"I wouldn't know about that. Only that he was there at the Swan and Sword only 'bout half an hour. He paid me to say it were longer, but it weren't."

"There are employees in the tavern who have also now come forward," Brom said. "They're willing to corroborate Mr. Gibb's story."

Rand nodded. "Take him to the magistrate's office. See that he tells them his tale. I'll take care of the rest."

Brom arched a brow. "And you, Your Grace? If I may be so bold, what will you be doing?"

Rand smiled thinly. "Speaking to Greville Townsend, of course. I am eager to see if his lordship's story changes along with that of Mr. Gibbs."

The Pig and Fiddle wasn't as bad as a lot of places Nick had been. It was constructed of brick, stood three stories high, and the rooms were clean. But it sat at the edge of a district north of the city called Saffron Hill, one of the toughest areas in London.

It was a dangerous place, prone to pickpockets and foot-pads. Whores lived down the hall from their quarters in the garret above the tavern, a small attic room that was clean but spartan, and smoke and bawdy laughter seeped up from downstairs through the cracks in the floors. Mice made scurrying sounds in the walls at night and the food was bland and badly prepared.

In truth, it was hardly the place for a lady, certainly not a woman he cared for as much as he did Elizabeth Woolcot. That he was the reason she was there ate at his conscience and left a foul taste in his mouth.

"You are pacing again, my lord." Elizabeth's soft voice dragged his attention from the attic window that looked down on the bustling dirt street. With her fiery hair glinting in a small patch of sunlight, she was such a contrast to their dismal surroundings that something tightened in his chest.

He sighed and glanced away. "I'm sorry. My mind was wandering, I suppose." Wandering from their grim abode to the equally grim future ahead of them, forced in the direction of reality and away from thoughts of Elizabeth's slender body, of his fierce need of her, of the desire he had been fighting since the moment she had stepped into his dingy prison cell, determined to help him escape.

He closed his eyes but he could still see her standing a few feet away, her lush breasts rising above her peasant blouse, the tiny curve of her waist, the small slippered feet beneath the hem of her brown wool skirt. He wanted her with a need that drove him insane, wanted to strip away her simple clothes, to lay her down on the rough-hewn bed in the corner, to spread her legs and thrust himself inside her. He wanted to take her so hard and so deep he could absorb the very essence of her.

Instead, he remained aloof as he had since they had arrived at the tavern, refusing to succumb to his unbearable craving, knowing it wasn't the time or the place. Knowing it was his fault her life had taken such a terrible turn, that he had failed her yet again, and that she was now in even more danger.

"Your mind has been wandering all morning. What is it you are thinking?"

That I want you. That if I come near you, I will take you and I don't deserve it. Guilt trickled through him as it had a dozen times since they had arrived in this place. His conscience refused to let him touch her, wouldn't let him ease his needs with the comfort of her body. Not when he had allowed her to risk herself as she had. She should have married the viscount. If she had she would be safe.

"I was thinking that I shouldn't have let you convince me to leave the prison. I shouldn't have let you put yourself in jeopardy as you have. It was wrong and now it is too late to do anything about it."

She moved toward him, frowning slightly. "That is what you have been thinking? You are worried about me? I thought you were thinking of the murder, trying to figure out who might have killed the countess. Worrying about me will do neither of us any good."

He sighed and shook his head. "I can't help it. It seems I have made your life miserable from the day I first met you."

She went to him then, slid her arms around his neck, pressed her soft figure the length of his. Heat slid through him, and a burning need so strong it made his body go rock hard.

"You are wrong, my lord. You have brought great joy into my life. Whenever I look at you, my heart expands with love, and I thank God and my father for placing me in your care."

"Ah, God, Elizabeth . . ." Then he was kissing her, taking her mouth as he had wanted to do every hour, every day, they had been apart.

"Nicholas . . ." She said his name as if she sensed his need, as if she needed him as well. "I've missed you. Dear God, every day was agony without you."

She stood between his splayed legs and he could feel every soft inch of her body. "I need you," he whispered, the words thick with longing. "God, I need you so much." He captured her face in his hands and the kiss turned hard, demand-

ing. He was conscious of her slight weight against him, the
pressure of her breasts and thighs as his tongue swept into
her mouth, stroking deeply, claiming her as he so desperately
needed to do.

She didn't fight him, just kissed him with equal demand,
urging him on, making the fire in his loins burn hotter. With
a groan of defeat, he lifted her into his arms and carried her
over to the bed, placing her there on the mattress, then coming up over her.

It was too late to remove her clothes as he had wanted to
do; he needed her far too badly. He simply shoved up her skirt
and white lawn chemise, unbuttoned his breeches, found the
core of her, and sank himself in.

A groan escaped at the hot wet heat and the tightness, and
some of the tension ebbed from his body. He was where he
had longed to be, where he so desperately needed to be. He
rested there a moment, basking in the feel of her warm flesh
wrapped around him, the soft heat of her body. Her fingers
slid into his hair and she pulled his head down for a kiss.

"I've been waiting for you," she whispered, and desire
flooded into his groin. "I've wanted you so badly." His body
clenched, making him harder still. He tried to be gentle, to
show her how much he cared, but his muscles shook with the
effort and sweat broke out on his forehead.

He wanted her now, wanted to drive himself deeper inside
her, wanted to possess her. Elizabeth must have sensed his
urgency for she shifted on the mattress, arching upward, fit-
ting them more closely together. He cupped her breasts, felt
the tight budding of her nipples, and a ragged sound tore from
his throat. Elizabeth wrapped her legs around him, taking
even more of him, and at last he gave in to the fire scorching
through his blood.

Pounding into her, he drove harder and faster, the rhythm
increasing, heat sweeping over him until he could no longer
think. He wanted to tell her he loved her. He knew that
now without the slightest doubt, but he had never said the

words, had never really believed in love, and he wasn't certain how to say them.

Instead, he thrust into her, allowing his release to come, letting it pull him into a deep, bottomless pool of pleasure. Elizabeth followed him down and they remained in the silvery depths for seconds that seemed hours, until the world around them began to right itself, and gradually return to focus.

Propped on his elbows, his hardness still inside her, he blinked at his surroundings, the shabby room that was the same, yet somehow different. Amazingly, the garret seemed less dingy, the air less stifling. He knew it was Elizabeth and the closeness they had shared.

She cupped his cheek with her hand. "If you wish it, my lord, we can give up the search, find a ship, and leave the country. There are places we can go, places where we will be safe."

He smiled then, feeling lighter inside. In the time he had lain with her, hope had somehow been resurrected. As long as they were together, life was worth any sort of risk.

"We'll do that if we must, but not yet." He rolled over, curling her against him. "First, we'll assess what we know of the murder. We'll list those things we think are probabilities, things that are only possibilities, and so on. Then we'll go over them until we discover what it is we might have missed."

Elizabeth looked up at him and smiled. "We should have made love sooner. Your best ideas seem to come when you are content."

Nick laughed. It was the first time he had done so in days and it felt remarkably good. "Come, love. It's time we went to work." Urging her up from the bed, he helped her adjust her clothes and inwardly he smiled.

She'd had her chance. She would never escape him now. He had only so much chivalry and where Elizabeth was concerned he had long ago used up the final measure.

Tricklewood be damned—he would never have her now. Elizabeth belonged to him and, whatever happened, Nick meant to keep her.

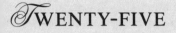

TWENTY-FIVE

$\mathscr{R}$and Clayton, Duke of Beldon, studied the small stack of papers on his desk. Since his discussion with Brom Small, he had been gathering information, discovering as much as he could about Greville Townsend, Viscount Kendall.

Rand had met the young man only once, but he had thought him likable and imagined that women found him attractive. He was also hot-tempered, and he could be jealous and possessive. They were interesting traits, under the circumstances. Could they drive a young man to murder?

Hearing tales of a duel Grey had fought over the daughter of a baron, Rand was more and more convinced it might be so. He was eager to confront him, but Kendall had retired to his home in the country.

Rand left the city early the following morning, riding his blood bay stallion out of London toward Kendall's estate, conveniently situated on the road that led to Castle Colomb. Convenient—or in this case, not so convenient, if Kendall was indeed responsible for Rachael Warring's murder.

Rand passed through the village of Upshire, a small town

not far from the castle. The Swan and Sword Tavern sat on a narrow side street, but Rand didn't bother to stop. He had the information he needed to confront Grey Townsend, and now that his friends were in even deeper trouble, he wanted to see it done.

A butler led him into the impressive entry of Kendall Woods, the palatial Townsend family estate. Grey greeted him in an elegant drawing room done in deep green and gold. From what Rand had learned, the viscount was a wealthy man, and the house reflected money and taste.

Aside from that, the first thing Rand noticed was the younger man's appearance—thin and hollow-eyed, his complexion slightly sallow, no longer the handsome, arrogant young lord, but a man who looked haggard, whose hands shook as if he had been taking a good deal of comfort from drink.

Kendall bowed politely. "I am honored, Your Grace, though I cannot guess what errand might have brought you into the country."

Rand absently slapped his riding gloves against his thigh. "I am merely the first of several visitors you are likely be having in the very near future."

Kendall arched a brow as he moved to a carved wooden sideboard, heavily gilded with a floral scene painted on the front. "Something to drink? Brandy, perhaps, or would you prefer something stronger?"

"Nothing, thank you."

Kendall motioned him toward the sofa, but Rand just shook his head. "You said you couldn't guess why I am here. Perhaps if you think very hard you can figure it out."

Kendall sipped his brandy, his face a study in control. "I heard you'd been asking questions, that you had a runner sniffing around the tavern."

Rand smiled thinly. "Mr. Small is extremely adept at his job. So adept, in fact, he was able to discover that you were lying about the time you spent at the Swan and Sword. It wasn't several hours as you claim but merely half an hour. Since that is the case, your alibi for the day of the murder is no longer valid. You had plenty of time to return to the castle. Since you had reason to lie, it would follow that there is every likelihood you are the man who killed Rachael Warring."

Kendall took a long sip of his drink. When he raised his eyes, there was a bleakness, an expression of utter defeat, that seemed to mire him in despair. It was followed by a look of resignation. "I wondered how long it would take before someone found out. I was hoping they wouldn't, of course. I am young yet, and I wanted to live. On the other hand, I am apparently more noble than I had believed. The guilt has been eating at me as if it were a flesh-and-blood being. I don't know how much longer I could have gone on, even if you hadn't arrived."

Rand forced himself to go slowly, but his heart was racing, his thoughts running ahead to where the viscount's words could only be leading. "Why don't you tell me about it?"

The glass shook in Kendall's hand. He took another long drink of his brandy. "I didn't mean to kill her. I loved her. We had a raging fight earlier in the day—just after Ravenworth left. Her husband wanted a divorce. I was happy because I thought that now we could be married. Instead, Rachael told me she didn't want to see me again."

He took a long, calming drink, but his hand continued to shake and some of the liquor spilled onto the Persian carpet. "I was angry—and terrified that this time I had well and truly lost her. I stopped at the Swan and Sword and started drinking. It didn't take much to convince me to return."

"And . . . ?"

"I came in through the back, an overgrown passage I often used in order to be discreet. Rachael was sitting on a stool in front of her dresser, admiring the jewels around her throat." His eyes looked vacant, as if they turned inward to study the scene. "She looked so beautiful . . . so incredibly beautiful. I wanted to take her right there."

"But this time she didn't want you."

Grey shook his head. "No. She was still angry, determined to end the affair. We argued and I lost my temper. We struggled. The last thing I remember was wrapping my hands around her throat. I squeezed and squeezed. By the time I let her go, she was dead. I left through the passage, climbed on my horse and started riding. I took a back road away from the house and nearly rode my horse into the ground getting back to my estate."

A hint of moisture glistened in the younger man's eyes. Rand couldn't help a twinge of pity. "I loved her," the viscount said. "I never meant to hurt her. I loved her more than anything in this world."

Rand said nothing. *Love*. It drove men to murder, drove countries to war. As he had a thousand times, he swore he would never fall prey to such a destructive emotion. "They'll be coming for you. It would be better if you went back on your own."

Kendall nodded. "Yes, I'm certain it would."

"I'll go with you, if you don't mind."

A sardonic smile curved Kendall's lips. "Of course." He left for a moment to retrieve his hat and gloves, then together they walked out to the stables.

It's over, Rand thought as he swung up into the saddle, and though he felt a trace of regret that young Kendall's life would be forfeit, he couldn't suppress a sense of satisfaction. The charges against Nick would be dropped. He and his lady would be able to go home, make the life together they deserved.

All in all, it was the first time Rand had felt a sense of accomplishment in a very, very long time.

"It's over!" Elias grinned as he stepped over the threshold of the small attic room above the Pig and Fiddle.

Elizabeth glanced up from the long list of notes she had

been studying, information they had assembled about the murder.

Nicholas stared in his friend's direction. "What the devil are you talking about? What's over?"

Elias just kept grinning like a fool. "Kendall did it. 'Tis the gossip on every tongue in the city."

"Kendall!" Elizabeth jumped to her feet, her heart beginning to pound. "Kendall murdered Rachael? But surely Bascomb—"

"'Twere Kendall," Elias repeated. "The duke—'e figured it out."

"Beldon?" Nicholas stood up, too, his black brows rising in amazement. "Beldon found the killer?"

"'E went to see Kendall and the viscount confessed to the murder. 'Is Grace brought the bloody bastard in." Elias extended the newspaper he clutched in a scarred, meaty hand. "I brung ye this. Can't read it meself, but they tell me it says they ain't huntin' ye no more."

Nicholas accepted the folded-up paper, spread it out on the table and began to read. Standing on tiptoe, Elizabeth peered over his shoulder.

"My God, Nick, it's true! Kendall's confessed—though it says here he claims it was an accident. They were arguing and he lost his temper. He didn't mean to kill her."

Elizabeth reached out to Nicholas and he dragged her into his arms. "It's over," he repeated, spinning her around, grinning from ear to ear. "Sweet God, Bess—it's well and truly over." He hugged her against him and she felt his heart pounding even harder than her own. Sinking down in a chair, he drew her onto his lap and she wrapped her arms around him.

A miracle, she thought. A miracle in the guise of the Duke of Beldon, to be sure, but a miracle just the same. Elizabeth stared at the newsprint, which began to blur behind the tears that sprang into her eyes. "Rand is a wonderful friend. We'll never be able to repay him."

"No," Nicholas agreed. She could feel him smiling as he kissed the side of her neck. "But we can certainly thank him." He turned to Elias, who couldn't seem to stop grinning. "I don't know about you, my friend, but I've had just about enough of the Pig and Fiddle."

Elizabeth sat next to Nicholas in the duke's private drawing room, both of them still dressed in their simple clothes, a contrast to their lavish, gilded surroundings.

"So on top of being eternally indebted to you," Nicholas said dryly, "I have missed my sister's wedding."

Beldon laughed in that husky way of his. "Perhaps, now that you will soon be home and safe, she will make him marry her again."

Nicholas smiled at Elizabeth. He hadn't let go of her hand since they had left the Pig and Fiddle. "If she does, we can make it a double wedding." She gazed up at him and he brushed a kiss on her lips. "There is nothing to stop us now, my love. You refused to marry Tricklewood—that leaves only me. You said yes before and I am holding you to it."

Pleasure warmed her insides. He loved her. In her heart, she truly believed he did. Perhaps one day he would say it. "I suppose, if I must . . ." she teased.

"There are a few things you'll have to do first," Rand reminded them. "You'll have to speak to the authorities, straighten a few things out."

Elizabeth smiled. "You mean like Nick's assault on poor Aunt Sophie."

A corner of Beldon's mouth kicked up. "Among other things, the guards, for example, that Elias coshed in the head."

Nicholas chuckled dryly. "That, no doubt, will cost me a pretty penny."

"Ah, yes, but worth it," Rand said. "If Kendall hadn't confessed, at least you could have left the country."

"Speaking of the viscount," Nicholas said, absently toying with a lock of Elizabeth's hair, "what did he do with the rubies?"

Beldon sighed. "I'm afraid, old boy, you're out of luck on that score. According to Kendall, he didn't take the necklace. It was still draped around the countess's lovely throat when he fled the castle."

His dark hand went still. Nicholas leaned forward. "Kendall didn't take them?"

"He is wealthy in the extreme. I don't think he would want to make things worse by lying about such a thing."

Tension crept into Nicholas's features. Elizabeth suppressed a shiver as she followed the train of his thoughts. "If Kendall didn't take the rubies," he said, "where are they?"

Beldon shrugged his powerful shoulders. "One of the servants must have stolen them. They would certainly pose a tremendous temptation. Perhaps we can question them, force the thief to come forward."

But Nicholas's jaw remained tight. "I don't like this, Rand. Something doesn't feel right. It all seems too easy, too neatly tied up. Kendall might have killed Rachael, but if he didn't take the rubies . . ."

"If he didn't take the rubies," Elizabeth said, her voice suddenly strained, "then someone else was there when the countess was murdered. If it wasn't one of the servants—"

"It could have been Oliver Hampton," Nicholas finished darkly.

Beldon's face showed only a hint of surprise. "The thought has occurred to me, as well." He strode to the wall and tugged on the bellpull, ringing for a servant. "'Tisn't so hard to believe if you consider the very convenient broken wheel on your carriage. Or who might have had something to gain by Rachael's death—and it certainly wasn't Grey Townsend."

Elizabeth's unease heightened. "Bascomb has had a spy in Nick's house," she said. "Elias believes it is the coachman. If that is so, Bascomb would have been privy to enough information to commit the murder and make it look as though Nicholas was the one who did it."

A knock sounded just then, interrupting them. Rand strode to the drawing room door and pulled it open.

"You rang, Your Grace?"

"Bring us some refreshment. We may be in here a while. And take a plate out to his lordship's valet. He is visiting a friend in the stables."

"God, I can't believe this," Nick said, raking a hand through his hair.

"Let us hope we are wrong. In the meantime, it is imperative, my friends, that you discover the truth of all this. If Bascomb is in some way connected to the murder, you won't be safe until the whole truth is unearthed."

Nicholas sighed. "I pray I am wrong, that Elizabeth will be spared more grief, but my instincts tell me Bascomb is somehow connected to Rachael's death. What I can't understand is why Kendall would lie."

"I don't think he would. I believe he is telling the truth—as far as he knows it. If your theory is correct, however, Bascomb may have been there, as well. He may have gone there to threaten Rachael, to insure, perhaps, that she didn't agree to the divorce. He could have taken the jewels simply because they belonged to you and he knew how much they meant to you and your family."

"Rand is right," Elizabeth said. "Whatever the truth, we have to know once and for all if Bascomb was involved."

Nicholas worked a muscle in his jaw. "I know one thing—as long as that man draws breath, there is a question of your safety." He came to his feet, his features hard and determined. "I'm going to call him out."

Rand tossed him a glare. "Don't be a fool. You'll only wind up where you were before—back in a cell in Newgate Prison."

"Not if I'm careful. If there are enough reliable witnesses to the duel—"

"If you kill him you will never know the truth and you will never get back your rubies."

"Damn the rubies."

"There is a way," Elizabeth put in, gently touching his shoulder, "something we can do that will not put you in danger. If we are careful, we can discover the truth of your coachman's loyalty as well as the facts about the murder."

Both men turned in her direction. "How?" they said in unison.

Elizabeth took a long, slow breath and steeled herself for the battle she knew she must win.

Choosing a particularly fetching green silk gown sprigged with embroidered roses, Elizabeth dressed with care the following morning. A note had been sent to Mercy Brown the night before, and the girl had arrived at the Duke of Beldon's mansion with an assortment of clothes which she hoped would serve their purpose.

Elizabeth studied herself in the mirror, thinking Mercy had chosen well, pleased with the way the tops of her breasts were exposed, liking the way the little maid had fashioned her hair in soft curls at the crown of her head, hoping the care they had gone to would produce the desired results.

She had gone over the plan a dozen times since Nicholas had at long last, grudgingly, agreed. It was decided she would arrive at his town house alone, seek out Jackson Fremantle and set things into motion. The hope was Fremantle would go to Bascomb, and the earl would take the bait.

"Bait?" Nicholas had raged when she had first presented her plan. "Tell me you are not speaking of yourself. Tell me *you* are not the bait!" But of course she was and only hours of pleading and the duke's solid support had convinced him to let her proceed.

She glanced in the mirror one last time, plucked her shawl up off the bed, and headed downstairs where the men would be waiting, Nicholas and Rand and a judge named Wilton

Sommers, a powerful friend of the duke's who had agreed to help them.

The plan was set, every possibility considered and hopefully prepared for. Oliver was obsessed with having her—or obsessed with revenge against Nick—or perhaps a little of both. He always believed the worst of people. She prayed, knowing the earl as she had begun to, the role she meant to play would prove convincing.

Enough so that the earl would admit the truth.

Elizabeth descended the stairs of the duke's town mansion. Beneath the crystal chandelier in the entry, Nicholas paced the black-and-white marble floor.

"I don't like this, Elizabeth. I never should have agreed. It is simply too risky." His eyes were dark and piercing. The Earl of Ravenworth was a formidable man, particularly when his protective instincts were aroused.

Elizabeth held her ground. "We've been over this time and again. Oliver Hampton has been the scourge of my life for years. I am sick unto death of the power he holds over us. I want all of this to end." She gently caught his arm. "Bascomb isn't going to hurt me—not as long as you and Rand are there."

Nicholas stared at her for long, disturbing moments, his eyes an intense bluish-gray. A muscle throbbed in his cheek. "It may not work, you know. Bascomb may simply send one of his henchmen after you instead."

"I don't think so. Not this time. They have failed him too many times already."

Rand squeezed Nick's shoulder. "Never fear, my friend. Should Bascomb appear, we'll be waiting. Elizabeth will be fine."

Nicholas said nothing more, but his features looked tense and grim. Wordlessly, he helped her into the carriage. Elizabeth arrived at the town house as scheduled at exactly ten o'clock and went directly out to the stables. Jackson Fremantle was there, a stout, middle-aged man with sharp blue eyes, waxing Nick's sleek black phaeton. If he was surprised to see her, he didn't show it.

It was certain he knew Ravenworth's name had been cleared. Everyone in London was aware of the viscount's confession. Elizabeth smiled as she gave him the message that Nicholas and Elias had gone to settle matters with the authorities.

"I'm not certain how long it will take them. Certainly not more than a couple of hours. His lordship wishes you to pick the two of them up at the magistrate's office."

"And you, miss? Are you to go with me?"

"I believe I shall wait for them here." She smiled at him sweetly. "It will give me a chance to read. I do so enjoy the soft light in the library."

It was the room they had chosen for their trap. With a small anteroom off one end, it was easily accessible from a door at the rear of the house that was only kept locked in the evenings.

"Are you sure you should be stayin' here by yourself, miss? I thought his lordship was worried about your safety?"

"They'll only be gone a couple of hours. No one knows I'm here. I'm sure I'll be fine until then."

Jackson grinned. "I'll fetch him home, miss. Don't you worry."

"Thank you." She returned inside the house and watched out the window till the carriage pulled out of the stables. By now the other men had arrived. Scowling and pacing like a frustrated bull, Nicholas waited in the drawing room, along with Rand and the judge, Wilton Sommers.

"I still don't like this," Nicholas grumbled.

"Relax, my friend. You've Theo and Elias for protection outside and the three of us in here. Surely that is enough."

"Where Bascomb is concerned, an army of men is not enough." But he didn't protest further, and as the time slid past, the men took up their places, the duke and Sommers behind the door of the anteroom, Nicholas behind a high wall of bookshelves at the back of the library.

Elizabeth sat down in a window seat that overlooked the garden. If Bascomb came in through the rear, as they hoped he would, he would know she was in the library as Fremantle would have told him.

She opened the heavy tome she had chosen and tried to read, but there wasn't the slightest chance she could concentrate on the words. The clock ticked loudly. Elizabeth thought that if Oliver Hampton decided to come, it would be soon. He would want her spirited away from the house before Nicholas and his tough-fisted valet could return.

Minutes ticked past. Twice, she heard a slight impatient noise behind the bookshelves, then the silence would thicken again. From the corner of her eye, she caught some movement on the path through the garden. No, just a shadow magnified by her nerves. Time was slipping away. Perhaps he would not come. A small part of her almost wished he wouldn't. The other half wanted this over and done.

It was a full fifteen minutes later by the clock on the mantel that the library door swung open and Oliver Hampton, Earl of Bascomb, walked in. She didn't have to pretend surprise. She had convinced herself he wasn't going to come.

"Oliver . . ." She closed the book with a shaky hand and stood up as he closed the door.

"You use my first name." A hard smile edged his lips. "I suppose that is a start."

"What are you doing here?"

"Surely you know the answer to that, Elizabeth. I have come here for you."

Her heart beat faster. The palms of her hands felt damp. She pressed them against the sides of her skirt. "I am surprised you would make the effort. You must know by now that I will not go with you. I'll scream if you come near me. Servants will come. You can't simply drag me out of here."

"I hoped I wouldn't have to."

"What do you mean?"

"I thought that perhaps, after all that has occurred, you might have tired of your dalliance with Ravenworth. I hoped it had finally occurred to you that in light of all the scandal, should you remain with the earl—perhaps even marry him— you will be forever relegated to a lifetime of boredom in the country."

Her gaze met his, held steady. She shrugged and glanced away. "Actually, it has occurred to me—rather recently, to be sure, but in truth, the thought did cross my mind. I am not entirely enthralled with the notion of being ostracized from Society for the rest of my life. On the other hand, Ravenworth has offered to marry me, while you want merely to make me your mistress."

"There was time I wanted you for my countess."

"I was younger then, less experienced. I was less certain of what I wanted."

A thick brow arched up. He studied her long and hard. "And now?"

She allowed the faintest of smiles. "I have to admit, you've begun to intrigue me, Oliver." She walked toward him, moving with what she hoped was a slightly seductive air. "You're stronger than I ever imagined—and far more clever."

"That is true, of course, but I am surprised you have finally realized it. What was it that convinced you?"

She paused a few steps in front of him. "Rachael Warring's murder. I don't believe there is a person in London who imagines you played a part in her death, but I do. I think you are the only man smart enough to have devised a means of placing the blame on Nicholas."

A smug smile curled the corners of his mouth. "And you find the possibility intriguing."

"In a strange way, I do." Only a man as corrupt as Bascomb would believe such a thing. Only a man who had no feelings for anyone else would believe she could turn away from Nicholas as if she had never really cared.

He took a step toward her and a faint noise sounded behind the bookshelves. She prayed Bascomb hadn't heard it, and that Nicholas wouldn't be too hasty.

"I could show you things, Elizabeth, take you places. I could give you riches—anything your heart desires. All you have to do is come with me. Leave with me now, and I promise your life will never be boring."

She stared at him, hiding the loathing she felt, the disgust that roiled in the pit of her stomach. With every moment that passed, she was more certain he was somehow involved in Rachael's murder.

She turned away from him, pretended nonchalance. "There *is* something I want. Something Rachael Warring had that Nicholas can no longer give me."

His expression changed, turned to wary regard. "Surely you aren't speaking of the rubies? Their theft was all over the papers. I didn't realize you had an interest in such things."

"I'm a woman, aren't I?"

A sound escaped, not quite a laugh. His smile became one of triumph. Reaching into the pocket of his coat, he pulled out a handkerchief, walked over to one of the tables, and set it on the top. "I thought these might prove tempting. Such a treasure would be hard for anyone to resist. Open it."

Her pulse trip-hammered, seemed to thunder in her ears. She followed him to the table, reached down to examine the small white bundle he had placed there. With trembling fingers, she parted the linen handkerchief embroidered with the Bascomb crest—and stared down at the Ravenworth rubies.

For a moment she said nothing, her gaze locked on the glittering bloodred gems that placed him at the scene of the murder. Slowly, she turned to face him.

"You were there. I knew it. I knew you were somehow connected."

He chuckled, a harsh, grating sound. "It was quite an ingenious plan—though it didn't go exactly as I had envisioned.

That poor fool Kendall actually believes he was the one who killed her—not that he didn't come close. His jealous tirade made the whole affair quite simple. I merely finished what that young fool started. I knew everyone in London would be certain it was Ravenworth who killed her."

Elizabeth said nothing. She couldn't squeeze the words past her lips.

"The rubies are yours if you come with me. We'll have them reset. They'll be our symbol of triumph. No one will ever guess the truth."

Her hand shook as she shoved the rubies away. "You murdered her and let Kendall take the blame." Her fingers felt numb as they crept to the base of her throat. "You lied about Nicholas, too—the night he shot your brother."

"Ravenworth killed Stephen. Everyone knew he was a far better shot. The fact that my brother was armed was entirely irrelevant."

"Not to the courts, it wouldn't have been."

Bascomb frowned. "I am tired of talking. It is time for us to leave."

"I'm not . . . I'm not going with you."

Bascomb's features hardened. If he was surprised, it didn't show. A hand disappeared inside his tailcoat and reappeared holding a pistol. His smile was thin and harsh. "Oh, but you are, my dear."

The door to the anteroom flew open the same instant Nicholas stepped out from behind the bookshelves. Both Rand and Nicholas held pistols.

Nicholas moved forward. "Put the gun down, Bascomb. Now."

A look of pure hatred washed over his features. He stared hard at Elizabeth. "I was a fool to believe you had changed. I should have known you wouldn't have enough sense to accept the gift I offered."

"I love him. A man like you can't begin to understand what that means."

Very slowly, Bascomb turned the gun in Nicholas's direction. "You think you have finally outsmarted me. You think this time you have won." His hand tightened on the gun and Elizabeth's heart constricted. "Does she really mean that much to you?"

"She means everything," Nicholas said softly.

Bascomb's mouth flattened into a thin, grim line. "That's too bad." With a single quick movement, he swung the pistol toward Elizabeth and squeezed the trigger.

"Nooooo!" Nicholas's cry cut the air and his pistol rang out as a blinding pain seared into her chest.

Rand's gun went off, but her legs had turned to butter, refusing to hold her up. She slid to the floor, Nicholas calling her name, his boots pounding toward her. Elizabeth could barely hear him. Her eyelids felt heavy and the pain was so fierce she clenched her teeth to keep from crying out. Her breath came in short, choppy bursts, and her arms felt tingly and numb.

She looked up to see Nicholas kneeling beside her, lifting her head into his lap, repeating her name again and again. She saw that there were tears on his cheeks. The pain burned hotter, sharper. She realized his hand held hers, but she couldn't feel it.

"Don't die," he whispered. "Please don't die."

"Nicholas . . ."

He smoothed back her hair with a hand that shook, pressed her fingers to his trembling lips, but she couldn't feel the warmth.

"Elizabeth . . . please . . . you can't leave me. I've waited all my life for you. I need you, Bess." His voice cracked on the last. "I need you so much."

She didn't want to die. Oh, God, she didn't want to leave him. She wanted to be his wife. She wanted to bear his children. She tried to tell him so, but her voice wouldn't work. She tried to lift her head, but it felt like a lead weight, impossible to move.

"Don't try to talk," he said to her, the sound of tears in his voice. "You have to save your strength." He swallowed and she could see the muscles in his throat constricting. "Rand has gone for a surgeon. You have to hang on."

Pain knifed into her chest and she closed her eyes. She prayed he would tell her he loved her. That the words he had said before were no longer true. She wanted to hear it so badly. If she were going to die, she needed the words to give her the courage to face the unknown.

And she had prayed so hard, hoped for so long it was true.

She tried to wet her lips. They felt cotton-dry. She tried to swallow but her throat felt tight and swollen. Her eyelids burned. She forced them open, saw Nicholas's dark head bent over hers, saw that he was praying. His cheeks were covered with tears.

With the last of her strength, she reached out to him, cupped his face in her hand. "I . . . love you," she whispered. "Do you . . . love me?"

A sound of anguish tore from his throat. She saw his lips begin to move, knew that he was speaking, thought that perhaps he was saying the words she so desperately wanted to hear. Elizabeth could no longer hear him. It saddened her to think she would never know for sure.

Darkness swirled in. The pain surged once, twice, then began to wane. She saw him reaching out to her, thought that he was begging her to stay, begging her not to leave him, then her eyes slid closed and his beloved face faded away.

TWENTY-SIX

$\mathcal{N}$ick pressed Elizabeth's pale, limp hand against his cheek. It felt icy cold, the pulse in her wrist barely discernible.

"I love you, Elizabeth. God, I love you so much." Nick had repeated the phrase a thousand times in the past three days—or was it four? He couldn't seem to remember. He only knew that Elizabeth hovered on the brink of death, that she had lost consciousness before he could say the words she had longed to hear, that he had waited too long to say what was in his heart.

He kissed her palm and carefully rested her cold hand beneath the blanket. With each of her shallow breaths, his heart ached more. A painful knot clogged his throat and guilt was a heavy stone crushing his chest. It was his fault this had happened. He should have kept her away from Bascomb, should have kept her safe. He had tried so hard and yet he had failed her again.

Nicholas dragged in a deep, shuddering breath and bowed his head.

Lord, I know I haven't been all the things I should be. I've

*done things I regret, things I wish I could change. I've failed
You more than once. Perhaps in the years ahead, I will fail
You again. But I am a different man now, a better man because of Elizabeth. I know I don't deserve her—I probably
never will. But the truth is, I love her—more than my own
life—and I beg you to let her live. I'll take care of her, Lord.
And I'll try to be an even better man.*

Nicholas released a slow, painful breath and leaned back
in the chair beside the bed he had sat in these past four days.
He felt like screaming out his rage. He felt like weeping. But
Elizabeth didn't need either of those things. She needed his
strength and he was determined to give it.

He hadn't lied. He loved her more than life and he was
damned if he would let death steal her away.

Maggie Warring Sutton, Marchioness of Trent, stood next
to her husband just inside the door to Elizabeth's bedchamber.

"I can't bear it, Andrew. I can't bear to see him like this."
Day after day, her brother had sat at Elizabeth's bedside. No
amount of coaxing could force him to leave. He hadn't eaten.
He hadn't slept. Dark circles turned his eyes a flat dull gray
without the slightest trace of blue. And still Elizabeth had not
awakened.

Andrew squeezed her hand. "You mustn't lose heart, my
love. The doctor says there is yet a chance she may live."

"She has to, Andrew. Nicholas loves her so much."

"He keeps saying he never told her the way he felt. He sits
there, praying she will open her eyes so that he can tell her
now."

Maggie's throat closed up. Her brother's face rose into her
mind, his handsome features ravaged by pain as he clung to
Elizabeth's hand. Downstairs Rand Clayton paced the floor
of the drawing room, nearly as distraught as Nick, blaming
himself for convincing his friend that Elizabeth would be safe.
Aunt Sophie fared better than the rest, determined her niece

would not die, seeing to her care from dusk until dawn, her own way of coping with her fears.

That Oliver Bascomb was dead no longer seemed important. Not if the price was Elizabeth's life.

"I can't bear it, Andrew. I simply cannot." But of course she would. She had her husband to lean on, to lend his strength and support. She never could have guessed how good it felt to love a man like Andrew Sutton, to plan for a future together, to look forward to giving him children.

She prayed God would grant Nicholas that same chance at happiness, that the Lord would spare the woman who was his one true love.

Nicholas paced the floor beside Elizabeth's bedside. For days he had wavered between anger and despair, had alternately raged and prayed. He was raging now and he hoped Elizabeth could hear him.

"You will not die—do you hear me, Elizabeth Woolcot? You will open those big green eyes and will listen to what I have to say."

She did not move.

"You are going to marry me—do you hear? You agreed, and now you will do as you have promised."

She did not awaken.

Nick paced away then back to the bed. "I am tired of arguing with you, Bess. You are stubborn and you are willful. You rarely do as I tell you, but in this you will do as I say. The doctor says that your wound is beginning to heal. There is no reason for you to lie there, pretending you do not hear me. I love you and I intend that we shall be married." He dragged in a shaky breath, wondering if his words were useless, feeling more alone, more weary, than he had ever felt before.

Still, he refused to give up.

"I'm talking to you, Miss Woolcot. I love you—do you hear? We are going to be married and—" He started to say something more when he noticed her eyes had popped open.

At first he thought he had finally gone mad, that all his ranting and raving had driven him over the edge, but those bright green orbs just kept staring in his direction and the softest hint of a smile curved her lips.

"Say it again," she whispered.

Nick dropped to his knees beside her, clasped her fingers with a hand that trembled. "I intend that we shall be wed."

"The . . . other . . ."

Tears stung the backs of his eyes. "I love you. I've loved you since that first day when you stumbled into my study. I loved you the moment I saw you in the garden gazing up at some fool bird. I loved you the instant you stepped into that foul-smelling cell and told me you had come to help me escape."

"I'm not . . . going to die," she said with such conviction that relief swept through him. He found himself smiling. God, he had forgotten how good it felt.

"No, you're not going to die. I won't let you."

"I love you."

A surge of love tore through him, so rare, so powerful, that for a moment he couldn't catch his breath. God had answered his prayers. He had returned Elizabeth to him, and Nick wasn't a man who took such miracles lightly. Leaning forward, he brushed a soft kiss on her lips. "I love you, too. From now on I shall say it until you can't bear to hear the words."

"Truly, my lord?" she whispered.

"I promise you that, Bess. I love you. I'll tell you well and often. I won't ever let you forget."

It was a promise he meant to keep.

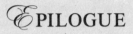PILOGUE

Elizabeth savored the feel of Nicholas's hard body curved protectively around her. They had just finished making love and the glow of contentment remained.

Today was the six-month anniversary of their wedding, a simple but elegant affair celebrated in the gardens at Ravenworth Hall. All of their friends had attended, Rand and the dowager duchess, Lord Trent and Maggie, old friends and new—far more than she had imagined. Off to one side, Elias had stood next to Theo, Mercy Brown, and the loyal Ravenworth staff.

Jackson Fremantle wasn't there, of course. He had been summarily dismissed, with no letters to recommend him.

After the wedding, in their bedchamber that first night, Nicholas had gifted her, not with the Ravenworth rubies, which remained locked up in Sydney's vault, but a lovely diamond and emerald pendant he had chosen to match her eyes.

Elizabeth smiled to think of it. She had worn the exquisite emerald at supper tonight, and Nicholas had surprised her with a matching bracelet and ear bobs. She had a different gift for him, more precious than any jewels.

She felt his fingers moving lightly over her shoulders, tracing the small line of ridges down her spine. He pressed his lips against the side of her neck and a little shiver ran through her. He was deliciously insatiable, especially tonight. He wanted her again and, as always, she wanted him.

She rolled onto her back to look up at him, saw the love and the wicked glint of desire in his eyes. "Thank you for the bracelet. Six months is hardly a true anniversary, yet to me every day has been special since the moment I met you."

He brushed a soft kiss over her lips. "You are the one who is special, Bess. And I thank God every day that you are mine."

She reached for his hand, laced her fingers through his. "I have a gift for you, as well. I meant to give it to you earlier in the evening, but you were so eager for . . . other things, I thought perhaps I had better wait until now."

A fine black brow arched up. "I thought you had given me your gift. I thought that when you ran your tongue inside my navel and all the way down to my—"

"Nicholas Warring! That isn't the kind of gift I meant and you know it."

He grinned roguishly. He was after all the Wicked Earl and, thankfully, some things did not change. "Sorry." But the unrepentant gleam in his eye said he wasn't sorry at all.

"The gift I have is something that will last through a lifetime and beyond. Can you guess what it is?"

He grinned and shook his head. "A new pair of riding boots?"

She smiled at him, took his hand, and placed it very carefully over the slight curve of her stomach. All amusement faded from his face.

"Tell me you are not jesting. Sweet God, Bess, say that the gift is a child." His gaze was so intense, his expression so filled with hope, tears sprang into her eyes.

"We are going to have a babe, my lord. If we are lucky, perhaps it will be a son."

His throat worked but no words came out. For an instant he glanced away. When he turned back, he was smiling. "It is the gift I have desired above all else. A gift I never thought to receive. Son or daughter, it doesn't matter. What matters is that the child will be ours and that we will love it beyond all reason." He bent and kissed her deeply. "I love you, Lady Ravenworth. I love you so damned much."

Happiness surged through her, and a ragged, almost painful swell of love. She was his wife now, and soon she would be the mother of his child.

In her wildest imagination, Elizabeth never would have guessed the joy she would find in the arms of the Wicked Earl.